A LEGACY WRITTEN
WITH BLOOD. AN HEIR
RAISED TO END IT

JENNIFER CHAWLA

First Printing, 2025

Book Cover Design by: Rebeca Ira

ISBN: 979-8-9992394-0-2 (Paperback)

ISBN: 979-8-9992394-1-9 (ebook)

To my husband — for supporting me through the late nights,
twisted plot-lines, and morally gray men.
You married this chaos.
That's on you.

To my family — who would've cheered me on if I had told
them I was writing a morally questionable love story.
(Hi! Surprise!)

And to *you*, dear reader — thank you for picking this up.
No judgment, okay?
We're all a little unhinged here.

CONTENTS

One

Crossfire

The air was thick with the smell of gunpowder and smoke.

The walls of the home, had almost buckled beneath the weight of the bullets that pierced them. The cracks and splinters stood as evidence of the violence that had shattered what was once a palace. The pavement bore its own scars as stones cracked and chipped under the fury of an unrelenting gun-storm. What had once been a city of laughter and family—a place of promise—was now a war zone, a gang-infested hell where every echo was laced with screams.

They were losing.

Daniel was standing at street's edge, all the way across from the open kill zone where the dilapidated mansion had been their last stand. The odor of sweat and blood filled his lungs, choking him. His glasses were broken, missing a lens, but that was the least of his worries. Warm blood was dripping down the side of his face mixing with the sweat and grime coating him. His side burned, a bullet wound that he had tied off with shaking hands, but the pain didn't matter now. All that mattered was the fight.

Chicago was unraveling. Block by block, the Russian gangs had sunk their teeth in, and now the city flinched at its own shadow. Detective

Allison Murphy wasn't surprised. She'd been waiting for this, in a way, bracing for it ever since she was a kid. Her adoptive family, all cops, had raised her on stories of justice and duty. She took it seriously. Too seriously, maybe. Years of her life had gone into studying the Russian mob. She knew their routines, the way they talked, how they moved money, who they trusted, and who they had disappear. But now that everything was falling apart, all that knowledge sat in her chest like a weight. *Useless.* Like a lifeline that kept slipping through her hands.

Allison pushed forward with uneven breaths, her once pristine uniform now torn and stained. The gun was cold in her hands, the metal cutting into her trembling grip. With every pull of the trigger, she felt the blisters split, raw skin tearing open beneath the strain. Each step forward was a battle, her boots slipping on stones slick with blood, but she wouldn't allow herself to stop. She couldn't.

Beside her, Daniel was silent, his jaw clenched in grim determination. He was the one who kept them grounded. When things started to spin, when they lost their grip on what mattered, he didn't flinch. But tonight, even he looked shaken. His glassy green eyes darted around the room, his breathing uneven as he tightened his grip on the weapon. There was a quiet anger in him, hard to name but impossible to miss. It sat just beneath the surface, steady and cold, with something darker flickering behind his eyes.

And then there was Rob Walker, his red hair making him look even more washed out than usual. The smile he always carried, the one that could cut through the worst days, was gone. His hand, unsteady, found Allison's shoulder and held on.

"We're... Allison, we're getting overrun!" His voice cracked, desperation clear in every word. His usual humor, that had carried them through countless sleepless nights, was gone.

All that was left was that sinking, bone-deep fear—the kind that told them this was really it, and there was no way out.

Allison came to a stop beside them, chest heaving as she tried to steady her breath. She didn't answer Rob, but she didn't have to. The fear in her eyes said enough. They had tried. *God, they had tried.* But the Russians had known. They had been waiting for them; every alley, another trap, every window a sniper's nest.

The mansion had once been a fortress. Now, its halls echoed with gunfire and screams. Shadows were dancing through the broken windows, the muzzle flashes were like lightning in the pitch-black sky. Walls that once held luxurious tapestries and fine art were now bearing stains of blood and bullets. Each room they cleared had been another nightmare, another chance for death to claim them. The Russian mafia had turned this estate into a slaughterhouse, and Allison's team had walked right into it.

Daniel swore violently, his voice low and raw. "It was a trap," he gasped as he peered up at the windows. "They knew we were coming."

Allison's mind raced. She could feel the weight of every decision pressing down on her shoulders, each second another chance to save a life or lose one. She saw the bodies of fellow officers, men and women she had once shared coffee with in the early hours, laughed with during late-night stakeouts, lying dead and bleeding. Her throat closed around a smothered scream.

She turned to Daniel, whispering beneath her breath," We have to get them out. They can't stay here... not like this."

Rob's hand was still on her shoulder, shaking her as if to snap her out of it. "Allison, they're everywhere. We're surrounded! We have to get out of here."

She looked up at the mansion, at the flicker of movement in the broken windows. The Russian mafia had been methodical, ruthless. This was their city now, their stronghold. The Chicago Police Department was crumbling under the weight of their empire, and Allison felt the bitter sting of defeat at the edge of her resolve.

But she wouldn't back down. She couldn't. She had spent her career preparing for this fight; every lesson, every late-night briefing, every moment she had spent poring over files in the cold glow of a desk lamp. She owed it to her family, to the city that had raised her, to every name on the memorial wall back at the station. She would not let the Russian mafia take that from her.

"Fall back," she said finally, her voice low and steady despite the fear that twisted in her gut. "We regroup, we come back stronger. But we can't die here. Not tonight."

Daniel nodded, jaw tight. Rob loosened his grip on her, but his eyes were still wide with alarm. Together they started to move back as the Russian gangs pressed forward with cold precision.

The city had become a place where justice was written in blood. But Allison knew this wasn't the end. It couldn't be. The Russian mafia had taken everything from them tonight—their pride, their brothers and sisters—but they hadn't taken her resolve.

There had been a moment when they thought they would storm the house and that this would be the very night to finish it. But Radimir, had actually played them. He had known they would come; had known they would attack.

He had let them think they had a chance.

Radimir served as the chief architect behind the city's takeover, commanding a Bratva renowned as one of the most formidable forces in the criminal underworld. His reputation for brutality extended well beyond his own faction, earning infamy across rival organizations. Among his most notorious practices was the branding of his followers with a double-R sigil—a permanent mark to signify their unwavering allegiance and serve as a constant reminder of whom they served.

A loud laugh erupted from the shattered doorway; through the smoke were a dozen shadowy figures, guns raised, striding forward with calculated confidence. The twisted delight on their faces sent a chill down Allison's spine.

At the front, Natalia Gordeev strode ahead, her lips curled into a feral grin. There was something wild in her eyes, a manic gleam that didn't waver as her finger tensed around the trigger.

Just behind her, Dimitri Malakhov stepped through the haze, taller than the others and impossible to miss. Smoke curled around him, catching in the waves of his dark, shoulder-length curls. Broad-shouldered and solid, his strength was evident—unmistakable, but not exaggerated. He moved with a quiet, deliberate menace, eyes fixed on Allison like he'd already decided she wouldn't make it out alive.

Grigori Gordeev came next, moving through the chaos with the quiet grace of a shadow. Tall and lean, his frame was strong but wiry, his muscle toned by years of endurance, not brute force. His face, marked by subtle lines and a touch of gray at his temples, spoke of experience and patience. He carried himself with a cocky authority. Beside him, the tension in Natalia's steps softened ever so slightly, a silent testament to the bond they shared.

And then there was Aleksei Kotov—composed, crisp, untouched. His suit was immaculate, not a crease out of place, and he walked as if the crumbling world around him were a mere inconvenience. Fear, clearly, had never been part of his vocabulary.

She knew these names, these faces. She knew what they were capable of, had studied their crimes and their mannerisms. Seeing them all together in person was her personal version of a nightmare. And behind them stood the multitude. The mafia's foot soldiers in black, their guns raised, their faces hidden beneath the smoke and sputtering light of the burning chandeliers.

Daniel kept a tight grip on his gun, but the barrel wavered in his trembling hand. His cracked glasses left his green eyes unprotected. He swallowed hard, forcing his breathing to steady.

Rob was already moving, his broad shoulders squaring in front of Allison as if preparing to shield her from the coming hail of bullets. His face was pale beneath the grime; his jaw was set, and his blue eyes were sparked with defiance.

Natalia's laugh pierced the thick air low and laden with mockery. She closed in, boots crunching on shattered glass and dry shell casings. "I'm going to enjoy this," she purred, raising the gun till the barrel was aimed just above Daniel's heart; her voice was dripping with condescension. "You look... tired, dear boy."

She fired.

The shot crackled like thunder in that confined space, and Daniel flung himself sideways just in time. The blazing missile went into the stone behind him, pulverizing it into a pile of dust and stone shrapnel. Pieces grazed across his cheek, the heat and sharpness almost paralyzing, as his blood dripped onto his collar. He sucked in a breath, pain flashing white behind his eyes, but he didn't lower his gun.

A sigh from her lips carried unconcealed mock disappointment as a smile curled upon Natalia's face. "Really," she said with a sarcastic tone, "still fighting? Don't you know when you have lost?"

"Not yet," Rob snarled, rage thickening his voice tilting with effort not to drown in fear. He planted his feet wide, gun raised, but Allison could see the faint tremble in his hands and the beads of sweat on his forehead.

Malakhov let out a dark chuckle while his eyes kept clamped on Allison. "You should listen to the others," he drawled, with words dripping in a tinge of cruel amusement. "Radimir's empire will not crumble. So this little *battle* of yours? It's already over."

"No," Daniel snapped back, his voice was raw but steady. "Not until Radimir's dead."

For a moment, everything went silent. Natalia's smile slipped away, her face tightening. Something colder flickered in her eyes: a sharp, ruthless edge that swallowed any trace of warmth. "You filthy little pig," she spat, the words dripping with venom.

She raised her gun again and fired.

The bullet crashed against Daniel's chest with a sickening thud. The bulletproof vest he wore absorbed the forceful impact of the shot, but the force of the shot shoved him back, knocking the air out of his lungs. He hit the wall with a yell, holding onto his vest where the bullet had hit him, his gun wavering as all the energy seemed to drain away from him, struggling to remain upright.

Allison's heart jumped into her throat. She took a step forward, her own gun trembling in her grasp, but Rob's hand was already holding her back. His eyes were wild, fear and fury warring behind them.

Natalia laughed again-an unforgivably sharp sound. "Look at you," she crowed viciously. "Still clinging to your *little hero* fantasies? This city was ours long before you ever picked up a badge."

Behind her, Grigori stepped forward and leveled his weapon at Allison, his voice coldly calm.

"You should have stayed in your little precinct, *girl*. This isn't your fight anymore."

Allison's thoughts tumbled over each other in a frantic blur, her breath catching in her throat. She could feel the deafening rhythm of every heartbeat in her throat. She could still see the shadows of their fallen comrades, eyes fixed blindly on the ceiling.

Her gun rose higher, steady despite her trembling legs. "This is still my fight," she whispered. "And I'll never stop."

The Russians grunted as they changed their stance in the door, guns rising with single-minded unanimity, black barrels blotting out their faint flicker of hope. The world seemed to shrink to a tunnel of smoke and darkness. Flames crackled somewhere far away, and the drip of blood filled the void.

There were more of them.

Allison clung more tightly to her weapon, her breath short and shallow. Daniel staggered back to his feet, his face was pale, but his eyes burned with fierce determination. Beside him, Rob squared his shoulders, teeth bared in a snarl.

And with that, there was the solemn understanding; this was not the end of the war. But, the battle was already falling apart.

With every step back, the police tried to regroup, only to be driven further into chaos. The more gunfire was unleashed, the more they retreated, their formations cracking under an impossible weight of the assault laid out against them by the mafia. Screams and frantic orders were swallowed by gunfire, each voice falling silent in turn.

They had lost.

Allison's throat burned as she gasped for air, sweat and soot matting her hair to her scalp. She tripped over a fallen man while her boots slipped on the pool of blood beneath him; she caught hold of Daniel's sleeve with trembling fingers, "We have to stop this," she uttered, low and urgent, barely above the crackling of fire and gunshots.

With blood and dirt streaked across his face and eyes wide with hollowed despair, Daniel said, "No." No sooner had he uttered the word than it sounded like rejection rather than hope. "No. We can still-"

"We have to go," Allison interrupted, ripping into his arm with desperate fingers. "If we die here, then it's over, *really* over."

A terrible silence fell, heavy and final, as if the world itself had gone still. Even the gunfire seemed to fade to a distant murmur, giving way to the ragged sound of their shocked breathing.

He arrived.

Through the haze of smoke and drifting dust, he stepped forward with measuring calm, knowing he could not be touched. Radimir glided like a phantom, his pale eyes catching the firelight with an unnatural gleam. The long coat was immaculate, unsoiled by blood or soot; each one of his steps was full of intent, signaling control—a power that could not be challenged.

The roar of battle now felt distant, *hollow* as he made his way through the broken hall as if it belonged to him alone.

Allison's pulse hammered, her throat tight. All of the officers who had been fighting alongside them now froze mid-fight. Their guns felt heavy in their hands, and there was fear etched on their faces in the flickering lights-this was no longer a fight. This was judgement.

At the center of the hall, Radimir came to a pause, smoke curling warmer and darker around his shoulders like a solemn halo. His eyes slowly swept over the scene with cold disinterest and flickers of amuse-ment, seeing broken bodies and smoldering ruins.

"I expected more from Chicago's *finest*," he said softly, as though nearly whispering, but those words pricked through the silence like a blade and crushed down the last shred of hope clinging to those battered officers.

Daniel already took a step back, an involuntary reflex, tightening his grip on a gun as if clinging to this crumbling moment. His lips parted in silent questioning, or pleading; no words came. Both knew—long before he had even set foot inside this place, the battle had already been decided.

Allison felt it in her bones, in the heavy air that pressed down around them like a weight. No victory lurked here for them. They were already dead—the final act of this tragedy etched in the silence that followed, marked by the smell of smoke and the stillness of bodies that would never rise again.

Radimir turned his head slightly, a faint smile stirred on his lips as if a cat was playing with a mouse. "This city... it was never yours to save," he murmured almost gently, as if bestowing upon them a last mercy in the form of truth.

It was then that Daniel lowered his gun. Not surrender, but quiet recognition that no bullet could carve away from what lay in shadows around this ruined hall.

Allison's hand dropped from his arm, her shoulders slumping with the last of her strength pouring away. She did not drop her weapon, but it became an empty act—sheer formality.

Radimir's pale eyes caught what little light there was, and for a split second, no one moved. No one breathed. It was like the air had been sucked from the room. They knew what was coming—had accepted it, in a way. Hope had bled out long ago. All that was left was the waiting. Waiting for the end. For the gunshot. The scream. Whatever came first. The silence stretched, unbearable. And still, he didn't move.

The Bratva moved in a controlled fashion, forming a loose ring around the group, which then slowly tightened like a noose. Every step they took was purposeful, the sharp scrape of boots against broken marble echoing ominously in the shattered hall. Their faces were masks of cold concentration, their eyes glittering with anticipation and cruel delight.

Allison felt cold dread beginning to snake down her spine, tightening around her chest like a clamp. Her eyes darted to any crack in the tightening circle, any sign of hope. There was nothing, there was only that tightening death circle and the hint of glimmer from gunmetal.

Aleksei Kotov moved with a beauty unworthy of nature, his fitted coat undisturbed by the chaos surrounding him. He leaned in close to Dmitri Malakhov and murmured something under his breath. The Russian's eyes darkened, and he let out a slight nod, glancing briefly toward Allison, enough to make her stomach turn.

Something was wrong.

A deep, low laugh came from Natalia, she licked her lips languidly while her handgun made for an amusing toy in her fingers. "Oh, what a perfect moment," she hissed, her voice thick with twisted delight. "Do we kill them now, Radimir? Or do we *enjoy* ourselves for a while?"

She was vibrating with anticipation, every breath heavy with the promise of blood and violence.

Radimir didn't even look at her. He moved without rush, but every step was intentional, controlled. His long coat brushed over the shattered floor, silent and smooth, trailing behind him like something alive. The firelight danced across his face, casting it in soft orange and shadow. He looked calm. *Almost peaceful.* And somehow, that was the most terrifying part.

He looked at Allison.

There was a catch in her throat, and she froze like a cornered animal... The gunfire, the smoke, the scent of blood and fear—all faded away into a dull gray haze. Allison could only see one thing; those cold, icy eyes searing hers in a gaze that sucked the air right out from her chest.

"Bring *her* to me," Radimir said quietly, but sharper than any blade, slicing through the chaos around him. His words silenced the ragged shouts of officers worn out by battle. Each word was a command; every syllable was an unbearable weight pressing down upon her.

A ripple of tension spread through the Bratva ranks. Some exchanged glances of vague puzzlement, a momentary flicker of confusion cutting through their otherwise crystalline discipline. Others smirked, their expressions curling with amusement, but no one dared to object.

Natalia stiffened, her grin faltering as disbelief flickered in her eyes. "*But*—Radimir—" she rasped.

Radimir turned his head, his gaze slipping over her as if she were ice. Natalia snapped her mouth shut, immediately dropping into a bow while clutching the edge of her coat with shaking hands, as if to hide her trembling.

"*Untouched*," said Radimir, voice falling softer now, and for that very reason agonizing. His eyes never left Allison. "If any of you harm her—you will *pay* for it."

His words hung in the air, heavy and final. A chill went through the room, as if all the fires had suddenly gone out. Allison felt as though something cold had plummeted into her stomach, cold sweat forming along the back of her neck.

Natalia's smile had vanished, replaced with something flat and unreadable, an uneasy stillness more terrible than her laughter. Aleksei looked displeased, a tight line stretching his mouth, but he said nothing. A flicker of resignation took over his pale eyes, a silent acceptance of a command he was powerless to question.

Malakhov remained staring at her.

His eyes, while cold and calculating, bore an additional, slow, and thoughtful gleam that caused her skin to crawl. It was almost like he was memorizing her, storing every flicker of fear and indecision; she did not know why.

"Doronin," Radimir continued lazily, the voice bearing no heat at all. His eyes slipped from Allison to Doronin, as if barely caught between breath. "You will ensure that my orders are obeyed."

Doronin's expression did not change. His eyes hard to read, dark slashes above them imparted quiet acceptance. "Of course, Sir," he said, voice flat and calm as if commenting on the weather. Allison's jaw twitched as she forced herself to stand a little straighter and glare back at his cold gaze with what little defiance she still had. Inside her mind, however, thoughts were swirling wildly, her breath shallow, fast, and her heartbeat thundered.

A faint smile appeared on Radimir's lips as he stepped closer toward her. That was the moment of realization for Allison; there would be no moment of mercy, no place for rescue. She was right where he wanted her.

And there was no escape.

Daniel finally snapped.

"She's not yours!" he shouted hoarsely, his voice torn by desperation and fury as he pushed himself before Allison. His arm stiffened, shielding her with what little strength he had left in his battered frame.

Rob likewise moved to grab Allison's arm in a desperate, almost painful grip. His eyes were wild, and from beneath layers of grime and sweat, his face stood pale. "We have to go," he muttered under his breath, the words rushing out in a panicked breath. "Abort this mission—try again some other time. Allison, *please.*"

Radimir watched them with a detached, nearly curious look. He tipped his head, angst-ridden, pale eyes flickering as a hunter appraising its prey. He sighed, a note of dreadful calm amid the rampaging chaos.

"You still think you have a choice?" he murmured, voice as soft as silk but weighing as heavy as an executioner's verdict. "I will remain in this city."

Carelessly now, with a wave of his hand, the night exploded with violence once more.

Gunfire tore through the air, muzzle flashes casting brief, blinding strobe-like bursts into the darkness. The smell of death filled the streets intermingling with the burn of gunpowder and blood. The echoes of death-cries gelled with the sounds of crumbling ruins, shouting the last stand of the police already collapsing under the Bratva's assault.

Daniel did not wait.

"RUN!" he shouted with all his might as he grabbed Allison by the shoulder and shoved her forward.

Without any hesitation, Allison took a vice-like grip on Rob's hand, and together they bolted over broken marble and cracked tiles.

Bullets cracked through the air, each impact sending shards of stone and glass slicing through the smoke-choked gloom. The floor shook beneath their feet, the world itself threatening to come apart.

But something had shifted.

Radimir's order had *changed* the battlefield—no one was firing directly at Allison anymore. The Bratva's cold discipline twisted into something new; they moved with purpose, closing in like wolves, cutting off every possible escape. Each turn they took only revealed another blockade, another line of mercenaries in black coats and silent eyes.

"The back alley!"Allison gasped for breath; her lungs were being torn to bits, as she fell down against the crumbled remains of a shot-up window. Her chest heaved with gasps as panic clawed desperately at her throat.

"There's a back street that leads closer to the downtown office... it's our only chance!"

"What?!" Rob panted, his voice raw, but he didn't slow down.

"The alley!" Allison repeated, her voice cracking under the strain. "Trust me—go!"

Daniel didn't question it. "Go!" he ordered, his hand tightening around his gun as he turned to cover them.

They turned quickly, heels skidding on loose stones as they plunged down a narrow alleyway forged fast into the darkened city. Smoke and dust hung in the air, thick as wool, and merely inhaling them burned the lungs. This alley was laced with rubble and broken glass, the hollow shells of homes.

But freedom lay at its other end.

Quickly, they were stopped.

Aleksei Kotov and Dmitri Malakhov came into view, their forms already blocking the narrow gap like specters from a nightmare. Aleksei still looked immaculate, his pale hair shining with the little available light, and his face forming an expression of bored amusement. Malakhov appeared casual at a glance, but his eyes held a shrewd glint of cold calculation.

"Going somewhere?" drawled Aleksei, almost pleasant, words laden with mockery.

Malakhov tilted his head, his attention focusing on Allison. Something about that look was disturbing-somehow thoughtful and deliberate as if he had already made a decision as to how best to cut her open.

Rob raised his gun with trembling hands, barrel steady as his breath rasped in his chest. "Get the hell out of our way," he growled, but otherwise steady.

Aleksei gave a thin smile; his eyes gleamed with amusement. "I don't believe we will," he said softly, more final.

Silence descended upon the alley, far away ringing faint flashes of gunfire; their hearts continued pounding within their chests.

And in that stillness, Allison knew—there would be no escape. No miracle. Only a cold certainty of a fight in the making.

Barely having time to react, an enormous blast blew through the night.

The force of the explosion collided with Aleksei, sending him crashing backward through the shattered doorway of the crumbling home next to the alleyway, his body flung about like a rag-doll. The masonry cracked and buckled upon impact, a shower of dust and splinters filling the air in a choking cloud.

At the last possible moment, Malakhov threw up an arm to shield his face from the mass of debris; his coat snapped around him as he swiftly proceeded to turn and track the source of the explosion.

And there he was. One of their undercover agents who had been embedded in the Bratva for years, performing his role so well, many on the force were convinced he had forsaken them for the power and status afforded to him in his posting. But Allison knew, or at least was the only one on her team to know of his true allegiance.

Nikolai Doronin emerged from the smoke like a phantom; his black coat flowed behind him; his gun was held low but ready. Calmness befitted him, he was unshakable among the destruction around him. He moved with quiet purpose, every gesture deliberate.

He planted himself between them and Allison, his gaze flicking to her face briefly then again coldly settling upon Malakhov's hidden frame.

Another officer appeared by Doronin, his gun raised, the steel gleaming faintly in the dim light. His face was in shadow; dark eyes beneath the brim rankled with unreadable coldness.

"You are wasting time," said Doronin, smooth, unhurried unlike the discord surrounding them. "She is already marked for capture. If you value your life, run to headquarters. *Now.*" Then Doronin laid down in the rubble as if he too was caught in the explosion, as Aleksei and Malakhov began stumbling out of the wreckage.

Aleksei was stirring now, coughing and shaking off the dust that clung to his pale hair and fine coat. He pushed himself up with a grimace, rage simmering behind his narrowed eyes.

No time to think. Only to run.

Allison listened to the hammering sound of quickened blood in her ears. A dry taste of smoke and panic lingered on her tongue, though she stared straight back at him, recognizing in his eyes the unspoken urgency, and without pausing, they turned and ran.

The alley fell away behind them, swallowed by darkness and fire. The city burned. Smoke billowed around them, the night sky alive with orange flames. Ash fell like snow, coating their hair, their skin, and the jagged ground beneath their feet.

They did not even dare look back.

Gunfire and dying screams followed them, the city wailing as it burned. Each breath was a ragged gasp, their lungs raw from the stale air.

Their boots pounded across broken pavement, down alleys that twisted like veins through the old district.

The battle was lost.

Radimir ruled the city now—his will stamped across every ruin and every shattered window.

And worst of all?

He had looked directly at Allison when he declared his victory.

When he told them to bring *her* to *him.*

Untouched.

Alive.

The memory of his eyes—icy, unblinking—sent a shiver down her spine, colder than the night air.

They weren't safe.

Not anymore.

Not ever again.

Two

The Ruins of Hope

As the lock clicked open, Allison barely noticed; her heartbeat was already drowning out everything else. She pressed the back of her head against the cold concrete wall, her breath ragged, the metallic taste of blood sharp on her tongue. They had battered their way out of the fight and slipped away into the alley's pitch darkness, grasping desperately for safety.

Flames still lit up the skyline, ash drifting down in soft, gray flakes. Chicago didn't even look like itself anymore.

An intense, aching silence settled around them. For the first time since the battle began, the alleys no longer echoed with cries. Bullets no longer ricocheted off the stone. There was no war raging in the streets—only the three of them, crouched on the floor, the last desperate survivors of a fight they had already lost.

Rob was the first to speak, his voice hoarse and breathless. *"Shit."* He turned toward the distant flames, his face pale and drawn, sweat glistening on his brow. "Did that just happen? Did we just—" He cut himself off, the words catching in his throat like broken glass. Saying it aloud would make it real—would make the defeat permanent.

Allison forced her head up, eyes flickering to the sky. Embers rose from the ruins of their city, dancing like fleeting ghosts. She swallowed hard, tasting soot and fear. Chicago had officially fallen to the Russian mafia—no, not just fallen. *It had been taken.*

It hadn't been a sudden siege. It was a poison, slow and insidious. Years ago, they had started small; bribes, blackmail, subtle threats whispered in the dark. Department by department, they crept in, coiling themselves around the city's heart. First, it was the shipping docks—greased palms turned a blind eye to crates of weapons and contraband. Then it was the unions, intimidation and *accidents* turning powerful men into puppets. The city council, the courts, the mayor's office... each piece of the puzzle fell, one by one, until the city was no longer Chicago, but the Bratva's empire.

The police had been the last to fall. Years of camaraderie and trust shattered under the weight of fear. Officers vanished overnight, families threatened, children used as leverage. Some gave in, taking the money. Others ran. And now, it was just them: Allison, Daniel, and Rob. The last embers of a dying flame. They were not sure how many other of their fellow officers made it out.

Daniel hadn't spoken at all. His fists were clenched, with his head bowed. In his silence, there was more noise than in a scream.

Allison swallowed. Her voice sounded like it belonged to someone else. "We need to move."

Rob let out a bitter laugh, raw and hollow. "Move where? There's nowhere left, Allison. That was it. That was our chance!" He raked a hand through his sweat-soaked hair, his fingers trembling. "We had one *fucking* job—kill the leader. Cut off the head of the snake. And we failed."

"We didn't *fail*," she said automatically, though the words felt like ash in her mouth.

Daniel finally lifted his head. His green eyes were dull, almost empty. "Yes, we did."

She recoiled as if struck. Every muscle in her body wanted to refuse, but Allison forced herself up. She simply could not just give up, not now, not with ghosts of the city pressing in around them. She clenched her hands, remembering Radimir's victorious cold glare in that fitful light.

He had known. That was why he hadn't rushed to finish them off. That was why he had let them run. Chicago was *his* now. His to rule, his to break.

Her legs were lead. Each step a small act of defiance; she kept moving anyway. "We need to find somewhere safe," she said in a thin voice. "Somewhere that won't occur to them."

Rob released an exhale, puzzlement and a trace of fear crossing his face, but he nodded. "Fine. But first, we —"

The sharp crack of a gunshot broke the night, smashing the thin thread of calm that had just started to form.

Daniel didn't say a word. Instead, his face turned to the never-fully-distant sound, shadows of a thousand grim thoughts passing over his face. What they had to do weighed on them all. The Russian mafia hadn't merely taken away the city-they had *smothered* it. Now that their last resistance was in ruins, the city was left without someone to save it. No cavalry welcomed there. No backup. Just the three of them, hearts still pounding, lungs still working, refusing surrender.

* * *

The Bratva's headquarters—the Kotov estate, a sprawling manor just outside downtown—had somehow come through the recent battle untouched. The polished black floor reflected the long table that stretched toward the raised platform where Radimir sat. His clammy fingers drummed a steady, maddening rhythm in the heavy silence.

Standing before him, Aleksei Kotov had become a statue; pale, trembling. His very demeanor was cracking, on the edge of some rupture, each breath coming shallow and quick. Next to him was Dmitri Malakhov, standing rigid and stiff in terms of military precision, eyes utterly void of expression.

At the opposite end of the hall, Natalia knelt down, hair wild and untamed, chest violently rising and falling. Her forehead rested on the cold surface of marble, her breath a faint whisper.

They had all seen this mood before. They all knew what silence meant. The girl had escaped. *Allison Murphy.* A name that still sent a flicker of anger—no, fear—through the room. Radimir's fingers stopped their tinkling rhythms.

"Tell me..." he said in an all too gentle voice, the very softness of it strikingly more terrifying than if he had shouted, "how this came about."

Aleksei hesitated, lips moving to form some words. "Sir, we—"

"Not *you*," Radimir said, not raising his voice but his words sliced the air like a knife.

Aleksei shuddered, bowing his head and falling silent as his hands slid about nervously.

Radimir's gaze, like an icicle, turned to Malakhov. "You were the closest," he said, almost conversationally. "You were watching. Tell me, how *did* she get away?"

Malakhov was unflinching. His eyes locked with Radimir's, calm and unwavering despite the tension thickening in the room like fog. He exhaled slowly under the pressure. "She was faster than we expected. She knew the mansion inside and out, passages we failed to consider."

Radimir's thin lips curled, though there was no amusement there. "So you underestimated her."

Malakhov did not avert his gaze. "Yes, Sir."

From the floor, Natalia uttered a whimper, while her fingertips twisted in the hem of her jacket. She knew what was next. They all did. The atmosphere held a crackling electric terror.

One long finger of Radimir's hand tapped twice on the polished table before coming to rest. "Find her," he said in a soft murmur. "Bring her back. *Alive.*"

Malakhov inclined his head, briefly glancing at Aleksei before returning his gaze to Radimir. "As you wish."

In the hall, a draft hurried in, and a single candle was extinguished with a soft hiss. The darkness seemed to grow even more oppressive. Radimir leaned back in his chair, his eyes half closed, as though he were already bored with the conversation.

"*Go,*" he finally spat out like the tolling of a bell sealing his fate. Malakhov bowed and turned around, his footsteps clicking against the marble floor as he left the room.

Silence filled the space.

Allison Murphy had escaped from their grasp. But Radimir's patience was not infinite. Somewhere in the shadows of the city, the chase had already begun.

Radimir leaned back into the chair, fingers beginning their purposeful tapping once again. He let the silence grow, minutes of tension mounting.

The temperature in the room dropped, darkness deepening all around them, a quiet but heavy threat hanging in the air.

The hunt was no longer just for capture. It was a *statement*. Radimir wanted her alive — for reasons no one dared guess, but all feared.

* * *

Allison's breath had become fast, and uneven as her chest felt too small to hold the panic. The damp undergrowth scratched against her legs as she rashly stumbled forward, taking heavy steps from exhaustion and fear.

Were they even pursued? How long had they been running? Hours? Days?

All this time had become a blur, and every doorway looked the same—dark, waiting.

Were they being followed? The thought gnawed on her all the time. She remembered not to look back; the darkness played tricks with her mind. It felt as if the city itself was chasing them. *Would it ever stop? Could it stop?* Her head brimmed with questions, but the darkness offered no answers.

"Allison!" Rob's sharp whisper cut through the fog and pulled her back from the brink of panic. Almost tripping over a root, she stumbled to a halt, turning towards the voices. Her two friends were standing within a few paces, breathless, faces drawn and pale beneath the moonlight filtering through the trees.

Daniel wiped a trembling hand over his sweat-streaked face and shook his head as if to clear it.

"We can't—" His voice in the middle of cracking. "We can't keep running like this forever."

"We *must*," Allison hissed, gripping her gun tightly. "If we stop... they'll find us."

"They're not behind us," Rob said, dropping with a heavy sigh on a fallen log. His head slipped into his hands like the weight of their defeat pressed down on him.

"We lost them. No one's followed us this far."

Allison wanted so badly to believe him. To tell herself that the worst was over, that the nightmare had passed.

Rob let out a shaky breath, the fight leaving his voice. "We need to stop. At least for a little while. We can't run on empty."

Allison hesitated, torn between stubborn hope and grim reality. Her muscles ached, lungs burned, and every step was an agony. Running without a plan—without a moment to catch their breath—would be suicide.

Even while she reluctantly nodded, another voice set its gaze upon her and rested cold and clear in the back of her mind.

"Bring her to me."

Eyes squeezed shut, as she tried to thrust the remnant of the cold voice away, but it latched on to her like a sickness.

"Fine," she said finally, her voice didn't match the chaos in her head. "But not here. We need better cover. Somewhere where they will have difficulty finding us."

Daniel straightened, forcing the fatigue off in his head piece by piece. "There's an abandoned shed up ahead," he said, glancing toward the dark tree-line. "We can rest there for a while, regroup."

Rob let out a long sigh but did not argue. He pushed himself upwards with each movement being weighed down with weariness before falling in step beside them.

As they pushed farther into the outskirts of the city, the cold stabbed at Allison, but she barely noticed. The biting chill was nothing compared to that wretched chill that was crawling down into her chest.

His voice had followed her into every corner of her mind, as though he were still standing right behind her. Even now, she couldn't shake the feeling she'd turn around and see those eyes.

Somewhere out there, the chase had already begun again.

And there was no escaping it.

* * *

The meeting had finally ended.

The Bratva members slipped away quietly into the shadows, murmuring unhindered with heavy undercurrents of unease and uncertainty. The events of the night had agitated them much more than they cared to admit. But Malakhov stayed back, his face unreadable, his posture rigid, but his mind was far from still.

Radimir had been calm. *Too calm.*

Malakhov had been in the service of his rein; fighting, betraying, interrogating brutally and being on the receiving end of the fury and wrath of Radimir. The same fury and wrath which broke prisoners to dust, which showed no mercy to the rebels, the wrath which ruthlessly wiped out the enemies.

But this?

Radimir's interest in the girl was different. Far from the usual contempt or cold dismissal. This was something else entirely—something almost *protective.*

Malakhov's fingers tapped lightly against the smooth surface of the armrest, his mind turning over every detail. The command had been clear; *find her. Retrieve her. Bring her back, alive.*

Yet, deep inside, a whisper of doubt crept in.

Why had Radimir spared her? Why had he ordered restraint where he usually showed none? Why shield her from his own followers, who would have gladly torn her apart without question?

He had been thinking about her, Allison Murphy. The girl who had eluded capture and had outwitted their forces at every turn. She was more than just a target or a prize. She was a *symbol.* A key figure in the police's attempt to dismantle the Bratva.

Malakhov knew power when he saw it, and the girl held something Radimir coveted beyond mere control—a secret, a threat, or perhaps a weapon concealed beneath her fragile exterior. She stirred something in

Radimir that even his most trusted soldiers couldn't understand. And that made her *dangerous*.

Malakhov was no fool. He understood that serving Radimir meant accepting the unknown, following orders without question. But this case was different. This mission carried a weight that no one else seemed to grasp.

Curiosity burned quietly beneath his disciplined facade. He found himself wondering not just about her, but about Radimir's endgame.

What game was he playing? And where did Allison Murphy fit into it?

* * *

The shed was small, a secret kept away by thick, tangled foliage and jagged stone jutting about sharply on one side of its wooden door. Muffled noises like leaves rustling were heard outside, reminding them that the city's shadows are always just around the corner.

Inside, Allison sat against the cold, stony wall, her knees pulled tightly against her chest. In her lap rested her gun; her fingers were curled around it as if it were a lifeline. All that could be heard were muffled breaths of Daniel and Rob nearby; the heavy silence. They had succumbed to exhaustion first; dragged into a restless sleep despite the present tension.

But Allison could not rest. Sleep was a stranger, a mocking illusion that left her the minute she closed her eyes.

Because, every time she did...

She saw *him*. Not Daniel. Not Rob.

Him. Radimir.

The memory burned bright, cruel; the smoldering ruins of their city behind him, the flickering embers casting fleeting eerie shadows upon his deathly pale face. His eyes, cold and calculating, darkly hungry, unblinkingly locked on to her.

Not on anyone else.

Her.

Why? Why had he wanted her taken alive?

She was no one extraordinary. No powerful officer or war hero. Just a simple detective, one of the last left standing from an almost abandoned police force that had long since been pushed out of the city by forces far darker than ordinary crime.

And yet...

One hand shot up to her mouth, while her fingers themselves shivered a little, trying to push back the wings of rising panic that were threatening to take her time.

Something was *wrong*—wrong in a way she couldn't name. Like a hand reaching out in the dark, waiting to close around her throat.

But she knew. She *felt* it, with every fiber of her being, that whatever was coming next would change *everything*.

Her last thought before she succumbed to sleep was that she simply did not know *how* or *when* everything would change.

* * *

Inside the dimly lit shed, Allison's eyes snapped open. For a moment, the fog of exhaustion kept her from understanding what had pulled her from uneasy sleep.

Then, a whisper of movement just beyond the fragile walls.

There was a quick take of breath as she swiftly straightened up, her weapon held in both hands.

Daniel's head lifted from where he lay nearby, sluggish but instantly alert, eyes narrowing.

"You heard it too," he murmured.

Allison gave a small nod, her heart thudding so hard it felt like it might choke her.

Rob stirred in his sleep and made small groaning sounds without waking.

Another sound. Closer this time, a sharp crack of branches breaking under cautious feet.

A prickle ran cold and hard down Allison's spine.

She sucked in a deep, slow breath, trying to keep herself under as much control as possible even while the dread pounded in her mind.

It could be anyone. Civilians fleeing, the Bratva, wild animals.

Or...

Her gut twisted so hard she thought she might throw up.

It could be him.

***

Malakhov crouched low, fingertips barely brushing against the leaves that dotted the forest floor. His eyes, piercing and calculating, scanned the faint impressions in the soil, reading a tale as if it were an open book.

Someone had passed here within the last two hours. Someone moving fast, but with care, trying not to leave more than whispers behind.

He let out a sigh of relief, and the cold air on his breath clouded his thoughts.

They had stopped running.

That was their first mistake.

A slow, almost imperceptible curl lifted the corner of his lips.

Perhaps this wouldn't take as long as he had expected.

Three

Don't Look Back

Every night, they moved. No plan, no map. Just three figures in a city that didn't want them anymore.

They only had survival instincts, and a desperate need to keep moving, to keep each other upright, even if the weight of it all was going to bury them.

Whenever they stopped, it was only long enough to catch their breath, maybe half an hour to shove down whatever scraps they could find, before the world came crashing back in. They ate whatever they could get their hands on: bitter, half-rotten apples hanging from gnarled branches, stale bread swiped from crumbling village shops, water scooped from slow-moving streams that tasted like metal and rot. Sometimes the water even burned going down. But they drank it anyway. They didn't have a choice.

The thirst for finding anything took them one night to an empty grocery store on the city edge. Windows broken, door hung down on twisted hinges, a faint fragrance heavy with mildew and mold drifting out into the night air, it appeared abandoned.

Rob insisted on going inside. His jaw clenched tight, each breath a rasping out fear. His fingers shook as he grimly forced the rusted door open with all his might, while it moaned softly in protest. They slipped inside quietly, moving carefully, every muscle tense, alert to even the smallest shift in the dark.

The shelves were half-collapsed, and they had been stripped of their goods a long time ago by those who had come before. Rats ran from shadow to shadow, sniffing the air with each turn down the narrow aisle. But there was still somebody among them in that silence.

There was movement in the dim light. A young man, barely older than Daniel, shifted into view. He slowly uncoiled his frame along a cracked window.

He was armed and wary, eyes as hard as the barrel of the gun slung across his chest. For a long moment, he didn't move. Just watched them with a cold calculation that made the hairs on Allison's neck stand on end.

She stopped in place, her heartbeat loud and uneven, making it hard to think. She could feel the blood thundering in her ears, could see Rob's grip tighten on his gun, knuckles stiff and trembling with barely controlled panic.

The man's fingers hovered over the battered radio at his side. *One word, one crackling call*, and everything would come crashing down around them.

Daniel kept his voice low as he walked in, "We don't want trouble." His words were soaked in marked weariness and a desperation that was impossible to hide.

The man hesitated, radio still lifted. For a moment, everything went still, just the low rumble of thunder in the distance, like even the storm was waiting.

Finally, the man lowered the radio. He didn't speak. Didn't offer help or threat. Just watched them with cold, assessing eyes that promised he would remember.

They slipped out moments later, hearts still thrumming in their throats. And though they were gone from that place, the warning lingered. They were never alone. They were always being watched.

Each night took another shred from Rob's unraveling. Every step into the dark, every empty promise of safety, stripped another piece away from him. His temper, once susceptible to the strict training of a soldier, grew at the slightest provocation.

"You're not *thinking*!" he snarled, spit flying forward from his lips one night, as Allison wavered at a fork in the path. She blinked back tears and pressed her lips together to force herself forward. There could be no room for weakness anymore.

Daniel was growing quieter by the day. Once, his voice had remained a steady calm in the winds of chaos; now, one could only recall how it had sounded. His empty eyes stared into the abyss, as if searching for something beyond the endless night. She wondered if he had already given up, walking forward merely because his legs had not forgotten how.

And Allison?

She refused to stop moving. Even when every breath burned through her aching body, even when everything around them seemed hellbent on crushing them to mere dust, she whispered into the chill of the night; words for them, and words for herself.

"We'll figure it out," she repeated, as though the mere utterance could stave off night.

Rob didn't believe her anymore. She could see it in his eyes, every time he turned away. Daniel barely heard her at all.

And still, they kept moving, three figures, clinging to the smallest threads of hope, even as the night swallowed them whole.

* * *

The glowing flame in the hearth cast shadowy silhouettes onto the rugged stone walls of Radimir's bedroom. The fire didn't warm him. *Nothing* did. Alone he sat, sharply tailored in his dark suit-almost with inhuman precision—fingers steepled under his chin, staring into the coals now burning slow and low.

The silence was absolute, save for the occasional crackling and popping sounds of the fire. Days had passed like this—without laughter, so deep with emptiness and silence one could drown in it, pressing on his temples like a vice.

She was still out there. Still running. Not from danger, no, but from the unknown. From *him*. She didn't see the path he'd laid out for her for what it was: a way forward, not a trap. But she didn't understand that yet, so she kept running, assuming the worst because the truth felt too uncertain to trust.

He should have been exasperated with rage. He should have felt this old, familiar resolve running through his veins. But for some reason, it never came. There was no surge of fury or frustration boiling just beneath his skin.

What came instead was the calm, though colder than the stone floor beneath his boots, an assuredness that steadied every breath he took, as though the weight of the world had at last settled in the cradle of his hands.

Because he *knew* how it would end.

She did not—not *yet*, at least. She still thought she could slip through the cracks, could find some sanctuary in the dark corners of the world where his reach might not extend. But he knew better. *He had always known better.*

His fingers tightened, almost imperceptibly at the memory of every inch of ground he had ever claimed in his lifetime. Every lie he had told. Every secret he had uncovered. Patience had turned into his most dangerous weapon-an edge honed to such perfection that it remained cold and sure.

The hunt was anything but a burden for him. It posed a challenge; a shadow and silence game he would gladly indulge in.

Because she would be his.

When she felt the pressure of the truth on her shoulders, when she came to understand that there were no other routes but the ones he had laid out for her, she would stop running. She would understand. She would realize that all roads led back to him.

And she would become what she was always meant to be.

For a moment, something like satisfaction crossed his mind—quick and faint, like a spark in the dark. She was his. She always had been. *She always would be.*

No matter how far she ran, no matter how many times she tried to slip his grasp, the truth would find her. And when it did, she would have no choice but to accept it.

He leaned back in his chair, the fire's light painting harsh lines across his face. His mind drifted to the first whisper of this truth, back when the world had still been torn open by war.

It had been nothing but rumor then. A half-heard murmur slipping through the net of spies and informants, a name spoken in hushed voices behind locked doors. A child, they said, taken from her mother in the dead of night. Smuggled away under cover of darkness by the mayor, Scott Sutton, himself, a man known more for his cowardice than any shred of loyalty.

Radimir had dismissed it at first. In a city full of broken families and whispered lies, children vanished every day. Some were lost to the chaos, some to the cruelty of desperate men. There was nothing special about one more child swallowed by the night.

But the rumor grew roots in his mind.

And when he finally looked closer, when the pieces began to fit together with unsettling precision, he could no longer ignore it. A child of unmistakable bloodline, placed in a home where no questions were asked, her past scrubbed clean like a slate ready for new writing.

Her story was a void, a blank space carved into the records so meticulously it was almost art.

That was when curiosity became resolve.

He dispatched his agents, quiet and thorough. They combed through forgotten archives, interrogated those who thought themselves safe behind layers of denials and forged papers. For years, the search dragged on, the trail growing colder with each season that passed.

Then, one night, Nikolai Doronin returned from a mission, his face carefully blank. But Radimir had known the man long enough to read the flicker of guilt in his eyes, the weight of something unsaid pressing against the stiff set of his shoulders.

Radimir didn't need to threaten. He didn't need to raise his voice or brandish the blade of fear. Patience had always served him better than any violence. So he waited.

Slowly, the cracks in Doronin's carefully maintained calm spread. In that silence, the truth spilled out.

The girl, the girl known to the world as *Allison Murphy,* was no orphan. She was not some nameless waif plucked from the ruins of the city.

She was his.

The blood in her veins was his legacy, the culmination of everything he had built and everything he intended to see endure.

The revelation shifted something deep within him. She was not a pawn, not a prize to be claimed and discarded. She was the future—a living testament to the iron threads of his will.

And every moment she remained lost to him, she was in danger. The world beyond these walls would eat her alive if he let it. She could not see that yet—could not understand how fragile her freedom truly was.

But she would learn.

Because he *would* find her. He would bring her back. And with that day, the end of a child lost, an orphan hidden behind a middle-of-the-road name would come into sight, in the harsh face of rehabilitation, as the rightful heir she had always meant to be.

Radimir offered a fleeting smile, sharp and cold, like a vulture circling.

The game was not over.

And he had every intention of winning.

* * *

Rob tripped over the rough bark of a fallen tree again, the thud echoing sharply in the still night. Another crack of snapping wood cut through the cold air, matching the tight frustration etched across his face. He breathed hard and ragged, each exhale puffing out like smoke in the freezing darkness as his shoulders rose and fell.

"This is pointless!" he spat, his voice hoarse and sapped with exhaustion and fury.

Allison flinched but said nothing; there was nothing left to say—no promises, no reassurances. Each derailed plan, dead-end, and close call weighed on her like a stone around her neck. She wrapped her arms around herself, the cold seeping through her thin jacket. Above them, the forest stood quiet and distant, completely indifferent.

Daniel was sitting not far away, slouched forward against a boulder, his hands making slow circles on his temples, that gesture bearing witness to his fatigue. He appeared older than she had ever seen him before, *haunted,* kept down by sleepless nights and far too many near misses.

His voice cracked. "We can't...*we can't* keep doing this."

Rob spun around so quickly, he almost lost his footing, "Doing *what*, Daniel?" Rob's voice shook. "Surviving? That's it. That's all we're fucking doing." He broke down on the last word but would not back down. "We're not fighting, we're not winning. We're just waiting to be found. Waiting to *die*."

Daniel remained silent, which was itself a rejection. The placement of silence lay between them, interrupted only by the soft rustling of leaves and the breaking of brittle twigs under their feet. Allison swallowed with great effort. Her mouth was dry. She couldn't remember the last time she'd swallowed without pain.

She closed her eyes for a moment, composed herself, then finally said, her voice low yet with unmistakable clarity, "We need information, something—*anything*. We're not going to outrun him forever."

Rob let out a bitter laugh, the sharp edge of it digging into her nerves. "Oh, *right*. Let's just stroll into city hall and ask them why Radimir's after you, Allison. I'm sure they'll be more than happy to help. Or maybe we'll just walk in and end up with a bullet in the head because everyone in that place is already bought and paid for!"

His words cut right into her. But Allison didn't flinch this time. She could see the truth of his words, and that only made them more difficult to bear. The twisting in her stomach, that awful, nauseating feeling rose at the thought of the words she'd never dared to say aloud. That phrase circled her thoughts like a vulture.

Bring her to me. Untouched. Alive.

She didn't know what was worse—not knowing why, or imagining it.

That memory made her skin crawl. She didn't know why he wanted her alive. Maybe she didn't want to know. Maybe she already did. And maybe some part of her didn't want to find out.

Daniel shuffled slightly, his face unreadable. But then the calm, steady, voice he only could manage came; "We have to figure it out, Allison. We need to understand why he wants you so badly."

There was something very heavy on her chest. She looked down, twisting her fingers, as she forced herself to finally acknowledge what she hardly even dared entertain, "*I don't know,*" she whispered. "I don't know why. I don't know *what* I am to him."

Rob sighed harshly, sitting down on a nearby low rock with a heavy thud. He rubbed his hands over his face, fingers trembling. When he looked up, she saw his bloodshot eyes from way too many sleepless nights and the strain of being hunted without an end in sight.

"So what the hell do we do, then?" His voice was strained, close to breaking. "Wait for him to catch up? For someone else to sell us out? Because that's all it feels like right now—like we're stuck in a slow death spiral and there's no way out."

Allison pressed her lips together, fighting through her own fog of fear and fatigue. She had thought through every lead they had chased, every scrap of information they had collected and subsequently lost. There appeared to be so little to hold on to—but something flickered in her mind, a thread of hope so fragile.

"We go to Findley Place," she said, and the voice came out firmer than she thought she could muster.

Daniel's head shot up, his wide eyes filled with disbelief. "Findley Place? *You're serious?*"

She met his gaze, her own steady even with the twisting of her stomach. "It's the only place left. Before everything fell apart, we hid files there—documents, notes, things that didn't make sense then but might now. If there's anything left that can help us, that's where it'll be."

Daniel ran his hand through his hair, mirroring the tight expression she wore. She saw the weight of the risk in his eyes, the unspoken question whether it was the end or their last chance to fight, but he did not argue. He only nodded in slow defeat.

"It's dangerous," she said, knowing those words would get stuck in her throat, "But we're out of options."

Daniel exhaled, labored in the quiet of night. "Then we go tomorrow. At first light."

For a long time, nothing was spoken by Rob; his jaw was clenched, and his eyes stared down at the ground. At long last, the slow lifting of his head was accompanied by a stiff-looking, reluctant nod of acceptance, and he muttered the words, "Tomorrow, then."

Allison took a shaky breath, heart pounding with dread and determination. Tomorrow they would have to face whatever was waiting for them in the ruined Findley Place. Tomorrow they might finally learn why Radimir had marked her—the reason she was at the center of this storm.

She didn't know if she was ready. Maybe no one ever was.

Four

Findley Place

The air in the old house felt damp, almost greasy on their skin. Dust coated everything—walls, shelves, the tops of door frames—like it had been waiting years for someone to come back. Every step on the warped floorboards let out a long groan, a sound that made Allison think of all the arguments and late-night confessions these rooms had swallowed.

This place had been something of a refuge. Back when they had just come out of the academy, alive with fire and dreams of saving the city that still lay ahead. Laughter had mixed within these walls with the clinking sound of beer bottles and the rustle of cards during those late-night games. It was home; a fortress where they could be themselves without the heavy badge or the even heavier sense of duty.

Daniel had inherited it when his parents died, a home meant to be filled with family and warmth. But after graduation, as the city's heart darkened and the Russian mafia's reach stretched like a cancer, they drifted away. The precinct closer to downtown called them, a siren song of danger and purpose they could no longer ignore. And the house fell silent, locked up and left behind.

Now, years later, it was like stepping back into a memory that hadn't aged well. A snapshot of their last fragile hope, frozen in time.

Daniel moved first, gun drawn and flashlight cutting a narrow path through the shadows. Dust floated through the pale beam of light, hanging in the air like the remnants of something long forgotten. His eyes were hard, scanning each corner as though expecting the past to lunge from the darkness.

Allison's breath caught in her throat as she followed. This house had once held all their plans, all their whispered vows to stand together against the Bratva's grip. But she could feel how those vows had withered, replaced by the frigid certainty of survival.

The air smelled of mildew and the deeper rot of time, memories steeped in wood and silence. Allison's hand brushed along the chipped banister as they entered farther; her fingers left faint streaks in the dust.

Daniel's voice was a low growl, filled with exhaustion from too many sleepless nights. "I'll go upstairs, check if it's clear."

Rob hesitated, looked at Allison, as if he wanted her to say that it was fine to leave her side. She nodded slightly, though her heart was pounding in her chest.

"Yeah," he muttered. "I will go with him."

She stayed downstairs, solidly grounded. Her feet were moving on their own down the narrow hallway, past the battered kitchen and the living room that still carried faint smells of stale cigarettes and laughter of times long gone. She stopped at the office library, her hand hovering over the door knob as if she was about to open a tomb.

This room had been their war room. They had spent long nights huddled over documents and witness statements, cups of coffee gone cold on the desk. Boxes were stacked in the corners, folders bristling with names they'd tried to bring to justice. Radimir's name had been there even then, an echo of a threat they hadn't yet understood.

She pushed the door open. The hinges groaned, the smell of dust and paper hitting her like a wave. The shelves were still lined with files, their edges curling with age. She moved to the closest box, her fingers shaking as she lifted the lid.

They had thought knowledge would be enough. That if they just found the right thread, they could unravel the Bratva's hold. That the truth, once uncovered, would set the city free. But standing there now, Allison could taste the bitter irony of that belief. She dug through the papers, scanning for names burned into her memory—Petrov, Antonov, Sokolov—tied to bloodlines and power, to investigations that had haunted her every step.

Then she found it. Her breath caught. A hand froze on the brittle paper. *Radimir.* The name was there, scrawled in ink half-faded with age yet still heavy with a curse. She flipped the pages, eyes darting through alliances and betrayals, through the tangled web of violence choking the city.

Nothing made sense until she reached the bottom of the box. There lay a small, battered ledger with its leather cover cracked and worn. She opened it with cautious hands, feeling the crunch of the thin pages like dried leaves. The handwriting was old, a careful script that felt almost reverent, as though whoever had written it knew how dangerous these words were.

She had never seen this ledger before. *How had it gone unnoticed all these years?* Her throat felt tight, her breath hitching in her chest.

"Allison?" Daniel's voice drifted down the hallway, but she barely heard him. Because her eyes had fallen on a name.

Her name.

Written there in that same careful script, tied to something she didn't understand—something that made her stomach twist and her hands go cold.

A name she didn't want to see. But one she couldn't look away from.

* * *

Dmitri Malakhov had always been a patient man.

A predator didn't rush its quarry. It didn't spring from the shadows at the first flicker of movement. A predator watched. It learned. It waited for the perfect moment—an opening wide enough to sink its teeth in.

He understood the fragile balance between fear and flight, how easily a cornered animal could turn savage when pressed. He'd seen it too many times to make the mistake of pushing too hard.

He wouldn't make that mistake with her.

Not Allison Murphy.

She was too valuable, too clever, too dangerous to be treated like any other target. She was the key to everything he didn't yet know—and he was never one to break his own toys before he understood how they worked.

He stood in the shadows of a narrow alleyway across from Findley Place, half-concealed by the crumbling brick and the damp reek of rotting refuse. The city was alive around him, breathing in soft gasps of mist and neon. Rain glossed the cobblestones, turning them into a mosaic of reflections. Somewhere, a car engine rumbled—a reminder that the city was still awake, even if this street was dead.

Dmitri adjusted his grip on the revolver at his hip, feeling the solid weight of it like a talisman. It was an old friend, as patient as he was, as certain.

He had followed them here, through the city's forgotten edges, the industrial husks and the hollowed-out towns that had become ghost stories. He had learned their patterns, their small hesitations. Their fear, which had begun as a flicker, had become a steady flame, consuming them from the inside.

They were getting sloppy.

Desperation was seeping into their movements like water into a cracked wall. It showed in the way they paused at every corner, the way their eyes darted at every creak of wood or hiss of wind. Even the sharpest mind could dull under enough pressure, and Allison had been under pressure for far too long.

But he wasn't fooled.

She was still clever.

Clever enough to know when to run, and when to fight.
Clever enough to know that running wouldn't save her.

He watched her now through the rain-slicked glass of the old house. Her silhouette moved with purpose, rifling through boxes, papers, the ghosts of old conspiracies. She was searching for *something*, he could see that in the tense set of her shoulders, the way her hands moved quick and sure.

Some scrap of truth she thought might save her.

But Dmitri knew better.

Truth was a luxury in this city. A currency traded by those who had the power to keep it hidden.

Radimir had given him simple orders; bring her back *alive*. He didn't need to know the reasons. He didn't particularly care, to be honest. Radimir's reasons were his own—layered in shadows, wrapped in the same oily darkness that had claimed the city years before.

And Dmitri had already guessed enough to know that Allison was more than she seemed.

A key, perhaps.
A lever that could pry open secrets meant to stay buried.

That made her worth more alive than dead. *For now.*

He let a smile curl at the corner of his mouth as he watched the scene unfold. The rain painted everything in quicksilver glimmers, masking the dirt and blood beneath. He let the moment stretch—watched her lean closer to a stack of papers, her breath fogging the glass as she read.

He would let them have tonight.

Let them believe the lies they told themselves—that they were still a step ahead, that the walls weren't already closing in.

And when they were done—when their exhaustion turned to complacency, when their fear became something jagged and careless—he would move.

Not too fast.

Not too soon.

Because he had learned long ago that the final moment of panic, when prey realized the cage was closing and there was no way out—was the moment he liked best.

And Allison Murphy was going to give him that moment.

She was worth the wait.

* * *

Allison's hands delicately trembled, following the trace of the inked words. Each letter represented a crack in what she thought was her reality. The page smelled of mildew and old secrets.

Murphy, Allison - placed into adoptive care under government order.

Her stomach flipped, the bitterness working its way back from her throat. The words attacked her, merciless and cold.

"Adoptive care?" Rob's disbelief echoed in the silent room. He leaned over her shoulder, his breath warm and uneven as his eyes scanned the page. "What the hell does that even mean? I thought... your parents—"

Allison's eyes blurred until the letters swam together.

"It means..." A sob cracked her voice as she whispered. "It means I was *hidden*."

The truth was too enormous to bear.

"It means I was someone else— before I was ever *me*."

She remembered her parents, whose real names were the Murphys- holding her close on stormy nights; their soft voices were promising that she was safe, she was loved. Never once did she doubt them. They were her family in every way that mattered.

But this...

This is different. This is a lie nestled beneath so many layers of false comforts.

Daniel registered the touch of his fingers on the ledger's edge as the very old leather cover groaned in protest, his knuckles pale against the aged brown hue of the book.

"Keep reading," he said, voice tight and jaw set in a hard line. "We need to know everything."

Allison swallowed hard, her throat tightened and dry. Yet, she forced her eyes back onto the page, forcing herself to witness what had been re- ally written there.

Paternal bloodline; Unconfirmed. Inconclusive.
Maternal bloodline; Confirmed via DNA genetic testing. Mother;
Katerina Petrov (deceased).

Petrov. The name thundered distantly in her mind and grew louder with each breath. She caught her breath; pounding at her ribs was her heart.

Katerina Petrov.

She had seen that name before, etched in the margins of case files and spoken soft in conversations that ended in blood and icy steel.

She gripped the sides of the ledger with all her strength; her fingernails bit into the worn leather.

"Katerina Petrov," Daniel whispered, his low, rumbling voice cast with a dark gaze that seemed unreadable. *"That name...* I've heard it before."

Rob's face went pale; the freckles across his palm looked like ink stains upon parchment.

"Petrov..." he half-whispered, unsteady in voice. "Do you think—like... *Pavel Petrov?"*

Dryness gnawed at Allison's mouth.

Shadowed by the enormity of the truth she was saying, she jerked her head just once in careful acknowledgment.

"Pavel Petrov," Allison muttered, numb across her lips, "One of Radimir's inner circle, a fanatic, a butcher. My mother... she was one of *them."*

The room seemed to shrink, bursting only with the dripping of water from a cracked pipe above.

Daniel placed his hand on Allison's shoulder, his brows knit with confusion. *"Allison,* listen to me. This does not define who you are. Blood doesn't—"

"That's *everything* to them!" she cut him off, panic sharp in her voice. "To the Bratva. Radimir. It's *everything.* And all of it is in me."

Rob slumped onto one of the old crates, hands still trembling as he ran them over his face.

"So what the hell does it mean?" His voice was hoarse. "Allison... what does it mean for you?"

She could not answer, because all she could see was the single jagged line—

Paternal Bloodline; UNCONFIRMED.

The name that should have been there, her father's name, scratched out as if someone wanted to erase him from existence.

The yellowed pages of the ledger seemed to pulse in her hands, the ink bleeding like old wounds.

"It means I don't know who I am," muttered the restless Allison with a trembling grasp of her words. "I am a phantom in my own story."

The silence again fell heavy; thick, suffocating. Daniel laid his other hand on her shoulder, his touch grounding while her mind spun.

"We will find out," he said in a low, steady voice. "Whatever has been buried, we will uncover it. *Together.*"

Allison nodded, but her eyes stayed fixed on the empty space in front of her—the place where the rest of the truth still lingered, just out of reach. She wasn't sure she wanted to find it. If her mother had been part of that darkness... what did that mean for her?

* * *

Leaning against the wall, Malakhov stood with his broad chest clasping his arms, each dreadful chilling breath entering his lungs. Moonlight caressed the icy cobbles beneath his boots with faint shadows that danced along the alleyway and then retreated into the void.

The house across the street had been silent for quite a few hours; its windows no more than mere shades with a plain facade to match every other silenced one in this forgotten street. His cold yet calculating eyes never wavered from that house.

He had been watching Allison Murphy from the very first day this war had truly begun. From that moment she stepped beyond her badge and into a world that had always belonged to someone else. She wasn't the strongest among them, he had seen others wield power like a blade, tearing apart reality at the seams. She wasn't the most ruthless, he had seen blood spilled by hands that wouldn't even tremble.

But power and cruelty didn't interest Malakhov at all. He watched her because she was *unpredictable*. And unpredictability, in his experience, is much more dangerous than power or brutality.

Unpredictable prey can become a threat in an instant. Unpredictable prey can turn a hunt upside down.

Tonight, though, it wasn't a question of what she *might* do that he was watching for. Tonight he was waiting for her to realize. She did not yet know the truth that was coiling around her like a sleeping serpent. But she was close. He could feel it in the air; it crackled like lightning.

She was not who she thought she was. Not the adopted daughter of good and kind people who had sheltered her from the dark world of the earth. Not the hard-working police officer who had sworn to uphold the law. *No, she was something else.* Something birthed out of war and violence and merciless power.

The very instant she knew what she was and what had all along inhabited her—that would be the moment when she would stop running. He shifted a little, that faint smirk breaking onto his lips. He had come to recognize that moment in others—that spark of realization that could harden into something monstrous even in a meek soul; something unstoppable.

He waited. The night was still. The world was poised. And he knew that very soon, she would walk out of that house a different woman. No longer afraid of the dark, because deep down she'd known it was in her all along.

That was when the real war would begin.

* * *

Allison forced herself to keep reading, while her throat constricted and her heart seemed to tear with every breath. The words blurred slightly as tears gathered at the corners of her eyes, but she blinked them away. She had to see them. She had to know them.

At the bottom of the page, beneath her father's name—scratched out so violently it nearly tore the paper—two final words waited. *"Erased. Hidden."* Beneath them, another line in handwriting she didn't recognize sent an icy chill down her spine; *"Radimir must never know."*

Her heart faltered, her ears roaring as dread flooded her veins. She read those words again and again, eyes passing over them as if they would begin to change or vanish if only she looked long enough. But they didn't. They remained there—four words and their weight; *"Radimir must never know."* Ink as dark and as final as the truth it intimated appeared before Allison; she felt the ground beneath her feet giving away.

Her hands shaking so much that she thought she might drop the ledger. Her fingers lacked coordination. Numbness swept through them. This was more than a carefully constructed lie meant to keep her safe. This wasn't a convenient story to protect her from the shadows of the past. No, it meant something else entirely. *Something deeper.* Something putrid with fear and desperation—something that had scared the very people who hid her away in the first place. Her breath came in quick, shallow gasps as her mind tried to grasp the enormity of it—but it was like trying to catch smoke in her hands.

Who am I? Her mind was now a frantic echoing jumble. *What did they try so hard to keep from him?* She saw her life crumbling before her eyes. Every memory. Every moment took on a darker tone. Her mother—*Katerina Petrov*, a name that had never quite felt real. The Petrovs— a name that sank right into the heart of the Russian Bratva, a family of violence and blood. Her father's name wiped out like it had never existed.

What could be so dangerous about her blood that even Radimir- with his reach and influence stretched across continents—had to be kept from it?

Her mouth tasted of bile. She swallowed again and again, but it wouldn't go away.

Who am I?

The question pulsed behind her eyes, too big to hold. She'd always felt...*off* somehow. Like there was a seam in her life she couldn't quite smooth flat. She'd told herself it didn't matter. That it was nothing. Forced herself to believe she belonged. But now-there was no denying it. This was not something she could ignore anymore or shove beneath the routine of daily living. This was the truth-and it was coming for her, whether she wanted it or not.

If this secret was so dangerous it had to be buried, if it was so important that even Radimir must be kept in the dark, then it could mean just one thing.

He already knew.

Because Radimir had a way of pulling secrets into the light, of prying open doors no one else could even see. He always had. And if he didn't know yet, he was close. Too close. She felt it, like feeling a storm brewing in the air, electricity that stood hairs on her arms and a nameless tension.

She shuddered as she slammed shut the ledger. *He's coming*, she thought, shouting inside her. *He knows. And I have no idea what he is going to do with me.* The walls felt too close. She needed air. She needed to move before she lost her mind.

She needed to get out of here, to feel the cold night on her skin, somehow make rational sense of the chaos detonating in her chest. *I need to get out of here. I need to figure out what this means.* The muscles in her arms tensed up, buoyed by that instinct to run, yet another voice whispered in her mind-the one much smaller, more sure, and colder.

You can't run from this.

Not anymore.

Because whoever she'd been before didn't matter anymore. The truth was out there. And so was Radimir, coming straight for it—and for her. She couldn't stop it. She took a shaky breath and placed the ledger gently on the table; her fingers lingered on the leathery worn cover as if to anchor her to the world she had always known.

But it could not. And she knew it.

The truth had found her.

And so had Radimir.

Five

One Problem at a Time

The smell of damp asphalt clung to everything as Allison, Daniel, and Rob moved quietly along the narrow street. This town was the kind you never noticed. People minded their own business and kept their heads down—exactly what they needed right now. But somehow, that still didn't guarantee safety.

Their boots collided with the wet street, producing faint echoes that seemed to fill the void. They looked worn down, hollow-eyed from hunger, drifting through the empty street as if they hardly belonged there.

Rob clasped his coat tighter around his shoulders, as if to hold the wind at bay. His eyes kept flicking from one doorway to the next, jaw tight, as if he expected something to lunge out at them. "I don't like this," he whispered with a hoarse voice emerging from sheer weariness. "It's too late, too exposed."

Daniel kept walking. "I know," he said shortly, as if his words were something that he couldn't bear to hear. "But we really don't have a choice."

Rob gritted his teeth. "There's always a choice, Daniel. Always a way out."

Daniel looked away, his features stretching into grim lines. "Not this time." He looked back at the empty windows lining the street. "We're down to scraps. We either take the risk, or we starve."

Rob shook his head, frustration etched into his features. "Or we get shot. Or *caught*. I don't know which is worse."

Allison had become completely silent as her fingers clutched the pistol was deep within her coat. Every breath scraped her throat, the cold sinking deep under her skin. She didn't let herself think about how close they were to the edge, or what might be waiting if they slipped.

Focus, she told herself.

One problem at a time.

The corner store loomed up ahead, shabby and silent. The store sign had cracked into oblivion, with its window panes coated with a thick layer of grime. Daniel eased his pace, all the while squinting at it with suspicion.

"We'll check here," he said faintly.

Rob's eyebrows went up. "*Here*? Seriously?"

Daniel simply nodded. "It's our best shot."

Rob's laugh was shaky, his breath fogging the cold air. "Best shot for what? Getting ourselves killed?"

Allison spoke gently but firmly. "*Stop*. There is no time for arguing."

Rob glared at her. "I'm not arguing, Allie. I'm trying to keep us *alive*."

Daniel exhaled, rubbing his forehead. "We're all trying to stay alive, Rob. But we need food. We can't keep going like this."

For one moment, there was silence. It seemed as if time stretched on forever, broken only by the slow rustle of the wind in the alley.

Finally, Rob muttered, "Fine. But I'm not going in there. You two can play hero."

Daniel's mouth tightened. "You'd rather stand out here in the open?"

Rob snorted. "Out here, at least I can see what's coming."

Allison put a hand on his arm. "We'll be quick. Just... keep watch, okay?"

Rob tightened his lips. "Yeah, I'll keep watch." A worried resignation settled across his face. "Just... don't be stupid in there."

She smiled weakly. "We'll try."

Daniel looked at her seriously. "You sure you want to come in?"

She nodded. "I'm sure."

For a moment, he hesitated, then just made one curt nod. "Alright. Stay close to me."

Rob shifted uncomfortably, glancing around the street. "If you're not out in five minutes, I'm coming in after you."

Daniel smiled faintly, "If we're not out in five minutes, then it's way too late."

Rob didn't laugh, but simply nodded shortly and stepped back into the shadows near a boarded-up doorway.

Allison and Daniel exchanged one last look and proceeded towards the store. The door gave a broken, rattling chime above the entrance as Daniel forced it open, and they entered.

The shelves leaned drunkenly, laden with cans of food whose labels had faded away. Allison's fingertips hovered near the pistol; all senses stretched to the limit as she looked down the aisles.

The weak fluorescent lights gave feeble glimmers above as Allison and Daniel continued into the dark, shack-like shop. Miserably overpriced canned goods, packets of dried meats, and stale, countrified bread sat on bent shelves. For this new world, it was better than nothing.

A weary cashier slumped behind the counter, eyes fixed on an old newspaper. He barely glanced at them, his eyes glazed and fixed on the spaper as the radio beside him croaked a soft tune—some old song that had once been lively but now only added to the illusion of normalcy.

Perfect.

Daniel picked up a plastic basket, the handle squeaking under the strain of being bent so many times. He moved quickly, deliberately, his fingers darting between shelves, snatching only what they needed—protein, carbs, salt—fuel for survival.

Allison moved alongside him, her mind a haze of calculation and exhaustion. She forced herself to focus, her lips silently counting each item, mentally tallying up the meager cash she had left.

They proceeded further past a stack of boxes that seemed poised to give way. A single bulb overhead flickered feebly, casting long, jittery shadows across the cracked floor.

"Check the back," Daniel whispered. "I'll cover this side."

She moved as quietly as possible, her boots barely whispering against the floorboards. Her pulse thudded in her ears, silence pressing in toward her. She snatched a can of beans from the shelf, dusted it off, and wondered what in the world she was going to do with it.

"Find anything?" Daniel called softly. She shook her head. "Just old cans. Nothing fresh."

He sighed. "Figures. Grab what you can. We'll sort it out later."

She reached for a small bag of oats, her fingers brushing against the cold metal shelf, the texture grounding her for a moment.

And then—

She felt it.

A chill crawled up her neck, prickling under her hair. It was the feeling one gets when one feels watched. Her breath caught in her throat, a knot tightening in her chest. She had to muster just enough strength to turn and take a sidelong glimpse through the grime-streaked window of the store.

Outside, Rob was still there, pressed to the cracked outer bricks of the wall. Arms tightly crossed to his chest, one foot tapping out a frantic rhythm, as if each second became a weight he could not bear on his own.

To him, nothing seemed out of place. Yet the silence was wrong. *Too still. The air felt thick, like it was waiting.*

This was not just nerves. It wasn't paranoia. It was real. In her bones lay the sick certainty that tightened knots in her stomach.

A breath escaped her almost inaudibly from her lips, "*Daniel.*"

His eyebrows knitted together quickly, "What?"

She didn't look away from the window, her knuckles white around the basket handle. "Something is *wrong*," she said, Her voice came out raw, scraping her throat.

Daniel stopped for a second. A faint temptation lurked in the back of his mind to insist on retrieving his weapon from beneath his jacket, but he refrained and kept his voice steady. "What do you mean?"

"I..." Her mouth felt dry like dust. "I just know."

Outside, Rob shifted and shook the shoulders of his discontent. He glanced quickly up and down the street, one hand lightly tapping his pistol's hilt beneath his coat, as if the faintest contact might afford him some semblance of comfort.

Daniel stepped in closer, lowering his voice. "Allie, focus. What do you see?"

She shook her head slightly, her breath quickening. "Nothing. But the air—it's too still. Too quiet. Like... like everything's waiting."

He glanced at the cashier, who really seemed half asleep behind the counter-oblivious to the creeping dread seeping into the room. Daniel leaned in closer to her, his voice an awful whisper. "Alright. We'll finish fast. Keep your eyes open."

"I don't like this," she said, eyes moving to the window. "Rob doesn't look right, either. He seems on edge."

"He's *always* on edge," said Daniel, though he didn't sound so sure. He grabbed another can off the shelf and tucked it away into his basket. "Almost done. Then we're off."

She gave a tight nod, forcing herself to walk on. Wherever she went, the atmosphere grew heavier. She was straining to hear anything but the scratchy radio and the sound of the basket. The silence here was a thick blanket pressing down on her.

Rob was pacing outside now, his foot tapping faster. His eyes kept flicking to the ends of the street, to the fog-draped corners that seemed to swallow up the night.

"Allie," Daniel said, "we're going to be *fine*. One more row. Then we're out."

She nodded again, but her fingers twitched at the thought of reaching for the gun in her coat pocket—the weight of it oddly comforting. Instead, she grabbed a soda can and a box of crackers, her movements automatic, like muscle memory.

Daniel's voice was calm, but all the tension threatening to explode.

"Almost done. Rob'll keep watch. We're fine."

She glanced at him sharply. "You don't believe that."

He gave a thin, humorless smile. "Doesn't really matter if I believe it. It's what we have to tell ourselves."

She almost laughed—*almost*. But the weight of the silence was too much.

But outside, Rob's foot suddenly stopped tapping. He stiffened, his head snapping to the side, eyes narrowing into the shadows.

Allison felt a drop in her stomach. "Daniel—"

"I see it," he said sharply, controlled and low. Daniel straightened himself and placed a can back on the shelf as if nothing was wrong. "Stay calm."

Outside, Rob's hand dropped down by the grip of his pistol, his knuckles white as bone. His wild eyes followed something or someone that they could not see from inside.

Allison forced herself to breathe, blood pounding in her ears, and she felt it in the back of her throat. "What do we do?"

Daniel caught her gaze with his hard eyes. "We walk out of here like nothing's wrong. If we run, they'll know that we are scared. We aren't giving that to them."

She swallowed hard, nodding in agreement.

Reaching for her hand again, Daniel brushed his fingers lightly over hers. "Ready?"

"Ready," she whispered, still not sure if she believed it.

Daniel looked at her for a moment longer before turning away. "Stay behind me. Let's go."

They walked to the door, opening it to the loud squeal of the hinges that cut through the suffocating quiet. The cashier didn't even lift his eyes, unaware, too immersed in his paper and music.

Allison stepped out; the fog hit her cold, against which Rob's eyes snapped to hers, and he gave a nearly imperceptible nod.

"There's something out there," he said quietly, his voice taut with tension.

"What did you see?" Daniel asked, his own hand resting near the gun at his side.

Rob's jaw worked, his breath slow and careful. "Three figures. Dark coats. *Watching*. They're moving slow—like they're waiting for us to move first."

Allison's blood turned to ice. "Are they armed?"

Rob nodded once, his face pale under the flickering streetlight. "I couldn't see it, but... I'd bet my life on it."

Daniel took a deep breath. "We walk back into the store. *Calm*. If they follow, we deal with it then."

Allison swallowed. "And what if they don't?"

His gaze darkened, glinting so hard and cold. "Then let us move on, shall we? Focus on one thing at a time."

Her nod was jerky, caught in little sharp bursts of breath. "Okay."

Rob shifted on his feet, moving fingers around his gun. "Let's just get the hell away from here."

And then, they appeared.

Three figures, stepping out of the fog like wraiths, their movements slow and deliberate. Coats heavy and dark, faces hidden in the shadows.

Daniel's voice was calm and low. "Back inside, don't stop. Keep walking."

Allison clenched her jaw, her fingers now so tight around the handle of her basket she thought it might snap.

One problem at a time.

They stepped back into the store, silence pressing down on them, heavy and infinite, with the only source of noise coming from the soft hum of the radio.

The world held its breath.

And so did they.

After a moment they saw that the three figures were advancing through the mist, each step on the wet pavement rendered inaudible from the store front window. The flickering lamplight would alternate between stretching and shrinking their shadows with every step that was taken. One was tall and broad of shoulder with a cruel smirk twisting his lips, as if tasting blood already. One was lean and monstrous, pressing forward with shoulders hunched and movements almost animalistic. The last was quiet, eyes sharp and cold, taking in everything with clinical precision.

Gordeev.

Romanov.

Malakhov.

Rob's breath caught, his blood turning to ice.

No. Not here. Not now.

They were walking straight to the store without putting any thought whatsoever into hiding themselves. They walked past the townspeople who were left to gather about, underneath the heavy gloom of silent doorways, broken window glass, and rejected shadows searching for sun. Their eyes fixed straight ahead.

And worse—

They weren't scanning the streets for signs of Daniel.

They weren't glancing at Rob's bright red hair.

They were looking straight at Allison.

Rob felt the air grow heavier, like the mist had turned dense enough to choke on. The room pressed in around him, leaving a sick, sinking feeling deep in his gut.

"No, no, no," he whispered with a trembling voice.

He whirled around, every nerve ablaze in panic. His hand slammed the door open with enough force to make the small brass bell above it scream into the silence.

"Daniel! Allison! We have to leave— we have to run!"

Too late.

Glass shattered as windows exploded inward, an eruption of sounds marking the destruction. One moment in calm, and the next it turned into chaos. The bullets followed their trails of fury across the shelves and opposite walls, the metallic smell of gunpowder merging with the musty aroma that emanated from mildew and old paper.

Allison didn't think. She grasped Daniel's sleeve and pulled him behind a display just as a shelf came crashing down with sparks and splinters.

The cashier let out a strangled scream and dived behind the counter. Gordeev's laughter pierced the silence like a knife. "There you are, you little *сука*," he intoned, his voice almost musical in its cruelty.

Allison's breath came in short, ragged bursts, each one caught in her chest as gunfire cracked again and again, sharp and relentless. Her ears rang with the noise, and her heart pounded so hard it hurt. Every part of her was screaming at her to run.

They're here.

They found me. This is it.

They didn't care about Daniel.

They didn't care about Rob.

They had come for her. And they weren't going to leave there without her.

Her thoughts fractured, pieces of half-finished memories and terror crashing into one another. Findley Place. Whispers in the dark. Threats that had never been idle. *Survive.*

She could feel Daniel's fingers brush against hers, an anchor in the storm.

They had each other.

They had to fight.

They had to *Stay alive.*

Dmitri Malakhov did not waste time.

While Gordeev stood back, laughing like a demon as the building crumbled, and Romanov grinned with teeth too large for his mouth, Malakhov was already moving. From his very first step, he kept them silent and slow, a deliberate attempt at holding control in all his movement. He floated inside a dust of gunpowder, an almost shadow figure against the sputtering lamps' swinging light.

Allison saw him clutch a gleaming bit of metal. She watched his coat flare with each stride of the silent predator. The pounding of her heart was forming exits through her throat. She fumbled for the small pistol she had tucked within her jacket pocket, only to find her fingers slicked with sweat.

Aim.

Shoot.

Move.

She raised the gun.

"Don't even think about it, *sweetheart*" Malakhov said softly. His voice was calm, almost with a hint of kindness, but there was no mercy in it.

A single step, and he was there.

He grabbed her wrist with an iron grip, twisting just enough to send the gun clattering to the floor. She gasped, her eyes wide. The world shrank to the feel of his hand—rough, callused, *steady*.

He didn't tighten his grip to hurt her. He didn't wrench her arm or drag her closer. He just... held her there, suspended in a breathless moment.

For one heartbeat, their eyes met. His were dark, like a midnight forest, older and watchful. But beneath that stillness was something else—something that flickered just beyond her understanding.

Recognition.

It wasn't just that he knew her.

It was that he understood her.

"Allison," he said in a low voice, her name coming from his lips like some kind of secret.

She shivered. Her skin broke out in goosebumps. "What do you want?" she could hardly choke the words out.

His jaw twitched, and he considered her for a moment, his head tilting. "You know what I want," he said hoarsely.

She swallowed hard, her voice a whisper; "Let me go."

"I could," he murmured, his voice hoarse but disturbingly gentle. "But you know I won't."

Her breath caught in her throat. The air between them was charged—hot, tense, and just this side of dangerous. She tried to pull back, voice low and shaking with fury.

"You are never going to take me," she snapped.

Malakhov's lips twitched, not quite a smile but close. "Take you?" he echoed, his tone just a little too amused. "You make it sound like an invitation"

Color rushed to her cheeks before she could stop it. "Stop that," she muttered, flustered and furious all at once.

His fingers caressed her jaw. "I will not hurt you, Allison," he said, and she chose to believe the words whenever her mind insisted that it should not have. "But I will not let you run away from me either."

Her eyes went wide, spinning with a quiet assurance in his tone.

No threat.

A promise.

There was still chaos outside; shouts, the sound of breaking glass, the metallic sharpness of blood in the air. Yet that instant, it was just them.

And in that moment, she could have screamed or surrendered.

Until then, everything around them was a faded roar; Romanov rampaging his way through the store, flinging bottles, and furniture around in search; the laughter of Gordeev ringing from afar, a sound that turned bitter and bloody in the air.

"Allison!" Daniel's voice cut through the chaos, raw and urgent.

Daniel crashed into Malakhov, shoulder-first, breaking the moment apart. The spell shattered, and Malakhov released her wrist, his fingers sliding away like water. Allison stumbled back, her legs trembling.

For a single instant, she saw something flicker in Malakhov's eyes—regret? No. *Something more.*

Then he was gone, shifting his weight and turning, calm as ever, coiled like a serpent ready to strike.

Rob was there, grabbing her elbow in a fierce grip. "Come on! We have to go!" His voice was a low growl of fury.

She let him pull her, her feet moving on instinct, her mind a storm of questions and fear. The rear exit slammed open, cold night air rushing in. The alley was dark and wet. The mist curled low around their ankles.

Rob was breathing in ragged gasps. "Did he hurt you? Allison, did he—"

"No," she whispered, her voice too soft. "No."

But her eyes were wide and unfocused, because he hadn't hurt her.

He hadn't even tried.

That was what terrified her most of all.

Inside, Malakhov moved through the wreckage with serene grace, stepping over shattered glass and broken wood. Romanov let out a growl of frustration.

"We had them, Malakhov! We had them—"

Gordeev's eyes burned. "Why did you let her go?" he demanded, his tone seething.

Malakhov didn't look at them. He exhaled, his breath fogging the air in front of his lips. He turned his head, looking out at the door through that they had disappeared. His gaze turned cold and distant, as if looking at something far away from him, something only he could see.

"She is not ready," he said.

Romanov growled, teeth bared. "Next time, I'm getting a taste."

Malakhov said nothing. The black barrel of the gun glittered with the broken light as it was lowered back into his coat. He stood silently, watching: the only point of calm amid the chaos.

He'd seen it in her eyes—a flicker of recognition she couldn't hide.

She knows.

And soon enough, she would stop running.

Because once she understood, once she let it in, she would come to him.

And he would be waiting.

He always had been.

Six

A Sacrifice in Silence

They ran until it felt like their lungs were tearing themselves apart.

Allison gasped, each breath a rasp of fire in her throat. Her legs threatened to buckle with every step, but she couldn't stop—*not now*. Not when stopping meant letting them catch up.

Around them stretched a maze of darkness and crumbling asphalt, broken alleys twisting off in every direction. The cold stung their faces, biting at every patch of bare skin. Still, they didn't look back. They couldn't risk it.

There was a calm steadiness in Malakhov's eyes she couldn't shake. That unblinking stare, like he already knew every move she'd make. Even when she tried to shut him out, she kept seeing him—his head tilted slightly, the ghost of a smile twisting his mouth.

Why had he let me go?

It didn't matter. She couldn't let herself think about it, couldn't even begin to slow. Just not a single second.

They slammed the pavement with their boots as they turned into another street. The street was deserted. Their footsteps echoed in the emptiness. A single streetlamp flickered, casting warped shadows that crawled across the cracked pavement like grasping hands. Every window boarded up, every door sealed tight against the night was a defiance of shelter.

Her heart slammed, each beat echoing in her ears like an ungodly drum. She was tempted to scream, to let the terror out, but she could not, she would not.

At the town edge, within a swirling blanket of fog, an ancient cottage came into view. Timbers in loose decay, half swallowed by shadow. Somewhere in the past, it might have been a home, but now it was just a hollow shell. Without a second thought, and with a gasp, she lunged forward to throw the door open and almost stumbled inside.

Rob and Daniel were right behind her as they closed the door with a thudding sound that went into her bones. For a few seconds, they stood there, chests still heaving, and sweat now cooling on their skins in the damp chill of the cottage.

Inside, the air was stale and thick with the reek of damp wood that clung to her throat. Shadows invaded, corners where darkness seemed to breathe. They could all hear it, the heartbeats, hers and those of her friends, a harsh pounding that filled the silence.

Rob doubled over and braced his legs as he gasped. *"Jesus Christ,"* he whispered, sweat dripping off his forehead. His hoarse voice was torn from his throat during their run.

Daniel leaned against the wall; the gun in his shaking hand glowed faintly in that dim light. His green eyes became wide-glassy, bordering on feverish panic. Clicking the safety off was the only sound he made.

Allison pressed her forehead to the door, her breath coming in ragged shudders. She closed her eyes to calm herself. *Breathe. Just breathe.* But her thoughts wouldn't stop.

Malakhov's touch had lingered on her skin like a phantom ache where his fingers had fastened around her wrist. Not a grip of violence or aggression, but something else entirely. Something that had left her cold and shaking.

Not the touch of an executioner. Not the touch of a man who wanted to kill her.

Recognition. Understanding. *Desire?*

Her skin crawled at the thought. She gritted her teeth and forced it out of her head. No time for that now.

"That was way too close," she whispered, brittle with fear, the voice rebounding in the hollow silence of the cottage.

Her eyes snapped open before she pushed herself back from the door, turning to face Rob and Daniel. She was breathing too fast, raggedly.

"We can't stay here," she said, voice barely standing the trembling weight of the words.

Rob let out a breath that was close to laughter but owned no humor. "*You think?*" came the dull retort, graceless for once instead of having its sharp bark. He wiped the sweat back from his brow, afterward slumping forward with exhaustion.

Daniel pushed off the wall, fingers raking his hair in an effort to stop the trembling in his hands. His eyes locked to Allison's own wild desperation. "They weren't even looking at us," he said, low, strained. "They only wanted *you.*"

The words hit her straight as a punch to the gut, but she didn't flinch. She swallowed hard, a bitter tang of fear on her tongue. She had known it from the first moment she'd seen Malakhov's eyes upon her across a crowded street. She'd told herself it was a coincidence, that it was nothing. But she wasn't that naive anymore.

She clenched her fists at her sides. "We should keep moving," she said. Her voice did crack; she forced it steady. "Get as far away as we can before they-"

A low hum filled the air, rising like a breath held too long. Seeping through the walls, it choked the cottage with cold energy unlike any Alison had felt before. Every hair on her arms stood up as she froze.

Daniel's eyes stretched wide and his skin grew pale, ashen. Rob's head snapped up, eyes wide and mouth agape in a curse without words.

They all felt it. The weight of it. An invisible presence that pressed against the cottage like unseen hands tightening with every tick of the clock.

Allison's heart popped in her ribs.

They're here.

Daniel whispered, his voice almost lost in the suppressing silence; "They knew we'd come here." The phrase caught and hung in the air like a poisonous mist.

Rob bolted to the window, adrenaline triggering his body to move so fast it felt numbing. He stuck his face to the narrow cracks in the boards, his breath fogging the splintered wood. "They're here," he rasped, "They're *everywhere.*"

Allison's hands were clammy. She stepped forward, pressing her back against the door frame for support. Peering through the crack she could barely square her stomach at what she saw.

Figures in the fog. Calm, patient, moving with the deliberate grace of hunters. They're not rushing the cottage. They're not battering the door. They're standing there, watching. *Waiting.*

Why are they not coming in?

She couldn't see his face, but she knew he was out there. Malakhov. Watching her. She could feel it like his gaze was a brand against her skin.

He wants me to see him. He wants me to know he's there.

A shudder ran down her spine, catching in her throat as the sound of his voice whispered through the darkness, so soft and low, it was as though he were whispering into her ear.

Daniel's grip upon the gun was tightening. "They want us to come to them," he told her, voice taut with tension.

Allison closed her eyes tightly, as if that would make it bearable. The questions kept circling around in her mind, rapidly and angrily; *Why me? What could they want with me?*

With so much effort, her gaze met Daniel's and she whispered, "We have to move," it came out in agonizing struggle with the fear choking her throat. "We cannot be trapped here with them."

Daniel sharply nodded with his jaw clenched. Rob's eyes met hers, widened with fear, but he gave a nod as well.

Outside, the fog was shifting, approaching. And shadows shifted, patient as death.

Then—the voice. As smooth and cruel as a winter gale.

The voice of Grigori Gordeev pierced the folds of darkness like an edged blade, laden with scorn. "We both know how this ends."

The air stood still for a moment when Allison's breath was paused in her throat, the sound of his voice making her blood chill in her veins. *They knew she was here.* They weren't breaking down that door for a reason of their own. They were toying with her. Drawing this out. Waiting for her to hit that weak point, *to break.*

She spun around, eyes sweeping the room. "Daniel, Rob..." Her voice cracked with urgency. "We have to run, there is a back entrance, a cellar door; if we can be fast enough, then we can—"

The explosions shattered the quiet of the cottage. It was as if the earth itself was tearing apart. Dust and bits of plaster cascaded down from the ceiling before blinding her. The floor beneath her had almost broken in two as splintered wood invaded the air.

Through the veil of dust, she heard Grigori's voice again. Grigori's voice was amused, mocked.

"Or," he whispered, "you can make this easy."

Daniel raised his gun. His jaw was clenched with fury. "We fight." The words were a promise.

Rob answered by raising his weapon also. "Damn right."

Allison didn't move. She didn't care to look at the battered door, nor at the figures in the darkness beyond—she looked on her friends, her *family*. They were the only people she could still trust left in this world.

If they fought, they'd die. Not because they weren't strong. Not because they weren't brave. But because Radimir didn't want them.

He only wanted *her*.

She felt it in her bones, cold certainty, like death. Outside, the cold pressed in from all sides, ready to swallow them the second they slipped. Her chest ached with it and with the knowledge of the terrible truth, that was the only way.

Tears prickled her eyelids, but she would not let them fall. Standing straight, she whispered, "*Go.*"

They exchanged glances with her that carried shock and fear, mixed with unspoken understanding. Rob's jaw tightened, disbelief filling his eyes—but Allison moved.

Her back hitting nothing, she had taken a step back. Because that was the only way.

"Run," she said, louder this time. No longer was she a girl begging for mercy; she was giving an order.

Rob bellowed hysterical laughter. "Are you *insane*?" he snapped. "We're not leaving you behind!"

"There's no other way," she said, stepping toward him. "They don't care about you. They only want me."

A heavy silence fell, thick as blood. The truth sank in for all present.

BOOM.

The door shattered inward, splinters shot like daggers. Shadows beyond the threshold seemed to spring into life and coalesce into the shapes of her nightmares. At the center was Grigori Gordeev, his eyes shining coldly and with ardent amusement; to his left, was Igor Romanov, his sneer promising violence; and to the right stood Dmitri Malakhov, his eyes locked on hers.

Allison felt her breath hitch, her chest heaving as she stared at his presence. Grigori moved forward; the soles of his boots made no sound against the broken floor. "It's over, *girl*," he said under his breath. "You know it. I know it."

For an instant, the room fell silent; nothing but shallow, ragged breaths could be heard.

Then—chaos.

Daniel fired. The single bullet practically thundered in its roar through the room, striking the door frame maybe two inches from Gordeev's head, splintering the wood. Gordeev gave no sign of a flinch. His gaze did not wander away from Allison.

"Stop," he said with a voice soft as silk. Daniel's arm bent at the elbow, his fingers shaking as he tried to hold the gun steady. He struggled to rise with it again, but his body froze at the quiet yet commanding presence in Gordeev's voice.

Rob lunged forward, his snarl muffled and furious-the butt of the rifle crashing terror into Gordeev. With flawless ease, Gordeev sidestepped him, almost gracefully. The other hand shot out and gripped Rob's wrist, twisting it with an extremely sickening crack. Rob shrieked his agony as the rifle slipped from his now useless fingers.

"NO!" Allison cried, rushing to Rob's side, but a hand clamped on her throat. The fingers were cold and calloused, clinging tightly.

Romanov. His face was mere inches away from hers, his breath hot and foul. His smile was a mockery. "Such a pretty little thing," he growled.

Her whole body shuddered and throbbed with panic. Out of reflex or defense, she clawed at his wrist, piercing the skin, trying to dig into him; but all those grooves cut into his skin were impotent agony; he would not let go.

"Let her go!" Daniel bellowed, his voice breaking with fury. He tried again to raise his gun, but Gordeev's gaze held him in place like an insect pinned beneath glass.

"I told you," Gordeev murmured, his voice like ice. "Stay out of this."

Romanov's grip tightened. Allison's vision began to whiten around the edges; the room was spinning. She was choking, struggling to suck the air that heaviness in her lungs refused to take.

Then, another voice. Calm, cold, so familiar it froze her blood.

"Enough."

The voice cleaved the chaos as if it were a blade. Allison's eyes snapped open, a hollow catch escaping her lips. The grip around her throat slackened just enough for her to gulp, but still, her lungs burned.

Through the almost palpable dust and shadows, she finally saw him. Malakhov, his coat dusted with plaster, expression unreadable.

The others stepped backward, falling into silence about him. Even Gordeev.

Malakhov's gaze met hers, a calm weight dropping and freezing her in place. "Release her." His voice was low, measured in tones that sent chills through her blood.

Romanov's fingers squeezed once, almost defiantly, before he dropped his hand from her throat. Allison staggered away, ragged gasps tearing into her lungs. Her knees gave way; her whole body trembled. She pressed one trembling hand to the growing bruises spreading across her neck but never broke eye contact with Malakhov.

With a step forward, the others seemed to fall back, almost as if pushed away through an unseen force. His very presence was its own entity, silent, suffocating, inescapable. For a moment, the rest of the room, all blood and violence, seemed to recede with the storm of chaos.

Malakhov's eyes glanced down to her throat, to see the coarse red imprints left by Romanov's grasp. His jaw clenched so faintly it might have been missed; she caught a fleeting hint in his glare, a sort of hybrid between sorrow and fury.

"Are you hurt?" The words came low again, but with a tenderness almost unknown to him, which stole her breath away for yet another time.

She blinked, startled by the concern behind his question. Her raw throat finally forced out a rasp. "I'm... fine..."

The smile that flickered across his lips was dangerous and, somehow, teasing. "*Liar*," he said, playfully. "You may be good at many things, but you are not good at lying."

"I didn't think you were paying so much attention..." she replied, voice thin and brittle. Her sarcasm was a fragile covering that was about all she had left.

The smile widened, but the warmth in his eyes was gone. "Oh, *Allison*," he murmured, going closer to her, so much so that she felt the warmth of his body heat, and could smell his scent of leather and smoke, "I see it all."

She caught her breath. "Oh, that is... disturbing."

He tilted his head while his fingers flicked lightly down her chin, inciting a shiver to run down her spine. "Only if there is something in your heart you wish to hide."

She started to say something, but no words came; instead, his hand fell away from her. His head turned, and he looked past her towards Daniel and Rob, the teasing glint fading away into an unforgiving and merciless one.

"Their business is no concern to me," he said harshly. "Let them go."

"No," Daniel said fiercely, his gun shaking in his grasp. "We are not going to leave her."

Malakhov's eyes narrowed, and his lips pursed in disdain. "If you stay, you die. This is not your fight. Leave. *Now.*"

The silence came down like a blade. Daniel was clutching his gun with white knuckles, his shoulders squared in a layer of stubbornness.

With a choked voice, Allison leaned forward and extended her hand to them. "*Please,*" she whispered, voice breaking. "Go."

Her eyes met Daniel's. For a split second, she saw a storm brewing; the battle between his need to protect her and the admission that to stay would mean death for all of them. His mouth opened. Then it closed. His shoulders slumped in defeat. A shuddered nod ensued.

Rob gave her a look that was half agony, half apology, and then he nodded too. Malakhov stepped aside with a silent order, and the others retreated, revealing a path toward the broken doorway.

As they passed her, Daniel squeezed her shoulder once in a silent promise.

"Don't you dare die on us," his voice was hoarse.

She smiled weakly. "I won't."

The silence swelled again like a coffin-lid, sealing her doom as their footsteps melted into the fog.

Malakhov's attention snapped back to her in a suffocating wash of darkness. Taking another step forward, he leaned in, voice dropping into a deep tender whisper just for her to hear. "Can you trust me, Allison?"

She looked at him, throat raw, heartbeat thundering beneath her in suspense. "Absolutely not," she said in a broken yet bitter voice.

"Good." A shadow of a smirk touched that predator-like smile, what almost felt teasing indeed. He brushed a strand of hair back off her face. His fingers radiated a heat that made her breath catch.

"Don't *touch* me!"

The smirk returned, he leaned forward with a thumb lightly caressing her jaw from her chin to her ear with a difference of tenderness from the steely hardness in his eyes. He stepped back, "I guess if you want your captor to be a little more... *charming*, I can comply."

Her laugh was short and weary, full of disbelief. "*Charming*? You just threatened my friends."

"And *spared* them," he whispered, helping her up, "A kindness you'd best not mistake for weakness."

Her pulse began to race, screaming to push away, but her body wouldn't move an inch. "*Why*?" came the strangled whisper. "Why are you doing this?"

Darkness slipped over his face, that temporally possessive gleam in his eyes. "Because," he said softly, "you belong to us."

Heart slammed against rib cage; the frantic, wild beat. "No," she countered, trembling, "I'm not yours."

Almost amused, almost... indulgent. There was that dangerous smile again. "Oh, Allison," he breathed. "You just keep telling yourself that."

Her mouth opened, ready to scream in protest, but no sound came out; the atmosphere in the room thickened with weight under his gaze.

Malakhov leaned in until she felt his breath on her skin. His voice was low, unyielding. "Now," he murmured. "We're leaving."

Seven

A Smile Without Mercy

The metal cuffs bit sharply at Allison's wrist, the ruthless rivets dug into her flesh with every jolt as the car bumped over an uneven roadway. The heavy weight of steel numbed the feeling out of her arms. She shifted slightly in a futile attempt to ease the ache, but there was none.

The car felt like a cramped metal box, the kind that squeezed the breath right out of you. Only the occasional flicker of streetlights cut through the dark. The air was thick with the smell of sweat, leather, and damp wool—clinging to her skin, heavy in her lungs, like it knew exactly how scared she was.

Fear forced her to sit rigidly between her captors, her back pressed hard against the cold wooden panel. Grigori Gordeev sat directly across from her, luxuriating in a confidence he wore casually, legs spread wide, spinning his gun between his fingers as if it were a mere trinket. His black eyes gleamed with enjoyment born of cruelty as he stared down at her, her anguish shrank under his gaze, as if he were eager for the performance to begin.

Her left side belonged to Igor Romanov, whose grin was that hideous, greedy seal, teeth unnaturally yellowed, leering. His gaze dragged over her like something feral sizing up its prey, and though she fought to keep her expression cold and unreadable, a flicker of disgust still slipped through.

Allison forced herself to keep her head up, holding her face in a carefully neutral expression. She would give them no indication how her stomach tightened in disgust or how dread gnawed slowly at her insides. Yes, she was their prisoner, but she would not give them control over her.

Not yet.

Not ever.

"Well, well," Grigori laughed, mockery thick within his voice, rough around the edges from an accent. "Never thought I'd see the great little detective in chains."

Allison said nothing.

His smirk grew wider, full of dark amusement. "What? Nothing to say? No clever words for me now?"

Igor chuckled, the sound low and threatening, his fingers drumming on the bench, "Maybe she is learning manners," he said, his voice loud with heavy sarcasm. "Knows her place now, yes? Little girl."

Allison's skin crawled at the words.

Igor leaned in closer, his foul breath hot against her ear. "I could teach you some manners," he whispered, voice low, thick with sick amusement. "Break you in proper, before we hand you over. You understand, yes?"

She felt bile making its way up her throat as she jerked away.

Igor let out a low, grating laugh. "She looks like she'd like it rough, yeah? Smart little thing like her—probably puts up a fight."

Allison bit down hard on her tongue, swallowing the retort burning in her throat.

"Dirty little pig," he muttered, licking his lips. "Bet you scream real pretty."

She stared ahead, silent, refusing to give them what they wanted.

Igor's grin stretched wider. "Or maybe you'll stay quiet. Maybe you'll beg. Guess we'll find out."

Grigori chuckled darkly beside him. "They always beg in the end. Always."

Igor shifted, hand sliding dangerously close to her thigh—

And then from her other side a new voice emerged.

"Enough."

Malakhov said it just loud enough for them to hear, the single word cutting through the tight space like a blade.

Allison's breath suddenly caught as she was caught between hope and despair.

Romanov's grin froze halfway through a sneer, his predatory eyes narrowing as the atmosphere thickened instantly with tension.

For the first time since they had captured her, the entire mood inside the car shifted.

Malakhov, who had remained silent and still throughout the whole tense ride, finally moved.

He slid smoothly across the wooden bench, settling beside Grigori Gordeev. His expression was unreadable, calm, but cold and the ease in his posture betrayed a lethal confidence. There was no unnecessary motion, no wasted energy, but the threat he carried was undeniable.

Allison realized then that, although Malakhov had been the only one in the carriage who hadn't laid a hand on her violently, hadn't sneered or threatened, he was clearly the one they all feared the most.

His dark eyes flicked sharply toward Romanov, calm but edged with a quiet, iron authority that demanded attention.

"You know the Boss's orders," Malakhov said, voice low and steady.

Romanov's sneer curled at the corner of his mouth, mocking yet hesitant. "We're just having a little fun, Malakhov. No harm in—"

Malakhov tilted his head slightly; his eyes became as penetrating as a knife's edge."Shall I remind you what transpired the last time someone dare disobey the Boss's orders regarding her?"

The question came soft, deceptively light, almost conversational. But the weight behind it was undeniable.

Romanov's grin vanished as if snuffed out.

The car fell into a heavy choking silence.

Even Grigori's trademark smirk dimmed for the barest instant, a flicker of hesitation running across his shadowed features.

Romanov muttered his disapproval and with a groan, reclined, mockingly raising his hands in surrender.

"Fine, fine," he mumbled through clenched teeth. "Didn't know you were so protective of her."

Malakhov's gaze never glanced to acknowledge him. Not a blink.

"I'm not," he said, quietly, coldly, "I am protective of my own survival."

The words hung in the stale air, curiosity-sated and heavy with finality.

Allison breathed out softly while her heart hammered in her ears. Malakhov had her baffled, she wondered about his real intention and why he had come to help at all.

But one thing was painfully clear, he was not her ally.

He was not there to save her.

He was simply a man following orders.

And that terrified her far more than any threat Romanov or Gordeev could make.

They pulled up to a sprawling manor, its iron gates clanging shut behind them with a metallic finality that echoed across the grounds like a sentence passed. The mansion doors groaned open, then slammed shut with a deafening thud, trapping Allison and the man inside a chamber so cold it seemed to seep straight into her bones.

The sudden stillness weighed heavily upon Allison, she was gasping, too fast, too shallow, and uneven. Her wrists throbbed painfully, still raw and sore from shackles that had been just recently removed, the memory of cold steel biting into her skin fresh and raw.

Far away at the other end of the chamber, Radimir stood frozen, almost petrified, his pale hands clasped neatly behind his back. His immobile gaze was penetrating in its silence—one that felt not unlike waiting but rather akin to calculating.

He didn't so much as utter a single word. Just watched.

The silence lingered, stretched too tightly over their presence, the weight of which somehow seemed to tighten Allison's lungs and constrict her breathing even more.

Then he stepped toward her, slow and deliberate.

"You are mine, *Malyshka*."

The words slid out softer than Allison expected. It was free of ridicule.

No cruelty.

Just quiet, unshakable certainty.

Like this was not a threat. But an unchangeable fact.

"You always have been."

Allison felt her stomach twist violently and a chill knot clenched within her gut.

Her fingers curled tightly into little fists at her sides, nails digging into her palms, sensation anchoring herself against the dread.

"I'm not yours."

Her voice stayed calm, steady even—but inside, everything was in chaos. Fear, defiance, and anger twisted together, pulling her in all directions.

Radimir slowly smiled, his smile full of insinuation.

"You think so?"

She met his gaze squarely. "I *know* so."

His silver eyes glinted with something unreadable—amusement? Pity? Something darker.

The man spoke softly, dropping a casual "I did always admired that about you. That stubborn fire. That never-give-in type of obstinacy. That sort of passion. It is a rare thing."

He then took another step forward; the sound echoed off the cold stone walls.

"And yet... here you are."

Allison refused to flinch even if her heart punched fiercely against her ribs. She tilted her chin up higher.

"You had me dragged here in chains. That isn't really being victorious."

A low, chuckling rasp came from him.

"Dragged?" His lips curled up almost amused, his head slightly tilted, as if toying with a curious conundrum. "You misunderstand, Allison. You were always meant to be here."

The words settled heavily, more chilling than the cold stones against which she stood.

There was something about that voice, a knowing certainty, as if half the secret lay with him. Something that ought to make her recoil, to stagger back, claw away, and flee.

But she didn't.

She wouldn't.

Though a part of her trembled, terrified.

"I was never meant to be anywhere near you," she said firmly, though her voice cracked slightly.

His eyes flickered with amusement at her defiance.

"Then tell me," he said quietly, "why do you think you're still alive?"

The question caught her off guard. Her mouth opened and searched, but no words came. Because the truth was simple, *she didn't know.*

Why was she still alive? Was it a mistake? A cruel joke?

Or was there some deeper reason, something tangled in fate, that kept her breathing under his shadow?

Her mind raced.

Was this some cruel game to wear her down?

Or had Radimir spared her for something far darker than she dared to imagine? The quiet settled around them, heavy as wet wool, smothering any thought she tried to form. Radimir's gaze pierced through Allison unblinking, waiting her answer. But she could only stare back; her fists clenched tightly, trembling slightly as her thoughts went spiraling into the unknown.

Why had they restrained her and dragged her here, only for Radimir to now stand before her silver-eyed, calm, and patient as if he had all the time in the world? Why had they left her untouched, unmarked, except for the bruising of her capture? Allison swallowed hard, grasping at her thoughts, trying to steady them as they rattled within her skull.

Her chest rose and fell with ragged breaths. She forced his voice out as firmly as she could. "You think I'll tell you something."

Radimir's head tilted, and a flicker of amusement showed across his pale face. "You think too small, Allison." His tone was light, almost gentle, and it sent chills racing across her spine.

Allison's pulse thudded in her throat, loud and sharp, while the chill in the room brushed against her skin like cold breath. She could feel the weight of him somehow—like invisible hands pressing down on her. Radimir looked at her with unsettling focus, something close to hunger in his eyes... or maybe something darker.

"I wonder," he murmured, almost to himself, "what do you think you are to me?"

Allison stood there, frozen. A moment passed and hitched a breath.

What was she to him?

A pawn?

A bargaining chip?

Or something worse?

A rush of nausea began in her stomach. Shaking it off, she forced herself to keep her voice steady. "I am *nothing* to you," she said, these words bitter on her tongue.

His smile did not waver, thin and humorless, barely reaching his eyes. But then a movement, a flicker of interest, or maybe something on the darker side.

"Your parents were always cowards," he said quietly, with all the deliberate, measured tones.

The accusation made Allison stiffen, tension locking her shoulders.

Radimir saw it. He pressed further, his voice almost conversational.

"They lied to you. They considered it the only way to protect you."

Allison felt her throat tightening as if an icy hand was sliding down her spine.

No. He was lying. He had to be. This was what he did. He twisted the truth, turned it into a weapon.

"They never lied to me," she forced out, though her voice cracked.

She needed to believe that. She had to.

Radimir exhaled slowly through his nose, almost like a disappointed sigh. "They lied to everyone, Allison. *You* were just their greatest lie."

Her hands trembled at her sides, and she clenched her fists so hard that her nails dug painfully into her palms. She echoed the hard and hollow words, "I don't believe you."

He began to walk toward her, each paces purposely measured and precise. His presence descended upon her with icy suffocation.

"You don't have to," the whisper came in reply. "The truth exists whether you believe it or not." She gasped for breath and almost drowned out everything with the pounding of her heartbeat in her ears.

She wanted to scream at him.

To deny him, to fight him. But she couldn't find her voice.

And then—

Radimir said the words that shattered everything she thought she knew about him, about *everything*. It hit her like a rush of ice, cutting through her thoughts and leaving nothing but cold, brutal clarity.

"You are my daughter."

Time stuttered and splintered around her. Allison opened her mouth, but nothing came. The words he'd spoken lodged somewhere beneath her ribs, sharp and unreal.

His daughter.

No.

It couldn't be.

It wasn't true.

She shook her head slowly, her voice barely a whisper. "You're lying..."

Radimir's gaze softened, or maybe it was just another mask he wore, a calculated move to throw her off balance.

"Would you like me to prove it?" he said quietly, with a drawl of kindness.

Allison felt weak in her knees; her heart pounded and it felt as if it would just leap out of her chest. She felt like screaming. *To run.*

But she stood frozen, trapped in the weight of those impossible words.

She was his *daughter.*

Allison swallowed, her voice raw. "Why are you telling me this?"

Radimir's mouth curved in something almost like a smile. "Because you deserve to know what you are."

He shifted back half a step. The chill of him remained lodged in her bones.

Questions collided in her head, none of them taking shape before the next one hit.

But she could not speak. She simply stood there, staggering from the reverberation of this one-shattering revelation.

Allison felt the ground shift beneath her, like the floor was slipping away into nothing. Her body froze, rigid and unyielding, while her mind hit a dead stop, like it forgot how to think. A tightness clawed at her throat, and the room around her melted into a swirl of colors.

No.

Her legs felt as if they too might have just given away beneath her. Clinging to the very last bit of her disbelief seemed like she was holding onto the only thing that could keep her upright. She choked out the words, "You're lying," her voice thin and far away.

Radimir smiled slowly, a cold amusement twisting her inside in bewilderment. "*Am I?*" he murmured in an almost indulgent tone.

Her head shook wildly, and the curls whipped about her face as desperation rose in her voice.

"No. No, that can't be." Her voice cracked on the last word, but she did not care.

"You were hidden," Radimir said, almost mocking that sort of calm certainty that flatly stated the obvious. "Erased. Buried in a lie so deep that even you believed it." His wickedly bright eyes cut into her gazing upon every twitch, every tremor of her body.

Her lungs felt as though they were turning to stone, as if she wasn't able to draw a proper breath. Every inhalation was ragged and shallow.

"They would never have..." she began, faltering like a candle in the wind.

Radimir's smile vanished, to be replaced by a far darker expression. "They *took* you from me," he whispered, so low that the words itself seemed to crumble into the air like lead ore.

Allison staggered back a step, her eyes wide in disbelief, her mind refusing to comprehend. The slow horror slithered around her throat, tightening step by step with her ever-shrinking heart.

No.

This wasn't happening. This was some twisted, psychological game—a cruel trick, a manipulation.

This was what he did.

This was who he was.

A small breath passed from her lips, forced out. "I still don't believe you."

Radimir gave back his smile, thin, and sharp as a dagger. "*You will,*" he said softly. There was such absolute certainty that her bones involuntarily shuddered.

She wanted to scream at him to take back what he had just said... Because if he was lying, then *fine*. She could fight him. She could hold onto that. But if he wasn't... If there was even a chance...

Her parents. Their quiet strength, their warmth. Their love.

They were hers. *They were hers.* They had to be.

Each breath scraped her throat raw, too shallow to steady her. She felt as if she was slowly drowning with the weight of his words, with each word that sank her deeper.

With a somewhat clinical curiosity, Radimir looked at her, his face unreadable.

He said no more and let the silence hang around them as the weight of his words settled into her bones.

Allison's eyes searched the room for something, anything, to anchor her, to pull her back from the edge of this impossible revelation.

She wanted to run. To tear at the walls until she woke up from this nightmare. But she couldn't move.

At last, her voice broke in a small, feathery whisper. "*Why?*"

Her question was raw, torn from her chest.

Shadow of disdain darkened Radimir's gleaming eyes as he stepped closer, his once clear voice waning into a silk whisper.

"Because, whether you believe it or not—the blood in your veins is *mine.*"

She felt the fragile edges of her sanity fraying now, and her thoughts scattering about like leaves caught in a storm.

She shook her head again as her voice broke into another sob.

The silence that loomed was inaudible.

She felt as if she were about to collapse.

She felt like she might shatter.

And still, Radimir watched her, patient, cold, and waiting for her to break.

Then—

"Malakhov."

The doors opened with a great reverberation, echoing through the silent room like a whip cracking. Allison's head snapped toward those doors with her chest rising and falling to the awful burden of Radimir's words. Malakhov stepped inside, his long strides measured, and his expression unreadable as ever.

His cold gray eyes flicked from Radimir to Allison and back, betraying nothing.

Radimir's voice remained calm. Absolute. "Take her to your estate."

Allison's thoughts stuttered to a halt.

The world tilted again. She had expected a cell. Expected chains and dark dungeons. Expected to be left to rot in some forgotten hole. Not... *this.*

Malakhov's jaw tightened, a flicker of something, *doubt? Uncertainty?* Passing across his face before he smothered it beneath the cool mask of obedience.

He bowed his head slightly, but his lips parted, the ghost of a protest catching there. "Sir..."

The words were soft, cautious, like he was choosing them carefully.

Inwardly, Malakhov's mind roiled.

The girl. Murphy. She was originally thought to be nothing. Just another detective taken off the street. But now... His daughter?

The idea was madness. *Dangerous madness.*

But Radimir's orders were clear, and Malakhov knew better than to question them aloud. Still... To bring her to his estate, to shelter her, even as a prisoner? It was a risk.

A risk that could cost him everything if he misstep.

He made an effort to keep his features in control, though a shadow of unease still lingered in his eyes. He had seen Radimir's wrath before. He would not test it.

Radimir didn't look at him, his attention still fixed on Allison with a possessive calm. "Ensure she remains unharmed," he said.

The words were soft but left no room for doubt.

Malakhov's mind churned. *Unharmed.* He was no fool, he knew what that meant. *No interrogations. No petty cruelties.*

She was... important. *His daughter.*

The thought still scraped against his reason, but he had seen Radimir's power. He knew better than to question it openly.

A pause.

Then—"*She is mine.*"

The finality in Radimir's voice settled over the room like a vice.

Allison's breath shook. She was unable to tear her eyes from Radimir, her mind trying vainly to understand the impossible.

Malakhov shifted; their eyes met momentarily. She looked so small. So breakable. He forced the thought away.

It wasn't his place to think of her as anything but what she was, a *prisoner*.

But Radimir's words, *she is mine,* they resonated with a dark finality that even he couldn't ignore.

Radimir wasn't exactly generous with his praise. If anything, he nodded like he was handing out a rare reward, not just giving orders.

"Welcome home."

The words dripped with cold amusement, and Allison flinched as if struck.

Malakhov's heart beat a little faster. This was no ordinary task. He inclined his head, his voice carefully neutral.

"It will be done, Sir." But inside, a sliver of doubt twisted in his gut. *What was his plan with her, truly?* And what would it cost Malakhov to stand between them if the Boss's mood ever changed?

Once they took her gun, she stood trembling, as though she'd already been shown her grave.

Malakhov forced the thought aside. He was Malakhov. He obeyed. He would take her to his estate. *That was all.*

He gestured curtly. "Come."

Allison's legs barely worked. She moved, because standing still felt worse.

Behind them, the doors shut slowly and firmly, sealing in the echo of Radimir's voice. His words hanging heavy in the air like a curse that wouldn't be broken.

Eight

The Gilded Cage

The car ride was silent.

Allison sat in the back, her movements mechanical, as if she were only going through the motions. She was still reeling from the conversation, replaying every word in a punishing cycle.

Malakhov sat next to her, legs spread, one arm casually resting on the back of the seat. He was relaxed almost to the point of boredom. He had not said a single thing from the moment they left the headquarters. His gaze was fixed somewhere outside and purposely away from her.

She wanted to scream at him; to demand answers, to demand the truth. *Why was she here? What did Radimir want with her? What the hell was any of this?*

But she refused to be the one to speak first. She wouldn't break the silence. Wouldn't give him that. Not when she already felt like she was losing everything else.

The car slowed down as it made its way down the cobbled street, lined with giant ancient trees and ominous shadows. A mansion loomed at the end of the drive, all stone and glass, its silhouette carved out of the dark like something that refused to be known.

Allison's hands throbbed where the restraints bit into her skin, but she barely felt the pain. All she could hear inside her head was Radimir's words echoing.

You are mine, Malyshka

You always have been.

The vehicle slowly came to stop, as the large iron gates swung open to admit them to the estate. The window on the passenger side creaked as the door flew open, the outside, cold wind entered inside the car, opposing the suffocating warmth of her fear.

Malakhov was first out of the car, his leather boots creaked as he climbed down on the gravel stones of the pavement. With a steady motion, his gaze swept over her and then he reached for her, his hand closed around her upper arm with a gentle ease that made her stomach unsettled.

She dug her heels into the earth, resisting out of sheer instinct, but Malakhov did not seem to mind. He did not yank her roughly or pull her. He just guided her forward. His grip was steady and firm, the pressure of his hands more grounding than painful. Her boots dragged against the stones made her balance waver.

She barely found her footing before he pressed her back against the car. The impact stole her breath, it was not violent, but unsettling in its steadiness, as if he were assessing her reactions.

He released her hand and slowly made it come around to lean on her waist. The very deliberate slowness caused her heart to race. The chill of the night air bit at her skin; because of this, she could only feel the heat of his hand.

His face hovered close, his breath warm against her cheek, expression unreadable. No threat in the moment, just the quiet inevitability of his hands and the closing of space that felt like a claim.

Calm. Amused. *Dangerous.*

"I am not staying here," she snapped, her voice dropping to a cold edge.

Malakhov tilted his head, his lips twitching in a faint smirk. "We'll see," he said lazily.

The fury bubbled up in her chest, white-hot and reckless. She lunged at him, her hands still bound but she put her weight behind the shove. It was a pitiful attempt, he barely shifted an inch.

He took evil delight in grabbing her wrist, turning her round, and pinning her to the car. His body was pressing against hers, and the heat of him seemed to seep through the thin fabric of her jacket.

She kicked out at him with burning frustration coursing through her veins, but he did not flinch. His grip was iron-like, unyielding, yet not cruel.

A low laugh vibrated in his chest, soft and amused. "You can't possibly think you'll win, little lion."

She drew a shaky breath. "You don't know me," she spat, her glare sharp enough to cut.

His grin curved slow and dangerous. *"Don't I?"* His voice lowered to something dark and velvety that sent chills down her back despite her anger.

She tried to wrench free. Still, he held her fast, his thumb tracing gently over her pulse. Almost gentle.

Almost.

His eyes gleamed with a cruel glint. "I *remember,*" he said, soft and teasing. "Last November—the shootout at the bank on 10th Street?"

Allison stilled. Her throat went tight.

He bent above her, his breath barely touching the edge of her ear in a warm caress. "I remember *you,*" he whispered, almost with fondness, as if recalling a pleasant occasion.

The memories blindsided her—blood spattering across tile, glass falling like rain, the searing impact of a bullet that nearly stopped her breathing. It had missed her heart only by a fraction, with surgeons working overtime to save her life, just barely.

Her chest heaved. Her fingers curled into fists. "I almost *died*!" she hissed.

Malakhov's smirk faded and his face went blank. "I didn't intend for you to survive," he said quietly.

Silence fell, heavy and suffocating. Her pulse thundered in her ears.

Then he started smiling again, slowly and deliberately. "But yet... here you are."

She wanted to scream; her hands wanted to claw off that smug look on his face. But her rage tangled with something colder, an acid dread she couldn't shake.

He suddenly let go of her wrist and stepped back just enough to give her a moment of space, his eyes never once departing from hers.

"I suppose I should be grateful," he said with a lightness almost as if it were just a passing thought.

Her lip curled. "*Grateful*?" she echoed, her voice dripping acid. "For what? That I didn't bleed out all over the *fucking* floor?"

He gave her a glancing look, with a slight smirk twinkling in one half-closed eye. He snorted before whispering, "Because if you had died, Boss would have surely killed me by now." His manner was fluid and teasing, like two people talking about the weather rather than about her near-death experience.

Cold sweat ran down her spine. *This was it. That was why*; not because she was alive, but because he was.

"You're a bastard," she snapped, tightly clenching her fists.

Malakhov tilted his head slightly, eyes glittering. "Ah, but you already knew that."

She glared at him. "You don't care about me."

The wicked smirk on his face widened, sweet honeyed sarcasm dripping from his smooth words. "Of course not."

Then, his fingers drifted over hers, just a fleeting caress, an invisible whisper against her skin; it made her breath hitch, made her heart miss a beat, as if he dared her to believe in something more.

She hated it.

Hated him.

She spat the words at him. "You're playing a dangerous game," she said.

Her smirk only grew wider. "And you're playing it with me, *little lion*," he whispered, deep and wicked. "Don't play innocent; and pretend you're not enjoying it a bit."

Her fury surged up inside her; she tugged away. "I'd rather die than be your plaything."

For a single moment, his eyes darkened-a flash of something she could not quite put a name to. Then, lazily, he smirked with a look of boredom. "We'll see."

Turning away from her then, she felt broken. A burning fury and confusion were choking her, tightening their grip on her, and she just could not rid herself of that feeling.

"Come inside," he said with a casual smile, gesturing toward the looming estate.

She hesitated now, every nerve screaming to run away. Her legs were heavy as lead. Her chest felt hollow, breathless. Braving each step, her feet scraped against the stones as she followed him inside.

The manor was beautiful in a cold, ancient sort of way-high ceilings, one could imagine the scent of burning firewood reaching their nose through the tall windows. It was a place that was meant to be safe. But she felt the presence, every bit like a noose choking her.

She spun around on him as the doors closed behind them, her breath ragged. "Why am I here?" she demanded.

Malakhov shrugged lazily at her, his smile veering toward the mischievous. "Because he told me to bring you here."

Her eyes narrowed. "Why?"

He looked at her for a long moment, something flickering in his eyes. "I think you already know," he spoke in a softer voice.

She clenched her jaw, not letting him in on how that made her stomach flip.

He smirked while stepping forward. "Come on; let me show you to your room."

She glared at him but did not struggle as he led her up the sweeping staircase.

The Malakhov estate hallways had an unnatural silence in them. Allison went through them one by one, with every step counted, her wrists beginning to throb with the old familiar pain from the strain of the manacles that were only just removed. A low persistent hum filled the air, a mixture of hidden surveillance cameras and the faint distant echo of the footing of some guards, stating in no uncertain terms that every move she made was being watched and her freedom squeezed dry.

She was trapped, but this was no dungeon. It was a gilded cage, with passages of opulence stretching far and wide; this was an idea that unsettled her ever so much more than cold stones and iron bars would have.

Shelves crowded the walls, books scarred by time. Portraits of unsmiling ancestors watched her pass. Decorated with somber oil portraits of grim-faced forebears who seemed to watch her in silence. Under glass were cases housing intricate artifacts and relics, worthy of display in museums or of noble families, that all spoke riches and power, not punishment. This place was to make her feel safe. To lull her into complacency.

To induce forgetfulness about her status as a prisoner. Allison had different ideas.

To her surprise, the room that had been opened for her was warm, with wood paneling, a soft bed, and a homey fire merrily crackling away on the grate.

Allison had been suspiciously staring around the small room, noticing the heavy wooden beams and the hazy glow of light from the fireplace. "Is this supposed to make me feel... *comfortable*?" She asked coldly, each word clipped.

He leaned back casually on the door frame in low light. His long, flowing jet-black hair fell in strands brushing a tan neck and a sharply-lined jaw. A sprinkle of freckles ran across his nose and cheeks, somehow softening the edges of an otherwise sharp face.

His physique was athletic, with half-a-dozen muscles coiling tight under a narrow shirt, yet he moved with a calculated grace. Not enormous but heavy on his feet, his broad shoulders tapered down to a slim waist. Across his chest and arms, the shirt was painted tight, sleeves pushed halfway up his forearms, which bore the faintest smattering of freckles with his sun-scorched warmth, the branded sigil just peeking out from underneath where the fabric bunched up.

He grinned at her, messy and almost mocking, flashing a wicked grin of white teeth. "Consider it... *a courtesy*," he said, his voice ragged with quiet amusement.

She crossed her arms and tightened her gaze on how the firelight played across his face. "What the hell am I supposed to sleep in?" she barked acidly. "You planning to keep me in these clothes forever?"

He started to hum, tilting his head in serious contemplation of the question she had put forward. Then, with a theatrical gesture, he removed off the dark button-down shirt that had graced his frame over his undershirt; his biceps flexing under the pleasant distraction as the fabric was stretched taut across his chest.

With a casual wrist flick, he flung the shirt in her direction. "Here," he said softly, as though presenting her with a glass of water. "This will suffice for tonight."

She grabbed hold of it instinctively. The warmth from the fabric and its softness caused her eyebrows to shoot upward in surprise. "What, there is no spare set of clothes from your wife lying somewhere?" she shot back, sounding as sharp and pinprick as steel.

His smile grew wider, as if a hilarity of some kind had materialized there on the spot. "No wife," he said darkly and with added emphasis. "Not really my style."

He let his eyes slowly and deliberately sweep all over her. "Though... if you'd like to play that role for a night, *sweetheart*, I might be convinced."

She snickered and tossed the shirt back to him, rolling her eyes. "In your dreams."

He caught it with ease; his fingers closed on the fabric with a hurried casualness that made her breath condense. "Oh, you will be," he said, gently closing it with an airy finesse over his arm. "But tonight—" plopping it back in her hands with a brushing touch of his fingers over hers, warm and firm "keep this. I'm sure it will look much better on you."

She narrowed her eyes. "Don't hold your breath for confirmation."

His smirk held on. "I will try not to be too disappointed," he said in that quiet voice, low and playful, rolling his shoulders in a slow, deliberate motion and pushing off from the edge of the door frame, never diverting his gaze from hers.

"Good night, Allison," he purred in mock courtesy, "I'll be right down the hall if you... need anything."

She glared, and said nothing—denying him the satisfaction.

He stood and watched for a long moment, his gaze unwavering with notable calmness before finally turning and closing the door behind him.

Darkness swallowed the room, the fireplace crackling in its corner. She stood there for what felt like an hour, the shirt heavy in her hands, her thoughts refusing to quiet.

In the thin light, Allison stayed awake, Radimir's echoed words ringing in her ears like a curse; *You are mine. You always have been.* She wanted to disprove it; she wanted to believe Radimir was playing some elaborate game, some cruel manipulation, but there was something raw and terrible deep inside her that told her it was the truth.

But she'd find a way to get out. She would.

Tonight, she'd wear his shirt, and survive, even if she hated every second of it.

Morning came too soon; Allison's eyelids fluttered open before the faint steal of first light entered through the heavy curtains. The room was cooler, but the weight of the silk shirt Malakhov handed to her still clung to her skin—a soft, alien comfort that unsettled her inside. She stood there, hesitant, every muscle screaming against it in exhaustion. But today was one day she knew she couldn't run away from.

When she finally descended the wide staircase, the shirt hung low and loose on her skinny frame, hem brushing barely above her knees, the loose fabric was completely swallowed by folds meant for a man twice her size. The sleeves bunched awkwardly at her wrists, the collar slipping low against her collarbone. Cautious, she moved through the vast estate while her bare steps were swallowed by thick Persian rugs. From somewhere, she felt Malakhov's stare—sharp, heavy, and unrelenting—following her every step.

"Well, little lion," his Russian-accented his words, almost licking them, enticing her along into the breakfast hall. "I have to say, that shirt looks far better on you than it ever did on me."

His eyes sparkled with a dangerous glint while humor tried to make a bid for its place, only to be overtaken by something darker; something possessive. For a brief second, the weight of his control pressed down upon her, not in chains or shackles, but by something as simple as that look. Allison squared her shoulders, unwilling to be broken.

The breakfast room matched the manor's grandeur but felt unnaturally cheerful. The air smelled of fresh herbs and something sweet she couldn't name. The table was ceremoniously set with fine china and crystal glasses. Silver trays held pastries lightly dusted with powdered sugar; bowls of fresh berries sparkled with all the gleam known to mankind. Black coffee and tea sat waiting in steaming cups. It was strange to see golden-yellow butter beside cloth-wrapped croissants, the steam still rising from them.

She seated herself at one end of the long table, her wrists now free, but her hands awkwardly clasped in her lap. Malakhov took his position at the other end of the table, reclining with an air of confident ease, impeccably attired in a suit seemingly chosen with him in mind. He lounged with practiced ease, but nothing about him suggested anything less than complete command.

Before her lay a full breakfast spread; more fit for a guest of honor rather than for a prisoner. Smoked salmon, thin slices of smoked cheeses, and warm bread with honey. But Allison did not lift a single bite toward her mouth.

Again, her eyes flickered toward Malakhov as his eyebrow went up and a very faint smile touched his lips.

"Still playing hard to get?" he murmured, swirling the dark liquid in his own glass.

Allison pressed her lips into a thin line. "I'm not hungry."

"*Perhaps*," he said, smooth as silk, "you simply are not hungry for what I am offering." His eyes held hers unapologetically, sharply. "Because refusing to eat only makes this harder on you."

Allison shook her head, refusing to crack. "I don't trust anything from the Bratva."

Malakhov chuckled softly, that deep, dangerous sound again. "Listen, Allison. If I *really* wanted you dead, you'd be in the ground by now."

Swallowing hard, she held onto that steady look. He was as much the mystery as was the man who sent her here. And the stakes were equally deadly.

An amused and impatient sigh escaped Malakhov. "You're just being dramatic," he breathed smoothly, as if he were unbothered by it all.

She did not look him in the eye. "You're holding me hostage."

"*Semantics*," he replied with that causal shrug, stirring his coffee.

She bit down hard on her lower lip.

He snuck a glance at her, that tiny shadow of a smile dancing about in his eyes. "I assume you have questions."

That sparked a flutter of hope in her, and she threw herself forward, eyes sharp and unwavering. "Why am I here?"

His eyes sparkled with amusement. "Because Radimir commanded it."

She let out a slow breath, barely keeping her expression neutral. "I meant—why *here*? Why with you?"

Malakhov set the cup down with a soft clink, tilting his head as if weighing her value. "You *think* I asked for this?"

Her lips pressed together tightly. "Did you?"

His smile widened just enough to unsettle her. Allison's fingers curled in her lap. He was enjoying this, playing with her like a cat toys with a mouse. But she refused to give him the satisfaction. She stacked her chin, forcing calm into her voice. "If I'm so important to him, why put me here? Why not keep me under his watch?"

He sighed again, almost bored, and said, "The Boss is not the type to hold a leash, Allison. He does not cage what already belongs to him."

Her breath hitched. She forced herself to stay composed. "You speak like he's already won."

Malakhov's lips curved into a slow, knowing smile. "Hasn't he?"

Her chest tightened with a cold dread.

No.

Not yet.

Not ever.

She pushed her untouched plate forward.

He met her eyes directly."You know, by refusing to eat, you only hurt yourself."

Her stomach twisted unpleasantly.

"Eat," he said, deliberately picking up a piece of bread.

She said nothing.

He leaned back, eyes sharp, watching her like a predator assessing prey. "You still believe you're leaving, don't you?"

She kept silent.

Malakhov's sigh was almost indulgent. "Escape is impossible," he said quietly. "You've seen the gates, the guards."

She had. She knew the house was a fortress, every window, every door warded and watched. And yet—

"Impossible isn't forever," she said quietly.

He smirked. "Spoken like a true detective."

Her jaw locked. He was toying with her, testing the limits of her resolve. But she wouldn't let him win.

Changing tactics, she said carefully, "You don't seem the type to *babysit* prisoners."

Malakhov raised a brow, curiosity flickering across his face. "I'm not."

"Then why keep me here?"

He tilted his head, considering her carefully. "You assume I have a choice."

She let a long silence stretch between them, then leaned forward, voice low and steady. "You do."

His expression held no emotions, but his fingers went on tapping to a rhythmic beat on the cup.

"I imagine Radimir is a difficult one to oppose," she pressed on, "but you don't seem the kind who would be a... what'd you say?—*leash-holder.*"

Malakhov's lips curled slowly into a dark smile, and then he laughed. It was not a laugh of cruelty or scorn but genuine amusement. It churned Allison's stomach violently, the first glancing miss since her arrival.

He leaned forward, his voice deepening, more amused as he said, "Do you really think you can *manipulate* me?"

Her chest tightened as she held his gaze, clinging to the idea that perhaps there would be a consideration on his part. But he had seen through her, and found it amusingly endearing.

Malakhov laughed. "Oh, *sweetheart*" he whispered, "you really have no idea what you're up against."

Her breath had come short and ragged.

He lifted his coffee, a slow smile tugging at his mouth. "Try again."

Nine

Crimson, Control, and Cruelty

The gown felt like a trap.

Layers of silk pressed against her skin, tight and unforgiving, the deep ruby shade making her feel like she was draped in Russia's flag. The corset was pulled tight, squeezing the air from her lungs. Every breath felt like a struggle, reminding her she was trapped.

The sunlight reflected off the tall mirror in front of her, the silver embroidery winding down the bodice like it had a life of its own. The delicate threads caught the light, tracing patterns over her skin like an invisible brand—*his mark*. Her bare shoulders and collarbones shone with warmth, while her hair tumbled around them in soft waves that kissed her skin with every movement.

She looked... refined.

Elegant—as if she belonged.

And that was what had her stomach clutching with anxiety.

In the first moments of this hell she'd been dragged into, there had been, perhaps for a split second, a notion that she was *meant* to be here. The girl in the mirror wasn't the same one who'd raced through forests without a care, whose hands had blistered from gripping a gun until her knuckles bled. *That girl* was no more; she had been buried beneath silk and illusion.

This deep-red silk hugged her as tightly as the chains once had.

A knock at the door.

Soft, deliberate.

The door opened.

Malakhov stepped inside.

He wore a handsome black tuxedo, silver-lined, which reflected the low candlelight. His hair was pulled back into a tight knot at the nape of his neck, his posture razor-sharp. But when he looked at her, he faltered—just for the barest breath; a quiver of something bare and fleeting, before he caught up with a wave of practiced calm.

Allison felt her cheeks burn against her will. She hated that flicker. She hated the way her body betrayed her.

The draw of his mouth did something to her. His cruelly amused word, "Wow," came out with a cold yet silken edge of mockery, as if he knew beforehand every protest that would be uttered against him.

Her heart skipped a beat. She froze unable to stop her chin from trembling. "Say what you want and be done with it." Her irritation felt fake, but the tension between them was real—like a threat waiting to ignite.

Malahov's smirk only deepened. The polished soles of his shoes traced a slow deliberate step across the thick carpet, sending a shiver down her back. "I had expected you to look... *presentable,*" he murmured lazily, eyes drifting over her figure, just long enough to rest on the soft swell at her waist and the hollow along her neck pulsing with her heartbeat, that betrayed the calm mask she wore. "Not..." He paused, his eyes locking onto hers with wicked amusement. "*Irresistible.*"

Her pulse stammered in her throat. She forced her jaw to tighten while her breath hitched. She refused to let any surprise or weakness show on her face. "I am not here to entertain you," She snapped, but the words felt hollow, like she was trying to convince herself more than him.

Malakhov chuckled low and smooth, the sound painfully slipping beneath her skin to coil down her spine. He stepped in closer until the heat from his body was warming her side, his shoulder lightly brushing against hers; a touch deliberate in itself. Their reflections blurred and tangled in the mirror, a silent battle of wills.

"No," whispered Malakhov, a silky voice grazing the shell of her ear, provoking a shiver against her will; "You are here to amuse *them*." His breath ghosted over her skin like an electric promise.

Her eyes were cold and her jaw clenched with tension as if she were steel under pressure. "Let's get this over with," she snapped again.

He just smiled, as if that had been exactly what he was hoping to see. He offered his arm, in mock chivalry, lips curled in a smirk of invitation and challenge, pale fingers flexed with intention, just enough to allure her.

"Shall we, little lion?" he drawled, his voice dripping with mock tenderness, a civility that only made the moment feel more wrong. His eyes darkened, slowly shifting to a shade thick with heat, hunger, and something dangerously magnetic.

For a fleeting second, she hesitated, but she finally reached out to lay her hand on his arm. She had no choice. A sharp, victorious smile ran across his lips.

As they stepped forward together, every hungry eye in the room settled on her back, on the game they were playing—a game she was not certain she could win.

But she lifted her chin. Because if she could not win, at least she could refuse to lose.

Her hand trembled as she curled her fingers around his sleeve. Her nails pressed into the soft fabric with enough pressure to leave a mark. He noticed. But that only made his smile grow wider, the dangerous shimmer in his eyes telling her how much he enjoyed her defiance, but would never really admit it.

Together they made their way through the room; she a woman draped in blood-red, he a man cloaked in midnight-black, their footsteps like whispers in the dimly lit hall, playing silent accomplices to a dance neither of them had consented to.

Kotov Manor had always been a place of splendor; tonight, however, it served as a statement of excess and cruelty. The chandeliers flickered, casting molten pools of light across the marble floors. The decadent fixtures sneered at the decay beyond these walls. The blood-red velvet drapes pooled atop the columns, caressing the stone while carving the shadows in stark lines.

A current of something electric hung in the air, making Allison's skin prickle. She felt it as a phantom touch; slipping under her dress, caressing her shoulders, and sliding down her spine. She didn't belong here. And she never would.

Scent of spiced wine and vodka mingled with the smoke from candles and overpowering perfume of men and women intoxicating and suffocating. Conversations hummed in low tones, fake laughter hiding the sharp edge of danger beneath the surface.

They weren't *just* Bratva dogs.

This was old blood—those who thrived in shadow and were drunk on the promise of Radimir's new dawn.

And now, they had come to see his *prize*.

Malakhov's hand was steady on her arm, neither cruel nor gentle, just... possessive. *Controlling*.

They moved forward together, and the room reacted in waves—like a stone dropped into dark water.

Eyes turned. Voices slithered. Whispers like poisoned honey.

"Didn't know filth could shine so bright."

"The boss must have plans for her."

"Or maybe he's offering her up tonight. A real treat."

A slow, oily laugh. "Maybe she'll be on her knees before midnight."

Allison felt her pulse spike, but she kept her face smooth, the muscles in her jaw tight as she forced her breath steady.

Malakhov's fingers shifted, just the smallest flex of control, reminding her; No reaction. No weakness.

She swallowed the bile in her throat and kept walking, heels clicking like a heartbeat in the hall.

Near the head of the room stood the Kotovs— one of Radimir's closest allies and oldest friends.

Aleksei Kotov's gaze was cold and distant, like a man who'd seen it all before, a hand curled tight around his cane.

His wife, Svetlana, had blue eyes that flicked between Allison and Malakhov like a scalpel, cutting straight through to the truth.

And then there was Andrei.

The last time she'd seen him, they'd been neighbors, polite nods in the hallways, the occasional stolen cigarette on the fire escape.

Now, his silver eyes locked onto her like a brand. The glass in his hand trembled, dark red liquid sloshing against crystal.

She held his gaze a moment longer than she should have, long enough for memory to twist in her gut, before Malakhov's hand guided her onward.

A sudden, sharp yank at her wrist. Claws digging in.

Allison felt her breath choke up as she was spun around, face to face with Natalia Gordeev. There she stood, untamed and electric, her tight curls, sun-bleached blonde, and just as wild as her reputation, framing a face that was half beautiful and half dangerous. Her pale eyes flashed with manic energy — like she thrived on the chaos she created. A malevolent smirk had twisted her lips with a wicked glint; a promise for mischief that she fully endorsed and already enjoyed.

The woman was crazy, utterly unhinged, but it was the kind of crazy that made everyone freeze in fear. She took on impossible missions, was first to leap from rooftops or run into burning buildings, and the last to back down from a fight. She would laugh in the face of death, and somehow, death would laugh right back at her—because however reckless she was, Natalia always walked away alive.

Others whispered she was a ghost, an omen, a *devil* wrapped in a woman's skin. Allison could now see it all in the gleam of Natalia's eyes, and in that unconcerned, dangerous confidence swirling around her like a storm about to break.

Natalia's lips twisted into a slow, serpentine smile, her fingers digging in just enough to bruise. "Well, look at you," Natalia crooned, her voice was sickly sweet, like decay.

"I almost didn't recognize you, dressed up so... delicately."

Allison forced herself to hold that dark gaze, refusing to let the revulsion show.

Natalia leaned in, her breath warm on Allison's ear. "Guess it's true what they say, *the dirtier the girl, the prettier she cleans up.*"

Allison's lips curled. "Funny. I've heard the same about you."

Natalia's grip tightened, fingers like steel.

"Oh, kitten," she purred. "I could snap you in two before you even begged me to let you live."

A sharp, bright pain as her nails bit through the silk of Allison's sleeve.

The crowd around them watched, some amused, some bored. Natalia leaned in closer, her breath warm on Allison's cheek. "Do you *really* think you're one of us now? Or are you just playing dress up?"

Allison's jaw tightened. "Sounds like you're afraid of me."

The words slipped out before she could stop them. Natalia's dark eyes flashed and her smile wavered.

A sharp slap. The sound sliced through the silence.

Allison's head snapped to the side, her cheek burning. A sharp tang of blood on her tongue.

Laughter, low and cruel, rippled through the air.

But she had not looked away. She turned back, raising her chin to watch. She smirked, voice low and dangerous. "Better than I expected. *Almost felt that one.*"

Natalia's smile was sharp enough to draw blood. "You're a mouthy little thing," she said in a soft voice. "Maybe I should find a better use for that pretty tongue of yours." Now her hand was tracing Allison's jaw—cold fingers, too familiar, too possessive.

Then a hand gripped Natalia's wrist, firm and sure.

Malakhov.

His face stayed quite neutral, almost bored, but there was a steel grip in his hand that could not be uttered.

"Stop, Gordeev." Soft as velvet and hard as iron was Malakhov's voice. "She is not meant for your breaking."

Natalia's lips parted into a slow, dangerous smile.

"*Protective*, are we?" she murmured, glancing to Allison and back. "Or is this your favorite new toy?"

Malakhov's smile was colder than the marble beneath their feet.

"I simply, do what the Boss orders," he said with that same even voice, with that same toneless restraint.

There was a ripple within the crowd.

The shift in power was enough to tilt opinion to a new tone.

Natalia let out a breathy little laugh of amusement and released her hold on Allison's wrist, tucking an errant curl away from her visage as though she had never intended harm.

"Of course," she said, washing her hands of the matter with an absent-minded step back.

"I'll play nice, Malakhov."

She gave him one last smirk before she melted back into the crowd, her perfume drifted like smoke.

Allison exhaled slowly while rolling her shoulders, chasing away the pain from her arm. Malakhov did not look at her or speak. He simply rested a hand on the arching curve of her back, guiding her forward again, the touch light, almost teasing. After a pause, he said in a casual tone, "You know, you're making quite the impression tonight."

"Is that what this is?" she hissed, her voice a low growl. "A debutante ball for the doomed?"

He chuckled, dark yet warming her skin, even as it twisted her stomach. "Don't sell yourself short," he whispered, leaning closer, his breath an exhalation against her ear. "You wear *ruin* very well."

She turned her face, eyes flicking up to his. "And you wear arrogance like a second skin," she said.

His mouth turned in a slow, inflected smile. "It's the only armor worth having in this place."

For a few moments, their eyes interlocked, a *look*, something dangerous, alive in the calm between them.

He turned away then, his hand never leaving her back as they ventured further into the room. The night was far from over.

And neither of them were done playing.

Allison had barely recovered from Natalia's attack before the ballroom fell silent.

A single voice rang through the grand hall, smooth and commanding. *"Officer Murphy."*

The cruel title sliced through the air like a whip, triggering a violent chill. A sudden breath stuck in her throat. Glancing back, she locked eyes with the man standing atop the dais with all the power in this twisted realm.

Radimir.

He was cloaked in black as if to absorb the light around him. His pale fingers rested lightly upon the intricately carved back of the throne, skeletal and exact; if he so wished, he could have bent the whole room to his whim with a mere flick of his wrist.

"Allison Murphy," he said, his voice a caress coiling about the name, shivering against her own skin.

Malakhov's hand pressed along her back, urging her forward with a needled insistence; it held no comfort; only power. He gave her no option. As if a wave, the crowd parted ahead of her, eyes ravenously drinking in every molecule with a tangled mix of curiosity, repulsion, and something much worse-*desire*.

She climbed up the marble stairs, her heartbeat pounding against her ribs.

And then—Radimir spoke.

"This woman," he said, his tone soft but unwavering, echoing effortlessly through the silent hall. "This *officer* you mock—she is my heir."

A gasp tore through the entire room, then a symphony of disbelief and outrage.

"Lies!"

"She's filth!"

"This is an insult to us all!"

The accusations flew like knives. A few of the older men surged forward a step, faces flushed with fury.

But Radimir lifted one hand, fingers splayed, and the noise died instantly, choked off in the throats of even the most defiant An unnatural hush fell over the room, as if the air had been strangled.

His gaze never left her.

He took his time, letting the weight of his declaration sink in. Then a slow, deliberate smile graced his lips.

"The state lied to you all," he continued, his voice silken snare. "Lied to her. Hid her away, thinking it could erase what she was." His silver eyes gleamed in the golden light, a predator's gaze. "But she is the future."

A concerned murmur passed through the crowd. Each word fell like a nail driving deeper into Allison.

Radimir stepped forward, his very presence filling every inch of the dais.

"And as my heir," he said, almost with reverence, "she will not just carry my name— she will carry my legacy."

A low hum of excitement passed through the room. Heads turned, eyes narrowed with sudden, hungry calculation.

Radimir's lips curled into a slow smile that didn't touch his eyes. "A bloodline as great as mine must not end. It must endure." His gaze swept the room, taking in every greedy, ambitious face. "And for that, my daughter will do her duty. She will ensure that the next generation is as powerful..." he paused, savoring the anticipation, "As dominant, as those who stand before me tonight."

The ballroom shifted. Silence broke into low murmurs of excitement. Eyes, cold and covetous, flicked to Allison with renewed interest, no longer dismissing her as some poor, forgotten orphan but instead as some prize to be won.

A few men near the front traded glances, their mouths curling into knowing, conspiratorial smiles. She saw them clearly, frozen in her mind like snapshots, watching her, weighing her, already calculating how best to take advantage of the opportunity Radimir had just handed them.

Her stomach did twists, nauseating in its intensity. She felt exposed, every nerve raw, like her skin was crawling under their eyes.

Radimir's voice dropped ever lower, a blade slipped between the tides of murmurs.

"Do not mistake my generosity for weakness," he said, each syllable weighed heavy and deliberate.

The room went still, again; greed-sick glances glimmered faintly under the weight of his declaration.

"She is *mine*," he said, his tone freezing the air between them, "and was always mine. If any of you ever forget this, if any of you even try to lay your hand upon her without my bidding..." His eyes flamed, voice changed to iron. "I will ensure your suffering is... *significant*."

A single, cold shudder ran through the gathered crowd. The smirks faded. The eager eyes turned away.

The silence was allowed to grow, the blossoms of fear having full opportunity to bloom before he looked back toward her. He tilted his head, looking at her with dark amusement. "You understand, don't you, *my dear*?" he whispered, his voice soft and taunting. "You won't let me down, *will you*?"

Allison opened her lips, but no sound came from her. The pounding of her pulse in her ears seemed to mark the intensity of every gaze in the room as it pressed over her skin.

Radimir stepped closer, his face inches away from hers, his breath icy. "You *will* do as you are told," he said softly, his fingers gliding along her jawline, seemingly gentle. "You *will* carry our blood, *or you will die*. There is no other fate for you."

The weight of it settled deep in her bones.

She felt her jaw clench, her entire body rigid. But her voice was lost to her, choked off by the weight of what he'd said.

Radimir's lips twitched again, seeing the horror in her eyes. "Ah," he murmured. "You see it now. *The truth*."

He leaned back, his hand falling away, a satisfied smile playing on his lips.

"Welcome home, *Malyshka*" he whispered.

The crowd was still silent, while Radimir moved to his throne and sat down, with a casual grace that spoke of a man who believed that he was holding the world in his hands.

Allison swallowed, walking upright, now terror clawing at her ribs.

Because she understood, finally, with brutal clarity;

There was no escape.

There never had been.

She realized, with a sinking feeling, that the game was already in play.

And she was the prize.

Her stomach twisted violently as nausea rose to her throat. This couldn't be happening—she had already made peace with death, having to be ridiculed and degraded before these men.

But not *this*. Not for Radimir to declare her his heir, his bloodline, his successor.

Her breathing turned quick and shallow, snagging against the tight fabric of her dress. She could feel it, the sudden shift in the room, sharp and disorienting. The confusion in the Bratva's eyes didn't last long. It was already twisting into something worse: curiosity... and *hunger*. Beneath the calculating stares and eager expressions, there was something else simmering—resentment, hot and sharp, like a thousand tiny needles pricking at the edges of her awareness.

The murmur, faint at first, swelled around her. Harsh whispers sounded like snakes hissing. She could feel eyes scurrying over her skin, peeling her layer by layer, weighing her value now that she was no longer an outsider to be dismissed but had instead been made into a conquest. And there, at the very center of it all, she could see Radimir's faint twist of satisfaction, a predator witnessing his prey beginning the painful choice of coming to terms with freedom girded in a cage.

"This is madness."

"She's filth! She can't be—"

"A lie. A trick."

Allison's hands clenched into tight fists, nails digging deeper into the flesh in her palms. She did not want to believe it. Every part of her mind was screaming that this was a lie, that Radimir was toying cruelly with the situation, twisting the truth to suit his dark ends. But then—

Radimir could only show calm indifference, tilting his head. There was a glimmer of amusement in his silver eyes, as though he was entertained by their disbelief.

And then he spoke again, his voice quiet and almost too sweet, yet carrying like a silk whip across the ballroom. "I do understand your skepticism."

His words traveled through the air, strangling each person in the room like a noose. His voice was soft, almost soothing, but it cut deep, shredding the last scraps of doubt.

"You question what you do not understand," he said, his gaze slowly crawling over the gathering. His eyes flickered with cold amusement, studying their faces, their wide eyes, their stiff postures, and watching their uncertainty begin to curdle into another feeling, a dangerous one.

"But doubts do not change the truth," he said, and there was a quiet finality that sent a chill down Allison's spine. "And tonight, the truth shall be undeniable."

He raised his hand, and the murmurs died instantly, as if someone had flipped a switch.

"Nikolai."

Allison's stomach took a plunge.

The the Bratva parted like a ripple as a tall figure clad in black stepped from the shadows, the flickering light stealing a moment to shine heroically on a silver clasp at his throat.

Doronin.

His dark eyes met her own for one split instant, a flicker of a feeling she couldn't quite name-whatever it was, *regret? apology?* But then that feeling was swept away, replaced by a carefully willed blank mask. Gone was the usual sneer he would put on, the cold disdain that had always curled his lips in the past. He was calm. Cold. Controlled.

Allison's fingers trembled at her sides.

Doronin was supposed to be on *her side.*

Or at least... on the side that wasn't *this.*

But he didn't hesitate. Didn't even blink in surprise. Which meant he had known. *For how long?*

The thought went around, twisting inside her gut in utter distaste while her knees buckled.

The cloaked figure of Doronin halted mere feet in front of her, the jacket falling like a shadow around his boots.

He inclined his head toward Radimir with rigid formality. "Sir."

Radimir gestured toward Allison with a flick of his long, pale fingers, his expression a mask of cruel amusement.

"Prove it to them."

Doronin turned a gaze her way, eyes barren and void as though looking into oblivion. Allison lifted her chin and threw her shoulders back. Behind it, the painful thumping of her heart pressed against her rib cage. Doronin withdrew a small envelope from within his coat; its all white facade stood out against his black suit. He moved it forward, his face a mask of stoic indifference.

There was that painful twinge rising in Allison's throat while her breath remained suspended within her chest.

"What... *what is that*?" She knew all too well, remembering the last time she had seen him, when he had almost leaned in with that inviting smile.

He had pressed a handkerchief to the cut on her arm-an accident, she thought.

An act of kindness.

But she saw it now. The truth, sickening and inescapable.

He'd taken her blood.

Without her knowing.

Without her consent.

And now... here it was, in his hand, the final proof.

Her jaw clenched, her fingers curling into fists at her side. "You took my blood," she said, her voice low, shaking with fury. "You took it without telling me."

Doronin's lips twitched as if he might speak—*an apology?*—but he said nothing.

Radimir watched her, his silver eyes bright with cold delight.

Doronin broke the envelope's seal and withdrew a single folded sheet of paper. He then read aloud with a clear and precise voice as if this were the final line in a deadly play.

"The DNA analysis confirms the lineage. There can be no mistake; she is of Ryabov blood."

The crowd murmured down in disbelief and awe, only to be dismissed by a sentiment of fear.

Radimir's smile grew wider as he kept his gaze fixed on hers and now stepped closer, uttering, in a quiet and defiling voice, "A Ryabov by blood. Bound by lineage. My true flesh and blood."

Allison's breath caught in her throat, the words hitting her like blades—sharp, cold, and impossible to ignore.

With an almost gentle smile, he now turned to the crowd, his voice breaking the stunned silence like an executioner's blade.

"And so it is proven."

He spread his arms, his silver gaze sweeping the room. "No more doubts. No more questions." He gestured toward her, a slow, deliberate movement that made her blood run cold. "My daughter stands before you. *My blood. My legacy. My heir.*"

A chill slithered down Allison's back, her entire body rebelling against the truth he had forced into the world.

And then he spoke:

"Allison Ryabov."

The name hit her like a curse, a brand searing her skin.

A hush spread all over the room. That name settled upon them like a stifling fog. She continued to shake her head, barely aware of her movements; her voice seemed stuck somewhere in her throat.

No.

No, no, no.

That was not her name.

She was *Murphy*.

She was herself.

She was not his.

But Radimir watched her with that same quiet certainty, as if he had already won.

And maybe, *he had.*

Because the moment the name left his lips, it existed.

And now... the world would never forget it.

Only whispers hung in the room, the space weighed down by the oppressive dankness. It seemed all sound had been silenced, until, a lone voice pierced through the stillness, incredulous.

"She's still a filthy cop."

There were no more words spoken until a bright gunpowder flash illuminated the room between them, almost simultaneously with the shot's crack echoing like a thunderclap.

A choked cry.

A heavy thud.

The noise made Allison turn her head while her stomach dropped.

One of the Bratva men lay sprawled on the marble floor, body twisted and eyes blank as the blood seeped onto the floor beneath him.

Radimir lowered his gun, his arm steady, his expression serene.

The room fell into a deeper silence, the kind that hummed with raw, electric fear.

Radimir's voice was calm, almost patient.

"Let there be no... *misunderstandings*," his lips moved almost unnoticeable around the last words as he considered her. His words carried across the carpet, filling the reverberating silence and reaching everyone who could hear. "She is my heir and will be treated as such."

A pause.

A long, terrible pause.

And then—

"Would anyone *else* like to object?"

No one moved.

No one spoke.

Because no one dared.

Ten

Shadows of the Past

Allison had been given an entire suite at headquarters—grand and overwhelming in a way that screamed her status as heir. There were no chains on her wrists, no cold stone walls or iron bars. Yet, somehow, she felt more trapped than ever before.

The room was almost too beautiful, too lavish to feel cruel. The towering windows, their panes almost starting at floor level, were bordered by heavy velvet curtains which were deep burgundy and black, which constantly cast long, shifting shadows across the silver carpets below. A massive bed draped in dark red silk took up most of the space, the fabric catching the candlelight like spilled blood. Its tall carved posts rose like fortress towers, adding to the room's suffocating grandeur.

The chandelier threw long, eerie shadows across the room. The quiet crackle of the fireplace was the only thing breaking the frozen silence. It might've felt welcoming, *almost*. She could've let herself believe it, if she didn't already know why she was really here.

This wasn't a dungeon. It was something worse, a cage draped in wealth meant to lull her into forgetting she was a prisoner.

She made her way towards the mirror, and touched the cool, polished wood, as she lingered over her thoughts. Her eyes panned down to watch her reflection. Her stomach gave a tight twist. This was no mere room; it was a statement. A declaration of ownership with plans, already being laid out like blueprints for her future.

It was a place filled with expectations and legacy, where unspoken commands tightened around her. She took a shaky breath and pushed down on the cool surface of the vanity to gain reassurance.

She would not give in.

Not to this.

Not to him.

No matter what they wrapped it in silk, velvet, and firelight, she wouldn't be their puppet. Because in the end, it was still a prison. And she was not going to let them break her.

A knock at the door pulled Allison from her spiraling thoughts. She turned sharply just as it creaked open.

Andrei. He offered a fleeting, almost cold smile as he looked at Allison, the somber expression in his eyes vanishing for only a moment. On other days, he had been the loudest presence, a neighbor in every sense. The easy smiles, the dashing laughs, he had always seemed as bright and effortless as a summer breeze to her.

But not tonight.

Tonight, this Andrei was different, stern, silent, his eyes gleaming like polished steel in the candlelight.

He glanced around the room slowly and casually, but Allison caught the tightness in his jaw and the faint strain at his mouth's corners. It was like he was holding his breath, and wasn't letting go.

He gave the door a soft click, sharp and final. He crossed the room and stopped a few feet away from her.

Allison squinted and crossed her arms over her chest. "Come to gloat?" she said, her voice harsher than she intended.

The corner of Andrei's mouth twitched. He squinted his silver eyes ever so slightly. "You *really* think that?" he asked in a low rasp, carrying a tone of tiredness.

She twisted and embraced herself tighter. "I do not know what to think anymore."

For a second, the thick silence tried to impose itself. Andrei examined her face, his visage unrevealing. Then finally, he exhaled deeply, accompanied by a mysterious slight shrugging of his shoulders.

"We've known each other for a long time, Allison," he breathed quietly, softer now. "Long before all... *this*." He waved his hand vaguely around them, taking in the dark walls and the heavy presence of the Bratva world.

She frowned. "We're not friends," she said uncertainly.

Ghost of a smile. Humorless. *Tired*. "No," he agreed. "We never were." His eyes sought hers, and for a fraction of a moment, she did not see the man in a suit, an heir to a great family. She saw the boy, the one who used to stand across the yard, peering into her, silent but intense and deep.

"You remember," he said, almost to himself. "Those summers, our families side-by-side, sharing fences and secrets they never told us. You in the garden with your mother, me with my father... always watching each other. Never speaking much."

Allison blinked as that image flashed in her mind; sunny afternoons with honeysuckle in the air blending with distant notes of freshly mowed lawn, Andrei's pale hair catching light some yards on the other side of a fence from her while he watched.

"Never friends," she said once again, softer this time. "But... we were never enemies, either."

"No," he murmured, his gaze steady. "Not enemies. Just... two children growing up in the same shadows."

She looked away, her throat tightening. "That was a long time ago."

He tilted his head, a faint glimmer of sadness in his eyes. "It was," he said. "Some things just don't change. I am not here to gloat, Allison. I am not here to hurt you." That low voice dropped almost into a whisper, "I am just here to *warn* you."

She swallowed, dropped her hands to her sides, and again met his gaze, "I don't know if I can trust you."

"I don't expect you to," he said quietly. "But... you need to know—I'm not your enemy, Allison. I never was."

For a moment, the room seemed to fold in on itself, pulling her back to childhood. Just two kids, standing on opposite sides of a fence they never really understood.

Never touching. Never quite part of the same world.

But now... there was no fence. No distance. Only the fragile space between them, and the weight of a past neither of them could outrun.

"Don't fight this," he said softly.

Allison's breath hitched. Something crawled beneath her skin, sharp and electric, and her stomach turned uncomfortably, like it was bracing for a blow. "So you want me to just... *accept* this?" she demanded, her voice shaking, "Become what he wants me to be?"

Andrei's jaw almost twitched for a moment. The fleeting flicker deep in his eyes might have been a glimmer of regret, and then his gaze became lowered to the floor. "It doesn't matter what *you* want," the soft utterance barely reached Allison's ears. "All that matters is what *he* wants."

She recoiled suddenly as a pain tightened in her chest. "So that's it?" she spat. "You're going to stand here and tell me to turn around and let him own me?"

He didn't answer right away but came closer. His voice fell to yet another depth. "I am telling you to survive," he said, harshly yet kind. "You don't understand yet, Murphy. You will."

Her throat bobbed as she swallowed hard.

"Understand what? That I'm just a pawn in all of this? That I'm supposed to smile and play along while he calls me his heir?"

Andrei's eyes darkened. "Understand that he *always* gets what he wants," he said, his voice hinting with some sorrow. "He doesn't care about your defiance. He doesn't care if you are angry. All that matters to him is for you to be his. And he will make it happen so that everyone else sees it that way, too."

Allison had parted lips but no words came out of them. The certainty in his voice-the finality-felt like a tightening around her throat. She lowered her eyes to the floor, and her hands could not stop trembling.

He looked at her for a long, quiet moment, something soft, almost hesitant, passing through his eyes. Then he reached out, his hand hovering near her arm, close but never quite making contact.

"I'm just trying to keep you alive," he said so quietly, it was almost a plea. "Don't be stupid, Murphy. You can survive this. If you play it right."

The words sank into her, cold and sharp. A warning. A promise.

And then—he was gone. Like a ghost, he slipped out the door without a sound. The click of the latch echoed behind him, sharp and final, like the slam of a prison gate.

Allison stood there, alone in the heavy silence, the weight of it pressing in from all sides. She could fight. She could scream. She could claw at the bars of this gilded cage.

But in the end, none of it would matter.

Radimir would still win.

And she would have to find a way to survive it.

* * *

Shadows clung to the carved wood panels that lined the walls, giving the chamber a brooding elegance. At its center sat a long expanse of black marble, cold and imposing. Surrounding it was a set of Victorian-style chairs, their dark polished wood catching what little light there was. The space felt heavy, like it was built to hold secrets.

Some of the members of the Bratva had assembled. The suits were dark, the expressions guarded. Some leaned forward from their chairs; others leaned back; all of them watched Radimir with a cautious hunger.

They waited.

Radimir was seated at the head of the table, fingers skeletal and tapping lightly against the armrest of the chair. His gaze ran over all who were present, measuring each man in turn. They had come with a request—one he had anticipated. One he had even let them believe they could put forward.

Grigori Gordeev cleared his throat, breaking the silence that was about to become too intense. His voice was smooth but went with a slight wavering underneath. "Sir," he started, his fingers almost nervously fidgeting with the edge of the table, "now that you have formally recognized your heir, there is... the matter of *securing* her future."

Radimir's lips curved faintly. He did not speak. Did not interrupt. He simply let them continue, his silence both permission and test.

Maslov, seated to Grigori's left, leaned forward slightly, his expression eager. "She is the first of your bloodline," he said, his tone thick with anticipation. "It is only natural that we discuss who is most... *fitting* to stand beside her."

Another pause followed. Then, a murmur of agreement rippled through the chamber, low and thick with shared ambition. Men straightened in their chairs, their gazes flickering with new intent. Several pairs of eyes shifted toward the door, as if imagining Allison herself standing there, imagining the power she represented.

Malakhov remained silent, *watching*. His fingers drummed once against the table before stilling. He saw it plainly. They didn't want *her*—not her mind, not her spirit. They wanted the throne beside her. They wanted the power, the prestige, the *claim*.

Idiots, he thought, his lip curling faintly. They saw only the surface.

Because she wasn't just a prize. She wasn't some delicate flower to be claimed and displayed. She was a wildfire. Brilliant. Sharp-edged. A mind that cut deeper than any blade, a will that refused to be tamed. And none of these men, *not a single one,* deserved to touch that.

Across the table, Aleksei Kotov shifted, his eyes bright with quiet calculation. He leaned forward, his voice calm but pointed. "Sir," he said, his tone deliberate, "if an alliance is to be made, I humbly suggest my son."

The room went still.

Malakhov's eyes narrowed slightly, noting the way Radimir's fingers paused in their steady tapping. Andrei Kotov—Aleksei's heir. A strategic match. A *logical* match. The perfect union of two powerful lines. Aleksei knew exactly how to play this game.

But there was more to it than mere ambition.

Andrei and Allison had known each other long before titles and bloodlines ever mattered. They had grown up as neighbors—two children in the same neighborhood, their lives separated by little more than a low stone wall and the unspoken weight of their family names. Before the Bratva had claimed them, before the heir had been recognized, they had seen each other in backyards and along quiet suburban streets. Summer afternoons filled with laughter they never shared, silent glances over garden fences. Always there. Always just out of reach.

Malakhov's lips curved faintly as he watched Aleksei. It was a calculated move, yes, but it was also an echo of the past, a thread of familiarity that Aleksei was betting on to sway the room. He was no fool. He knew the power of shared history.

Radimir's gaze flickered, the faintest hint of amusement in his eyes as he let the silence stretch. He knew the history, too. He remembered how they had grown up side by side, two children too young to understand the future that waited for them.

But childhood familiarity was not the same as loyalty.

Radimir's fingers resumed their tapping, his expression impassive as he considered the suggestion. Around the table, the other men shifted, exchanging glances—some intrigued, some envious. Andrei Kotov was a respected heir, a capable strategist. But more than that, he was someone who had known Allison before the weight of her bloodline had turned her into a prize.

For a moment, Malakhov almost pitied him.

Almost.

Because in the end, Radimir would decide.

And whatever Andrei's childhood memories of Allison were worth, they would not be enough if they did not serve Radimir's purpose.

Aleksei sat back, his calm expression hiding the flicker of uncertainty in his eyes. He had played his hand. Now he waited.

And Malakhov, watching it all unfold, thought that perhaps Aleksei had overplayed his advantage.

Because Radimir never let sentiment cloud his judgment.

Not even for a history that began in childhood.

Radimir said nothing at first, his gaze turning to Aleksei with a slow, deliberate sweep. Malakhov could see it, the faint glimmer of amusement in Radimir's pale eyes. He let the idea hang in the air, watching them imagine what it could mean.

For a moment, hope flickered in the room, soft and dangerous. Men weighing their own worth against Kotov's, already calculating new alliances, new ambitions.

Malakhov let out a slow breath, his lips twitching faintly. *Fools.* They still didn't understand.

One of the younger men, Yegor Ruzinsky, leaned forward, his voice soft but insistent. "If she is to be wed, Sir, it must be someone with the strength to match her. Someone who can stand beside her, not... beneath her."

Maslov nodded eagerly. "Someone with lineage, of course," he added quickly, glancing at Kotov and then back to Radimir. "And proven loyalty."

Yegor's lips curved in a faint smile. "My family has served you faithfully for three generations, Sir. My father was at your side in the early years. I would consider it an honor to carry that loyalty forward, to be the one who guards her future as you would."

The heavy undertone of slight murmuring went inside the room in agreement.

Across the table, Boris Lukin shifted in his chair, his eyes piercingly calculating. "She will need somebody who understands the heavy burden of leadership," he said smoothly. "I have spent years in negotiation, in building alliances. I know how to secure loyalty, not just from her, but from all who would stand in her shadow."

He paused, his gaze steady. "Give me the chance, Sir, and I will not only secure her, but expand your legacy."

Maslov licked his lips, leaning forward, eager to seize the moment. "She needs a partner who can provide stability," he insisted. "Someone who has proven he can hold territory, command respect. My lands are secure. My men loyal. She would have nothing to fear with me beside her."

Aleksei Kotov watched them all with a faint, knowing smile. When the others had spoken their piece, he let his voice cut through the din, calm, deliberate. "Andrei is not merely a man of power," he said, his tone smooth. "He is her equal in a way no one else here can claim. They have known each other since childhood, grown up in the same shadows. There is no unfamiliarity between them, no doubt about *intentions*."

He spread his hands lightly, as if offering the perfect solution. "My son would give her a partner who understands her—not just as an heir, but as the woman she is. Their history is woven together. Let that be the foundation for the future."

Malakhov watched it all in silence, his lips curling faintly. Each man thought he saw the prize. Each man thought he could tame her fire—bind it to his own advantage.

But none of them really understood the woman they spoke of.

None of them saw the quiet defiance in her eyes or the mind that would never be content to be conquered.

Malakhov snorted quietly. Strength, loyalty, none of it was real. They just hid their greed behind fancy words. Their need to carve out a piece of her power for themselves.

Radimir, too, listened in silence, his pale eyes half-lidded with amusement. He let the offers stand, let the silence stretch long enough for them to squirm, for the weight of their ambition to settle in the room.

Then, his fingers resumed their tapping, slow and deliberate. "You may make your cases," he said softly, his voice echoing in the dim light. "But remember, she is *mine* to give, not *yours* to take."

There was a flicker of warning in his eyes, a silent reminder.

In the end, none of them would matter, only Radimir's will. And the woman they were all so eager to claim... she would not bend so easily to their designs.

Radimir let the silence stretch, his eyes flicking from one face to the next. His lips curled into a smile, sharp, cold, and anything but comforting.

The room grew colder. No one moved, no one dared to speak. The crackling of the fire filled the silence like a heartbeat.

Radimir's fingers resumed their slow tapping. He let them stew in the cold weight of his authority, let them remember who held the reins.

"You may dream, my friends," he said at last, his tone almost gentle. *Almost.* His gaze swept the room, lingering for a heartbeat on each man who had dared to hope. "But in the end, you will remember your place."

Malakhov's lips twitched into a smirk. *Let them dream*, he thought. Let them imagine their futures wrapped in her fire. Because in the end, they would all learn, just as she would—

Radimir always got what he wanted.

And Allison Murphy was *his*.

The last of the inner circle filtered out, leaving only one behind. Smoke hung in the air, sharp and clinging, mingling with the scent of old paper and ink. This wasn't a room meant to impress, not like the ballroom or the thorn room. This was built for strategy, for control. A war room, reserved for the highest in Radimir's ranks.

And when it was nearly empty. Radimir sat in quiet contemplation, his steady gaze locked on the figure standing before him.

Dmitri Malakhov.

The fire cast shadows along Malakhov's sharp features, but he remained composed, his posture loose, yet disciplined, as if he already knew what was coming.

Radimir studied him for a long moment.

Then, he spoke.

"Tell me, Malakhov... you are one of my most loyal soldiers. Why is it that you are the only one who has not pestered me for my daughter's hand?"

Malakhov did not flinch. He met Radimir's gaze evenly, his posture calm and measured. The corners of his lips twitched faintly, but he did not smirk. Not this time.

"Because I don't need to ask for what will already mine," he said, calm and certain, every word dripping with quiet confidence.

A beat of silence. Then, Radimir laughed.

It was soft, low, a sound of amusement laced with something darker.

He leaned forward, steepling his long, skeletal fingers as he watched Malakhov intently.

"Practical. Patient," he murmured, his eyes glinting with approval. "Just as I expected of you." He let his gaze linger, searching Malakhov's face. "They see only a throne, a conquest... a *body* to claim. You see... *more.*"

Malakhov inclined his head slightly, his expression composed. "I see her mind. Her will. She is not something to be taken, but someone to be respected," he said quietly.

Radimir's lips curved faintly, amusement flickering across his features. "And yet, you have made no move to challenge their ambitions," he observed, his voice low, almost curious. "No grand displays of interest. No declarations of intent." He tilted his head, the flickering firelight dancing in his dark eyes. "Tell me why."

Malakhov met his gaze unflinchingly. "Because I am here to serve you, Sir," he said simply. "I know my place. And I know that if I am meant to stand at her side, it will be because you decide it and not because I pushed others aside."

Radimir studied him, his fingers tapping idly on the polished wood. "Some might call that weakness," he said, his voice soft, testing. "A *lack* of ambition."

Malakhov's jaw tightened, but he did not look away. "Ambition is a blade, Sir," he said evenly. "It can cut clean... or it can turn in your hand. My loyalty has always been my strength."

Radimir's eyes gleamed, something like approval, cold and calculating, settling in their depths. "Indeed," he murmured. "Good."

He leaned back, watching the fire dance.

"Let them scheme," he muttered softly, a sort of underbred idiocy. "After all, the final decision will be mine, and I have always respected those who know when to wait."

Radimir nodded slowly, clearly pleased.

"She is yours to train. She is yours to guard." Radimir's voice was calm, but every word carried weight. "If she is reckless, you will *correct* her. If any of my followers lay a hand upon her in a way I do not approve, *you will handle it.*"

Malakhov raised a brow. "How far am I permitted to *handle* it?"

Radimir's smirk was a flicker of amusement in the firelight. "Anything but ending their life. That privilege remains mine."

Malakhov inclined his head, his face an unreadable mask. "Understood."

A long and heavy silence settled onto the room, as heavy as the stones outside. Radimir looked at Malakhov with cold curiosity as he lightly drummed his fingers on the table. Finally, he said, again in a low voice, with a careless facade.

"And tell me, Malakhov...what is there about my daughter that appeals to you?"

The question came out soft, almost uncertain, but somehow the air grew colder in its wake. Malakhov didn't answer right away. The weight of the question hung between them—heavy, coiled with quiet implications that felt like something slithering just out of sight.

He thought carefully before speaking his measured words; "She is not weak."

Radimir smiled slowly in satisfaction. "No," he breathed, reclining in his chair with his eyes flashing with dark approval. "No, she is not."

He let the words linger in the silence, allowing them to enter their ears fully before saying anything else. "Train her well, Malakhov," he said softly but with absolute authority.

"Teach her to stand where others would fall."

Malakhov bowed his head. "I will."

Radimir's fingers paused in their idle drumming, his gaze fixed and sharp. "And remember," he added softly, "strength is not only in the arm or the blade. It is in the mind... and the will."

"I understand," Malakhov said quietly.

Radimir's lips twitched faintly, a whisper of approval. "Good," he said again, his tone final, a command and a blessing all in one. "You may go."

Malakhov straightened, turning to leave, the air behind him thick with unspoken vows.

* * *

Radimir found her private room silent when he arrived.

Allison was sitting in front of the fire, her gaze lost in the spell of the dancing flames, casting a golden glow over her silken frock. She kept her gaze low until the intruder appeared; her fear already replaced by resignation

For a moment, there was silence; the crackling hearth mocking them in brittle laughter.

Then, "You have questions."

Allison felt her jaw tighten as one of the muscles in her cheek twitched.

"*Questions?*" she repeated, sharply, with the voice of a knife. She slowly turned her head, meeting his cold, steady gaze with a fire of her own. "You've already decided on my future, so what could be the use of asking anything?"

A faint curl seemed to twitch around Radimir's lips, a glimmer of fleeting amusement appearing in his dark eyes. Moving toward the ornate chair opposite her, he sank into it with the unhurried ease of one who has never felt fear, much less hurry in his life.

"You assume I am cruel," he said softly. "That I will sell you off like cattle. That I will take pleasure in binding you to a man you despise."

Allison didn't flinch, but her eyes sparked. Because she *had* assumed that.

Radimir tilted his head, studying her face with a calm that only made her fury burn brighter. "You misunderstand me, my dear."

The words cut through her like ice. He had called her that before, *my dear,* but it felt different now. Different because he meant it.

Because he believed it.

"You *will* be wed," he continued, his voice calm, almost gentle. "And you *will* continue my bloodline. That is inevitable. But I will not treat you like a mere pawn to be traded away."

Allison swallowed, her throat raw with dryness, her hands curling into fists in her lap. "And yet this is what I am, a *pawn* in your game," her voice fought to resist the surge of anger welling up inside her.

Radimir's eyes glittered, amusement playing on the edges of his ice-cold expression. "No," he said softly. "You will have a say in the matter. I will take your input into consideration." He leaned forward but did not avert his gaze.

"But the decision will be mine. My bloodline will continue, and your husband will be one that I approve."

Allison's fingers dug into the arms of her chair, gripping so hard the old wood let out a faint, strained creak beneath the pressure. "You talk as if it's a kindness," she spat. "As if you're giving me a gift, but it's still a cage."

Radimir's smile was slow, indulgent. "Call it what you like, *Malyshka,*" he said, his voice soft as velvet. "But you will not refuse."

"And if I do?" she demanded, her voice rising, fierce and desperate. "If I refuse to play this game? Will you kill me, too?"

The smile widened slightly, a flash of teeth beneath the cool calm. "You will not refuse," he stated, uttering his last words, a quiet promise. "Because you already know what happens to those who defy me."

A suffocating silence fell between them. Radimir leaned back, his gaze never leaving hers, watching the fury in her eyes like a man studying an unpredictable fire.

Then, with a near-casual cruelty, he added, "Don't fool yourself into thinking your husband will be Daniel. Or Rob. Or any of those *precious* officers you cling to. That's not how this ends."

Allison felt the words like a blow to her chest, her breath catching, her vision swimming with sudden, blinding hatred. She clenched her hands so tightly her nails dug into her palms, drawing thin crescents of blood.

Radimir rose from his chair. "Rest, my dear," he said softly. "Tomorrow, your training begins."

Allison didn't move. Didn't breathe. Didn't dare speak.

Because for the first time since this nightmare had begun, since she had been dragged into this world of shadows and secrets, she felt it:

A cold truth settled over her.

She wasn't herself anymore.

Not free.

And the worst part?

Radimir knew it, too.

* * *

Katherine Walker was crying. Her shoulders shook with muffled sobs, her breath coming in ragged gasps. At long last, Rob and Daniel had arrived at the home of Rob's parents, where Allison had spent so many summers, a place that somehow felt like a second home to her.

Allison used to laugh in this room, used to spin barefoot across the warm wooden floors like nothing could touch her. Now, the only sound was the soft creak of the house settling, and the kind of silence that grief drags behind it. Katherine hadn't said much since the news came. Her hands kept trembling, pressed tight against her mouth like she was holding back something too heavy, too terrifying, to let out. Her eyes were red and puffy, swollen with tears she couldn't stop, the kind of grief that looked a lot like mourning the dead.

"She's just a girl," she whispered, her voice so faint it was almost drowned by the thick silence of the room. "My Allison, my clever girl... she sacrificed herself. She gave herself up for all of us."

Beside her stood Heather, her true daughter, stiff as stone, arms locked around herself like she was the only thing holding her together. At just twenty, she was always the wise one, but now, she looked like a child lost in the middle of a storm, eyes vacant, barely blinking. Her knuckles were white where she gripped her own sides, and her mouth was drawn in a tight line, like if she let it part even an inch, the sobs would pour out and never stop. Allison had always been more than a friend, she was like a big sister. The kind Heather leaned on, learned from, laughed with. And now, she didn't know what to do with the space that was suddenly left behind.

Across the room, Charles Walker, Rob's father and the man who had always been a quiet rock, stood behind the mantle, shoulders stiff and jaw clenched so tightly that it appeared painful. A man of very few words, his eyes speaking for him in that moment.

"We don't know what they're doing to her, Daniel." Scott's voice cut through the thick silence, low and rough, his face drawn tight. But there was no mistaking the weight behind every word. "We don't have the faintest clue of what is being done to her."

His jaw clenched, another thunderous beat pounded in his ears.

"She is still alive." The voice that came was harsh; the words seemed to catch in his throat, but that very voice echoed with unmistakable defiance against the fear gripping the room.

Brandon Mitchell, another older officer, snarled, "For *now*." The words etched themselves like a knife through the thick air. "But she's in his hands."

A shiver passed through everyone. That was what scared them the most.

Not just that she had been taken by the Bratva.

Not just that she was a prisoner.

She was in *his* hands.

Radimir's hands.

Daniel's breath caught.

His best friend—his sister in all but blood—was *gone*.

Trapped with the monster they'd all feared.

And he couldn't reach her.

Suddenly, Rob jerked up from his seat, his chair dragging across the floor with a harsh, scraping noise and falling to the ground. The noise was thunderous in the silent room. Everybody turned around. The face of Rob was pale, his eyes wild, and his chest heaving in irregular breaths. His fists were clenched, "I—" His voice broke; it was raw and tearful. Yet, he swallowed hard, forcing the words out; "I can't—." His shoulders started shaking, fighting to hold himself together.

"We have to do something," his voice was shaking with desperation now. "We can't just sit here and wait. We have to..."

His voice was gone for good as he stood abruptly and pushed past the door's edge, storming out of the room.

No one stopped him. No one tried. Because they understood.

Rob loved Allison.

It wasn't loud or dramatic, not the kind of love people wrote stories about. It was quieter than that, steadier. He'd always been the one to pull her out of her head when she got too wrapped up in her work, slipping in a joke or some ridiculous comment just to make her laugh. And when she did, when she actually let herself ease into the moment and let go, he'd be there, catching every second of it like it was something fragile and rare.

But Allison never really saw it. Not the way he hoped she would. She was too focused, too stubborn, too convinced they were just kids still figuring things out. She had plans. *Timelines.* Dreams too big to leave room for something as unpredictable as love.

And Rob had accepted that, or at least, he *thought* he had. He told himself it was enough just to be close to her. To care from a distance. To love her quietly.

But now... *now* he stood in the wreckage of what was left, and the weight of it was unbearable. It hit him all at once, how much he'd already lost. Not just the chance to tell her, but the thousand little moments they'd never get back. The laughter that wouldn't come again. The future he'd never dared to hope for, but had always secretly held onto, tucked away like a kept secret.

And the worst part?

He couldn't go back and do any of it differently.

He couldn't change a thing.

Everything in the room came to a deafening silence, the heaviness gnawing. At last, Scott's deep voice broke through the tense atmosphere, low and steady but iron-hard. "We need intel. Now."

Daniel blinked, the fuzz of fear glare and fury fogging away his mind. His breaths came raggedly, and everything whirled in his mind. "Intel?" he rasped, the word tasting like dust.

Scott was grim now; he set his mouth in iron. "We can't storm headquarters blind, Daniel. If we don't know what's waiting for us, we all will be slaughtered, and we will never get her back."

With a worried look, Captain Hunter nodded, "If we go in blind, we'll lose everything. We have to be smart."

Daniel felt a cold dread settle into his bones.

He wanted to act—wanted to charge in, tear the whole damn Bratva apart with his bare hands if that's what it took.

But they were right.

They had one chance. And they had to make it count.

He exhaled sharply, his hands balling into fists.

"Who do we have on the inside?"

Scott's jaw worked. He looked away for a moment before turning back. "Doronin."

Daniel's blood ran cold. "*Doronin*?" His voice was sharp, incredulous. "You mean Doronin is an undercover agent?"

Scott sighed, "He was. Or... he used to be. Before he got in too deep with the Bratva." His mouth twisted. "It's getting harder and harder to know if the intel he brings is real. Only he might have some real insight as to what is happening on the inside."

Hunter's face hardened, a fleeting shadow of conflict upon his eyes.

Scott met Daniel's gaze, hard expression, and said;

"I don't trust him either, Daniel. But he's all we've got. If we want Allison to see daylight again, we've got to take that risk."

Daniel took a hard swallowing, nails digging into his innards with fury and fear.

Doronin.

The man who for years had tormented them, who worked with the mafia and laughed about it.

The man who may well save her now.

He forced the words out, his voice low and unyielding.

"Find out what he knows."

In response, Scott nodded, his expression was dark and steely. Then suddenly, the air shifted, as if the world had stopped holding its breath.

Because they knew what this meant. The first move had been made. The war for Allison's freedom had begun. And they would not stop until she was back with them, no matter what it took.

The Art of Breaking

She stood in the center of the room, breath steady yet forced, grasping the polished wood of her practice gun. The floor was smooth and almost reflective, state-of-the-art obsidian floor carved with symbols in Russian that Allison had failed to recognize yet. All her instincts told her that the room was alive, humming with a power that did not belong to her.

And upon the other side stood Radimir; not on a throne, not above her, but before her.

He didn't need height to be intimidating—he carried power like a second skin. It pressed into the room, thickening the air, making it feel harder to breathe. His suit was black—so black it seemed to swallow the light around him. There was nothing soft about it. It didn't move, didn't shift with him. It clung, heavy and still, like even the air didn't dare brush against him.

He did not speak immediately.

He only watched.

His silver eyes tracked her calmly, studying her like someone re-reading an old story, one whose ending he already knew. His gaze remained fixed on her, patiently, an eerily predatory patience.

"You do not trust me," he finally said amid the heavy silence.

Her jaw tightened. "No." The voice came hoarse and cold.

A slight twitch now concerned the corner of his mouth, the faintest hint of amusement passing over his pale features. "Good."

Her breath caught. She had expected mockery or perhaps some thinly veiled threat—not *approval*.

Radimir never took his eyes away from hers. His tone was deliberate, almost as if he were pronouncing some eternal truth. "Suspicion is a powerful weapon. It keeps you from falling into traps. It keeps you alive. It sharpens your instincts."

The air in the room shifted. Heaviness settled over everything, thick and tense, as if the space itself knew something was about to break. Allison felt it immediately. It wasn't visible, but it tugged at her edges, pressed against her chest, made her lungs tighten. Her breath caught, sharp and fast, like her body was already bracing to run. But she didn't run. Before her mind could even register what was happening, she was already moving. Her arm lifted. The practice gun came up with it, both hands locked in place, her aim set on him.

Radimir's gaze glowed with quiet approval.

"*Instinct*, see?" His voice was a whisper of a blade being drawn. "You are learning already. As my Heir, it is imperative you strengthen your skills."

Allison's stomach twisted violently. She knew exactly what he was doing. He was not forcing her into darkness. Not yet.

He was waiting for her to choose this path on her own. Which, somehow, made it all the more dangerous.

"Again."

The order whistled across the room. Allison had barely enough time to catch herself when she hit the cold stone floor, air escaping her lips with a harsh gasp. Pain raced up her arms as she struggled to push herself up, her heartbeat pounding wildly against her ribs.

Radimir stood a few feet away, his hands still raised in a relaxed, almost indifferent guard. His expression was unreadable, his silver eyes glinting. He had not truly hurt her. Not really. But he had been ruthless.

"Again."

Allison gritted her teeth, her whole body stubbornly protesting against her forced rise. She threw an uppercut just in time, landing it just below his jaw. He nodded happily, her padded gloves muffling the impact.

"Your defenses are adequate," he said calmly. "But adequate will not save you in war."

His fist came forward again, faster this time, a blur of motion. Instinct taught her to barely escape; as if the world's hum burst all around her, everything else drifting away in the rush of adrenaline.

She almost forgot whose was fighting.

For an instant, there was nothing but the sharp, reckless thrill of moving faster than she could think. She countered with a sweep kick; low, fast, precise, and aggressive. Not a cheap shot, but one meant to end a real fight.

Radimir sidestepped effortlessly, a faint smirk tugging at his lips. "Good," he murmured.

She was breathing hard, arms shaking, half expecting the disgust to catch up with her. But it didn't. She only felt alive. Each breath was a spark, each movement a surge of heat through her veins.

And Radimir saw it.

"You like this," he said, sounding almost curious.

Allison's gut clenched. "No."

His smile deepened, a hint of teeth showing. "You will."

She hated how calmly he said it, how certain he was. And worst of all? She hated that a small, terrible part of her feared he was right.

* * *

Allison barely had time to catch her breath before she was ushered into the fighting chamber. This time, it wasn't Radimir waiting for her.

It was Malakhov.

At first, he stood with his back to her, his hands loosely clasped behind him, looking at the old wooden dueling floor. He spoke the moment she stepped inside, his voice light and tinged with mischief.

"A year is a long time, Murphy."

Allison blinked, momentarily thrown by the familiarity in his tone. Malakhov turned, his expression neutral but with a spark of amusement glinting in his eyes.

"I remember how you were in the bank," he said, lips curling slightly. "You were skilled then. *Reckless*, but skilled." His gaze swept over her like a lazy current, measuring something invisible. "And *now*? Now I expect much more."

She straightened, the faint challenge in his words making her bristle. "Much more? I didn't exactly spend those years training for street fights."

Malakhov's brow rose, and he let out a soft, knowing hum. "Нет," he said, the Russian word for "no" slipping easily from his lips. "But you had something better."

That was a question that became tinged with a trace of bitterness.

He approached, agitating the air between them, yet not so close as to drive her to flinch. "You had *fire*," he said plainly, as if it were an absolute truth. A wry smile ghosted across his mouth. "I'm not here to break you, Allison," he added, almost like a secret. "At least... *not yet*."

Her breath hitched. She'd heard him say her name before—more than once—but this time, something about it unsettled her in a way she couldn't explain. It was different now. Colder. Before she could even respond, he was already turning away. Whatever glint had flashed in his eyes a moment earlier was gone, snuffed out like it had never been there at all.

"Let's begin."

The word cracked through the air, and she lifted her hands automatically. The sounds of fists hitting padding, bodies colliding, and ragged breaths echoed around them. But as she moved, she realized something she hadn't expected. Malakhov wasn't fighting her like a captor. He wasn't toying with her or pushing her to break. He was *testing* her. Pushing her to see how far she could go, how much she could take.

Malakhov had fought countless opponents over the years, men twice her size, women who moved like predators, soldiers who had seen far too much blood. But none of them felt like this. As he watched Allison move, fierce and wild, he didn't feel the casual boredom he'd expected, or the superiority he usually carried so easily. He felt... *intrigued.*

Because she wasn't weak. Not at all. She fought like someone who had learned survival the hard way, who had been cornered and clawed her way back out again and again. There was no polished technique, no careful dance of moves drilled since childhood. Just instinct and raw, furious determination. It was that same spark he'd glimpsed two years ago outside the bank, and it was brighter now, *sharper.* And for the first time, Malakhov understood what Radimir saw in her.

"Again," his voice was softer this time, almost coaxing.

She breathed hard, her arms screaming with exhaustion, but she did not hesitate. She adjusted her grip on the practice gun, her gaze locked on his. Malakhov watched her, no longer with detached amusement but with a flicker of respect that hadn't been there before.

And that, more than anything, made her stomach twist. Because he wasn't going easy on her. And, she realized with a sick thrill, *she didn't want him to.*

She lunged, swinging the gun low, and he dodged just in time. His mouth twitched, that half-smile that was more challenge than praise.

"Better," he murmured.

An adrenaline surge coursed through Allison's veins. But as they moved together, her body on instinct, his steps calculated—every motion was one she could not deny. She saw the crack in his mask, the slip in that icy calm. And she didn't know if that should terrify her more than Radimir himself.

She wasn't like the others. Radimir had seen it, and now Malakhov saw it too. Her strength wasn't a birthright, a title, or a lineage. It was forged in war, shaped by desperation and survival. And that, he realized, was more dangerous than any noble bloodline.

Blood could be traced, tested, controlled. But *fire*? Fire was wild, unpredictable. It could burn even the hand that tried to hold it.

As he parried another strike, feeling the heat of her determination crackling in the air, Malakhov understood something else. Something that sat low in his gut, unsettling and undeniable.

He didn't want to put that fire out.

He had spent years following orders, never questioning, never wanting more than what he was given. But now, standing across from her, he couldn't help but *wonder*. Wonder if she was meant to be *just* Radimir's heir—or something far more dangerous.

His grip tightened around the practice gun. Their eyes met; hers shone with challenge and something he didn't want to name. "Again," he said, his voice low and edged with a grin.

Truly, he was not sure if he was teaching or being taught.

By the end, her body was aching all over in places she had long forgotten could.

Her arms ached, weighed down with exhaustion. Her legs throbbed, sore and unsteady beneath her. The bruises hadn't surfaced yet, but she could feel them coming, deep aches blooming like the last sparks of a dying fire. It had been a long time since she'd trained like this. Not just reacting out of fear or survival, but pushing herself with focus and control. This was different from the frantic, chaotic fights she'd been forced into during the takeover. This was something she chose.

It felt *good*. She hadn't expected that.

Hadn't expected the rush of satisfaction that came with fighting, with throwing up defensive blocks, with feeling her heart pulse and shift and surge as she pushed herself beyond exhaustion.

Allison let out a slow breath, pressed her fingers on the fine finish of the ornately carved wooden railing, and grounded herself. She had missed it, that feeling of power at her fingertips, and the feeling of control. She slowly closed her eyes, her breath slowing in an attempt to hold onto a moment of peace, a fleeting illusion of normalcy.

It didn't last. Reality crept in slowly, cold and unwelcome, like a shadow slipping beneath her skin. The truth of where she was, and who had been watching her, hit hard and sudden. Her eyes flew open. Her stomach twisted violently, and the warmth she had carried just moments before was swallowed by a creeping chill.

This wasn't the academy. It wasn't a safe training room surrounded by friends who trusted her. She wasn't under the protection of the resistance. And she wasn't preparing to fight *him*—not anymore.

She was *his* student now. She was in *his* home. In his world. And no matter how much she had enjoyed the training, the fight, she was still a captive. Allison swallowed hard, her fingers curling into fists. She would not forget that. *She could not forget that.* That's how it started. First the cage felt familiar. Then it felt safe. And then, one day, you just... stopped trying to leave.

She would not let that happen.

Not to her.

Never.

Allison's heart pumped fast, her hands raised above her head, muscles aching from the never-slowing pace of the duel. There was sweat at the base of her neck, in strands stuck to her temples as she circled her opponent again.

Malakhov remained calm, collected, completely unshaken. He watched her with the cold focus of a predator. For the past hour, he hadn't eased up. If anything, his pressure had only increased, pushing her to move quicker, to think faster. Every blow he delivered forced her to block or dodge at the last possible second. And every time she struck back, he countered with fluid, effortless precision.

But she was getting better, she could feel it. More than that, she could *see* it in his eyes. Not approval, at least not yet. But expectation. And something else too. Something she couldn't quite name.

She took another step back, calculating. Her ribs throbbed from some wrong landing earlier; she was trying to dismiss the pain. Malakhov tilted his head ever so slightly; the corner of his lip traveled in that flicker of a smirk. Quick. Precise. Unforgiving. Allison barely *barely* had time to raise a block, shooting her arms up hard and brutally as he shoved her back—the blow went through her bones like a rattling shock. He watched her mobilize herself again, his gaze sharp and unreadable.

Then he spoke, his tone quiet but cutting through the air. "You hesitate."

Allison clenched her jaw. "I think before I act."

Malakhov let out a soft chuckle, the sound barely audible over the crackling torches. "That is why you lose."

A pulse of anger shot through her, hot and sudden. Before she could question it, before she could even think, she lunged forward—fast and aggressive, striking as if she meant it. Malakhov's smirk vanished, and he was forced to dodge, *actually dodge*. A flicker of surprise crossed his face before it melted into something else. Something that looked dangerously close to satisfaction.

She never should have felt this way, *satisfied*. And Malakhov noticed. "There you are," she heard him whisper to himself.

Her breath caught, but she barely had time to react before he stepped back. "Enough for today. We move on."

For an instant, adrenaline gave the illusion that she might faint. One forceful nod of affirmation, and she felt she had never truly been victorious in training until now.

Malakhov strode toward the door, as effortlessly commanding as ever. "Stay here. I'll bring more of the training mats," came his steady yet unwavering voice.

Still catching a breath, she absently nodded, rolling her shoulders as Malakhov vanished behind the heavy wooden doors.

The chamber was too quiet. Just the crackle of torches and her own heartbeat drumming in her ears. The pressure built; she found a moment to stand in her calm center and let the quiet wash through her to calm her core, until, suddenly, something shattered that dreadful silence.

A voice slithered through the air like a snake. "Well, well...are you a sight, *little Ryabov*."

Allison froze; she almost did not recognize her *new* name, but slowly, too slowly, she began turning.

Grigori Gordeev leaned in the doorway, his presence sinking into the space like a poison, his lips curled with a smile that betrayed ill will. Her hands tightened around the grip of her practice gun.

"What do you want, Gordeev?" she said flatly.

"Just curious to see what Radimir's new toy looks like up close."

She didn't move, but lifted her chin with a brave face, refusing to compromise an ounce of fear. Grigori swept his gaze upon her, lingering where he should not. "I must say, you clean up *quite nicely*."

Her jaw tensed.

He took another step, closing the space between them too quickly, too easily. "I'm wondering if that spark of yours holds up when it's not a fight."

The air was suffocating. Grigori was close now, *far too close*. She clenched her fist just as his hand shot out, grabbing hold of her wrist and slamming it against the chill stone wall.

Panicked, she gave out a sharp breath. "Get off me!"

He smirked. "Why fight, little Ryabov? You'll have to belong to someone eventually."

Disgust unfurled like bile in her throat. She twitched her wrist; his grasp was steadfast, unrelenting. "I will *never* belong to you."

Grigori chuckled, breath hot on her skin as he leaned in; "We will see." Then—

The air shifted. Suddenly, like a flash, a solemn blow hit Grigori off-balance, sending him flying across the room. Allison gasped, the impact shooting through her whole body as he thudded with a sickening sound against the far wall.

Malakhov stood there, only one step away from her, his body coiled and protected full of lethal energy. His eyes bore into her with a look she had never seen before—an angry, threatening glow.

Without a moment's hesitation, he stepped forward to put himself in the way between her and Grigori. "Are you hurt?" His voice was grave and fully controlled, yet she perceived the hint in it—a possessive tone that gave her the chills.

Allison blinked, surprised by the question. She opened her mouth but closed it again, still struggling for breath. "I'm fine," she managed to say.

Malakhov gave a single, decisive nod.

Then, he turned.

Grigori was still groggy, coughing as he forced himself back up against the far wall. Malakhov took steps one by one, deliberate, while the room closed in darkness around him.

Grigori looked up and froze; the empty bravado lifted off his face.

Malakhov said in a soft, almost whispering voice. "*You dare* put your hands on what belongs to Radimir?"

Grigori wiped blood from his mouth, chuckling weakly. "Oh, come now, Malakhov. We all know she—"

Malakhov's hand came snapping forth, seizing Grigori's throat. The change was instantaneous and terrifying; one moment there was space between the two, the next, Grigori was pinned, wide-eyed and gasping for air. Malakhov's grip did not waiver; it did not tremble.

His voice was chilling. "You need to be punished."

Allison took in a sharp breath, her pulse hammering away. Malakhov turned to look at her, with an unreadable expression on his face. "Would you like the honor?"

She knew what he was offering, what it meant. *A chance.* A show of *power*. A way to put Grigori in his place.

She swallowed, her heart thudding painfully in her chest. And then, "No."

Malakhov's eyes flickered, but not with anger. Not with disappointment. What she saw instead must have been close to admiration. His lips parted, and for a moment, he looked at her as if she were something rare and precious.

A chuckle rumbled from within his chest, the sound was not mockery, but something deep and knowing, a lonely whisper. "What a *rare* little thing you are."

And Allison's chest tightened, and she caught her breath.

Somewhere beyond them, hidden in shadow, Radimir smiled.

Their training went on. Allison was drawing ragged breaths, her muscles cramping with each new movement, but she felt the strength beneath her skin-pulsating and hungry to be freed.

Malakhov watched her intently, and something fluttered in her gut beneath the intensity; it wasn't mockery or impatience, but something else, one that sent heat spiraling through her chest and made her mouth dry.

"Again," he said in a low, persuasive voice.

She had no thought at all. She lunged at him.

Suddenly, the movements were no longer only practice. It was a dance of bodies, a push and pull dangerously close to something else. Allison ducked under a strike; the sleeve of Malakhov brushed her shoulder, the warmth of his breath all over her skin. She twisted away and then felt her back pressed against his chest for half a second too long before she rammed her shoulder into him, pushing him back with a heavy thud.

He stumbled just slightly, a smirk upon his lips. "*Aggressive*. I like it."

Her face grew hot. "*Shut up.*"

The chuckle came from him and the sound sparked again some blaze to her.

He moved again, faster, more deliberate. A stomp aimed at her foot, she twisted away, barely avoiding it.

A quick snatch at her wrist, she slipped free, her skin tingling where he'd touched her.

Then a shift.

A step.

And suddenly, she was on her back, pinned against the mat.

She took in a sharp breath as Malakhov's arm pinned her arms in place, locking her body under him. She felt the heat from his body, smell the faint leather and steel of him, and for the first time since they started, neither of them moved.

The air between them shifted. The tension was still there, but it wasn't anger. It was something deeper, unfamiliar, and it unsettled her.

Allison's heart hammered as she tried to free her wrist, but she couldn't. Couldn't even think. Because he wasn't attacking her. He was watching her, studying her with dark eyes that felt like soft caresses.

He shifted his head slightly; his gaze grazed over her, invoking feelings so dangerous and thrilling. Then his lips brushed her ear, leaving his breath like a warm shiver across her skin. *"So much bravery in such a small little lion... how long do you think it will last?"* he whispered. The voice that hit her was low and lost in ambiguity.

A jolt shot through her, something hot and unsettling.

She pushed him away, *hard*.

He let her.

And that, somehow, left her completely off balance.

Twelve

A Touch too Human

In the depths of Radimir's headquarters, the study was dimly lit, the only illumination was the lamp on the desk. Shadows began their slow dance along the walls, twisting into forms that seemed to bear witness to the two men standing in the center. The air had a weight to it, as though they both shared a quiet understanding they didn't care to name.

Malakhov stood before Radimir, hands clasped loosely behind his back. His posture was disciplined, shoulders squared, and chin held up without a shade of doubt, while an air of nonchalance hung about him, a kind of casual confidence that, in Radimir's presence, most other men dared not show.

Radimir did not yet speak. He sat in silence, silver gaze steady and patient. Malakhov did not flinch at the stare. For he was one of few who would not be intimidated by the stare, even one so fiercely intense as Radimir's.

Finally, after a deliberate lingering pause, Radimir exhaled softly through his nose and gave a slight tilt to his head. "She challenges you."

A slow smirk curved Malakhov's lips. "She tries."

Radimir let out a low hum, the sound almost indulgent. "And yet, you have not grown tired of her." His voice did not carry a single question; it was simply a statement.

Malakhov arched an eyebrow as a surge of fleeting curiosity crossed his face. "Should I have?"

Radimir's mouth twitched at the corners slightly. "No."

Silence stretched in between them again, and with it came another element; a deeper realization. Leaning slightly forward, Radimir's eyes went over him sharply. "You do not treat her as your lesser."

Malakhov didn't answer immediately. There really was no need. A thousand signs were in his bearing, one of them being that faint softening of his eyes whenever the name Allison was pronounced. Radimir took notice of it and smiled, slow and indulgent, while his fingers tapped on the polished wood of the desk in front of him.

"You have never been one to covet power for its own sake," he said, musingly, as if almost musing aloud. "But you have always appreciated strength."

Malakhov made no move, the light in his eyes serving as an answer.

Radimir's smile deepened as a glint of amusement kindled in his pale gaze. "She amuses you."

A slow exhale found its way out of Malakhov; a telltale smile threatened to tug at one corner of his mouth. "She does not bore me."

A low cackle reverberated within the walls. "Good."

He waved a long, elegant hand dismissively, but pleasure laced his voice, twisted with something darker—something possessive. "Tomorrow, she trains with the others. Let her measure her strength against them." His lips lifted just enough to hint at a smirk, sharp and knowing. "And let them see how much restraint they really have."

Malakhov inclined his head in a silent promise, but he didn't move to leave. Radimir was not finished.

"And Malakhov?"

Malakhov tilted his head in silent question.

Radimir's voice cut through the quiet, deceptively soft, carrying the steel of a command wrapped in courtesy. "Make sure she does not grow... *too attached* to anyone else."

Malakhov gave that slow and knowing smirk. "That won't be a problem."

There was a low chuckle from Radimir. "No. I didn't think it would be."

* * *

The dueling chamber was cool and dim, the scent of damp stone hanging in the air like a quiet weight. There was none of the usual sparring tonight, no sharp clang of spells or the rhythm of fists meeting shields. Instead, Allison sat on the cold floor across from Malakhov, her legs stretched out before her, hands resting loosely in her lap, the silence between them heavy but charged.

It felt strange, almost intimate. He said nothing as he simply gestured for her to sit, and every bit of her instinct was telling her to refuse. But she had obeyed without question. A tension neither of them dared to name, though both felt it pressing in.

Malakhov finally broke the quiet with his low voice. "Tomorrow, you will train with the others."

Allison's brows rose. "*Others?*"

He cocked his head slightly, an almost wicked smirk playing at his mouth. "Did you really think you would be able to just fight me forever?"

She exhaled slowly, rolling her shoulders nonchalantly. "I suppose you are not about to tell me *who*?"

His lips curled into a teasing smile. "Now, where's the fun in that?"

She glared at him while forcing herself not to scowl at the heightening amusement on his face.

"You will hold your own, Murphy," his words rippled from his gaze, seemingly measuring something invisible. "I expect nothing less." His tone sounded casual, yet there was no hint of derision; it was just that calm certainty.

"You've taken a toll physically. I will not pretend to deny it."

Allison stiffened slightly at the acknowledgment. She met his eyes warily. "And yet, you're still expecting me to take a beating tomorrow."

He chuckled softly. "Of course."

More of an exhalation left her lips. "You're relentless."

"I prefer the term *dedicated*," was his smooth reply.

She rolled her eyes despite no real anger in the action.

Malakhov looked down at the faintly bruising wrists from the earlier defensive drills. For a moment, something almost like regret flickered across his face. "You can handle it."

His were not words of compliment, or even soft reassurance; They simply bore the truth.

Allison swallowed, surprised by the heat in her chest. She looked away so he would not see just how much she needed those words to mean something.

Malakhov's smirk deepened. "That's what I thought."

"You're insufferable," she retorted with a scowl.

He gave a low amused laugh. "And yet, you still listen when I speak."

She shook her head in disbelief, but could not really deny the small smile fighting to break through.

She stood tall, and he stayed seated as his gaze lazily swept over her. "Go to your room, Murphy. You'll need rest."

She bristled at the command. "I can decide that myself."

He arched a brow, his tone almost playful. "Not tonight."

She started to argue, but he cut her off with a single phrase that stopped her in her tracks. "Your bath has already been prepared."

Allison froze, her brow furrowing as she turned to face him fully. "What?"

His smirk softened, just a touch. "I had one of the housekeepers prepare it. You'll find the water is still warm."

She stared at him, momentarily at a loss for words. This wasn't a command. It wasn't a taunt. It was... a gesture. An acknowledgment of her aches, of the strain she'd put herself through. A silent admission that he'd noticed. It was clear that he cared—even if it was only in his own cryptic manner.

"*Why?*" Her whispery voice hardly crossed those already shadowy walls.

With a shrug for sheer indifference, "You will fight better if you are not limping."

Her mouth opened, but no words came. She simply could not conjure any sort of reply.

Malakhov got to his feet, stretching his arms behind his head as if the conversation had not just taken a strange turn that left her feeling off balance. "*Enjoy your night, Murphy.*"

And then he turned and left, leaving it to her to determine whether or not he was joking or not.

Radimir did not miss much. Not the way Allison lingered just slightly when Malakhov turned to leave, or the way he hesitated before walking away. He noticed how Malakhov had taken it upon himself to ensure she was not only strong but also cared for, a subtlety that did not escape his keen gaze. It was... *amusing*, to say the least. And, more importantly—it was useful. A slow, knowing smile curled at Radimir's lips.

Yes. This match would do just fine.

* * *

Allison's muscles ached while pulling the training robes over her shoulders the next morning. All the soreness kept reminding her about how much she had improved. Despite the bruises and the tiredness weighing down on her, she felt stronger. She hadn't expected that. Hadn't expected to wake up and not feel helpless. A small victory, perhaps. But in this place, small victories mattered.

She tied the belt around her waist, ignoring the way her body still hummed from the training session with Malakhov the night before. The closeness, the sharp contrast between their duels and the stillness that followed.

The moment when he had told her, *Enjoy your night.* The bath he had prepared for her before she even knew she would need it. *It was practical.* That's what she told herself. But something about it felt different.

She shook off the thoughts, squaring her shoulders as she left her room, heading toward the training hall. She needed to focus. She needed to prove, to herself, to him, to everyone, that she could handle this.

The moment she entered the room, she felt it. The wrongness. The silence. And then—someone jumped from behind a mat. A right hook, sharp and fast. Allison barely dodged in time, heat searing the air beside her as the fist slammed into the stone wall. Another swing. She twisted, raising her arms just in time to shield herself. The force of the impact sent a sharp pain up her arm, her body shifting backward as her attackers came into view. Maslov and Vasili.

She barely had time to think before they struck again. Two on one. Unfair. *Ruthless.* But she had fought worse. She had fought for her life. And she would do it again. Allison dropped into pure survival mode, her body reacting faster than thought, her anticipation flaring hot and bright.

Maslov lunged from the left, Vasili from the right. Allison deflected one, then the other, her heart pounding as she adjusted, spinning, attacking, blocking. They were playing with her. Testing her. Trying to break her. But they didn't expect her to fight back. Didn't expect her to *thrive*.

Maslov flicked his arm, a sharp, slicing motion. Allison countered before he landed, kicking him hard in the thigh. The impact forced Maslov to stumble. She used that moment, pushing forward. She ducked low, twisting on her heel, sweeping her leg out in a sharp, brutal kick. Maslov crashed onto his back. Vasili snarled, lifting his hands, Allison was already moving. She twisted her body, crackling through the air as she sent a palm hit straight to his chest. The force sent him stumbling, but they weren't done. Maslov rolled to the side, grabbing a dagger from inside his coat, lunging at her, Allison twisted, barely dodging the sharp edge slicing toward her ribs. Her breath came fast, ragged, her pulse hammering as she realized—he was trying to *actually* hurt her now.

Her temper flared. She turned sharply, her hand raised before she could think. "You bastard!" The force of the blow went straight to his jaw, and sent him backward against a stone wall, striking him about the chest and knocking the air out of his lungs. All went silent in the room. Maslov puffing, furious; Vasili staring at her dumbfounded; Allison trading glances, chest heaving, blazing eyes; her fists still raised.

Then came a cruel slow hand-clap, resounding through the oppressive silence. Allison turned around, still breathless and still filled with adrenaline. Malakhov stood in the doorway, clapping, a slow smirk curling from the corner of his mouth as his dark, unreadable eyes glinted back at her. *Dangerous.*

"Not bad, Murphy," he drawled, low and amused.

Allison swallowed. She tried to catch her breath and steady the pounding of her heart. But she could not help it. She smiled. Malakhov stepped further inside, his gaze dwelt on her for a moment, a languid consideration that set her stomach aflutter with warmth. "You're pleased with yourself," he said in a teasing tone, each word carrying a challenge. She never denied it. She didn't have to. His smirk deepened. His eyes dipped for a moment toward her mouth before returning to her. "You should be," he murmured.

A flush rose in her chest, unwanted, *undeniable*. Allison felt a shiver of delight going through her spine.

"I'm going to the cellar for a bottle, *to celebrate*," he added with quite a casual air, but somehow, the look he gave her was enough to make her catch her very breath.

Allison raised her eyebrow with a challenge.

"Celebrating what, exactly?"

Malakhov tilted his head with an almost wicked smirk. "*You*," he said quite simply.

He shot a pointed look her way with a flicker of humor in his eyes. "I assume you drink?"

Alison hesitated, and slowly, she nodded.

A deep, rich chuckle from Malakhov sent yet another chill down her spine. "Good," he said as he turned away. "I'll get us something decent. Try not to cause any more damage while I'm gone."

And with that, he disappeared from sight, leaving her alone with the lingering warmth from his gaze and a hiding hint at possibility.

Allison slid down against the cold stone wall as her sore muscles willed her to stand. She rolled her shoulders with a wince every time a sharp sting of pain radiated through a bruise. Her whole body throbbed, but beneath the bruises was something close to pride.

She had won.

She had beaten both of them. And for the first time in weeks, she felt good, like herself again.

But it didn't last.

The room grew quiet, broken only by the distant sound of fists striking and clashing as others kept practicing. Behind her, just barely audible, came her ragged breath, shallow and uneven against the cold stone wall that seemed to seep chill into her skin. A deep ache pulsed through her muscles, heavy with exhaustion. Her legs shook, but it was the kind of trembling that felt *earned,* a quiet satisfaction after a hard-fought win.

She should have known better.

The air shifted in a way that felt wrong, like a sudden chill crawling down her neck, making every hair stand on end. But it was too late.

"That was quite the show, little Ryabov."

The voice emerged from the shadows—cold, indifferent, carrying that twisted hunger that made Allison freeze. Her muscles tightened, her spine stiffening as she turned her head... just a moment too slow.

Maslov.

He stood there, eyes shining with the glint of a predator that sickened her stomach. His smile was a slow glide, seeping into her skin like poison. Allison swallowed hard; she was trying to steady her pounding heart, her other hand now clenched into a fist as she forced herself to look in his eyes.

"What do you want?" she almost whispered.

Maslov chuckled, stepping forth slowly and deliberate. "What, no *victory* speech? No grand declaration of how clever you are?" His tone was mocking, but beneath it was something, heavy and suffocating.

She swallowed hard, her heart racing as a flood of adrenaline surged through her. Before she could even gather her thoughts or react, Maslov was already moving. Faster than she expected, he closed the distance in a single stride. His hand slammed against the wall just behind her head, trapping her in place. He loomed over her, eyes burning with intensity, a smirk curling on his lips that made her skin crawl.

"You move well in battle," he said in a whisper, far too intimate for her liking and one which gave her yet another shiver. "Makes a man wonder how well you'd move elsewhere." His words were rich with dark promises, his meaning clear.

Revulsion crawled up her throat, making her want to gag. Allison sank her back against the wall, trying desperately for any semblance of space between them, but Maslov grinned as his eyes consumed her fright.

"I saw the way you fought," he said softly. "The way you threw your body into it..." Reaching out to tuck a rogue curl behind her ear, his fingers brushed across her cheek. She jerked away from him, a slight sob catching in her throat.

"Get off me," she spat.

Maslov's smirk only deepened. "You didn't say *please*."

He grabbed her.

The sudden switch was harsh and suffocating. His hand closed tightly around her wrists. He slammed her hands up in the air and pressed her down against the cold pavement. Her weapons lay underneath her, completely useless.

With almost a choking sound, her breath escaped, ragged and desperate. "GET OFF!" she screamed, panic flooding over every molecule in her body.

Laughter. Low. Amused.

Cruel.

He was stronger, and she had no one.

Maslov's hand knotted tightly around her wrist while his knee caught forcibly between her thighs, forcing them apart. He brushed his body against hers, grinding his hips down upon her, and she felt his excitement through the thin cloth that separated them. Until then, she thought that maybe Maslov had been playing with her, but now, the bile was rising in her throat.

"No, no, no—" she uttered choking while scrambling under him, terror filling up her mind.

His lips just barely grazed her ear as he whispered while his hot breath brushed against her neck, "Such fight, *little Ryabov*... I think I like that." His hands moved down her sides, their touch a cruel mockery of tenderness.

The chamber wasn't empty.

She could hear them, the other men who had been sparring earlier. They were watching. *Laughing*. Some moved closer, their amusement cold and sharp in the air.

"I thought she was supposed to belong to the Boss," one of them muttered.

"Oh, he won't mind a little fun first, will he?" another answered with a sneer, as Maslov's lips moved lower, kissing down her throat.

"I would hate for you to be married off without *some* Bratva *experience*, little Ryabov. You have to know what you are in for before your husband initiates you... and I am only *happy* to help."

The laughter continued to echo through the chamber, the pounding of her heartbeat deafening Allison as tears filled her eyes. She bucked wildly against him and screamed, "STOP!"

And Maslov just chuckled gleefully; "Shh... no need to be so dramatic," he whispered, slipping his hand under her shirt as his calloused fingers brushed the forming bruises across her stomach and upward. He moved with her sobbed breaths.

"No, please—"

"I think I like it when you *beg*," he said softly, undoing his belt as he pressed and ground his hips with greater force against her. It was as if her entire body had gone rigid and she choked out a sob as she truly felt him. Tears burned down her cheeks as she realized— she was going to be raped.

Here.

Like this.

This was how her first time would be stolen.

The wails came tearing from her throat, raw and in pieces. All she could do was pray, pray for someone to stop him, to end this, but she knew she was on her own.

A gunshot cracked through the chamber, echoing off the stone like a brutal verdict. Maslov's body jerked back with the force of the bullet, his limbs snapping as he was hurled away from Allison. The impact sent him crashing to the ground beside her with a sickening thud, even as she shoved his weight off her trembling body.

For a single breath, Allison didn't move. She didn't dare.

Then, she gasped.

She scrambled back all at once, away from the blood that was already pooling thick and black beneath Maslov's body. Her stomach heaved. Her hands scrabbled over the stone floor, scraped and trembling, her heart slamming against her ribs in frantic, terrified rhythm.

And then, *hands*. Warm hands. Rough, strong fingers holding her face with a gentle touch that dismantled her completely.

Malakhov.

Kneeling before her, his solid frame formed a shield between her and the world, instilling a sense of promise with his solid presence. Fury darkened his face, his eyes hard and cold, leaving no doubt what he would do again if he had to. But his hands, were all gentle.

Calm.

Safe.

"My *little lion*," he whispered hoarsely, thick with feeling, "are you hurt?"

Allison's lips parted as if to say something, but no noticeable words came, just a heavy sob.

Her head shook as hot and fast tears streamed down her cheeks. "I... I thought—" Words crumbled on her lips. She breathed in sharply and was shaking so hard she thought she would crack.

"He was going to— I... I... my first time..." She could not complete the sentence.

His hands froze in place, and with his full body stiffening, malice dark and absolute washed over him and made her shiver. His jaw clenched, muscles taut and tightening as he gazed, taking harsh, short breaths.

"You're a virgin," he rumbled with disbelief and rage, not at her, *never at her*, but at the man who dared to touch what was his to protect.

Allison hung her head. More tears came, falling more quickly now, her fingers digging into his shirt tightly as if clinging for dear life.

For a moment, Malakhov closed his eyes as if fighting something dark and vicious inside him. Then he exhaled.

The fury did not vanish, nor did it relent. It was instead shaped and tempering into something physically hard to break. His hands softened as his thumbs brushed with reverence over her tear-streaked face.

"That will never happen again," he whispered fiercely. "No one will hurt you like that. Do you hear me? *No one.*"

She clung to him. *Body and soul.*

Her sobs were ragged, yet he did not flinch.

He wrapped his arms around her, drawing her close and tucking her head under his chin.

His scent of smoke, musk and just a whisper of cologne held her steady in the chaos.

And Malakhov held her.

He held her as though she was something he'd sworn to protect, something he would kill for again without a second thought.

Around them, the chamber had descended into silence.

The air still lingering with the scent of gunpowder and blood.

Maslov was dead, with his twisted corpse sprawled upon the stone floor, a testimony to what would happen to those fools who dare try and touch her again.

But for Allison, there was just the warmth of Malakhov's arms, the steady beat of his heart steady against her cheek, and the unspoken promise on every breath he took;

"You are safe. And I will never let anyone - I repeat, no one—hurt you again."

The others? The others were suffering. Radimir saw to that, for *allowing* his heir to be attacked while standing around indifferent to her desperate cries for help. Those screams filled the air; raw, echoing, drawn-out just long enough to almost satisfy his cold curiosity. His pale gaze flickered back to the scene before him, back to the woman clinging to Malakhov's shirt as though he was the only solid thing within a world turned mad.

Even Malakhov was quite still, his strong arms wrapped in a protective embrace around her, his whole body curled over as a shield. To anyone else, it might have seemed as if a man was cradling something broken, but Radimir saw the truth.

Radimir lifted his head, his lips curling into something that was not quite a smile. "Never have I seen you so *soft*, Malakhov."

Malakhov didn't move. Didn't even blink. He didn't acknowledge the words, didn't so much as glance at the man who spoke them. He only tightened his hold on Allison, as though, for a moment, nothing existed beyond the space between them.

And Radimir?

Radimir was pleased.

Thirteen

A Dangerous Truth

The air felt thick, pressing in on her chest as Allison sat rigidly in the high-backed chair, hands clasped tightly in her lap. Smoke curled lazily through the room, mingling with the scent of old books and something harder to name—something that made her skin prickle. A fear slid cold and quiet down her spine. Maybe it wasn't the room that unnerved her.

Maybe it was him.

Radimir sat opposite her, the gaze of his silvery eyes measuring hers like a hawk studying its prey. Fingers steepled, he had an expression of almost boredom. But inside that placid exterior was a tension-filled calculation that sent a tightening sensation into her throat.

"You're becoming quite... *close* to Malakhov," he said at last, in a voice as smooth as velvet.

Allison forced her shoulders not too tense. Weeks she had spent learning to survive here, weeks spent training herself to hold her facial expressions, to hide her reactions. But she felt it; a cold twist gripping at her gut, an ominous warning.

She drew in another careful breath and set herself. "He is my trainer," she said softly, nearly reverent.

Radimir's lips appeared to uplift slightly, just a splash of amusement. "That is a formal answer, not an *honest* one," he corrected.

She said nothing. The silence grew longer, becoming heavy and oppressive. Her fingers curled into a tighter fist in her lap, her nails digging into her palm.

"He killed one of my best fighters for you," Radimir said gently.

Her breath caught; she forced herself to release it just as slowly and deliberately. "He did what was necessary," she stated, coolly.

Radimir's eyes caught faint glimmers in the light. "*For you*," he went on gently but insistently.

Allison's mouth went dry. Her heart thundered against her ribs, yet she tried to keep her breathing even. She did not know what to say—what he *wanted* her to say.

Radimir leaned forward, resting his elbows on the desk. "Tell me, *my dear*, do you think he would have acted so quickly, so *decisively*, if it had been any other woman beneath Maslov?"

Those words made her flinch because they went so deep she could not answer them without admitting she had a sneaking suspicion at the truth.

"I don't know," she said at last, her voice constricted.

Radimir held his gaze unwavering on her. "You are no fool, dear. I know you see what I see."

She looked away and swallowed hard. "What is it you see?" she whispered.

Radimir let out a slow, almost indulgent breath. "You're used to men like Daniel, Rob, others from your force—men who would die for you out of duty, out of *brotherhood*. But Malakhov..."

He paused and gave a little injunction to his words. Allison almost felt her skin prickle.

"What about him?" she asked softly, her voice betraying her before she could stop herself.

Radimir's eyes seemed to glint with a quiet intensity. "Malakhov would burn the world to the ground before he let you stumble," he said simply.

Her breath hitched. She wanted to call it a lie, wanted to believe that this was just another one of his manipulations. But deep down, she knew he wasn't wrong. And that—*that* was the most dangerous truth of all.

Radimir leaned back in his chair, lips curling in that faint shadow of a smile. "You do not punish the Bratva yourself."

Allison swallowed painfully. "I didn't want to."

"Or *perhaps* you knew Malakhov would do it for you," Radimir said, his voice low and patiently understanding.

The thought knocked her a bit. She hadn't thought about it like that... *had she?* Her lips parted to speak, but nothing came out.

Radimir let the silence settle heavy. He slightly tilted his head. "Any man who makes you *uncomfortable*, you may punish as you see fit."

She blinked, caught off guard. "*What?*"

"You are my heir... my *blood*," he said quietly. "You have power now. *Use it.*"

A chilling mist passed through her, more cold than even the air in the room. She shook her head, small in voice. "I don't want that kind of power," she murmured.

Radimir chuckled softly, a knowing expression gracing his lips. "Then it is a good thing Malakhov seems quite content to wield it for you."

Her stomach twisted at the thought, but she could not deny that something faint had stirred in her; fear, relief, confusion.

Radiating a fresh sharpness, something indecipherable flashed behind Radimir's eyes. "Perhaps he should no longer be your trainer," he said. "Maybe someone else should be assigned."

The words felt like a dagger plowing deep into Allison's very guts. She raised her head, refusing to stop herself from uttering the reply; "No."

The firmness had come out of her mouth unexpectedly, even to her. Slowly spreading across his face was the smirk of man who knew the truth she refused to admit.

"*Interesting*," he murmured, softly and insistently.

Allison pressed her lips together, her pulse roaring in her ears. She did not want to know what he was thinking. She did not want to see the *amusement* in his eyes, and yet she looked, aware that he had found something in her; an essence she had not wanted anyone to possess.

Radimir leaned back into his chair, still calm, and spoke with ease, "You're dismissed."

Allison stood on shaky legs, her chest tight; she bowed her head ever so slightly and stepped toward the door, clinging to the very weight of his words as if it were her second skin.

And as Allison stepped across the threshold into the corridor beyond the door, the air seemed to shift, as if the world had tilted on its axis.

* * *

Malakhov entered into the private study with deliberate calm, each step measured, his face carefully blank. But he knew why he was here.

He knew in exact detail the way the conversation would unfold. Radimir set his sharp eyes upon Malakhov, catching every flicker of hesitation, every unspoken word.

"She is important to you," Radimir had almost casually said.

Malakhov's lips had gone tight, thin, unyielding. "She is my assignment," he had said, curtly, coldly.

Radimir's smirk was faint but undeniable. "That is not what I asked."

The silence that followed was heavy, a slow, creeping pressure between them. Then, Radimir rose from his chair, moving with the careful grace of a predator. He began to circle the desk, every step deliberate and smooth, his voice a low murmur that wrapped around the room.

"I know my followers well, Dmitri. I know their ambitions, their wants, their hungers. And I know *you*."

Malakhov didn't flinch, didn't betray a single emotion. But Radimir saw it anyway. *He always saw.*

"I have watched you," Radimir continued, his tone soft, almost hypnotic. "The way you guard her. The way you anticipate her needs before she speaks them. The way you provide what she doesn't yet know she needs."

His voice dropped even lower. "The way you *look* at her..."

Malakhov's jaw tightened, his body going still, coiled.

Radimir's lips curled into a knowing smile. "Do you *want* her?" His voice sliced through the air like a blade.

Malakhov exhaled slowly through his nose, while something dark and ferocious flickered in his eyes. The battle within him was unmistakable, and every line of his body was taut with it. "I am loyal to you, Sir," he ground out, the words rough, scraped raw.

"And yet," Radimir pressed, his voice a gentle, insistent probe, "if you were given the choice?" He leaned closer, the red gleam in his eyes softening, almost warm. "I am not asking as your leader. I am asking as a father. I want her to be happy—if she is not, she will continue to fight me, and fight what I am building here."

Malakhov's breath caught, every muscle in his body tense. The idea of her, Allison, being *given* to another man sent a violent burn through his veins, jealousy and something deeper, something more dangerous, clawing at his throat. He didn't want to imagine it. *He couldn't.*

Radimir's gaze was relentless. "If I give her to another, will you stand aside?"

The question sank into him like a knife. Malakhov's heart beat fast in his ears, his vision narrowing. The thought of her in someone else's arms—*it was a poison*. His skin prickled with it, sharp and electric.

Radimir's voice softened further, becoming almost coaxing. "I do not want a man who obeys only out of duty. I want a man who would put her first above all else."

Malakhov felt as though his chest was painfully tightened and his breath shuddered out. There was truth, deeply buried within him; he was aware of it more than of anything else. But he could not bring himself to give voice to it.

Not yet.

Not here.

So he gave the only answer he felt safe enough to give. "I will serve you, no matter the outcome."

Radimir smiled more widely, slowly and with pleasure, a sliver of something darker, a gleam of amusement in his crimson eyes by the corner of his mouth. "That is not an answer," he murmured, "but it will do." His voice was warm and velvet-smooth.

Malakhov turned away; his footsteps were quiet. Yet something called to him. Once more, Radimir's voice sounded. Soft, barely a whisper,

"Dmitri," he called, stopping him cold.

Malakhov froze, every nerve alive.

Radimir's tone was light now, almost teasing. "Have you considered what it would be like... *being married to a cop?*"

Malakhov's breath stilled in his chest. His mind spun with it, a thousand images crashing behind his eyes. But he didn't speak. He couldn't. With one last glance, haunted, longing, dangerous, he turned and walked out of the room.

* * *

There was tension in Findley Place, the unspoken fears lying heavy upon the nervous atmosphere. Daniel sat there at the table's head, holding on tightly to the wood as if it were his only anchor. Beside him, sitting motionless, was Rob, his jaw clenched in anger and resolution, almost white as though his face was drained of any blood.

Across the room, Scott exhaled slowly and rhythmically. "Doronin has confirmed she is alive and well taken care of," he said quietly.

Rob flinched at the words, and Daniel's breath caught, a faint hitch in the silence.

Hunter spoke then, his voice calm but weighted with the gravity of the situation. "We do not know where she is being kept at all times. We know only what he allows us to know."

Rob's reply came in a tight, almost broken whisper. "But is she still *Allison*?"

The words hung heavy in the air, and Daniel felt his throat ache, the question twisting inside him.

"What if she doesn't want to come back?"

The silence that followed was absolute.

Then, cutting through the quiet, Heather's voice rang out, sharp and absolute. "Then we remind her who she is." The certainty in her tone was a blade, slicing through the uncertainty.

No one spoke after that, the weight of her words settling over them.

Scott finally straightened, his shoulders squaring with purpose. "We move soon." His words were a promise, a vow.

The war for Allison was far from over.

* * *

Allison stared at herself in the mirror, barely recognizing the woman looking back. The reflection wasn't the same girl who had once run through forests with Daniel and Rob, starving, desperate, always afraid. This woman stood taller, stronger.

Her clothes fit differently now—no longer loose or ill-fitting, but tailored to her form, designed to move and to fight. The deep ruby fabric clung to her curves, lined with silver, the Russian colors mocking her. Even her dagger felt different in her grip—heavier, more dangerous, despite being the only weapon she was allowed since she hadn't been trusted with her gun back yet.

She had always wielded power, but this was something else, something that made her chest tighten with guilt. She had been in Radimir's world for months now, telling herself she was only surviving, only playing the game until she could find a way out. Yet a traitorous voice inside her whispered; *Are you sure?* Because here, she had *real power.* No longer the sidekick or strategist in the background, she was the one who drew every eye when she entered a room, the one who inspired fear even though she had never lifted her hand to harm anyone.

It felt good.

Allison clenched her jaw, gripping the edge of the wooden vanity to ground herself. She should have been thinking of Daniel, of Rob, of the resistance. She should have felt disgusted with herself for not aching to return to them every moment of every day.

But she wasn't thinking about them at all.

And Malakhov—*Malakhov* was the reason why. That thought sent a wave of nausea through her. She had never once hesitated to hate the Bratva; not Natalia, not Aleksei, not Maslov or Vasili. *But Malakhov?* He was different. He was the one she trained with, spent her days and evenings with. The one who knew how she moved, how she fought, how she thought. The one who had killed for her without hesitation. Her breath shook because, for the first time, she wasn't sure if she hated him. And that was terrifying.

The dueling chamber was different today. Malakhov felt it the moment she entered. It wasn't the air or the torches or the layout—it was *her*. The way she stood, poised and controlled, her chin slightly lifted as she faced him.

The way she didn't wait for him to make the first move anymore. The way her energy crackled hotter, brighter, sharper than ever before. The way she smirked when she disarmed him for the very first time. Malakhov responded by flicking his foot, knocking her over with a single, sharp motion. But then he stopped.

Allison frowned. "What?" she asked.

Malakhov lowered his hands. "You enjoyed that."

She tilted her head. "Shouldn't I?"

Malakhov exhaled slowly. She was playing with fire, and she didn't even know it. "You're playing a *dangerous* game, Murphy," he said.

She arched a brow. "And am I playing it *alone*?"

Malakhov gave a smirk that didn't quite touch his eyes. In truth, for the first time, he was doubting who might be the leader among them.

He sat cross-legged on the marble floor and rested his elbows on his knees while observing Allison leaning on the freezing stone wall and drawing deep breaths. The silence wasn't uneasy but rather thick. Allison breathed out slowly, looking up at the torches, its flame flickered, casting dramatic shadows on the stones. Then—softly, almost in a whisper—she spoke.

"Do you regret it?"

Malakhov's eyes flickered. "Regret what?"

She turned her head, meeting his gaze. "Killing him. Maslov."

Malakhov's expression didn't change, but something in his posture shifted. "No," he said.

Allison's chest tightened. She should have been horrified. But she wasn't.

Malakhov tilted his head, his voice lowering. "Do you?"

Allison exhaled slowly, her pulse pounding in her ears. "I *should*."

Malakhov's lips curled slightly. "But you don't."

Allison swallowed, looking away. And for the first time, Malakhov let himself really look at her. At the way her fingers twitched against her jacket. At the way her breathing had slowed, carefully controlled. At the way her expression was so carefully blank that he could see the war inside her. And that was when it hit him; she wasn't afraid anymore.

Not of him.

Not of this.

And he should have felt triumphant. He should have been pleased. But instead, for the first time in his life, Malakhov felt like he had made a mistake.

* * *

Radimir positioned himself at the opposite end of the grand marble table, his imposing stature overshadowing the gathered Bratva. His cold, calculating stare moved across the assembled men, momentarily locking eyes with just one; *Malakhov.*

He had watched Malakhov with great interest, studying every subtle change in posture, the way he would unconsciously position himself between Allison and the others, the way his shoulders squared in readiness whenever anyone else dared cast an eye at her.

He had watched how Allison moved around him, no longer wary or reluctant, her footsteps bold as if she were aware of the assurance his very presence conferred on her. He had seen the silent attraction between them, they were drawn to each other even if they were without touch, as if simply being there together served as an unspoken agreement.

Radimir had seen it all, and it pleased him. But it was time to push this matter forward and see whether these hushed movements between them would actually materialize.

Radimir's voice was low and measured; it broke the heavy silence that had filled the chamber.

"Dmitri."

Malakhov held his chin high, poised as always. "Sir."

Radimir inclined his head, a slow smile appearing at the corner of his mouth.

"You have had time to *consider* your answer."

Malakhov's pulse didn't quicken—he refused to let it show. But he knew. He knew exactly what was coming.

Radimir's gaze flickered to Allison, a deliberate, lingering look, before settling back on him. "Are you ready to *claim* her?"

The room fell silent. The men around the table shifted uneasily, eyes darting between Radimir, Malakhov, and Allison.

They hadn't known, hadn't suspected what had been growing between them. Allison's breath caught in her throat, her fingers curling against the edge of her seat. Malakhov didn't move. Didn't even breathe. Because this was it. This was the moment everything would change, the moment when lines would be drawn and loyalties tested. And for the first time since all of this began, Malakhov didn't know what his answer would be.

Fourteen

Devotion Against Fate

The dining hall was quiet after Radimir's decree. The tension hung heavy in the air, thick with the weight of something looming and inevitable.

Allison sat stiffly at Radimir's right, her pulse pounding in her ears as every eye in the room fixed on Malakhov, waiting for him to accept his *prize*, waiting for him to claim what they all wanted. She felt suffocated by the expectation that pressed in from every side.

Malakhov, however, remained silent. He didn't immediately bow or accept, didn't reach for her, didn't take what was being offered so easily.

Instead, he turned to Radimir, his voice calm, controlled, and steady with something unrelenting. "Sir, may I request something?"

Radimir's brow arched slightly, intrigued by the challenge in his voice. "You may," he said.

Malakhov inclined his head. "I would prefer to speak with her privately before I give my answer."

A ripple of shock shot through the others around them. Allison's stomach twisted, her own fingers knotting the fabric of her dress. *He was supposed to accept.* That was how it always worked. That was what they had all been waiting for; Radimir to name her match, the chosen man to stand and take what was now his.

But Malakhov wasn't playing by their rules. And Radimir noticed.

His lips curled into a slow and dangerous smirk. He inclined his head, studying Malakhov as if he were a puzzle that needed to be solved.

Then his gaze swept over Allison, sharp and assessing. "Do you object, my dear?" he asked.

Allison swallowed hard, her breath coming in slow, controlled draws. *She didn't want this.* Didn't want to be paraded before them, to be fought over like some prize to be won. But she also didn't want to be alone with Malakhov in a private room, discussing the reality of what was happening to her. She didn't want to hear the truth—*his* truth. And yet, she shook her head.

Radimir's smirk widened. He turned back to the room, his voice silken and indulgent. "How charming. A true gentleman in our midst. Those of you who *begged* for her hand should take notes—perhaps you lacked the refinement to deserve her."

Some of the men around the table stiffened visibly. Aleksei looked away sharply, his fingers tightening around the head of his cane. Grigori sneered, and Vasili's jaw tensed.

But Malakhov didn't react. He simply nodded once, his voice calm and sure. "Thank you, Sir." And with that, it was decided.

The delightful crackle of the fireplace brought only a touch of warmth to the dim chamber as Malakhov stood near one of the windows, gazing above the darkened sky.

Allison sat on the edge of the long velvet sofa, her back stiffened, arms crossed tightly on her chest. Heavy silence settled over everything left unsaid.

When she couldn't handle the silence any longer, she forced the words out, her voice low with anger. "I don't want to marry anyone."

Malakhov did not turn around immediately. His broad shoulders shifted slightly, but his voice was calm, measured. "I know."

Allison let out a sharp breath, her frustration finally bubbling over. "*Then why are we here*? "Why would this even be a conversation if what I want *doesn't* matter?"

He turned so slowly, his face impassive and unreadable, his dark eyes locking on hers quietly yet intently. "Because, you well know, neither one of us has a choice in this."

Allison clenched her jaw, her fingers pressing into her arms. "That's a lie. You have a choice—more of one than I do."

Malakhov took a step closer to her, his voice quiet but unyielding. "I asked for this conversation because there were a few things I wanted you to understand— *important ones*."

She swallowed, her heart thumping wildly. "What?"

He came and stood in front of her, the grave look of his face momentarily softening so that she knew he truly meant what he said. "That no matter what happens next, no matter what Radimir decides—*if we marry*, I will be devoted to no one else but you."

Her breath caught, and the weight of that statement filled her heart with pain. Little by little, Allison began to shake her head, scarcely able to utter, "Everything is happening too quickly. I don't even know who I am anymore."

Without a hint of hesitation, Malakhov bent down before her, placing his hands gently on the front of his thighs while never averting his gaze from her.

"You are Allison Murphy. You're the youngest detective Chicago has ever seen. You're the remarkable woman who disarmed two of Radimir's best fighters and walked away victorious."

She let out a choked laugh, shaking her head. "I'm also his *daughter*."

His jaw tightened slightly, but his eyes never wavered. "Yes, you are both," he said quietly. "And neither part of you deserves to be caged."

Allison looked down at her trembling hands. Her voice was barely a whisper. "I don't know which part of me is winning anymore."

Malakhov lowered his voice to that same soft murmur. "Neither do I," he said, a tone of honesty raw enough to wrench her heart.

She forced herself to meet his gaze through a tight throat. *"Are you scared?"*

He exhaled slowly; his lips parted little by little. *"Terrified,"* he said simply, this one word hanging in-between them like a confession of something they had both been trying not to say.

Her chest ached for he was speaking the truth, and that, somehow, had become the most frightening thing of all. Slowly, Malakhov stood, his face quickly going back to that mask of careful inscrutability, but the determination in his eyes was impossible to hide.

"I will tell him yes," he said softly but firmly.

Allison drew a sharp breath; her fingers curled into the fabric of her blouse.

"Why?" she whispered.

Malakhov's jaw tensed, his eyes softening just a fraction. "Because I won't be forced to claim you in front of them. I won't let him decide how this ends."

She blinked, her breath catching. "Then what do you want?" she asked, her voice trembling.

Malakhov tilted his head slightly, a small, almost wry smile ghosting his lips. "I want you to know it's *me* choosing you, not *him*. I want you to understand that whatever this is, it's because I want it. And because I won't let anyone else decide what we become."

The silence then fell, deep and heavy, broken only by the crackling of wood in the fire, and the frantic pounding of her heart. Her pulse was echoing in her ears, and she knew-there was a strange thrill and fear to the knowledge-that everything had just shifted.

Forever.

* * *

The morning air was cold—even inside the great hall of the manor, but Allison felt nothing. She stood alone by the large bay window of her chambers, arms wound tightly about herself as she looked out upon the bleak gray sky, her mind empty and heavy with the load of the days ahead. She had scarcely allowed herself any sleep the previous night. She had barely eaten. Today was the day Malakhov would decide. And she always felt in her heart that this was peculiar, her future being molded at that very moment.

Softly there came a knock at the door. She spun around, and there her heart pounded; she did not want to see him, *not really*. The very air around Malakhov felt taut for her, as if the room wanted to hold its breath.

He stepped into the room quietly, the quiet force of his presence was calming yet terrifying all at once. For a long while, they looked at each other in silence. He was dressed in a formal black suit, with a gun tucked away by his side, he remained perfectly controlled and stoic. She felt the exact opposite, unwinding.

"Are you ready?" he softly questioned.

She let out a choking breath that rattled her even more. "I don't think I ever could be."

Malakhov's jaw muscles tightened just for a second, then he stepped closer still. "You don't have to be ready for them... You just have to be ready for me."

Swallowing pain hard, Allison's pulse was frantic. "Do you want *this*?"

His eyes glanced briefly into shadow, and his lips curled into a faint smile that did little to lift them. "What I want is not as important as what you want."

She barked out, "That's not an answer." The anger in her voice clear.

"It's the only answer I have," he whispered, inched toward her, coming close enough for her to see the lines around his mouth and the softened eyes with which he regarded her.

"I don't want to be forced into this," she said shakily.

Malakhov's eyes darted away. "Then I won't force you." He almost hesitated, his expression serious but there was a hint of the almost-playful inside. "Though I certainly could be very *convincing*."

There was a catch in her throat, the blush in her cheeks contrasting against the terror churning in her gut. "You enjoy that don't you?" she accused, half-angry, half-breathless.

He smiled faintly. "I enjoy seeing you flustered, *yes*," he admitted, making her stomach flip in a way she hated. "But the circumstances? No, I am not enjoying that it has come to this."

She stepped closer, anger and need boiled together. "Then why are we here?"

Malakhov tilted his head but his gaze remained steady. "Because if I must be *yours*, then you must be *mine*." His voice was calm, almost teasing but there was no misunderstanding the burden in those words.

She clenched her fists at her sides. "I don't belong to anyone."

"Then let me ask," he said quietly, tone shifting from teasing to something much more serious. "I will tell him that you will be mine... only if you will have me."

A sharp breath escaped Allison's lips. She had been expecting a demand. She had been bracing herself for a *command*. She was not prepared for a request.

"You're asking me?" she whispered.

Malakhov nodded, dark eyes locked in hers. "Yes."

She gave a slow shake of her head. "I don't want to marry."

"I know," came his reply, softer now. "But I won't let anyone else have you."

His eyes glimmered, and his lips curled up in a faint smile. "You can go on and call me possessive if you like."

She let out a humorless laugh. "A little."

He raised an eyebrow, that smile deepening. "Only a *little*?"

She glared at him, no real flame in that look, though. "A lot."

His grin was fleeting. "Good, because I'm only asking you to be mine. I'll see to everything else."

She swallowed hard, The ache constricting her throat. "You're afraid," she whispered.

"Aren't you?" he said softly in retort.

"Yes," was her reply, and for a while they simply looked at one another with two people caught in something that was thrust upon them, something neither of them knew how to fight.

Malakhov took a step forward and lowered his voice. "Will you let me protect you, *little lion*?"

Her heart pounded in her chest while she hesitated, finally, she nodded slowly.

Then he exhaled, "Then we will stand together," he said, just as he reached out for her wrist, caressing it with his fingertips.

Allison felt her breath hitch; the warmth emanating from his touch moved with intention as his eyes traced her face, and with almost reverent solemnity, he cupped her cheek with one hand, his thumb trailing ever so lightly. The shivers raced through her.

She did not pull away.

Just before the ghost of a kiss touched her lips, he bent toward her, a soft, tentative whisper giving her every chance to recoil, but she did not.

Instead, she leaned in, soaking in his warmth, a real, tangible, and present force.

When they parted, his thumb was again caressing her cheek, his voice low and soft as a whisper. "We will be just fine, *sweetheart*."

Allison swallowed hard, looking for a lie in his eyes, but came up empty. "Are you reassuring me?" she whispered. "Or yourself?"

His smiled faintly but never reaching his eyes. "Both," he admitted as he pressed his forehead to hers. "But either way, I'm not letting you go."

In that moment, she believed him—*terrifyingly so.*

* * *

The Bratva filled the great hall, occupying every seat. Their keen eyes harbored either a promise of violence or of triumph. Allison sat beside Radimir with her fingers clenched tightly in her lap, her nails biting into her flesh. Every thud echoed strongly in her ears mirroring her heartbeat, but she forced herself to remain still and to stay strong. She would not allow fear to show.

She could not afford to.

Malakhov stepped in, his presence quiet but commanding, each footfall deliberate, like time itself was pacing with him. It felt like the air shifted around him, slowing down, as if he moved in his own world and the rest of them didn't matter. The room fell into silence, thick and brittle, tension pulled tight.

Radimir, always watching, tilted his head with a smile that didn't reach his eyes—a warning more than a welcome.

"Dmitri," he said, voice low and smooth, the kind that sank under your skin, "you've had time to think."

Malakhov lifted his chin, gaze steady and cool. "Yes, Sir," he said simply, without hesitation.

But when Radimir's pale eyes glanced at Allison, a chill ran through her. That gaze weighed on her as a reminder that she would have to endure whatever came next; there could be no escape. "And what is your answer?" Radimir's voice nearly bored, but the glance he cast was full of eager interest.

Malakhov then turned to her... and something changed in his dark eyes. For weeks, she had seen nothing but cold calculation and unreadable determination in those eyes. Now she saw something final, something unyielding and yet, *somehow gentle.*

"She will be mine, but only if she will *have* me," he said, his voice calm but strong. In that moment, he was not addressing Radimir or the Bratva but was speaking to her alone.

A ripple of shock swept onto the room.

Murmurs followed as the men exchanged glances because, while they expected Malakhov to claim her, none of them had expected him to *ask.*

Radimir gave a mock-astonished raise of the brow and a slow smile of pleased approval; "Wise answer," he softly uttered, leaning back in his chair and looking once more to her."And what say you, my dear?" His voice came with a wicked glint in his eyes that made her stomach twist.

Allison swallowed hard and tried to meet Malakhov's eyes as her mouth became dry. She felt the room pressing over her with the certainty of Radimir's expectation and the glancing eyes of the Bratva. But there was warmth from Malakhov's eyes, steady and unwavering. He was *asking*; he was giving her the only choice she would ever get.

Her voice was tiny but resolute, "Yes."

That word glided across the hall, as if time itself paused to hear it. There was a murmur among the men, exchanging glances, some curious, some begrudging.

Radimir lifted a hand, and the room fell silent again—heavy and stifling, like the air itself had thickened. His smile stretched wider, but there was no warmth behind it—just sharp amusement and something colder lurking beneath.

"A splendid match indeed," he murmured, the words slick and slow, brushing against the room in a way that made her skin crawl. His gaze slid over the crowd and landed on Aleksei Kotov, whose jaw was locked tight, fury written all over him. Then Grigori turned away, lip curled in open disgust.

Radimir leaned ever so slightly forward, lowering his voice to something akin to a conspiratorial tone. "How rare it is to see a soldier who knows devotion," mocking yet indulgent. "I would advise the rest of you to learn from him. Loyalty to one's partner is almost as important as loyalty to me."

The words were a warning as much as they were a taunt, and Allison felt the shift in the room, the way the Bratva straightened in their seats.

But Malakhov never looked away from her. His deep eyes had locked with Allison's, his expression one of calm certainty as though the rest of the world no longer exist. Allison felt a heartbeat skip. For in that gaze, there was not only the promise of possessing, but also of protecting her, and being willing to stand beside her through whatever journey lay ahead.

Radimir's smile widened as he leaned back, his voice smooth and quiet, almost like a purr. "Now... about the wedding," he said.

The words hit like a drop down a steep cliff, Allison's stomach plunged at the weight of them. But just before the dread could take full hold, she caught Malakhov's gaze. There was something steady in it, something unspoken but firm—he would stand his ground, with or without her, no matter what came next.

And for now, that was enough for her to hold on to.

The doors burst open with a thunderous crash. A blast of gunpowder tore through the air, sending the guards flying like rag dolls—bodies crashing into walls and columns, dust and debris swirling in the cold air. Chaos erupted instantly.

Allison struggled to breathe, a sharp, burning panic clawing at her chest. She knew that sound—that pungent smoke. Her heart pounded wildly, hammering so hard it felt like it might break free from her ribs.

A voice beyond all that chaos, urgent and desperate, screamed "Allison!" Daniel—and just behind him, Rob. The resistance.

They were there for her, somehow, they never really gave up on her. That hope she had so far down in the recesses of her mind suddenly started its resurgence, so raw, so relentless. For a split second, her chest was pressed underwater, and she was clawing for air.

They were here.

They have come to save her.

She should have sprinted into their arms, thrown herself at them, screamed at the top of her lungs, *I'm here. Take me home.* But her body froze. She didn't move. She couldn't. Because before she could even blink, Malakhov was already there—his presence a wall of steel between her and the storm.

He stepped forward so fast it was as if he'd anticipated the moment before it happened, his body shielding her instinctively. His gun was raised, steady in his hand, eyes dark and unflinching as he faced the chaos head-on.

Radimir's chuckle rose low and slow from the hall, interspersed with smoke-like curls from a dying fire. "How *adorable*," he sneered so casually as if to amuse himself, each syllable drooling smugness.

That sound hooked her gut, painfully reminding Allison of the game she had been thrust into. It was more serious than ever before. Bile made its way into her throat, constricting it with a thousand different emotions.

Then came that *damned*, moment that would shape everything from then on.

A choice.

A single choice, stretching wide across the raging battlefield within her.

Should she run to Daniel? To Rob? To the resistance that had never stopped fighting for her freedom? Or should she remain behind Malakhov, the man who had lodged himself between her and the storm and had become her shield, her protector, her anchor? Her heart cried out to run away, while the body quaked with hesitation.

The room froze, every eye locked on her as if the next breath might shatter the silence. The weight of what she was about to decide pressed down like a storm ready to break.

One choice.

One moment that would split everything apart—and there was no turning back.

Fifteen

The Price of Protection

The hall exploded into chaos. Gunfire tore through the doors, ripping the heavy iron-reinforced wood into splinters that skidded across the stone floor. The sharp, choking scent of gunpowder filled the air, tangled with the noise of battle: shouts, metal, the pulse of violence.

Allison froze, her breath caught in her throat, body rigid with shock. She turned toward the entrance, where smoke and light clashed in the doorway—past and present colliding with a force that felt like it might tear her in two.

"Allison!" Daniel cried again, nearly choking on his words from desperation. Rob stood alongside him, one horrified grimace etched across his face, a pistol in hand. The resistance had come for her. They had not given up.

Malakhov's body was a barrier between her and the oncoming conflict. His gun was already in hand, eyes blazing with warning. "Do not move," he breathed, low and certain. "Stay behind me." He quickly flipped a table on its side, thick steel and wood screaming in protest, and laid a reliable barricade before the oncoming bullets.

Allison stood there momentarily. Breathless. Mind-empty. This wasn't the right way.

Daniel took a step forward, gun raised and shaking. "Move, Malakhov! You don't have to protect her, she's coming with us!"

Malakhov didn't flinch. Instead, he let out a low, humorless chuckle, the kind that made the hairs on the back of her neck rise. "You're mistaken, Diaz," he said coolly, tilting his head. "She is not yours to take."

Daniel's jaw clenched. "So this is what it's come to?" His voice cracked under the strain, equal parts disbelief and fury. "You're holding her here? Forcing her to stay in this goddamn chaos like some kind of prisoner? Look at her! She's terrified!"

"She's terrified because you kicked in the doors like a lunatic and started firing," Malakhov shot back his eyes flicked down to the weapon, then back up with icy calm. "I also don't recall her *asking* to be rescued. And I certainly don't need a weapon to keep my fiancé by my side."

The word hit the air like a detonation.

"What the hell did you just say?" Daniel barked, his aim faltering for the first time. "Fiancé?"

Rob's head snapped toward Allison, then back to Malakhov. "No. No way. That's bullshit."

Malakhov didn't look away. "Did I stutter?"

"You've got to be kidding me," Rob said, his voice rising with disbelief. "Allison wouldn't just—she wouldn't agree to that. What the hell did you do to her?"

"Oh, here we go," Malakhov muttered, half-laughing, his voice laced with venom. "Always so quick to assume I must've manipulated her, brainwashed her, drugged her. Couldn't possibly be that she made a choice you didn't like, right?"

Daniel shook his head, gun still half-raised, but uncertain now. "You're saying she agreed to marry you? In this nightmare?"

Malakhov's smile was razor-sharp. "I'm saying she didn't need a rescue because she already chose her side—*and it's not yours.*"

Rob stepped forward, ignoring the tension of the guns between them. "You think throwing a ring on her finger gives you some kind of claim? You think that's love?"

"No," Malakhov said, voice low and deliberate. "But I know what it is to fight for someone with everything you have. Can you say the same—or were you just hoping she'd eventually notice you standing in the corner, playing the noble friend?"

Rob bristled. "You don't know a damn thing about what I've done for her."

"No," Malakhov said, stepping in to close the space. "But she chose me. And I will burn this whole place to the ground before I let any of you take her from me."

Silence crackled between them, thick with heat and unsaid things.

"This isn't a contest, and she's not the damn prize at the end of it." Rob said quietly, anger simmering just beneath the words.

Malakhov's voice dropped, quiet and dangerous. "No. She's not. *But she's mine.* And if you think I'll stand here and let either of you parade in and play savior, you're both exactly as stupid as I expected."

He turned slightly, enough to glance at Allison—just for a heartbeat. And in that flicker of a moment, something softer lived in his gaze. But when he looked back, it was gone.

Around them, the hall had become a battlefield. The Bratva surged against the resistance, green and black smoke curling to the ceiling as bullets ricocheted off the stone walls and bodies clashed in the chaos.

Allison was frozen. Paralyzed. She could only watch as Malakhov stood in front of her like an impenetrable wall, refusing to let anyone near.

"Allison, come on!" Rob yelled, trying to push past Vasili, who stood unmoving with his gun aimed at him. "We're getting you out of here!"

But she didn't move. Because she didn't know if she wanted to. Shame and fear twisted inside her like a knife. She hated herself for the way her heart pounded, not from terror, but because she knew if she took a single step toward them, Malakhov would not let her go. And a part of her, dark and undeniable—didn't want him to.

"She's too far gone! We're too late!" Brandon's voice rose above the fighting, rough and final. Allison's head snapped up, her heart slamming against her ribs.

"She's one of them now!" he shouted.

Brandon raised his gun and fired towards Allison.

She barely had time to register it. Malakhov moved faster than she ever thought possible, twisting to shield her as he shoved her to the ground and returned fire in the same breath. A single, deadly shot rang out, and Brandon Mitchell fell, dead before he hit the floor. Allison's scream tore through the hall.

"No!"

The world blurred. She couldn't breathe. Her vision tunneled, her chest heaving with ragged gasps as she sank lower behind the barricade, still shielded by Malakhov. Daniel met Malakhov's eyes, and the two men held each other's gaze across the chaos, but neither moved to attack.

"Just go," Allison whispered, her voice breaking. "Please... just go."

Daniel's face twisted in horror. "Allison, no—"

"No, Allison," Rob yelled out, his fists clenched tightly around his gun. "You don't have to do this. You can come with us—we'll figure it out—"

"Just go!" The words tore from her throat, raw and broken, tears streaming down her face.

The battle raged on around them, but she didn't hear it and couldn't feel anything except the crushing weight of what had just happened. Brandon was dead. And she had let it happen.

Across the room, Radimir's cold gaze found her, fury and calculation burning in his eyes. He studied her reaction in silence before turning to Malakhov, the room falling into a tense, breathless hush. "Get her out of here."

Malakhov's voice was calm, controlled. He nodded once and, before Allison could even protest, she was being dragged down a back alley and shoved into a waiting car. Malakhov drove in silence, his jaw set tight as the city blurred past them. When they finally reached his family home and crossed the threshold, Allison broke.

She shoved him hard, her hands trembling violently. "You killed him!" Her voice was raw, the accusation echoing through the quiet entryway.

Malakhov didn't flinch. Didn't argue. "Yes," he said simply.

Allison's breath caught in her throat, her whole body shaking with anger, grief, and confusion. "How could you?!" she screamed, her voice hoarse.

Malakhov let her hit him. Let her yell, her fists striking his chest as tears streamed down her face. And then—his voice dropped low, cold and steady. "He aimed first."

Allison's stomach lurched at his words.

"He fired at you, Allison."

She shook her head, denial clawing at her chest. "No—no, he wouldn't—"

But Malakhov's voice remained calm, edged with something dark, something possessive. "He did. He shot first."

She felt sick, the room spinning around her. Malakhov took a step closer, his expression unreadable. "It would have killed you," he said quietly.

Her chest tightened painfully. "You don't know that—" she choked out, her voice breaking.

"Yes. I do." His words were final, sharp as a blade.

Allison's hands shook, her world crumbling around her. She had believed, *hoped,* that she could still go back. That there was a way to undo the past. But Brandon had aimed at her, seen her as too far gone. And for the first time, she wondered if he had been right.

Malakhov watched her, his eyes never leaving her face. "I held back because I knew you were conflicted, I did not fire at Daniel or Rob or anyone else, until they threatened you," he said softly. "I will never stand by and let someone harm you."

Allison's world tilted as tears filled her eyes. Her legs wobbled uncontrollably as she sank down with a thud onto the sofa. Malakhov lowered down to his knees in front of her, all careful deliberation, his movements smooth and controlled. Placing his hands on either side of her with firm yet gentle pressure, his voice poured low. "You are not alone."

The weight of everything she couldn't say choked Allison's throat. She had struggled for so long; she had tried to be strong for so long.

But now? Now she wasn't sure what she was fighting for anymore.

* * *

Back at the safe house, the mood was heavy. The resistance had gathered once again to discuss their next moves after the failed attempt to rescue Allison. Rob paced back and forth, his mind racing, trapped in anger as the words came, "I cannot believe this. I just cannot believe she is *with him,*" he muttered under his breath. "If he touched her, I swear to God I'll kill him... "

Heather sat there in silence, watching Rob. "Rob," she said softly, "I know this is hard for you. It is hard for all of us. But you have to understand, Allison has had to survive for months there."

Rob stopped pacing and looked at her. "What?"

Heather nodded, her face full of emotion. "I was there, in the back... Malakhov didn't fire *any* shots. He didn't attack us until Allison was in danger. When we moved in to approach her, he stood down, let us get close enough. He even protected her from the others." Rob let out a low mutter as he sank into a chair.

"That's insane," he said, shaking his head. "He's just keeping her locked away."

Heather's expression softened. "It's more than that, Rob. Malakhov actually cares for her. That much I could see."

Rob sighed, slumping in his chair. "I don't know what's worse, the fact that she's really chosen this life... or that she's actually *happy* in it."

Daniel clenched his fists, frustration and determination mingling in his expression. "We need to get her back. We need to keep fighting. This isn't over."

But in his heart, Daniel knew it wasn't just the battle they needed to win. It was Allison. And somehow, he had to find a way to bring her back, before it was too late.

* * *

Across town from Radimir's estate, the sitting room turned cold, sudden and sharp. Allison stiffened as a chill slid down her spine, instinct flaring just a second too late.

A deafening crack split the room. He was here.

Radimir didn't enter so much as *consume* the space. His presence hit like the first crash of thunder before a violent storm: immediate, impossible to ignore. The fire in the hearth sputtered and dimmed, its flames shrinking back as though suffocating under the weight of him.

Allison sat on the couch, frozen, trembling from what the evening's events brought upon her. Malakhov shifted slightly, placing himself half a step forward from her in a posture clearly casual yet protective.

"Such a strong reaction, *my dear*," spoke Radimir, smooth and almost amused, yet sharper undertones hid behind.

Allison clasped the fabric of her clothes tightly, breath coming raggedly in short bursts. She wasn't sure if she could even manage to speak.

Radimir's pale gaze darted to Malakhov. "Did she cry for the others as much as she cried for them?" Malakhov's expression was unreadable, but his jaw stiffened ever so slightly.

"She has spent her entire life with them, Sir," he answered smoothly, low but respectful, and firm. "I do not think it is a weakness to mourn the loss of what she knew."

Radimir stilled, his eyes narrowing thoughtfully.

Malakhov's steady voice continued, "She did not try to flee. She did not fight. She did not betray you."

Allison swallowed hard, her chest aching with emotions she couldn't name.

"She has accepted this life," Malakhov added quietly. "That does not mean she must do so without grief."

Allison sucked in a sharp breath. Malakhov was standing up for her, *against Radimir*. A lifelong servant and soldier of the Russian mafia was arguing in her defense. And Radimir... he was *listening*. For the first time since she'd arrived, someone was speaking for her, not just to use her.

Radimir's expression remained blank, but his fingers drummed lightly against the arm of his suit. The tension was palpable, a heavy, thrumming current in the air. Finally, after what felt like an eternity, Radimir exhaled softly. "You have always been... reasonable, Malakhov," he murmured.

He turned his cold, red gaze back to Allison. "But grief must not outweigh purpose."

Allison's throat tightened as Radimir stepped forward, his long, skeletal fingers folding together. "You have a place here, Allison. You are Ryabov's blood. *My blood.*"

She flinched, because despite *everything* she had survived, he wasn't wrong. She stood in place as his magnified gaze seemed to see straight through her, beyond her anger, beyond her sadness, beyond her confusion, down to the deepest and most fearful parts of herself. "You belong to me," he continued, the words a dangerously smooth promise. "This is your cause now. This is your world. *Learn your place.*"

The finality in his tone struck her like a blow. Malakhov's hands tensed at his sides, but he remained silent. Allison exhaled shakily, her entire body folding in on itself. She thought she would fight him, thought she would scream that she was still Allison Murphy, not Allison Ryabov—but the words wouldn't come. And Radimir knew it.

His smirk widened ever so slightly before he turned to Malakhov. "Take care of her," he said softly. "I will return soon."

Malakhov nodded. The door slammed again. Radimir was gone. Allison let out an incoherent shuddering breath; her vision was too blurred for tears, and her hands shivered. She had just lost her last lifeline to the world she once knew—and she wasn't even sure she wanted it back.

The silence set in the room was disturbed only from the intermittent crackling from the weak remnant dying away in the fire. Allison did not move. *She couldn't.*

Malakhov slowly turned to her, his gaze holding something she couldn't quite name. Wordlessly, he glided toward her, bent upon kneeling, his every movement weighed with calmness and tender care. "You are allowed to feel this," he whispered hoarsely, an unrecognizable echo away from his usual sharp tones.

Allison had a shaky, sobbing laughter. "Am I?" her voice broke.

Malakhov exhaled slowly; now, steady and calm was his gaze. "Yes," he uttered, wrapping her in warm blanket.

Her lips trembled; she squeezed her eyes shut and clenched her fists hard in her lap."Brandon is dead," she was whispering, those words heavy and poisonous.

Malakhov clenched his jaw but his eyes did not move away. "He tried to kill you," he spoke in a quiet voice.

Allison shook her head, tears dripping down her cheeks. "He thought I was lost."

"Then he should have tried to *save* you, not kill you," Malakhov speculated softly, but firmly.

Without thinking, Allison caught herself staring, mouth open; never before had she looked at it that way. "I've always thought the resistance would fight for me. That they believed I could still be saved. *But they didn't.*"

Malakhov stretched out his hand and laid it gently on her wrist. "You are only alive because of me," he murmured. "Not because of them."

His voice dug into Allison's throat because it was true. This time, Malakhov's voice dipped lower, more intense. "I told you once, I will always protect you," and she could hear the utter truthfulness in his tone.

She looked at him then; really looked at him, the assurance in the way he gripped her wrist, his steady, calm breathing, and those dark eyes, brimming with something raw, real, and terrifying. Then the realization hit her, making it hard to breathe; *she did not want to be anywhere else but here.*

A violent twist in her stomach made her drop her gaze, but he did not move. He did not press her; he did not demand. He only stayed there, holding her hand as she completely fell apart. For the first time since the entire ordeal started, she let him.

She wasn't sure how long they stayed like that. Minutes? Hours? Time, she realized, no longer mattered. Her breathing finally steadied; she stopped trembling, yet the ache in her chest had not gone away.

Still, Malakhov did not let go. His fingers loosened just a little to allow her the space to pull away if she wished. But she did not. She let his warmth seep into her skin. She let the weight of his presence sink into her, grounding and steadying her enough to keep her from falling any further into the storm raging inside.

A small, shaky breath escaped Allison, and she lifted her gaze. Malakhov was already watching her, neither expecting nor demanding anything but offering patience, the kind of patience from a man who had been waiting for her to see him. And for the first time, she did, she saw *him*.

Her heart was pounding against her ribs, filling her ears with its loud beat that drowned out every rational voice and warning telling that this was wrong. *But it did not feel wrong.*

Not when he reached up slowly and carefully brushed a stray curl from her face.

Not when his fingers lingered against her skin, warm, gentle, and grounding.

Not when his thumb traced her cheekbone, eyes flickering down to her lips and back to hers in silent solicitation.

Allison swallowed hard, almost choking on her breath. Then she nodded. Malakhov seemed to suck in a breath, as if he had been holding it for days, weeks, *eternity*. And then he kissed her. It was slow and deliberate. It was not a claim, not an assertion of dominance, but a promise. A promise that she was not alone. That he would not let her break. That whatever this was, whatever it was becoming—it was real.

Allison found herself leaning into him, allowing herself to fall just a little. Just enough so that there was no turning back.

Sixteen

Summoned by Shadow

Allison awoke to absolute silence. For a moment, her mind went blank, empty, floating somewhere between waking and sleep. Her body felt weightless and exhausted, with all muscles aching from the hard days before. Then everything came crashing back at once: the battle, Brandon's death, her impending marriage to Malakhov, and the sheer terror she'd seen on Daniel's and Rob's faces. Her chest constricted, and a wave of nausea drifted across her as she finally opened her eyes, blinking at the dimly lit space awash with faint colors.

This was not the Manor. Nor Findley Place. No, this was Malakhov's estate, what would soon be her new home.

The bedroom felt warm but unfamiliar, with dark wooden beams running across the ceiling, while bookcases as tall as the wall stretched along the walls. Heavy emerald-and-black curtains framed a tall window where a sliver of morning light slipped through a gap in the fabric. She moved a little, feeling the slightly soft mattress beneath her, the heaviness of thick blankets hanging around her. It all felt too comfortable.

Too normal.

And that terrified her.

Allison spent most of the morning avoiding Malakhov. He hadn't tried to speak to her when she woke up. He hadn't hovered, hadn't forced her to talk about what happened. Instead, he had simply left breakfast waiting for her on the table, along with a change of clothes, and then disappeared into whatever work he had to do elsewhere.

For that, she was grateful. Because she wasn't ready. She wasn't ready to look at him; she wasn't ready to hear his voice; she wasn't ready to bear the pain of realizing what he had done for her and what he had become for her.

She stayed the whole day in the library, in an armchair close to the fire, silently gazing at the glowing embers, trying to make sense of the chaos pressing in on her thoughts. She should be drawing plans, thinking about some way to escape her situation. But somehow... she couldn't. Somehow, she wasn't sure if she actually wanted out anymore.

By the late afternoon, the gloom was shattered by a brisk knock at the door. It came soft yet persistent. Before Allison could look up, the door's handle turned, and Malakhov stepped into the room. His face was carefully neutral. She looked away, unable to accept the hard intensity contained within his gaze.

"Radimir has summoned you," Malakhov explained in smooth, calm tones which somehow lacked all warmth.

Allison's stomach fell. "For what?" she nearly whispered, clutching the arm of the chair as a means of keeping herself grounded.

Malakhov pressed together his lips, and, perhaps, a shadow flickered across his face. "To determine where you stand."

Those words fell upon her with the weight of a thousand stones, crushing her dry throat. She could only swallow her pain and nod, letting go of the crippling silence that sealed her in. Slowly, she forced herself to stand to face Malakhov.

Malakhov watched her closely, his gaze tracking something unreadable in her expression. His shoulders tensed, just slightly, and his fingers curled before he clasped his hands behind his back. Like he was bracing himself, like touching the moment might make it too real, too vulnerable. Whatever was coming, he was already preparing for it.

Allison gave out a shaky breath. "Then let's go." she muttered in a half-whisper, more really to herself than to him.

Their eyes met again for just a moment. She thought she saw something, maybe a fleeting regret or maybe something infinitely deeper... But the moment passed, and it was replaced by the single-minded coldness of a man with his decision already made.

Together, they walked away from the library into the corridor towards the front door. The silence in the estate pressed down on them, heavy and unrelenting. Side by side, Allison's footsteps turned heavy with the weight of all that was to change, and with the knowledge that there was no turning back.

* * *

Radimir stood near the tall windows of his study, long fingers resting against the worn surface of the old desk. He held himself still, a towering figure whose presence seemed to press in on the walls themselves. The fading light from outside cut across his angular features, carving them in stark contrast, part dignity, part threat. His pale eyes caught what little light remained, glinting as they shifted toward Allison the moment she stepped into the room.

She did not flinch, nor did she bow; she certainly did not cower. Because she was not going to give Radimir that much. She would not let him see her fear if it existed deep inside her.

Malakhov stayed near the door, just behind her, his presence barely audible but he never left her alone. She felt his weight steady behind her, just enough strength to sit tall in her own pride.

Radimir threw his gaze on her straight away, a smile forming on his lips, not a smile of comfort or warmth but one that conveyed that he already knew the outcome of this conversation. That he held all the cards in this game.

"Come closer, Allison," he said softly but with authority.

She stepped forward, forcing her legs to move, each step deliberate, and one slow, measured breath followed.

Radimir had grown silent for what felt an eternity, his gaze almost unreadable, and he finally looked up and spoke. "You have had time to *reflect.*"

She remained silent because she didn't know what to answer. *Would there ever be anything she could say that wouldn't damn her one way or another?* So she just kept looking at him, silent but resilient, waiting for him to come to the point.

Radimir's lips curled slightly. "Your reaction last night was... expected."

Her fingers curled into tight fists at her sides, nails biting into her palms as she forced her expression to stay neutral. The memory of last night, of everything she had seen and done, started to blaze behind her eyes like a brand.

Radimir's eyes went dark, and his voice, laden with dangerous promise, dropped. "And now, I ask you plainly, are you fully committed to our cause?"

Allison's breath caught. She knew what he wanted to hear. She knew what would keep her alive, if only she could say it. But she could not muster the words. Because she did not know. *She simply no longer knew.*

Radimir noticed her hesitation, and it did not escape him. There was the faintest change in the room, demanding that she answer.

"You hesitate," he said smoothly. "Why?"

Allison forced herself to breathe, to think. "I..." She swallowed hard, throat dry and tight. She could not tell him the truth. She could not say that she did not know who she was anymore, that she was not sure she was still Allison Murphy. That part of her liked the power she held here. That part of her felt safer standing next to Malakhov than she had in years.

"This is not an easy transition, Sir," she finally said, her voice controlled but steady. "I am adapting."

Radimir's expression was unreadable. Then he smiled, a slow, knowing smile that made her stomach clench. "Good."

Allison exhaled slowly. But then, Radimir glanced at Malakhov and a chill ran down her spine.

He said, "She needs a little *direction*."

Malakhov gave a curt nod, the jaw visibly tightening.

Radimir turned back toward her, an expression gleaming from his silver eyes that made her skin crawl. "Your training is done. This means you are no longer a student, Allison. You are my heir, and it is time to assume your responsibilities."

Allison's stomach churned at the finality in his voice. She disliked the way he said it, like it was already decided. Like who she was didn't matter anymore. What she wanted didn't matter anymore.

"And if I refuse?" The words barreled out before she could stop them, sharp and defiant.

Malakhov stiffened next to her, his whole posture becoming rigid. Radimir's eyes shimmered as a soft chuckle passed between his lips, smooth, almost indulgent, as if he found her defiance funny.

"*You will not,*" said Radimir, calm and sure.

Allison's breath hitched, but she looked him squarely in the eye. She couldn't look away. Radimir gave a deliberate step forward, his long bony fingers folding neatly before him.

"You have a place here, Allison. You are mine, my blood."

She flinched at those words, at the truth she didn't want to face. Despite everything she'd done, everything she'd survived—he wasn't wrong.

She didn't move as his gaze pierced through her, cutting through the layers of her anger and sadness and confusion. Seeing straight into her deepest fears.

"You belong to me," Radimir continued, his voice dipping into something dangerously smooth. "This is your cause now. This is your world. *Accept it.*"

The finality of his words hit her like a punch to the chest. Malakhov clenched his hands at his sides but said nothing. Allison sighed sharply, the last threads of her old life seemed to give way to something dark and cold.

"What will you have me do?" she whispered, her voice low.

Radimir's smirk grew, a flash of satisfaction fleeting across his sharp features.

"You will assist in matters of strategy. We are preparing for our next campaign against the rebels who still fight against us. You will learn how to command, how to lead. And if you are truly my daughter, *you will learn to love it.*"

Allison's lips parted slightly, her heart racing in her chest. *This was it.* This was her final step into this new, dark world. And there was no way out.

"Dmitri will escort you to your first duty," Radimir said, sealing the decree with his finality.

Allison only nodded stiffly, feeling an odd twinge of detachment; before anyone could even blink, the moment had slipped through their fingers and further into the past.

Malakhov led her out of the study, down a long empty corridor with flickering sconces scratching out elongate shadows against the stone walls. Their footsteps were muffled by the heavy silence that clung to the cold stone floor.

The two walked in silence for a long time, the quiet stretching out, heavy and uneasy, like something unspoken was creeping in around the edges, thick with uncertainty and the faint sting of dread.

Cautiously, the silence broke. "You hesitated," Malakhov said, his voice low and equal, more stating a fact than passing judgment.

Allison felt her chest tighten, the constriction catching her breath. "Noticed that, didn't he?"

Malakhov nodded once, his expression calm but unreadable. "It was expected."

Allison slowly exhaled, her fingers rising to press against her temples as if she could press her confusion and doubt away from her thoughts. The admission was hushed and raw; "I really don't know what I am doing."

Malakhov didn't mock her. He never scolded her or tried to lecture her. He merely walked alongside her, in steady companionship. The quiet footsteps echoed strangely through the hall. To her, he was the only steady thing left.

"Then stop thinking about it," he intoned. Gentle yet firm.

Allison scrunched her brows, narrowing her eyes in frustration. "Impossible," she whispered, half a protest, half a plea.

The dimmest smile flickered on Malakhov's lips, an enticing promise; "Not if you trust me."

Her heartbeat rose and she looked across his gaze. And for the first time since last night, *since everything had changed*, she uttered it.

"I do."

Malakhov stilled, his gaze locking with hers. And though neither of them said it aloud, they both knew. In that quiet, dark hallway, that was the real beginning of her new life.

When they arrived in the dungeons the air was cold and damp, the corridor was filled with the usual smell of wet stone, there was also an aroma of blood and sweat. Allison tried to take a shallow breath, but choked on the stench. The echo of her footsteps was a cruel contradiction to her resolve.

Beside her, Malakhov walked with measured calm, his presence silent and steady, grounding in a way she didn't understand, or maybe didn't want to understand. *It was easier not to.*

She had not asked where they were going. She had not asked why. Because deep down, she already knew. The moment Radimir had smiled at her in that way, like he was pleased, like he was waiting for something more, *she had known.*

This was her test.

And it would break her.

The cells below were steeped in shadows, lit only by flickering torches that threw shaky light across the stone. Heavy iron doors lined the corridor, each one sealed tight, silent, but it was the kind of silence that didn't feel empty. It pressed in, thick and uneasy, broken only by the occasional shiver of movement from somewhere deep in the dark. The kind of sound that sank into the walls and stayed there.

Then, Malakhov stopped.

The door in front of them creaked open, groaning along with old hinges, revealing a tiny chamber with no windows. The air felt old and close, thick enough to choke on.

And inside—

Hunter Maddox and Bailey Hayes.

Two of her commanding officers. Hunter, who had pinned the badge to her chest the day she graduated, who had looked at her with pride and hope. Hayes, her first sergeant, always bright, always unshakable.

They were good people. New parents.

Allison felt a strange sensation rising in her throat. The world seemed to move around her with the edges of her vision blurring into clouds and darkness. Hunter, sitting with his back against the far wall, his head tilted slightly, his gaze sharper than she could have ever imagined for someone who had been beaten. Hayes, next to him, her usually vibrant hair now a dull, sickly brown, her shoulders slumped as if weighed down by exhaustion, yet her eyes shone brightly.

Still alive.

When their gazes met hers, Allison wanted to collapse.

Because she could see it.

Not hatred.

Not disgust.

But understanding.

And that... *that* made it so much worse.

Radimir stood before them, his posture easy but still commanding, the look in his eyes making her skin crawly in response. "They are rebel spies," he said quietly. "They know about our enemy's next move. I want to know what it is."

His gaze shifted to her, heavy and suffocating. "*And you will get it for me.*"

Allison froze.

The air in the chamber felt thin, pressing again her lungs as if invisible hands would squeeze the very breath from her body.

"But... Sir," she began, carefully, voice only low enough for his ear though her fingers trembled with anxiety. "I do not have the skill."

Radimir's smile grew broader, slow, and indulgent as though he were savoring the taste of her fear. "Nonsense, my dear. You are my heir. This is your *birthright*."

Her stomach flipped violently, bile rising in her throat.

This was it.

The moment.

The line she could never uncross.

Her breath came sharp and uneven, her mind racing, searching, desperate for any escape.

"She is untrained, sir," Malakhov's voice cut through the suffocating silence. Calm. Respectful. But firm.

Allison's eyes snapped to him, a flicker of hope sparking in her chest.

Radimir's gaze shifted, his eyes narrowing as they landed on Malakhov. "Are you suggesting I made an error in judgment, Dmitri?"

Malakhov bowed his head slightly, his expression unflinching. "Not at all, Boss. I am merely suggesting that she observe first. She must learn before she can execute your wishes effectively."

The silence that followed was deafening. For a moment, Allison was sure that Radimir would strike him down where he stood, his authority questioned, his command challenged.

But then, Radimir laughed.

Soft. Amused.

"Very well," he said, his smile returning, sharper than before. "You will do it in her place. And she will watch."

Allison felt her stomach churn, and a cold heavy feeling settled in her chest.

Because saying '*no*' would not stop the inevitable.

Malakhov might have only delayed her hand, and that was almost worse.

He moved forward with precise and measured steps, as if this were the thousandth time he had done this. Without any delay, hesitation, or doubt in his eyes, he pulled back his right fist and smashed it into Hunter's stomach.

Hunter shuddered, his breath caught in his throat, but he did not scream.

Hayes held herself stiff, her shoulders tense watching her husband take a blow, but she did not cry out either.

Allison's nails bit into her own palms, sharp pinches that kept herself grounded and not sinking down under the weight of what she was seeing.

She couldn't breathe. Couldn't move. Could only watch.

And they knew.

Hunter knew.

Hayes knew.

They saw her hesitation, saw the way she was splintering from the inside out. But still, there was no hatred directed at her. Hayes' lips twitched, just short of a smile, something kinder, gentler. "It's okay, Allison," she murmured in a gentle-but-firm tone. "*We know.*"

Before Allison got a chance to say anything, Radimir chuckled lowly. Moving close to her, his eyes sparkled with amusement as he looked at Hayes as though she were merely some small pitiful creature.

"Oh, do you?" mused Radimir, his head tilted as he pondered her words. "And what exactly do *you think you know?*"

Hayes swallowed and her fingers curled in tight fists at her sides. She glanced at Allison briefly, determined, as her jaw set. "That she's only here because she has to be—*you* are forcing her hand."

Allison stiffened, a sudden catch in her breath. Radimir's smirk deepened; delight curled at the corners of his mouth as he turned toward her. "Is that true, *my dear?*"

Allison's throat went dry. Because she didn't know how to answer. Because she didn't even know if it was the truth anymore.

And Radimir—he saw it too.

His expression shifted, growing more pleased, more knowing. He turned back to Hayes and Hunter, his gaze dismissive, cold, as if he were looking at something already broken, already done.

"You know *nothing*."

The words were still echoing in the chamber when his hand moved to his gun.

A loud bang.

Hayes gasped, but the sound was cut short as her body crumpled to the floor, lifeless.

Allison flinched, her breath stuttering in her chest. She barely had time to move, to think, before Radimir struck again.

Hunter had only just turned, his mouth opening to shout, when another gunshot rang out. He fell beside his wife, his expression frozen in something caught between horror and resignation.

A scream built in her chest, clawing up her throat. She swallowed it down and forced herself to stay upright. Her nails drawing blood from her palms.

Radimir exhaled as if he had snuffed out a candle. "There," he said, almost absently. "No more distractions."

For a single, fragile moment, Allison trembled. Just enough for Malakhov to see it. His gaze locked on hers, jaw tightening as he watched her struggle to keep her expression calm.

But he saw it. The cracks forming, the weight pressing down on her chest until it was hard to draw breath.

Radimir turned back to her, his satisfaction tangible in the cold air.

"That is why you are mine."

Allison clenched her fists tighter, fighting against the tremor in her fingers.

Because he was right.

And that—that was the most terrifying part of all.

Seventeen

In the Quiet Between Us

The moment they got back to Malakhov's estate, Allison collapsed on to the couch, her limbs shaking profusely. She didn't feel the cold until she stepped into the sitting room, where the hearth's glow cast shifting shadows across the walls.

Her thoughts chased themselves, tangled between Hunter's pained restraint, Hayes's silent empathy, and the lingering bite of Radimir's words.

"She's here because she has to be."

"Is that true, my dear?"

Her stomach clenched at the memory of her hesitation. She squeezed her eyes shut, willing the memories to vanish. But they clung to her, stubborn and heavy.

She felt the couch beside her dip under Malakhov's slow, deliberate weight. Not one touch, nor a word, nor even a push; he just waited.

"What am I becoming?" The question slipped out before she could stop herself, barely above a whisper, and she hated herself for asking it, for sounding so weak, *so lost.*

Malakhov had no immediate comeback. He exhaled slowly; then, his voice came low and weighed carefully. "Something stronger."

A choke of bitter laughter escaped from her lips. She shook her head, still in disbelief. "Something *darker*," she uttered.

Malakhov's gaze turned to hers, intention unwavering. "Perhaps." He stopped, staring at her as if searching for something buried beneath the layers of fear and uncertainty. "But you are still *you*."

Allison threw her hands up in the air, "Am I?" she breathed. Because she didn't feel like herself anymore.

Allison Murphy wouldn't have stood in that room and watched her mentors be tortured and murdered. *Allison Murphy* wouldn't have let Radimir's words settle in her bones instead of rejecting them outright. There wouldn't have been something for *Allison Murphy* to feel if Malakhov had stepped between her and the world, shielding her.

She felt his stare, heavy and pressing through the skin. Slowly and intentionally, his hand was extended. His fingers traced lightly over her wrist, and even that gentle contact sent a jolt through her.

The fingers were tracing the faint bruises there. Those were the marks she had inflicted upon herself with clenched fists and punishing nails.

"You *are* still you," Malakhov said, unfailing in his touch. "But you are learning how to survive."

Allison's throat tightened. She wanted to argue, to deny it. But she couldn't. Because she wasn't sure if she was surviving anymore...or adapting.

"I already told you," he softly whispered, barely audible, "you don't have to go through this alone."

Her heart gave a sudden, uneasy jolt. His fingers were still there, barely touching her wrist: slow, deliberate, like he was waiting to see if she'd pull away.

She didn't. And he felt it.

"And I will always be there to help you if you refuse or hesitate," he continued, his voice low, steady.

Allison swallowed hard. "That doesn't make it better," she said with a raw voice.

Malakhov relaxed and let out a long slow breath, while his dark eyes fixed onto hers. "But it makes it bearable"

Her eyes were burning, with pride in her pounding jaw.

"It should not have to be *bearable*," she spat, every word steeped in bitterness and self-loathing for her utter helplessness.

"But it is," he spoke as if it were some inescapable truth.

She hated that.

Hated that he was right.

Hated, even more, that she was relieved he had done it in her place. Because what did that make her? What kind of person stood back while someone else got their hands dirty?

She hated herself for *not* hating him.

And he knew. He saw it in the way her shoulders tensed, in the slight tremble of her jaw as she tried to hold herself together. Every small shift gave her away, the cracks in the careful mask she kept trying to wear.

Malakhov's fingers traced slowly along her palm, each movement careful, intentional. His voice was low, steady, barely more than a whisper.

"I'll always be the one to carry the burden if I have to. But this... *this* is bigger than us now, Allison. We're both being tested."

Allison closed her eyes, her chest heaving. Because she knew. Radimir wasn't just testing her resolve. He was testing Malakhov, too—seeing how far he would go for her. Seeing what lines he would cross.

And Malakhov—he was already crossing them.

A shiver chased down her spine. She opened her eyes with a hoarse voice. "And what will happen when there is nothing of me left to test?"

Malakhov's hand froze on her skin, his thumb pausing against her knuckles. "Well, I will still be here, because I have chosen to be."

The words settled inside her, heavier than she wanted to admit. Yet, she didn't choose to pull away. Didn't flinch.

Because some small, secret part of her, one she hated to admit even to herself, needed to hear that. Needed to believe it.

And Malakhov saw that too.

How long they sat there, Allison was unsure. Minutes, perhaps hours? Time had lost all meaning, dissolving into its margins until all that remained was the faint crackle of the fire and the drumming of her heartbeat.

Her breathing had gotten slower; the tremors in her hands ceased, yet the ache in her chest, that was heavy and tangled, stayed. But still, Malakhov didn't let go. His fingers had loosened slightly, giving her every opportunity to pull away if she wanted to.

But she never did.

She took in his warmth and the steady weight of his presence, grounding her before she slipped any further into the shadows at the edge of her mind.

A soft breath escaped from her lips. She slowly lifted her head, her gaze meeting his.

Malakhov was already watching her. There was no expectation in his eyes, no demand—only a quiet patience that took her breath away. The quiet, unwavering patience of a man who had been waiting for her.

Her heartbeat thundered, every rational thought slipping away. It should have felt dangerous. But it didn't.

Not when he reached up to tuck a stray lock behind her ear, his forefinger holding onto hers a little longer to brush past her cheek ever so tenderly, *so tenderly* that it brought tears to hers. Softly, almost as if caressing, his thumb glided along the curve of her cheek; his gaze held hers with such intensity, more meaning was conveyed in that look than his lips ever could.

Allison swallowed hard as her chest felt a tightening cluster of all she could never voice. There was fear, and there was want, sharp and sweet; she experienced both all at once in that instant.

Then—she kissed him.

He kissed her back slow and careful, like he was offering her something precious. No force, no claim, just a quiet assurance in the softness of his kiss. A promise that she wasn't alone. That he would carry the weight of this with her. That whatever this was, *it was real.*

And it was theirs.

Allison felt something inside her move, something fragile, yet strong with passion. She leaned toward him with one hand on his chest, feeling the slow beat of his heart beneath her palm. She let herself fall, just a touch.

Just enough to know for sure there was no going back.

Just enough to know she didn't want to.

His warm lips glided over hers, a tempting invitation, never a demand, each brush of his lips a soft promise that she could take if she wished too.

And she wanted it.

He leaned in again, pressing the tip of his nose to her forehead while his breath was ragged and warm.

"Allison" he whispered the name like promise from his lips.

She closed her eyes, fingers curling into his coat's fabric. "I know," she whispered back. "*I know.*"

For a moment, everything went still, their heartbeats loud in the hush of the dark. He tilted her chin up, his thumb warm and careful against her jaw.

A final meeting of their lips followed, slow and sensual, catching her breath and forcing her entire body to sway closer.

This time it felt different, less hasty and more sacred, as if the kiss were an actual vow between two souls. His eyes were half-lidded when he finally drew back, a slow smile curving across his mouth. "Come," he uttered softly but without command. He took her hand in his and led her from the room.

They walked the halls with soft footfalls. He spoke no word, neither did she, words felt unnecessary, unable to cut through the charged silence between them.

At the door of her room, he stopped again, turning to her and tracing one last time along the line of her lower lip with his thumb. He studied her face as though memorizing every line.

"Sleep well, little lion," he whispered, his words as soft as a caress.

Then he left her standing there, lips tingling, pulse roaring, and the taste of him still warm on her mouth.

* * *

Malakhov found her by accident.

He had left his bedroom sometime after midnight. Sleep wouldn't come and the day's events held him like a heavy cloak. His body was drained, but his thoughts refused to allow him some peace.

He walked towards his study to pour himself a drink and find something to read, some old text or half-forgotten scroll to divert himself from the chaos ongoing in his head. But after pushing open the heavy wooden door, he realized he wasn't alone.

Allison sat in the leather armchair, a bottle of whiskey before her, the empty glass held so faintly in her hand. She seemed utterly lost in thought, her gaze fixated on the dancing flames of the fireplace. The flames lit her face in shifting hues of amber and shadow. Auburn curls served as a halo for her shoulders while her lips parted just enough as she inhaled, slow and steady.

It was the first time Malakhov could remember hesitating—and it was because of her. She had not yet noticed him. But would it be better to allow her to enjoy her solitude?

The silence was interrupted by her voice.

"You're staring, Malakhov."

A smile played on his lips as he moved further into the room, almost clicking the door shut behind him. "I am simply admiring the view," he said.

She snorted and lifted an eyebrow at him. "Yeah, sure you were."

He shrugged as he made his way to her, eyes flicking toward the bottle. "Drinking alone tonight, sweetheart?" he asked teasingly.

"Not really," she muttered, twirling the empty glass between her fingers. "I've just been thinking."

Malakhov crossed to the cabinet and pulled out another glass, his movements unhurried. "Careful, Murphy. Thinking can be dangerous."

"Mm." She tilted her head, a small smile tugging at the corner of her mouth. "So can most things these days."

He set his glass down beside hers, poured them both a drink, and lifted his glass in a silent toast. "To dangerous things, then."

Allison huffed a soft laugh and tapped her glass to his. "*To dangerous things*," she said gently, echoing his voice.

They drank for a while, with the crackling fire being their only companion.

She put her glass down; her eyes were full of unspoken things she wanted to say, "Do you really believe in all of this?"

Malakhov wavered and slowly put his glass down. An amusement gleamed in his eyes as he said, "Define *this*."

She sighed, "Don't play dumb. You know what I mean.... Radimir's cause. The war. All of it. Do you really believe in any of it?"

Malakhov leaned back in his chair, rubbing circles around the rim of his glass with his fingers as he observed her. "Belief is a ... complicated thing."

She raised an eyebrow, unimpressed. "That is not an answer, and you know it."

He laughed, rich and low. "That's all I've got for tonight, sweetheart."

Eyes rolling, Allison had slipped backwards into the chair, crossing her legs. "You are impossible," she murmured, her lips twitching as if she were fighting back a smile.

His gaze dropped to her legs and unwillingly dragged itself up to her face, where he displayed a devilish and unrepentant smirk. "And yet, here you are, at midnight drinking with me."

She snorted out a laugh. "I'm here out of a certain curiosity—about *you*."

Malakhov's eyes narrowed slightly, his amusement ebbing into cool calculation. "Be careful, Murphy. Curiosity can become very dangerous."

"Oh, I know," was her softly unyielding response. "Then tell me—if not for belief, what is it? Why do you fight for him?"

Tilting his head at the sight of her, he then pondered on the puzzle before him, "Survival. Power. Strategy," he dissected and offered slowly. "Always preparing for the long game."

"That's it?" she said, sharply low in tone.

There was a smirk on his lips, heavy coldness in his eyes. "That's *everything*."

Allison gave a quiet sigh, shaking her head. "So you don't care about the nonsense of Russian dominance? About the killings? About *any* of it?"

Malakhov laughed deeply, dipping again into the bottle. "Please, Murphy. If I believed in that garbage, I wouldn't be wasting my time drinking in the dead of night with a cop I intend to marry."

The emptiness in his promise twisted her stomach with something hot and uneasy. She tried to keep a composed expression but a glimmer flitted across her face which he caught, only encouraging another smirk.

"So why stay?" she pressed softly. "Why keep fighting for something you don't even believe in?"

Another drink was poured; he sipped slowly and then set the glass aside. "Because power keeps me alive. Because war never really ends—it just *shifts*. And because it is better to be feared than to be forgotten."

Leaning forward, he dropped his voice lower, eyes drilling into hers in a way that completely stole her breath away; "And because of *you*."

Her breath caught, her fingers tightening around the glass. "*Me*?" she whispered.

Malakhov leaned back in his chair, his wicked smirk coming into full bloom. "Oh, *little lion*," he drawled in a mixture of velvet and smoke, "you're a dangerous thing all on your own. I don't care about ideology. I care about survival. Power. And I care about what is *mine*."

She gave a wary look, her heart thumping madly. "Oh? And are you saying that I'm yours, Malakhov?"

His own eyes darkened at the thought, dangerous sparks flashing in them. He leaned forward, fingers just brushing against her knee. "Are you not? You *did* kissed me last night."

Allison's skin prickled at his words, her pulse thudded in her ears, the taste of him still lingering on her lips. "You kissed me back," she shot, but her voice cracked on the last word and was barely as sharp as she'd wanted.

His wicked smile appeared and Malakhov went closer while his fingers traced inconsequential, lazy circles against the cloth of her nightdress above her knee. "And I'd do it again," he whispered low.

She rolled her eyes, the shameful heat climbing her cheeks though. "You're insufferable," she hissed.

Malakhov put his glass down, tilted his head, and held her gaze with an intensity so strong she struggled to breath normally. "Tell me, did you really think I wouldn't *want* you?" The caress of his voice made chills run up her spine.

Allison swallowed and changed her seat position; her fingers started to twist nervously in her lap, "I... I don't know," she stammered. "I thought maybe... you were forced into this as much as I was."

He didn't move, holding her gaze with those dark eyes. Slowly, a dangerous smile curled over his mouth. "Perhaps," he murmured, almost teasingly, "But that doesn't mean I didn't want you, Allison."

His fingers traced lightly over her arm, sending waves of goosebumps along it. "In fact... I wanted you from the very start," His voice low, charged with something electric. "From that first fight—I saw the fire in you. The way you wouldn't bend, wouldn't give in. That *spark*... it drew me in."

Allison felt her cheeks burn under the heat of his gaze. "That's...that's not fair," she whispered.

Malakhov let out a soft chuckle, but there was no amusement in his voice—only a promise. "Oh, but fairness does not come into this equation," he once again whispered, leaning in so close to her that his breath kissed hers. "Your mind... the way it works, the way you challenge me—is *intoxicating*."

His fingertips followed the thrum of her pulse. "But let's not pretend I don't also want to pin you against this chair and taste every inch of you," he murmured, heavy and low.

Her body shivered as she gripped the glass with all her might. "I—" she started but was unable to utter any more words.

Malakhov's smirk deepened as his eyes locked onto hers with a heat that made her shiver. "Any man would go crazy for your beauty, Allison," he purred, the tone half-teasing and half-in-reverence. "But that fire—the way you refuse to back down, the way you refuse anyone to break you, *that* is the sexiest damn thing I've ever laid eyes on."

He held her gaze, fingers just hovering above her wrist without touching, while he spoke once more. "Getting to know you? That was just... an unexpected pleasure," he said softly with that wicked smile appearing once more. "But make no mistake, Allison— I wanted you long before I ever had the chance to touch you."

Her breath came sharp and uneven, her heartbeat pounding in her ears. And in that instant, she knew—this wasn't a game. He wasn't just toying with her.

He wanted her.

All of her.

That knowledge was both terrifying... and thrilling.

Allison's chest was tight. She *should* push him away. She should say something... *anything* to stop this. But she didn't. She didn't want to.

And he knew it.

Malakhov's fingers brushed her cheek before holding the back of her neck. His thumb traced gently along her jaw, soft and purposeful. "Say the word, and I'll stop," he whispered, voice low and unhurried.

Allison's lips parted, her breath catching. Inside, her mind fought between want and fear, yet instead of words, she leaned forward and bridged that last inch of air beneath them. Her lips were met by his in a fragile, angling kiss.

There was no hesitation. A rush of heat and longing, his kiss deepening in spite of the restraint he'd tried to hold. His hand tangling in her hair, gently tilting her face upward toward his. The whisky had burned in her veins, but nothing burned with more fire than the touch of his.

He kissed her slowly, deliberately, as if memorizing the feel of her mouth. His other hand traveled upward along her thigh while his fingers brushed her skin, never quite getting to where she longed for.

Each brush of his lips asked something she didn't have words for.

A soft, breathless noise escaped Allison; she lifted her hands to press against his chest. She felt the hard lines of muscle behind his shirt and the rapid beating of his heart echoing hers. She felt weightless, intoxicated with his presence and his mouth that fit so perfectly against hers.

But with warmth spiraling low within her belly, a seed of doubt had wormed its way in. She pulled away just enough to break the kiss, their lips reddened and tingling, breaths ragged. "I... I don't have a lot of experience," she whispered, trembling, her eyes darting away.

A smirk crossed Malakhov's mouth but softened, his thumb toying with her lower lip. "That makes you all the more irresistible, *little lion*," he murmured, almost tender in tone. "The way you taste of curiosity and uncertainty... It's a challenge I can't resist."

Her heart tripped over his words. Heat prickled across her skin. She ached to surrender to the want curling low in her belly. But she couldn't. Not yet. She turned her head in her mind to close her eyes, shaking breaths forcing her to lean backward.

He let out a low sigh, but his expression was far from angry. He brushed a final kiss to the corner of her mouth. "Another time," he murmured.

His hand rested on her knee, warm, steady, grounding, and his voice took the air right out of her lungs. She knew this wouldn't be the last time.

Because, deep down, she wasn't sure she wanted it to be.

Eighteen

The Test of Loyalty

The Bratva meeting hall was quiet.

Allison was sitting in Malakhov's usual place, the seat to the right of the head of a long polished-black obsidian table. She could feel every flash of darkened eyes filled with amusement or jealousy. Those sitting around the table were some of Radimir's closest men, his hardness and most dangerous, and the fact that *she* was sitting next to their leader was a challenge they hadn't expected.

She had grown accustomed to the weight of their gazes by now. She was the heir, *Radimir's bloodline* and the woman promised to Malakhov, his most dangerous soldier. She had been *claimed*, and however much that claim might offer some form of security, it never lessened the tension in the air. Sitting opposite her, Grigori Gordeev, reclined in his chair, dark silks falling about his lithe frame, one corner of his mouth at a half-smile. He twirled his glass and watched with the lazy interest of a predator biding its time.

"Really, Malakhov," he drawled with thin irony, "you *really* got away with that one, didn't you?" He raised his cup in mockery. "Radimir's little heir. Quite the prize."

Malakhov just tapped the table with his fingers in response, his expression unreadable. "Got away with what, exactly? "

Grigori's smile grew wider, his eyes were sharp with the glint of a knife. "Claiming her, of course. I would have thought Radimir might... object. But perhaps he's not as possessive as I assumed."

Allison held her face impassively, though her pulse thudded relentlessly in her throat. She kept her expression neutral. She would not give that victory to Grigori.

Finally, Malakhov's eyes settled on Grigori, a flicker of amusement curling at the edge of his otherwise calm expression—sharp, knowing, and laced with quiet disdain.

"And yet," he said softly, "here I am... still standing."

The smirk on Grigori's lips altered into something sharper and mocking. "Or maybe, Radimir just hasn't yet decided to take back what's his."

The words were meant to prod Malakhov, and Allison felt the shift in the atmosphere without having to look at Malakhov's face. It felt as though every person in the room had gone still, waiting for the inevitable strike.

With deliberate slowness, Grigori raised the goblet to his lips for a sip; the whispers of torchlight were glancing off the glint of his eyes. "Tell me, Malakhov...how did you get her to agree? She doesn't strike me as the sort who'd be easily won over. Has she come around to you yet, or does she still require some... *convincing*?"

The last word rolled off his tongue like a venom, and in that heartbeat, no one made a move. Malakhov clenched his jaw, his whole body went still, and when he spoke, his voice uncoiled, smooth but edged with threat. "Jealous, Gordeev?"

Grigori's smirk faltered behind which was cloaked a wave of unease. "Hardly."

Malakhov pushed back in his chair, folding his hands behind his head with the calm ease of a man entirely in control—more predator than peer, relaxed but watching.

"Do you want to pretend, Grigori, that you ever stood a chance with her?" His voice was low, almost casual, but there was something colder beneath it, something sharp and deliberate.

"She's not some docile little plaything to be bent to your will. She would have crushed you."

He paused, letting his gaze drift lazily across the room before landing back on Grigori.

"And remind me—don't you already have a wife?" Malakhov's smile didn't reach his eyes. "You might want to focus on the one you're legally bound to, instead of daydreaming about mine."

Grigori's lips thinned. "And you think you are the man to handle her?"

Malakhov's smile stretched slow and feral, a dangerous gleam lighting his dark eyes.

"Oh, I don't think," he said, voice low and steady. "I know."

The tension thickened, humming with unspoken threat. Grigori clenched his hand over his goblet, knuckles turning white.

"Maybe," he said softly, "you're being selfish, Malakhov. Keeping something so... *tempting* all to yourself — you really should *share*."

Twisting with revulsion, Allison's nails dug into the arm of the chair. Malakhov moved before she could speak. One moment he had been a man reclining back in the chair; the next, there was a dagger at Grigori's neck, gleaming as it was cruelly pressed against him. The knife's tip forced the man's head back against the chair, the steel drawing a single bead of blood.

"Say that again," Malakhov whispered dangerously low, "and I'll cut your tongue out myself."

Grigori froze. His breath came out in a shudder as the hall filled with the deadly promise of Malakhov's voice. The other men around watched in tenseless silence. No one moved; no one dared intervene.

This was the Bratva. This was how power was claimed, and how stains of blood sullied the ground in defense.

Malakhov's eyes burned through Grigori's, and his voice low and almost seductive, but under it simmered lethal rage.

"She is not yours to speak of, Grigori. She is mine. The next time you even think of her that way, I will do more than draw blood."

For a long moment, Grigori said nothing. Then he swallowed hard, losing the smile from his lips. "Understood."

Malakhov held Grigori's gaze for a moment longer, the dagger gently pressing under his chin, staying put. Then, with icy calm, Malakhov slowly brought down the dagger while staring into the man's eyes. He leaned in close, his voice low at Grigori's ear, each word steeped in calm malice. "If you ever look at her like that again, I'll carve out your eyes. Do you understand me?" The voice was so soft, almost gentle, and yet it was laden with deadly intention.

Before Grigori could answer, the heavy doors at the other end of the hall flew open, and the very atmosphere in the room changed. Radimir entered like a shadow coming to life and the flickering torchlight dimmed as if in respect. The silence was instantaneous, as the men at the table stiffened, losing all their bravado. Some cast down their gaze; others stood upright in silent homage.

Radimir's icy gaze swept across the room with bored disdain, until it fell on Malakhov. A slow smile spread across his face; it was one of those knowing smiles that somehow never quite made its way to the eyes.

"Dmitri, Dmitri..." he drawled teasingly. "I feel as though every time I walk into a room, I find you threatening, *or killing,* my most loyal men."

Malakhov didn't so much as blinked. The dagger still hovered near Grigori's throat; his stance was relaxed and unconcerned. "Only to the ones that deserve it, Sir," was his grim reply, as though exchanging thoughts on the weather instead of violence.

Radimir's eyes narrowed in amusement; however, there was a suspicious glint lurking beneath. "Your devotion to my daughter is quite ... *admirable*," he whispered. His eyes landed on Allison, who sat upright with her hands folded neatly in her lap, fully aware she mustn't meet his gaze or show any reaction—maintaining a careful balance of calm and control.

Radimir's smile didn't touch his eyes. "I do hope it does not blind you to your other duties."

Malakhov finally stepped back from Grigori, his movements unhurried, casual. "Not at all, Boss. But I find offense when men forget their places and attempt to *solicit* certain things of a woman of her status."

Radimir's expression didn't change, but a flicker in his gaze was enough to chill everyone present. "*Solicit*?" he queried in a low voice.

The corners of Malakhov's mouth lifted into a smirk as his voice turned dark and mocking. "Grigori believes he should be given a night with her, believes, *your daughter*, is something to be *shared*."

An absolute silence that set in. His words pressed down, suffocating the air itself. A paleness went over Grigori's face; his bravado crumbled in an instant under the piercing gaze of Radimir.

Radimir stood still for a long moment; after which, he let loose a soft laugh that sounded more chilling than a threat. "Did he now?" he uttered.

Grigori opened his mouth, desperation creeping in, but Radimir silenced him with a single pale hand. "Do not bother, Gordeev," he said softly. "There is nothing you can say that will make me believe otherwise. I have seen the way you look at her."

The amusement in his expression vanished, replaced by something cold and absolute. His voice dropped, each word sharp and final. "Let me make myself very clear to all of you. She is *not* to be touched. She is *not* to be used. She will not be some vessel for your bastard heirs or your drunken fantasies." His gaze swept over the table, his tone like ice cracking in the silence. "She is my daughter—my heir. And if any of you even think about treating her as anything less than that, you will die *screaming*."

No one moved. Grigori very nearly swallowed his fear, his face going pale.

Radimir cast a glance back at Malakhov, tracing a smile faintly upon his lips. "And you, Dmitri... how lucky you are to have so wisely chosen."

Malakhov inclined his head in return, his smirk unchanging along his calm demeanor. "I've always been a strategist, sir," his tone stated, polite but with an edge of assuredness.

Radimir gave a soft chuckle, shaking his head slightly, and then turned his attention to Allison; his silver eyes gleamed with amusement and an unreadable edge. The mood switched instantly in the room, giving just enough momentary relief to breathe, yet beneath the surface still crackled the promise of a different kind of violence.

"Now, *my dear*, let us discuss something of actual importance." Sitting up straighter, Allison forced herself to maintain his gaze despite the flood of anxiety pulsing in her throat. Radimir studied her, his pale eyes gleaming with something predatory and amused. "It is time you prove your loyalty."

The room seemed to still around them. Allison's chest squeezed, but she didn't let it show. "I am at your command, Sir," she said, steady.

Radimir smiled broadly. "The rebels still fight. They still hope. That is a mistake. And I believe you will be the one to correct it."

She said nothing. The weight of his words set in upon her like frozen ice, but she kept a calm expression. Radimir sat back in his chair; his long fingers tapping idly against the carved wood.

"There is a rebellion hideout. We know its general location, but not its defenses. You will infiltrate it. You will disrupt their plans."

Allison felt a faint movement beside her as Malakhov shifted, his face utterly blank. A thousand thoughts filled her head, but she let none into her expression. "And if I refuse?" she asked quietly, calmly, the world now a tightening vise around her. Radimir shrugged his brow, half amused, his cold eyes piercing hers.

"Then I will assume you are not one of us. And I will treat you accordingly." His tone stayed light, almost casual, but the threat underneath it was impossible to miss. The meaning was clear. The warning was final.

Allison forced herself to remain steady, though she felt the flicker of fear deep in her chest, regret *perhaps*, but there was no room for that now. Radimir was waiting. She had only seconds to answer. Seconds to decide. She drew in a slow breath. "When do I leave?"

Radimir's pleasure was evident, his smile faint but unmistakable. He gestured toward Malakhov. "Dmitri will accompany you. But he will not interfere. This is your test, my dear. Pass it well."

Allison swallowed hard. The silence stretched until Malakhov finally spoke, his voice smooth, controlled. "She won't fail."

Radimir's smirk widened, something almost mocking in his gaze. "See that she doesn't."

Once the heavy doors closed in their midst, Allison turned her back on Malakhov, her voice low and sharp. "You knew he was going to do that."

Malakhov breathed slowly and brushed back his hair; his expression was cold and steel-like. "I *suspected*," he replied quietly.

A vise gripped her chest, her thoughts spinning in all directions. "And you're just going to let me do this?"

He looked at her fully now, the shadows in his eyes hardening his features. 'It's beyond us now, Allison. He's testing you. He's testing me,'" replied Malakhov.

A humorless laugh slipped from her lips. "And if I fail?" Malakhov's jaw clenched, his voice quiet but firm. "You won't."

She shook her head, her breath now coming in short, panicked gasps. "I can't betray them," she whispered, the tones on these words breaking away.

Malakhov stepped nearer to her, his own face expressing some faint dismay. "I understand, but don't allow them to betray you either, because they would if given the time."

Allison swallowed hard. Dread knotted her thoughts together. This was it; time at last to decide which side she was on and she hadn't the faintest idea.

Malakhov let out a breath before peering into the gloomy corridor ahead. "We leave at dawn," he said under his breath. "Try to rest."

She nodded slowly, her heart weighed down, mind tangled in a knot of panic and dread. Malakhov turned to leave; he paused and then spoke softly, "Whatever happens and however dark this gets, I will stand next to you."

A shiver ran over Allison as she closed her eyes. Because she couldn't decide if that was any comfort, or the worst part of it all.

Nineteen

Loyalty's Edge

Allison was lying in bed, staring at the ceiling, unable to sleep. The weight of tomorrow settled in her chest like a stone she couldn't shake." She always knew this time would come, a final test, a decision she could never take away. But knowing it would come and actually facing it were two very different matters.

She was going to see Daniel, Rob, Heather—the resistance, her brothers in arms. And she wasn't going back as their friend.

Her breath hitched, and her fingers twisted the blanket. She tossed and turned, trying in vain to find some semblance of rest, but she knew it was hopeless. All she could think about was what new horrors tomorrow would bring when she saw her old comrades again.

Frustrated, she kicked the blankets aside and went threading down the hall, her bare feet silent even on the icy floor. She stopped outside the door of Malakhov's bedroom; her heart hollow in her throat, an inner voice screaming at her to turn back. But she did not.

She lifted her hand and knocked.

A pause.

Then, his low voice; "Come in."

Allison took a deep breath and pushed the door open. The darkness in the room was only broken by the flickering of the candle, which cast long shadows on the walls. Malakhov was still in bed, balanced against the headboard, reading. *Shirtless.*

She froze.

His skin glowed in the dim light. She noticed faint scars she hadn't seen before, his own sigil burned into his arm. The silhouette of his muscles was sharply defined. The blanket had been slid down across his waist.

Of course, she had seen men like this before, living with two before, she was familiar with seeing them running around the home without shirts on, but this time it was different. A blush swept through her body, the feeling was entirely new and discomfiting.

She opened her mouth and then closed it again. She realized she was staring. Malakhov glanced up at her, an eyebrow raised and the beginnings of a smile edging his lips. "What's the matter, little lion?"

There was a rapid blink from Allison as she tore her eyes away. "I couldn't... I couldn't sleep," she whispered.

His smirk grew wider, eyes glinting with amusement. "...and you thought I might be able to help you with that, did you?" he teased.

Finally fidgeting, she felt silly. "I... never mind, I shouldn't have—"

He interrupted. "Stay." She glared at him, shocked by the gentleness in his command. His smirk softened to a quieter, more sincere one. "Would you like to join me?"

Her cheeks burnt. "I-what?"

The smirk returned, his voice dipping lower. "Just to sleep." A pause, then almost as a challenge; "Unless you had something else in mind, in which case, I'm happy to oblige."

Her eyes widened as her jaw dropped. "I— Absolutely not!"

Malakhov chuckled in delight at her reaction. "Relax, Murphy. I won't touch you... until you ask me to."

Before, that promise would have made her heartbeat skyrocket, but now she just wavered for a moment and brushed it off. "I just... I didn't want to be alone tonight."

The playfulness wiped off from his face, turning to rather a solemn one. "Come here."

She hesitated. Then she breathed deeply and walked forward. Malakhov lifted the blanket to invite her in, and she slid in underneath it, careful not to brush past him. But as soon as she was in place and comfortable, he moved nearer and lofted one arm about her back, drawing her tightly to remain pressed against his bare chest.

She rested one cheek on his warm skin and listened to the steady pounding of his heart. She felt every hard contour and every subtle flex of muscle beneath his skin as he breathed into her; feeling the heat pouring from him and soaking into her.

His chest let out a low rumble as his fingers began tracing lazy patterns on her arm. "You're tense," he murmured, the amusement concealed in his words. "What, afraid you'll touch something you shouldn't?"

She swatted at him, cheeks burning. "You're insufferable."

His laughter fell, silk dark, shivering up her spine. "I do try," he said almost playfully.

She rolled her eyes, but she could not stifle the small smile that tugged at her lips. "Honestly, how can you be so... *so smug* about everything?"

Malakhov tilted his head in slight curiosity as the smirk softened. "Because I like seeing you flustered. It's endearing."

"Endearing?" she asked, attempting not to sound too intrigued. "You're impossible."

"And yet," he pointed out, his voice soft, almost teasing. "You are still sharing my bed."

She snorted, cheeks ablaze. "Only because I didn't want to be alone."

"Mm," he whispered, the faintest smile tracing the edge of his mouth. "Whatever you'd like to tell yourself, little lion."

She gave him a dirty look, yet she was forced to return a reluctant smile. "Absolutely terrible."

With a mock-serious face, he said, "Terribly *charming*, you mean."

She snorted and shook her head without pulling away.

He took the book he was reading, opened it for her to see. "Here," he said softly. "You read. I'll hold."

She let out a shaky breath, feeling a warmth spread through her chest along with a strange, new sensation. Slowly and steadily, she began to read aloud. With every word she spoke, the tight knot of tension inside her loosened, replaced by a quiet comfort that seemed to radiate from him. It all happened so quickly she barely had time to think, her breaths evened out, her eyelids grew heavy.

Malakhov looked down at her head on his chest, her hair spilling down his arm. His fingers were drawing slow absentminded circles on her arm. For weeks he had been falling for her, but this was the moment he realized it. *She was his*. And he would always be hers.

He pressed a soft kiss to the top of her head, his lips curling into a small, private smile. "Sleep well, little lion," he whispered. "*I've got you*."

The sunlight barely trickled through the gloomy curtains when Allison moved, wrapped in a warmth that did not seem entirely hers.

Few seconds went by before she remembered the exact place where she was and *who* she was with.

Her cheek rested against Malakhov's warm skin, her arm draped across the hard lines of his torso. His skin was warm under her palm; his breath was slow and steady, the rise and fall hypnotizing and soothing.

And for a half-second, however fleeting, she allowed herself to pretend. That there was no mission. No betrayal. No war waiting just beyond the walls.

Just warmth.

Just him.

Then it all came crashing back.

The Resistance. Daniel. Rob.

Today.

She inhaled sharply and shifted to sit up, every muscle in her body stiff and uncooperative.

Malakhov stirred under her, but only barely. His eyes fluttered open, already focused, too sharp for someone who'd supposedly been asleep. *Of course he slept like a cat, with one eye open, already ready to strike.*

A slow smirk curled across his lips.

"Morning, sweetheart," he murmured, voice gravelly from sleep. "You drooled on me."

Her head snapped around to glare at him. "I did not."

"You absolutely did." He gestured lazily to his chest. "Right here. Evidence of your uncontrollable desire."

Allison rolled her eyes and threw the blanket off her legs. "That's not drool. That's sweat. From the oppressive heat coming off your insufferable ego."

Malakhov grinned wider, watching as she stood and ran a hand through her tangled hair. "You say that like my ego isn't exactly what helped you sleep like the dead last night."

"I was exhausted," she muttered.

He raised a brow. "Exhausted from what? All that nervous pacing? Or was it the intense mental gymnastics you did trying not to stare at my abs?"

She turned slowly to face him, arms crossed. "Oh, you bet I stared."

Malakhov's smirk faltered for half a second, just long enough for her to catch it, before he recovered. "Well, I aim to please."

"Yeah," she muttered, mostly to herself. "That's the problem."

She reached for her jacket, but the weight of the day settled back onto her shoulders like a burden she'd foolishly let go of only hours before. Her heart caught, climbing slowly, tight and heavy in her throat.

He was watching her now. Not grinning. Not smirking. Just watching.

Then, voice softer, lower, more serious, he said, "It's time."

Allison froze. And there it was.

No more warmth.

No more stolen moments.

No more pretending.

She nodded, once, her fingers tightening around the fabric in her hands.

Just like that—the peaceful morning was over.

But she felt the ghost of it cling to her skin. The quiet heat. The way he'd held her like he wasn't afraid of her breaking.

Or maybe... like he was.

* * *

The plan was simple. They were to act like they were escaping from Radimir, just a couple of lost souls who had stumbled too close to the camp. Their job was to get close enough to make the guards drop their defenses, letting the rest of the Bratva sneak in for a false attack. While the Resistance members were distracted dealing with the fake assault, Allison would plant a false lead to Daniel—a trap that would lure them in a few days.

Malakhov laid a map of the Resistance's hideout on the table, his fingers tracing over the faded parchment. "We know their main defenses," he said, voice calm and sure. "A few watch guards, double-locked doors, and some barriers around the perimeter. The weak point is here." He tapped the map at the eastern entrance.

Allison crossed her arms, her brow furrowed. "It's not going to be that easy," she said. "There will be guards. And there will be defenses we don't even know about; traps that aren't on this map."

Malakhov smirked. "That's where you come in. "You know them, their habits, their patterns, their vulnerabilities."

Her fists clenched tight; a mixture of fear and anger rushed in her chest. "And if I don't do this?"

The sharpness in his dark eyes did not miss anything; he tilted his head slightly, remaining in his place.

"Then Radimir will know you're hesitating," he said simply. "And hesitation means death."

Allison swallowed hard. She *knew* he was right. But still, doubt lingered in her mind, weighing her down like a stone.

Malakhov stepped closer. His voice softened, but it didn't loose its strength. "You are stronger than this, Allison. You'll go in there. You won't break. You'll come back to me—and we'll deal with whatever comes next, together."

Her breath stuck in her throat. Because she believed him. And for the first time since all of this started, she didn't feel like she was facing it alone.

She nodded once, her decision made.

Malakhov's lips curved into a smirk. "Good," he said. "Now let's go."

The resistance hideout was an old manor, hidden deep in the countryside, wrapped in layers of defenses and shrouded by overgrown trees. As dusk fell, Allison and Malakhov approached, their bodies battered, clothes torn, both of them playing their parts as desperate, hunted runaways.

Thin rivulets of blood traced down Allison's forehead, some real, others painted on for effect. A cut split her lips, sharp and raw with every breath she took. Her heart pounded fiercely beneath her ribs, matching the heavy rhythm of his steps beside her. Anxiety twisted tight in her stomach. Bound but unbroken, Malakhov moved with her, a predator in chains, holding his head high, dangerously proud.

They crossed the threshold, and immediately a shout rang out. "Stop! Who's there?" A guard stepped into view, face half-hidden by a hood, his gun already raised.

Allison shook on a forced sob. She stumbled ahead, her face down and hidden by the hood. "Please—don't hurt us!" she panted, every breath ragged. The guard seemed to hesitate, narrowing his eyes. More footsteps echoed farther down the hall of the home; more voices arose in alarm. Then through all that noise pierced a voice she could have recognized with her eyes shut.

"Allison?"

Her body froze; every muscle locked. Nails dug into her hood as it was being ripped away. Her pulse kicked hard in her chest when she met Daniel Diaz's stunned, stricken stare.

Rob stood beside him, his gun trembling in his grip, his face deathly pale. Behind them, Heather grimaced in pain and disbelief.

"Allison..." Daniel's voice was thick and shaken with something between rage and brokenness. "What the hell are you doing here?"

"I—I had to see you," she stammered, trying to force a weak, tiny voice. "This was the only way..."

Rob stepped forward, eyes blazing with fury.

"You came with him?!" he spat, jerking his gun towards Malakhov. "You brought the worst of them?"

Malakhov chuckled softly, his eyes glinting with dark amusement. "Oh, Walker. You wound me."

Rob's jaw tightened, and his gun snapped towards Malakhov. "Shut the hell up, Malakhov!"

Allison forced her hands to stop shaking, to stay focused. "Please," she said, her voice cracking. "We just need somewhere safe. We can talk later."

Daniel's eyes were hard, his jaw set like stone. "You expect us to trust you? After everything?"

"I expect you to believe," she explained, desperately building in pitch, "that our history wouldn't be wiped away in a few months."

Heather glared at her with icy intentness, calm and sober in her voice. "You look well enough. For someone who's been running from the Bratva, you don't look that hurt."

Allison's breath faltered. She could feel them slipping through her fingers. "Daniel—"

"Tell me the truth, Allison," he cut her off, voice low, shaking with betrayal. "*Are you still with us?*"

The question sliced through her. Her limbs seemed powerless, and she could hardly breathe in those few moments. Malakhov said nothing, all eyes were on her, waiting for her.

Testing her.

She clenched her jaw to overcome the tremor in her voice. "I am here because— *because* I was sent here...." Her words drifted away in an even and flat tone.

Rob flinched; his face appeared to be distorted by pain.

"No," whispered Heather, shaking her head. "No, you're not one of them. You just... you can't be."

And with those words, a shadow fell in Daniel's eyes, the pain of betrayal hit them like a sharp knife. "If you're not with us, Allison... then you're *against* us."

She shuddered, a sudden block in her throat; tears stung fiercely in her eyes. She could still choose. She could still turn back. But as she looked at Malakhov, standing calm and confident, and then at her old friends, she realized she didn't know what she wanted anymore. And that terrified her.

Before she could even respond, a bullet cracked through the air, whizzing so close to her head she felt the heat of it. Chaos exploded around her, shouts and scrambling feet filled the room, bullets ricocheted, and splinters of wood flew through the air like deadly rain.

"Allison, get down!" Rob's voice roared through the noise, but she didn't move.

Malakhov's hands were on her, yanking her behind him as he drew his own weapon with lethal grace.

"Time's up, little lion," he said, his voice calm, even gentle.

Her heart thundered in her chest. Daniel was watching, and his face turned into anguish and fury as the resistance scrambled to take their shots, every bullet flying through the air and fists crashing into one another.

She pressed herself back against the wall, her eyes darting from Malakhov to her friends, *her friends who now looked at her like a stranger.*

The battlefield had become a storm of dust, blood, and whispers that refused to fade. The air was thick with the lingering haze of gunpowder and sweat. The scattered resistance members now faced the broken room, panting, their eyes darting warily between Allison and the figure casting a stony shadow behind her.

Several feet away stood Daniel, his death grip on the gun making his knuckles shake, as his green eyes burned with a crush of disbelief and betrayal. Slightly closer was Rob, much too close; his hands shook at his sides as if silently begging.

Heather stayed glued to the door, her face obscenely pale and deeply pinched, her rigid posture suggesting that the only thing standing between her and a mad dart at Allison was the looming promise of answers she dared not know.

Malakhov was there, behind Allison, standing steady and almost relaxed, arms folded casually across his chest while observing the whole show. His gaze was calm, yet the faintest glint of something darker-steel pride or some cruel amusement-wrung the corner of his mouth. He was permitting her to act her part; permitting her to declare her truths or her lies. But he was watching her every move, every breath.

Waiting. Measuring.

Allison could feel it, his quiet approval going down through her heart like a knife. Her stomach flipped; she felt like drowning under the weight of her own decisions.

"You need to move," she said finally, with a calm voice, yet her heart pounded loud enough she wondered if they heard it.

Rob took a slight step closer. "You'll stay, won't you? We need to figure out what's going on—"

"No." The word slipped out before she could stop it, cold and final.

Rob's face fell, pain flashing across his features. "No? Allison, what the hell does that mean? You can't just—"

"I don't have time for this." Her voice grew tight as she forced herself to look at Daniel, locking onto his hard, assessing gaze, the very one she knew could see right through her. "I came here with information. That's all."

Daniel's jaw tightened, his voice dangerously low. "*To talk?* Allison, you've been gone for weeks. You show up now with *him*—" he jerked his chin toward Malakhov, "—and you expect us to just *believe* you?"

Rob's voice cracked, desperation shining in his eyes. "No. You wouldn't be here if you didn't care. You wouldn't come back unless you had some faith in what we're fighting for—"

The pain was sudden, sharp, but she kept her expression calm. "I have information," she repeated, her voice as steady as she could manage.

Malakhov gave a low chuckle and stepped up beside her, a satisfied glint in his eyes. "Believe her or don't, but we both know who she'll be leaving with tonight."

Rob's eyes narrowed at Malakhov, fury flickering beneath the desperation. "You're delusional if you think I believe this... *this*—whatever *this* is."

Malakhov raised a brow, his smirk infuriatingly calm. "Then perhaps you should ask her yourself whose bed she slept in last night."

Rob's gaze snapped back to Allison, searching her face for any sign of denial. Her silence only seemed to confirm the worst. He clenched his jaw, hurt and jealousy warring in his expression.

Daniel's eyes never left hers, sharp and unyielding. "Is that true, Allison? Is this what you've chosen?"

She swallowed hard, her voice low. "It doesn't matter. What matters is the information I have. That's all you need to know."

But even as she spoke, Malakhov's smirk only widened, his hand brushing against her lower back, a silent, possessive claim that was all too clear.

And in that moment, she knew, no matter how much they wanted to deny it, they all saw the truth in the way he looked at her. And in the way she didn't pull away.

A heavy silence settled between them. Heather's lips twisted into a sneer.

"Information? Or just orders? Because if you're lying to us—" Daniel's voice cut through the room like a blade. "You're one of them."

Allison swallowed hard, refusing to let her gaze falter. "I came on orders from Radimir. And I'm sorry I led them here."

Rob's face twisted with confusion and heartbreak he began reaching out to her. "*Allison*, no—"

Malakhov's voice was a low purr, his amusement evident as he tilted his head slightly. "Careful, Walker. She's still my fiancé, after all."

Allison dug her nails into her hands, the pain somehow grounding her. "I came to give you a chance," she said, her voice crackling with the barest hint of a sob.

Daniel's countenance grew darker, a conflict of suspicion and fury warring in his eyes. "A chance?"

She nodded once. "Radimir knows about your movements. He knows about the bases being shifted, the people being relocated. There's an attack planned."

For a moment, there was only silence. Heather's hands curled into fists at her sides. Rob's breath hitched, his shoulders shaking as he tried to process her words. "When?"

She paused. "Three days. On the northern border of the city."

It wasn't true, it was a lie she'd crafted carefully, deliberately, and only Malakhov knew it. She didn't look back at him, but she could feel his gaze on her like a brand, silent approval lacing his posture.

Rob turned to Daniel immediately, his voice urgent. "We can prepare for that. We have time to—"

"Wait." Daniel's voice was hard, his eyes narrowing. "Why lead them here if you wanted to help us? Why let them find us at all?"

Allison's stomach lurched. She forced herself to keep her breathing calm, her expression neutral. "He sent me here for this attack—he doesn't know I'm telling you this." She let her voice drop lower, softer. "You have to trust me, Daniel. Please."

Daniel's jaw tightened, his green eyes boring into her. And she knew he could see it; the uncertainty within her, the war she was undergoing inside herself. For a moment, he had eyes of steel but just the tiniest glint coming from the boy she used to know. But that fleeting glimpse was gone as quickly as it had appeared.

Rob stepped forward, desperation turning his voice raw. "Daniel, we have to act on this. We can't waste time... You heard what she said..."

"I know what she *says*, Rob," Daniel snapped, his voice tight, but his eyes never leaving Allison's face.

She met his gaze head-on, her pulse thundering in her throat. "Radimir is distracted. He's focused on another target. This is the best time to strike."

Daniel inhaled sharply, his fingers twitching as he processed her words. Doubt and conflict were clear in his eyes. He did not want to take her word. He did not want to give her entry, It was the possibility that, against all reason, she might be telling the truth.

A long, tense silence.

Then, Daniel turned to the others, his voice steady. "We move in an hour. Get ready."

Rob exhaled in relief, his shoulders sagging. An unyielding look was painted on Heather's face, but she gave a slight nod before turning away to relay the order.

Allison stood frozen, her hands clenched at her sides. She had just betrayed them. Lied to them. And the worst part was—*they still believed her.*

She felt Malakhov's hand brush against hers lightly, almost tender. "Very good, little lion," he murmured, so softly that only she could hear. "Very good."

Her stomach churned, but she forced herself to keep her face calm. She'd made her choice. And the worst part was, it hadn't even been that hard."

The plan had been flawlessly executed.

Allison and Malakhov slipped away to rejoin the Bratva members as they were retreating.

No one suspected a thing.

Except Daniel.

She could feel his eyes on her as she walked away, heavy with doubt she didn't dare look back to see.

Not yet.

Not until it was too late.

They drove back to the estate, parking just beyond the gates of the manor. As soon as the car stopped, Allison stumbled forward, her whole body shaking.

And then—her stomach twisted violently.

Malakhov barely had time to react before Allison dropped to her knees, retching into the grass.

Her body convulsed, bile stinging her throat as her hands dug into the cold dirt. She didn't even realize she was crying until a hard and steady hand landed on her back.

"Easy, you're okay. *Breathe.*"

Malakhov's voice was softer than she had ever heard it.

She pressed her eyes shut while the realization of what she had done hit her like a wave. She had sent them into a trap.

A beautifully constructed, well-placed, devastating trap.

And she had done it with terrifying ease.

Malakhov didn't say anything at first. He just let her breathe. Let her feel it.

Then, after a long, heavy silence, he spoke, his voice low. "That was well done."

Allison let out a shaky laugh, a bitter, hollow sound. *"Don't."*

Malakhov tilted his head slightly, his hand still tracing gentle circles across her back. "You knew this was inevitable."

Allison shook her head, her voice breaking. "I told myself I wouldn't break."

A hint of softness flickered in Malakhov's expression. "And yet, here you stand. Still whole."

She turned to him fully, her breath ragged, uneven. "Then why does it feel like I just shattered?"

Darkness washed through Malakhov's eyes, then he considered the strange impulse to reach for a stray curl and tuck it behind her ear. "Because you are still fighting. Still surviving."

Allison closed her eyes and leaned into his touch. And for the first time, she let herself believe that maybe, *just maybe,* she didn't have to fight alone.

The weight of the mission still clung to her, the deceit, the way Daniel had looked at her, the way Rob had still believed in her. The trap she had carefully laid at their feet.

Yet, as she stood beneath the looming estate, all of that faded into something else.

Radimir was waiting for them.

He was just beyond the entrance with a couple of guards flanking him, the eyes shining with satisfaction. When the gaze was on her, a slow smile emerged on his lips, pleased with the sight. "You have done well, my dear."

Allison forced herself to breathe. She shouldn't crave his approval. She shouldn't feel anything when he looked at her with something close to pride. And yet, she did.

She dipped her head slightly. "Thank you, Sir."

Radimir took a slow step forward, his gaze flicking to Malakhov, his expression unreadable. Then, a smirk. "And you, Malakhov. You have proven yourself more than just a soldier. You have shown unwavering devotion to my daughter. You will not only be her husband, but the father of my heir."

Allison's stomach tightened. She had almost managed to forget about that part.

Malakhov inclined his head smoothly, his voice calm, assured. "It will be an honor, Sir."

Radimir's smirk widened. "A strong union. A powerful one. It will be celebrated accordingly." Then, his eyes flickered back to Allison. "Tomorrow, you will be wed."

Allison's breath caught. She knew it was coming, but not this soon. Radimir stepped closer, his head tilting slightly. "You have cemented your place in this world, Allison. You are no longer a Murphy. You are no longer one of them. Tomorrow, you will be bound to Dmitri, and you will take your place as my legacy."

Allison swallowed, forcing her voice steady. "Yes, Sir."

Radimir smiled, lifting a thin, pale hand to brush a curl from his child's face. "Sleep well, my daughter. Tomorrow, you become something greater than you have ever been." He turned and entered the estate, leaving them with the stillness of the night.

Silence dropped over them like a heavy curtain. Allison exhaled a slow, shaky breath. Her senses spun in a dizzy haze.

Tomorrow.

She was getting married tomorrow.

Before she could sink into the gravity of the thought, Malakhov moved closer, his voice low but firm. "Stay with me tonight."

Her head snapped up, her eyes wide. "Malakhov, I–"

He let out a soft laugh and shook his head. "I mean in my bed, in my arms. Not anything else—unless you ask nicely, of course."

A blush flooded Allison's cheeks, and her lips parted in astonishment. "You're impossible," she muttered.

Malakhov smirked, his voice teasing. "You didn't sleep much last night. You won't tonight, either, if you're alone."

She inhaled sharply, glaring at him even as she couldn't deny the truth in his words. "Fine. But no *funny* business."

Malakhov raised a brow, his smile turning wolfish. "I make no promises, little lion."

Allison huffed but followed him inside anyway.

Twenty

A Legacy Forged in Fire

The first thing Allison noticed when she woke was the warmth at her back, steady, solid. It took her a moment to register the weight of someone lying behind her, unmoving but unmistakably real. Then it hit her—where she was, how she'd ended up tangled in Dmitri Malakhov's sheets, and the night that had brought her there.

Then, she felt it.

Her breath snagged, her eyes going wide when she realized what was pressing into her lower back. Her cheeks became a blaze of scarlet; she froze, uncertain as to whether she should move or stay perfectly still; whether she should wake him or merely close her eyes and pretend she hadn't been very cognizant of the very, very obvious situation.

Breaking her out of her thought, Malakhov shifted behind her with a parted sigh of contentment, muffled against her hair. It was only a moment before his arm tightened fractionally around her waist, pulling her close in a sleepy embrace. She let out a small yelp.

He chuckled, low and warm in her ear. "Well, good morning, little lion."

Allison could feel the heat of her embarrassment rise between them, impossible to hide. Malakhov laughed, low and amused, and it only made her shift uncomfortably, wishing the floor would swallow her whole.

"Didn't mean to startle you," he murmured, teasing, yet sleep-coated his voice, "but I really can't say I'm not delighted about having woken up this way."

Allison wriggled in an attempt to get away, her hands planted firmly on the bed, trying to wrench herself from his grasp. Malakhov, though, only tightened his grip to pull her closer.

"Where are you going?" said his voice, amusing. "I like having you right here."

"Malakhov!" she hissed. "You—your—"

"Ah. Yes. That." He let out an exaggerated sigh, feigning innocence. "I can't help it, sweetheart. You're a bit too tempting to ignore."

Allison buried her face in the pillow, groaning in mortification.

"Stop talking!"

Malakhov just laughed again, this time a deep, velvety undertone continuing to tease her.

"Maybe you should do a little exploring before you judge. I won't mind."

"I am not exploring anything!" she snapped, muffling her words on the pillow.

"Shame," he said playfully. "It could have been a nice little pre-wedding gift."

Allison finally pushed him, her eyes bright with defiance and her cheeks flushed with frustration. Malakhov caught her hand before she could pull it away, bringing it to his lips with infuriating calm. He kissed her knuckles: slow, deliberate, almost tender.

Then the teasing disappeared into a more intense expression. He raised her chin so she had to look into his eyes; the look was dark and heavy.

"You do know you are beautiful, don't you?" he softly asked.

Allison's breath caught again. "Malakhov..."

"I mean it, my lion," he said firmly. "You're stunning. And today, when I see you in that dress, when I stand before you and vow myself to you, I want you to remember this—I choose *you*. Not because of Radimir. Not because of the war. Because I want you. *You*."

Her heart tightened painfully. His words rang in her ears. She didn't know how to react to them, what to feel, or even say. She swallowed hard, scrambling out of bed so she could do something to break the spell his words had cast upon her.

"I—I need to get ready," she stammered, her voice shaking.

Malakhov smiled maliciously, watching her. "What a pity. I was hoping for a little more wedding celebration this morning. But I can wait until tonight."

"I'm leaving now," she said, this time, more firmly as she scrambled to get her things.

Behind her, he let out a quiet chuckle, clearly entertained by the whole scene. Despite herself, Allison felt a smile tug at her lips—one she didn't want to give him, especially not with her face burning and her heart racing as she all but fled the room.

* * *

Allison sat in front of the grand mirror of her vanity, gazing into her own reflection with hardly a recognition of the woman looking back at her. Her fingertips hovered over the fabric of her wedding gown—black and gold, traced with symbols of ancient Russian script. It was fit for a *queen*, not for a girl who had once only dreamed of books and heroics.

But she wasn't that girl any longer. And maybe... *maybe* she didn't want to be.

She had fought it for so long. Fought who she was becoming. Fought the pull of power, of belonging, of *him*. But there was no more fighting now. Because this? This was what she was meant for.

Her reflection smirked back at her, and for the first time, she didn't hate what she saw.

And Malakhov... she exhaled sharply, her stomach twisting—not in fear, but in something far more dangerous. He had been *unexpected*. She had never imagined falling for a man like him. A man who should have been her enemy—who *was* her enemy once. A man who had slowly, deliberately broken down every wall she had built. A man who had never forced her to submit, but instead made her want to choose him.

And now, today she was.

Allison inhaled deeply, pressing her hands against the vanity to steady herself.

This is who you are now. And you are not afraid.

A knock at the door pulled her from her thoughts. She turned just as Radimir entered, his presence immediately consuming the space. For a moment, Allison froze, unsure why he was here. Then, he smiled.

"You are beautiful, my dear," he said, in a quiet voice, measured and calm. Allison swallowed hard, her throat dry; she did not know how to respond. He approached closer and his pale fingers lightly touched the fabric of the dress she wore. "I always knew you'd take your place next to me. It was just a question of time," his tone calm, not cruel or mocking, yet it was that calmness that made the words worse.

Allison clenched her hands in her lap. "I was never meant for the world you wanted."

Radimir hummed, tilting his head as he studied her. "And yet, here you are. You cannot deny what you have become, Allison. What I always knew you could be."

She lifted her chin, meeting his gaze head-on. "And what exactly am I?"

His lips curled into a slow, pleased smile. "My legacy." Then, in a tone that was almost... human, he added, "My greatest creation."

Her throat tightened at his words. For the first time, she saw an expression she'd never expected in his eyes, *pride*. And it terrified her.

Radimir reached forward, brushing a stray curl from her face with cold, deliberate fingers. "Do not disappoint me today, dear."

Allison exhaled shakily, nodding once. And just like that, he turned and left the room.

Leaving her alone.

Leaving her to decide if this was truly the life she wanted.

Malakhov stood in the hallway, waiting. He had never been nervous before, not for battle, not for war, not for anything. But today? Today, something close to it stirred in his chest. She entered his view, and for the very first time in his life, Dmitri Malakhov forgot to breathe.

His dark eyes went wandering slowly over her, drinking in every bit of transformation that was laid before him. She was a vision of darkness, full of power, her gown cascading in waves of black satin and gold, a swirling mosaic woven with symbols that spoke of strength, of legacy, of things older than time itself.

And *fuck*—he was completely undone.

His mind whispered things he had no business thinking yet; a life with her, a home with her, a war beside her. The moment he realized he wanted all of it, he knew he had already lost himself to her.

Allison caught the way his throat bobbed, the subtle clench of his fingers at his sides, the way his gaze darkened—and gods, *she liked it.*

Malakhov stepped forward, his voice rougher than usual, low and deep. "*Fuck*, Allison."

Her cheeks flushed with heat traveling down her neck and dropping into her stomach. He raised his hand slowly, fingers barely touching the delicate gold embroidery on her bodice. "You are *breathtaking*."

Allison swallowed hard, her breath catching as his eyes held hers. Malakhov let out a quiet breath, his voice softer now, almost reverent.

"I thought I understood what it meant to want someone... but seeing you like this..."

Her heart pounded violently, and his fingers trailed lower, just teasing the fabric of her gown. "I'm going to enjoy stripping you out of this later."

Allison's breath hitched, barely able to keep the scandalized look off her face.

Malakhov chuckled again. "Don't look so shocked, little lion. You belong to me now. And I intend to make sure you know *exactly* what that means."

Suddenly, Radimir's voice echoed from the end of the hall, snapping them both back to reality. "It is time."

Malakhov stepped back, offering his arm. "Are you ready?"

Allison inhaled deeply, nodding. "I have to be."

Malakhov stood opposite her, his dark eyes unwaveringly fixed on hers.

The atmosphere was somber, bound with something nameless, old. Unknown faces, members of the Bratva, formed a circle around her, voices scarcely above a whisper, uttering the ritualistic incantations of an ancient tongue. Deep within the manor, in some secret hall lined with ancient tomes and lit by flickering torches, they held the ritual.

Allison realized, at that moment, that this was new for him as well. He had never belonged to anyone or anything besides the war, the bloodshed, the power he wielded, and now, *here*, he was about to bind himself to her.

And she to him.

Radimir stepped forward between them, his voice steady and commanding. "This is no simple contract. No fleeting bond. This is something ancient, something unbreakable. You will be tethered to one another in life, in war, in blood."

Her pulse quickened, but Malakhov's expression didn't so much as flicker.

A dagger sat carefully placed between them, its silver blade catching the low light with a soft glint. Faint, unfamiliar script ran along its edge, seeming to throb gently, almost like it was breathing. From the far end of the chamber, Radimir called out, "Cut your palms. Let your blood join. Let your lineage bind."

Allison's throat was suddenly dry. She reached forward, fingers curling around the dagger's hilt. Malakhov mirrored her motion. They hesitated for a breath, then together pressed the blade to their palms. The sting was sharp, the trickle of blood warm and real.

Radimir's eyes gleamed with approval. "Now, speak your vows. Bind yourselves in will and in power."

She inhaled slowly, steadying herself, then faced Malakhov. "I bind myself to you, Dmitri Malakhov." Her voice was steady, clear, unwavering.

A faint, almost imperceptible smile curved his lips as he replied, "I bind myself to you, Allison Ryabov."

The torches flickered ominously, the air thickened around them. Allison drew a short breath before continuing, "I vow my loyalty. My strength. In war and conquest, in fire and shadow."

His voice sank deep and smooth as silk; "I vow to stand beside you, to fight for you, to hold what is ours—in darkness, in blood, in power."

And a shiver ran down her spine. This was no mere ceremony; this was real.

This was them.

Radimir raised his voice, triumphant. "Let the bond take hold. Let the generations to come weave its will."

All of a sudden, the weight of the realization hit Allison, causing her to gasp out loud as his gaze clung to hers. There was something about his look that was hard to define; dangerous, possessive, convinced.

Then it was done.

A heavy silence fell over the hall.

Radimir smirked. "Rise, Mrs. Malakhov."

Allison sighed, stood up, and in that split second knew she would never be Allison Murphy again. When Malakhov pressed his lips in one final sealing kiss, the very last remnants of her former self dissolved in the air. She did not mourn for that loss anymore.

The dark whispers and knowing glances were carried into the closing of the ceremony. The Bratva stood around with glasses raised, making a toast to their marriage born of the power and blood. Their murmurs spoke of fate sealed and alliances bound, but Allison barely registered any of it. Her mind was foggy, her skin still tingling from what they'd done.

She felt Malakhov's presence beside her, solid, real, tethered. Without thinking, she let her hand slip into his and he didn't pull away.

He leaned close, voice lowered in intimacy, so only she could hear. "Are you ready now to accept it?"

She turned toward him and took a deep breath, feeling the crushing weight of their bond. There was a brief moment of silence where she did not answer, probably because she didn't know she had the choice anymore.

Then a slow, crooked smirk rose on her lips. "We'll see."

Malakhov chuckled, raised her hand, and gently kissed the knuckles.

And just like that, Allison was gone, and Lady Malakhov took her place.

The reception hall was royal and opulent, made to display all the pride, money, and success of Radimir's reign. The long tables were dressed with silks of deep black and scarlet, with goblets that held a deep crimson liquid. A few chandeliers hung low offering a warm light that glowed against the gleaming floors. At last, right there in the midst of all the grandeur sat Allison and Malakhov, now officially bound by name and marriage.

Hushed fluttering talks ensued, the members standing behind their goblets and saw them with unhidden curiosity, jealousy, and amusement. Some were in awe, some furious, and some simply wished they were him.

Radimir rose first, lifting his glass. The room fell instantly silent. His gaze swept over the assembled soldiers, allies, and rest of the Bratva before finally settling on Allison and Malakhov. "Tonight, we celebrate not merely a union, but a legacy," he said smoothly, with finality gravitating his voice. "A bond of strength, of loyalty, of power. My daughter and my most trusted soldier, bound in blood, bound in war, bound in purpose."

A murmur rippled through the hall as he continued, "Let none question their place. Let none dare interfere. This union is the foundation of the future we are building. And from it, our legacy will grow." He paused, letting the weight of his words settle like a carefully laid spell. Then, his eyes gleamed with something sharper. "An heir will come soon. And with it, the continuation of our great work."

As these words hit Allison like a physical blow, the weight of the new reality pressed on her chest. Malakhov remained still and controlled; his hand went to her thigh and gave a light squeeze beside her. Around them, the Bratva toasted loudly, some with amusement, others with barely concealed envy.

Radimir smirked. "Drink well tonight. Celebrate. For the future of our world has begun." In raising his goblet, the hall erupted in cheers.

In the obscurity of the night, laughter rolled, wine poured, and knowing glances were exchanged. Then, in a mixture of low, teasing tones, Malakhov turned to her; "Dance with me."

Allison blinked. "What?"

He grinned, inclined his head. "You heard me. Dance with me, *wife*."

The word sent a shiver through her. Before she could protest, he stood and offered his hand. She hesitated, this was something different. But there were far too many eyes watching, and the faint hoops and whispers in the air did not give one room for a polite refusal. She placed her palm in his and he took her to the floor.

The music shifted, lower, darker, smooth, and slow. Malakhov pulled her close, too close-one hand dangerously low on her back, the other holding her fingers. "Relax, little lion. Let them see you belong here."

Allison exhaled shakily as they moved, the room fading into the background. His voice dropped to a murmur against her ear. "Did you enjoy your toast from our leader?"

She swallowed hard. "You mean the part about producing an heir?"

His smirk deepened. "Yes, that part." His fingers pressed lightly into her lower back, warmth seeping through the layers of fabric. "I believe he expects us to get started on that rather soon."

Her face burned, and Malakhov chuckled, watching her reaction.

"Careful, wife. You blush so beautifully. You'll make me want to rush the rest of this evening."

Allison huffed, looking away, but she felt his smirk against her temple as he leaned in.

"Don't worry. I'll be gentle... *at least for tonight*."

She stepped on his foot. Malakhov let out a sharp laugh and pulled her closer. "Ah, there she is. My little fire."

Allison hated that she smiled, but she let him hold her just a little longer. Because despite all the whispers, all the expectations, this moment was theirs alone.

When they returned to the table, they were not left alone for long. Several others approached, some smirking, some cold, and others openly resentful.

Vasili was the first to lean in, a smug smile curling his lips. "A good match, Malakhov. But tell me, will she keep up? Or will she break like the rest?"

Malakhov's smile was slow and dangerous. "Break? Oh, I assure you, if anyone's getting broken in this relationship, it will be *me*."

Allison smirked as Vasili's confident expression faltered slightly. But before anyone else could speak, Grigori stepped forward, his tone dripping with envy. "You're lucky, Malakhov. I could have had her myself if the Boss had given us all a fair chance."

Malakhov chuckled, his voice mockingly smooth. "*A fair chance?* My dear Grigori, if you ever had a chance with her, I'd be genuinely concerned for our Leader's judgment."

Grigori's face darkened, his eyes narrowing. Allison lifted her goblet with a teasing smirk and took a slow sip. She enjoyed the game unfolding before her.

"Poor Grigori," she murmured, "it must be difficult knowing the only time you get to be in my presence is in moments like these."

Malakhov laughed low and dark beside her. "Oh, I married a wicked woman."

Grigori stormed off in frustration, leaving Allison to tilt her head and turn to Malakhov. "That was fun."

He grinned, brushing a finger lightly over her wrist. "I do love a woman who enjoys playing with her prey."

She met his gaze, smirking back. "Then you're going to love me."

Later in the evening, the Kotovs approached, their expressions un-readable and cool. Aleksei raised his goblet in a slow, deliberate toast. "You wear power well, Allison."

Andrei stood beside him, eyes sharp and calculating. "You've changed."

Allison's smirk deepened. "Have I?"

Andrei exhaled slowly, the weight of his words hanging in the air. "I hope you know what you're doing."

She took a measured sip of her wine, confident. "I always do."

Aleksei chuckled softly. "Then I look forward to seeing what you be-come."

Near the end of the night, Radimir rose once more, and the room im-mediately fell silent. "Let us drink to the future—to power, to unity... and to the consummation of this great union."

Allison froze. Her stomach twisted violently. She had forgotten about that part. And judging by the way Malakhov was watching her now, he hadn't.

She swallowed hard as the room was caught up in celebrations. Malakhov put his ear to her lips, his voice low, amused, and smug beyond measure. "Shall we retire, wife?"

Her heart was hammering. This night had only just begun.

* * *

The weight of the evening hung thick between Malakhov and Allison as they moved through the dim halls of the manor, away from the clinking glasses, the polished smiles, and the too-curious stares. The further they got from the reception, the louder her heartbeat felt in her ears.

She'd felt their eyes on her all night, waiting, *watching,* ever since Radimir raised his goblet in that final, suffocating toast. The realization had crept in then, heavy and certain: this was expected. This moment had always been coming.

And yet... beneath the dread curling in her chest, she wanted it, more than she could bring herself to say aloud.

As they walked, Allison couldn't help but steal a glance at Malakhov. A familiar, twisting knot tightened in her stomach, not fear, but something heavier, more complicated, and far more dangerous. Every step he took carried a quiet calm, like he hadn't just sworn his life to her, like he wasn't leading her toward the room where everything would shift between them. His hand stayed firm and warm around hers, steadying her when she felt like she might drift away.

Once inside their shared chambers, and the very heavy doors from outside clicking behind them, Malakhov exhaled deeply and faced her. His dark eyes burned-without expectations, but full of patient promises.

"Allison."

Her breath hitched. He so rarely used her name in this tone that it sent chills down her spine. He stepped toward her, slowly, giving her time to stop him if she wished, yet she did not. His hand rose to cup her cheek, his thumb brushing over her skin so delicate that it felt completely out of place on a man so often fierce and unyielding.

"I need you to understand something."

Allison swallowed hard and nodded. Malakhov's voice dropped lower, steady, absolute.

"I will not take you unless you want me to. Not because they expect it. Not because it's *required*. But because you want me. Because you crave me as much as I crave you."

Her stomach churned violently. She knew him as an annoying tease, flirting incessantly, a predator when it came to getting what he wanted. But *this*—this was something else.

"I-I do want this," she said in an almost inaudible whisper.

Darkness flooded his gaze. "But?"

She had looked away for the minutest fraction of a second, forcing herself to raise her eyes back to meet his. "I've still never done this before."

Malakhov stopped. Something, as quick as a flicker, crossed his eyes; raw, possessive, reverent. He let out a slow, measured breath, raised a hand to her chin, and tilted her face up to meet his.

"I will not hurt you."

His voice dipped even lower, a promise laid on her to comfort, without shattering the fragile tension between them. "I will *worship* you."

Allison shuddered, never before in her life had she ever experienced being desired and seen so intensely, so utterly claimed. At that moment, she wanted to relent to it.

"Then take me, Dmitri." The restraint in his eyes shattered instantly. But Malakhov did not rush.

He bent slightly, sliding his hand to her waist and drawing her close. Allison had barely a moment to feel the warmth of him and the strong lines of muscle beneath his shirt before his lips found hers.

The kiss was slow from the very beginning, a deliberate, teasing torment; his tongue brushed the edge of her lips, inviting her to yield. Allison melted into him, her hands grasping the fabric of his robes, her silent plea for more.

Malakhov smirked into her mouth, delighting in her enthusiasm, in how much she pressed against him, in the barely audible hitch in her breath at the touch of his fingers' glide down her hip. Then, the kiss deepened. It became less patient, less gentle, more urgent—hungry and demanding. It was a claim she felt in her bones.

Allison issued a tiny breathy sound, to which Malakhov responded by murmuring low against her lips.

"So eager, little lion," he whispered.

"You're the one who told me to want you," she said, a mischievous smile playing at her lips.

He chuckled, low and dark."Well, color me impressed—you actually took my advice."

An icy shiver ran down Allison's spine as his hands traveled further below, steady and sure, pausing ever so slightly at the small of her back. Steering her almost silently toward the bed, she could hardly register anything else, for her senses were overwhelmed by the way he kissed her, his lips brushing against her jaw, the faintest pressure against her neck.

The back of her knees hit the side of the bed, he set her down with great care, like something precious and worthy of cherishing. Very slowly, very deliberately, his fingers moved over her gown, removing it only by inches and revealing the soft, skin beneath.

His breath caught as if he still found it difficult to believe she was truly his to hold.

Suddenly feeling exposed and vulnerable, Allison shifted. Malakhov naturally had the usual sensitive presentation; He had grabbed her hand and kissed tenderly on her knuckles, his touch reverent and soft.

"You are the most beautiful thing I have ever... seen."

Her heart squeezed at the honesty in his voice, and she bit her lip, trying to steady the rush in her chest.

His hands continued their patient exploration; his fingertips had tracked her collarbone, journeyed down the smooth swell of her shoulders, and settled lightly on her waist, committing every curve to memory.

"You were made for this," he said under his breath, his lips following the path of his hands with soft, reverent kisses.

Allison shivered, and for the very first time, she truly believed him.

Malakhov wanted nothing less than making their first night together unforgettable. He explored her body with deliberate slowness, each touch making her shiver. Each movement was deliberate; he awoke every nerve and left her breathless. Allison arched beneath him, soft gasps slipping free as his fingers and lips pushed her closer to the edge again and again.

When he finally positioned himself at her entrance, he was slow and gentle, carefully ensuring that she did not feel any discomfort. He watched her face intently, noting in the mixture of anticipation and need within her wide eyes. Then with the husky voice unable to contain love and desire, he began to say soft words, proceeding with controlled and purposeful movement. Wherever Malakhov's hands moved, Allison's skin seemed to be burning; every touch of his left behind a trail of warmth and fire.

With sensations threatening to overwhelm her, Allison let herself go and wrapped her legs around his waist, urging him downward. The muscular strength in every one of his deliberate movements made her body tremble. She gasped his name, squeezing his back with her nails, fueling the fire of their growing passion.

Their bodies shaking in perfect rhythm, panting raggedly, wet with sweat, holding her close; Malakhov and Allison found themselves melting into each other. There were no words, just the heat shared between them and the unspoken truth that this moment had been destined to arrive.

After pressing a final, lingering kiss at her temple, Malakhov whispered a promise against her skin. "You are mine now, Allison."

She curled against his chest, still trembling and whispered back with a fierce certainty, "And you are mine."

Twenty One

Entwined Fates and Fractured Loyalties

The sun rose, soft ripples of light came through thick curtains, casting a golden hue across the room. Shadows crept gently along the walls as dawn edged into the room. The air was still and warm, carrying the quiet heaviness of a night that refused to let go.

Allison stirred, her body aching in a satisfied exhaustion. She blinked into the light of the early morning and shifted gently, wincing as her muscles protested. The aches were in her shoulders, in her thighs, even in the curvature of her spine, but good aches—reminders, marks of possession.

Malakhov still lay next to her, the steady rise and fall of his chest comforting. But with her movements, his eyes flung open instantly, sharp despite being half-gone to sleep. A faintly amused smile tugged at his lips as he turned toward her.

"Good morning, my wife," he breathed against her skin, voice low, hoarse with sleep; his accent wrapped around his words, stirring something deep inside her.

She faced him, her hand gliding across his cheek, long fingers brushing the short stubble along his jaw. "Morning, Dmitri."

Not a word. His lips met hers in a kiss, soft, lingering, almost tender in a way that felt unexpectedly gentle coming from the man who had held her so fiercely just hours earlier.

"I knew you'd be sore," he said, smug almost. "Let me make you a bath." His arm slipped round her waist to hold her close.

Allison blinked, suddenly touched by the sweetness of such an almost unheard-of gesture. "You want to make me a bath?"

He raised an eyebrow. "Of course. I'd very much enjoy watching you recover from my *enthusiasm*."

She let out a short laugh and swatted his chest playfully. "You're hopeless."

Malakhov slipped his hand over hers, his lips brushing her knuckles in a slow, gentle kiss. "And yet, here you are. Barely able to move, wrapped up in my arms, sighing like I've ruined you."

She rolled her eyes but could not keep the smile from spreading across her lips. "You always take care of me."

"That's because I'm not done with you yet," he said, darkening his eyes and trailing his thumb across her bottom lip, "You'll be sore again by tonight."

Her eyebrows rose, challenging. "I thought you were the one who needed a rest."

He gave a low chuckle, tugging her closer, his mouth brushing the shell of her ear. "You think I wore myself out? Oh, sweet girl. I was pacing myself."

Allison snorted, pushing lightly at his shoulder. "You're incorrigible."

"And yet you look at me like I hung the stars," he replied easily, his grin widening. "Or at least like I made you see them."

She laughed, breathless now, her cheeks flushed. "I'm leaving before your ego expands to fill the room."

Malakhov leaned back, hands tucked behind his head as he watched her with open admiration. "Too late. But please—enjoy your bath. Give me just a few minutes to warm it exactly how you like it."

She sat up gingerly, the sheet sliding down her back as she swung her legs over the edge of the bed. "You remember my favorite temperature?"

"Darling, I remember everything about you," he said smoothly. "Your bath preference. The sound you make when you're pretending not to like something. The way you say my name when you're angry—*Dmitri*." He mimicked her tone, mock-scolding. "Very sharp. I find it motivating."

She managed with great difficulty to throw on the nearest robe. "You're too much."

"But charming," he called after her as he strode off toward the bathroom. "And I might say, I'm still owed a proper thank-you for last night's... attentions."

She looked over her shoulder; her cheeks were rosy. "Later."

"Looking forward to it," he winked.

Malakhov then watched her disappear behind the bathroom door, a satisfied smile playing on his lips. He then threw himself back onto the pillows, hands behind his head, and sighed contentedly.

"My best conquest yet," he muttered to himself.

From behind the door came her cheerful retort; "I heard that!"

He grinned wider. "I *meant* for you too."

* * *

They moved down the corridor, where Radimir was already waiting—tall, still, and unmistakably imposing in the low light. The flicker from the sconces caught the silver in his hair, turning it to cold steel, and his eyes gleamed with a sharp calculation that sent a chill straight through her.

Allison felt it immediately, every pair of eyes weighing on theirs as they entered the hall. Bratva men lined each side of the corridor, chatting with one another, but they all froze the moment the visitors stepped inside. These were the same men who had watched her dance with Malakhov last night, speculating over half-finished vodka bottles and cigarette smoke about what his marriage to her might mean for the hierarchy. Now all these eyes, with a mixture of curiosity and respect, followed her, along with something else a bit colder- envy, perhaps. Or suspicion. She couldn't be sure.

Malakhov's fingers tightened briefly around hers, a steadying pressure that kept her rooted. No words needed; both knew what this meant. But even with that reassurance, the air between them was taut. Unspoken questions curled in the silence; *What now? What will they ask of us next?*

Radimir turned slowly away from the table; his eyes faded over them as if casting a blade. He rarely smiled but the slight twisting of his mouth, half-smile, half-sneer, communicated all that needed to be said.

"Ah," he drawled, his voice smooth as silk wrapped around broken glass. "The newlyweds. Or should I say, the empire's new favorite couple."

Allison straightened her spine, ignoring the pang of unease in her gut. Last night had been about surrender. This morning was about survival.

"I trust the night was to your... *satisfaction*?" With that, Radimir's voice carried an innuendo, followed by a dark note of approval, subtle and chilling."

Malakhov tilted his head, slight upward curve forming on his lips as if mocking, aggravatingly unreadable. "It was productive," he said at last, voice like velvet dipped in arsenic.

Allison fought the urge to elbow him, but a flicker of reluctant amusement passed through her all the same. *Bastard.* She turned her gaze on Radimir instead, eyes calm, voice carefully measured. "It was," she said simply, her tone cool but firm.

Radimir's brows lifted, his amusement edged with something colder. "Efficient. I like that." His eyes lingered on her a moment longer than necessary, then slid to Malakhov. "You've taught her well."

Malakhov's expression didn't shift, but Allison could feel his fingers twitch slightly where they touched hers. Whether from anger or amusement, she couldn't tell.

"Good," Radimir said finally, turning his back to them and pacing slowly to the war table. "Now that your bond is sealed, your position is no longer theoretical. You're not symbols anymore—you're weapons. And I intend to use you both."

The atmosphere shifted, something heavier sliding into place.

"I do not forget the task at hand," Radimir continued, his voice lower now, threading between the cracks in the stone floor like smoke. "The rebels believe they have us flanked. That we are too caught up in our rituals and celebrations to see what they are up to."

He stopped for a moment, placing his hands on the table, fingers spread like a spider ready to strike.

"But they are fools."

Allison's throat tightened. This was it. The moment her manipulation, her careful lies, would either collapse or bear fruit. Her mouth felt dry.

"I gave them the information," she said quietly, stepping forward. "The coordinates. The convoy time. They'll walk straight into the choke point outside the pass."

Radimir turned toward her again, eyes sharp with something like pride—but darker.

"You did well," he said, and unlike praise, the words dropped like a verdict between them. There was no hint of warmth; he just sounded very calculating. "Very well, indeed."

His gaze returned to her left hand, where the ring glimmered in the firelight.

He looked at the ring on her finger. "That ring doesn't just bind you to him, it binds you to all of us."

Allison didn't answer. She didn't flinch. But inside, something coiled.

Malakhov, however, stepped in, his tone deceptively light. "She belongs to me first."

The room quieted even more, a tension rising like fog. Radimir's eyes met Malakhov's, and something unspoken passed between them. A warning. A challenge.

After a long moment, Radimir smiled; thin, cold. "Of course. But *you* belong to me."

Malakhov didn't reply. He didn't have to.

"Go," Radimir said, straightening with a dismissive wave of his hand. "Report to the War Room. Finalize the positions. I want blood before midnight."

Allison turned, already moving toward the inner chamber, her hand slipping from Malakhov's as they passed the line of silent onlookers. But just before she stepped through the door, she glanced back at Radimir.

He was still watching them, *watching her*, with eyes that said that this was just the beginning.

The War Room was silent except for the occasional rustle of papers and the dragging of wood against metal as a chair was moved, boots shifted, or weapons were being readied. The scent of wax, ink, and gun oil lingered in the air. Maps spread out on the central table were weighed down by blades, empty glasses, and half-burnt candles, wax dripping slowly into the marks drawn with ink and blood.

As Allison and Malakhov stepped through the threshold, every conversation stilled. Heads turned. Gazes snapped toward them like triggered traps, sharp, dissecting, assessing. No one bowed. No one spoke.

This was the kind of silence that would weigh someone down and fill her lungs. She felt it, *them*, each calculating mind trying to piece together the meaning of her presence. Not just as Malakhov's wife now, but as a figure of consequence.

Her gaze flicked toward Malakhov beside her. He stood there, impermeable, a living testament to restraint and quiet command. His presence had the effect of a strong calming agent, a quiet reminder. The warfare above all was the path voluntarily taken.

No turning back now.

She took another step forward.

Radimir's voice cut through the quiet, sharp and commanding as he entered behind them. "The trap has been set."

It echoed through the vaulted stone chamber, dark and sharp, a note of theatrical menace that made the hair on the back of her neck rise.

"The rebels believe they are walking into an assault along the northern borders." Allowing the sentence to hang, he let anticipation and tension settle in the hard stone of the room. He continued, lips curling into a grin too much like a snarl to be counted among smiles; "What they don't know is that they are walking straight into their *graves*."

A murmur went through the gathering; dark approval and restrained appetite for blood. Several men leaned forward over the table. Others exchanged looks, their mouths twitching with cruel amusement.

Radimir's eyes found hers again, glinting like obsidian under firelight. "This will end tonight. And with it, our hold over this city will no longer be questioned. No shadows. No rivals. Only fire and silence."

Her heart hammered, a tight coil of tension settling low in her chest. She didn't move, but she could feel the pressure mounting in the room, *and within herself.* Every deception she had spun. Every whispered lie she had planted. They all led here.

Radimir stepped slowly around the table, letting his gaze linger on her like a challenge. "Allison," he said, and her name rang colder than the stone beneath her feet, "you were instrumental in this deception. Without your misdirection, without your precision, this plan would not exist."

His voice dropped slightly, intimate in a way that made her skin crawl. "And now we will see if your work was clever enough to stand without you."

She met his gaze without blinking. "It will," she said quietly, the steel in her voice quiet but undeniable.

Radimir's mouth twitched in something that might have been approval, or a warning.

"We shall see," he said simply.

He turned then, his eyes shifting to Malakhov. "We begin when you give the word."

Malakhov gave a single, clipped nod. "Everything is set," he said, his voice like flint on steel—calm, certain, ready to strike. "The convoy's been rerouted. Our snipers are in place. The perimeter will collapse in two waves, timed to the false retreat. They'll think they've won. Until they're surrounded."

Radimir nodded once. "Then let them bleed."

A tension seemed to snap across the room like a drawn bowstring. Men began to move, papers collected, coordinates double-checked, final commands whispered and barked.

Allison inhaled slowly. She stepped forward, toward the war table, her spine straight, shoulders squared. She could feel the eyes still on her, but something in their gaze had shifted. No longer just suspicion. No longer the half-concealed contempt once reserved for a woman walking among wolves.

Now there was something else.

Calculation.

Wariness.

Maybe even respect.

She leaned over the map, her finger trailing along the northern ridge where the trap was set, her voice calm as she spoke. "They'll send a forward scout unit just before nightfall. They'll expect light resistance here", she tapped a narrow crossing, "but we've left enough behind to sell the illusion."

A man to her left, broad-shouldered, face scarred, grunted in approval. "If they bite, they're boxed in within fifteen minutes."

"They will bite," Allison said, straightening. "Their commander is too prideful not to. He'll see what he wants to see. *Victory.*"

"...and instead," Malakhov said, stepping up beside her, "he'll find ash."

Allison didn't speak. She didn't need to.

This was no longer about proving herself. It was about owning the blood-soaked path she had chosen.

Radimir's voice cut through the last few murmurs like a knife. "Then let the city watch what happens to those who think they can challenge us."

The scout reports arrived like whispers of doom, hurried footsteps, a knock on the iron door, the low murmur of confirmation.

"They're en route," someone announced, laying the missive on the war table.

Allison stood motionless as the implications sank in. Rob and Daniel had taken the bait. They were heading straight toward the northern ridge, the false location she herself had described in intricate, believable detail. The lie had been elegant.

Seamless.

Cruel.

Radimir stepped forward, casting a long shadow across the table. His smile was not wide, but it curled at the edges with something far more sinister than glee—*certainty*. "They will be caught," he said, voice cutting through the silence like steel across flesh. "And then we will have them—alive."

A ripple of approval coursed through the room; Allison remained silent.

She clasped her hands behind her back, willing the tremors away. Her fingers locked into fists, each knuckle burning in pain. The weight of what she'd done came crashing down in a suffocating wave. *Rob. Daniel.* Friends. Loyalists. People who had trusted her once.

She had betrayed them.

And yet, underneath the crashing guilt, there was something else, something darker and more dangerous. A current of exhilaration that she couldn't deny.

She had power now. *Influence.* Her words carried consequences. Her choices shaped the tides of war. Her proximity to Malakhov, her role in Radimir's grand design, it all placed her at the very center of something enormous, unstoppable.

This was the world she had stepped into.

And now, there was no escape.

Malakhov's voice was low but steady. "The trap worked, no mess, no loose ends. They were intercepted by the second unit, exactly where expected. No fatalities. They've been separated, secured."

"They will serve us well," Radimir said with wicked satisfaction. "A symbol. A message." He turned toward Allison, his gaze hard and unreadable. "And you, my dear, have earned your place here."

He tilted his head, and, with a slight change in tone, he said something that made Allison's stomach turn.

"You have a choice now, Allison."

These words hit her harder than she wanted.

She raised her eyes to his, something tightening in her chest. "What kind of choice?"

Radimir's smile returned, slow and sharp. "Stand beside me. Beside Dmitri. Embrace what you've become. Or free them. Help them escape. But understand that if you try to leave, if you betray *us*... well, you know what will happen."

The room fell into silence, and the air grew heavy, electric with anticipation. Every eye was on her.

Malakhov stood to Radimir's right, arms crossed over his chest, his face unreadable. He didn't speak. Didn't move. But his gaze was locked on hers, unwavering.

There was no threat in his expression. No fear. Just waiting. Watching.

Trusting.

She realized then that this moment, *this test*, wasn't Radimir's alone. Malakhov had known it was coming. And he had said nothing.

Her breath caught in her throat.

Her mind spun through every possible outcome. If she turned against them, she wouldn't make it out alive. Rob and Daniel might. But she wouldn't. And if she stayed, if she accepted this life, this allegiance, she would be choosing blood over loyalty. Power over innocence. Them over everything she had once fought for.

And yet...

She looked at Malakhov again. At the quiet intensity in his eyes. The man who had never forced her to stay. Who had never taken her by force or by fear. The man who had given her space to decide, who had stood beside her in silence, through fire and strategy and sleepless nights.

In her eyes, she saw the truth. There was no manipulation; rather, there was conviction.

Allison felt her throat constrict and began stepping forward in small, very careful footsteps. Her heart roared.

She stopped just in front of him, raising her chin toward his gaze.

Her voice was barely more than a breath. "I choose you."

Her voice wasn't loud; it didn't need to be.

Those words fell like the final act of an earthquake, unleashing shockwaves no one could ignore.

Radimir inclined his head, satisfied. "Then it is done."

A breath slipped from her lips.

And just like that, her fate was sealed.

There was no turning back. No room left for doubt. The past was behind her—only the future stretched out ahead, cold and certain.

Twenty Two

Torn Between Two Worlds

Allison felt the crushing weight of her choice settle over her as Rob and Daniel were dragged in, their hands tied, their faces a mix of confusion and disbelief, *both betrayed by her*. She had done this. She had betrayed them, and nothing had prepared her for the searing pain of seeing it laid bare.

They had trusted her. They had believed in her, and she was the one who had taken them into the trap. She had set them up and now there was no turning back from it.

Rob's voice caught, rough with pain. His eyes darkened with betrayal, his features twisting like he was fighting to hold back a flood.

"Allison... why? Why are you doing this?" His voice cracked, the hurt plain in his eyes, the same eyes that once stood steady beside her, the man who had been there with her, fighting by her side through everything, standing before her to question every belief he had ever held.

Daniel looked at her as if his entire world had come crashing down. His eyes, once steady with iron resolve, now flickered with desperation and confusion.

"Allison, please, we need you! You don't have to do this." His voice cracked under the vulnerability that was almost untouchable. "You don't belong here."

She said nothing, the words caught somewhere deep inside, stubbornly refusing to surface. She knew the role she had played in their downfall, and it tortured her, but she forbid herself to show it. She had made her decision.

"I never wanted to hurt you, Rob. Or you, Daniel. But you never saw what I saw." Allison's voice was low, but steady. "I had to make a choice. This world is broken. I'm not going to sit here and pretend I can fix it anymore. I'm with them now."

Rob's jaw clenched tight, his eyes flashing with pain and rage, his voice barely holding steady as he spat out the words. "You can't be serious! This—*this* is what you've chosen? You actually think joining him will make things better? You really think—"

"Enough." Malakhov's voice dropped low, sharp like a blade. He stepped forward, his tall frame blocking the space between Allison and Rob. His towering figure casting a shadow threatening to press down on everything.

Rob stepped forward, his rage twofold, but Malakhov's cold and calculated gaze stopped him dead in his tracks.

"Stay back, Walker." His voice was low, dangerous, each syllable carrying a threat. "She is no longer yours."

Rob's fists clenched, his frustration boiling over. "You think you can just take her from us, from *me*?" He turned towards Radimir "Turn her into one of your followers?" His contempt filled tones carried the venom of words as he gave a look in Allison's direction. "She's a murderer just like all of you."

Malakhov took another step forward, lips twitching in a smirk that didn't quite reach his cold eyes. "She is no longer part of your world,

Walker," he said, his voice final. "She has chosen her side, and I will ensure that you grasp what that means, Allison is my *wife* now."

Rob staggered back, the shock and horror flooding his face. "What? No... Allison, you can't mean that." His voice cracked, a mix of disbelief and desperation. "I loved you. I thought... I thought you'd never choose this. Never choose *him*."

She looked at Malakhov, and for the first time, the truth of her feelings rose to the surface. She drew a deep breath, steadying herself. When she spoke, her voice was clear. "I love him, Rob. I love Dmitri. I love everything he is, everything he stands for. And I am proud to stand beside him."

Her words hit the room with a sudden, sharp weight.

Malakhov froze beside her, his eyes wide with surprise, shocked by her confession, though the emotion that flooded his chest was far from anger. There was a strange affection, something gentle that passed through his gaze.

And then, as if compelled by an inner need, Malakhov bent down to brush Allison's forehead with his with a tenderness she had never expected. "I never thought I'd hear those words from you. But you know what? I've never been more proud of you than I am right now." His voice was whisper-soft, sincere and only for her to hear.

The kiss was quick, but it stirred something new in her, a quiet warmth she hadn't allowed herself before. It was the softest admission of love, a bond made of fire and shadow.

"She loves *me*, Walker," Malakhov said, his words final and unyielding. "She is bound to me, by law and *blood*. She is my wife, and there is no place for you in her life anymore."

"You turned your back on us!" Daniel's voice cracked, sharp with raw hurt. "You've betrayed everything we fought for! *How can you do this?*"

Rob sputtered in disbelief, his face twisted with anger and grief. "You can't mean this! Allison, look at yourself! This is the man who's turned you into one of them!"

Allison swallowed hard as the realization dawned on her of what she had done, locking eyes with both Rob and Daniel.

"It's not about who's right or wrong now, Rob. It's about survival, and I've made my choice."

And she meant it. The finality in her voice said it all. There was no more doubt, no more second-guessing. There was the woman she had been, and the choices made along the way had forever shaped her, there was no way she'd turn back.

The room was silent when Radimir gave a slight nod, his eyes gleaming with approval. The man had gotten what he had wanted, and now Allison was his loyal heir.

"Very well," said Radimir with smooth voice. "It is as it should be, Allison. Your bond is clear. And your loyalty is assured. You are now more than just my daughter. You are a key part of the future we are building. This was the final test."

"This is your place now, Allison," Radimir continued, his voice quieter but more commanding. "You've chosen wisely. And you will continue to do so. *There is no going back.*"

Allison felt something deep within her shift as the gravity of the situation settled in. She wasn't just a pawn anymore, she was integral to Radimir's vision for the future. She had betrayed her friends, and in doing so, had chosen a side. *The dark side.*

Strangely, with Malakhov standing next to her, a part of her felt reassured. Rob and Daniel were shackled and defeated, but the moment now belonged to the past. Going back was out of the question.

Malakhov's hand rested lightly on her back, a reassuring touch; she already knew in her heart that she could never return to the girl she was before this.

There was no going back now; every step forward sealed her fate. Her heart ached, but regret was a luxury she couldn't afford, not when the path ahead was so clear.

Radimir stood behind a long table, his presence alone enough to fill the room with tension. The weight of his glare pressed into the space like a held breath. He was calm, *too calm,* the kind of stillness that comes just before a storm breaks. His face gave nothing away, all sharp edges and unreadable quiet. His gaze moved slowly over the prisoners... then locked onto Allison, cold and precise.

"The rebellion ends tonight," he said, voice low and deadly. "They are but pawns. You've done well, Allison. You have brought them to me. And now, I will finish it."

His eyes turned to Daniel and Rob, who were bound tightly, their faces full of confusion and disbelief as they glanced from Allison to Radimir. It was clear, they had no idea what was coming.

"Their lives are no longer important." Radimir continued, his voice growing more malicious. "The rebellion dies with them."

Allison's pulse quickened. The finality in his words felt like a clawing pressure on her chest. *This was it.* The choice she had made was not just a commitment to the dark side, but a decision that would seal the fate of her oldest friends.

But she had to choose. She couldn't falter. Not now.

Radimir's words hit Allison with the force of a physical blow; however, she could not afford to show weakness—not now, not in front of anyone. Malakhov's presence beside her was an opposing force that she leaned into, absorbing his strength. She had made her choice, but it still weighed on her with remorse.

The silence in the room was suffocating, every breath weighed down by unspoken threats. Radimir's gaze flicked toward Daniel and Rob, who now stood silent, awaiting their doom.

"*Execute* them," Radimir commanded, his voice cold and sharp, a sentence passed without hesitation.

The Bratva stood still watching and waiting for that particular moment to be. Allison saw pain etching itself into the very pores of Rob's face and the gaping expression of disbelief on Daniel's. They could not weigh what had, in their minds, happened to her and could not understand why she was here, betraying everything they had fought for.

Allison wanted to avert her gaze, to not see the end of it all. But she could not.

But something inside her began to shift. She didn't want this. *Not like this*.

There had to be another way. She had never been one to just sit back and let fate decide for her. She had always fought back; she had always tried to find a way to make it right.

Radimir's gaze weighed her down as though she were expected never to show weakness. But those words, those last words, stirred something deep within her. The humanity she had fought so hard to save began to waver.

To watch her friends die like this, and knowing she could have stopped it, set in. She was unwilling to be part of this brutal act.

For once, she didn't weigh the consequences. She stepped forward, her voice firm and defiant. "No."

An eerie silence filled the room as everyone turned her way; the moment was heavy, suffocating. Radimir's eyes narrowed ever so slightly, irritation flickering across his canvas.

"*No?*" he said, cold but amused. "What do you mean, *no, Allison?*"

She stood her ground, her back straight. "I will not let them die. Not like this. I cannot."

All the people looked at each other, trying to decide what to do. Radimir's eyes flashed with fury and surprise, and his hands clenched. The command was clear, and yet, Allison had outright refused to carry out his wishes.

Malakhov's eyes flicked to Allison, his expression unreadable. He had always sensed that the moment would come; even if he once thought that she would remain loyal to him, the thought of an outright defiance had never really made it onto his list of possibilities. This time, it really was not about her love for him. This was about her refusing to sacrifice her friends to secure her place.

His stare darkened, but he didn't speak at first, allowing Allison to stand before Radimir without interference. He had given her the space to make her own decision, this was hers alone to own.

But as Radimir's anger swirled, ready to strike, Malakhov stepped forward, steely resolve in his eyes. "Sir, please. Let her speak." His voice was calm, controlled. But there was a measure of defiance in it; he, too, was challenging the finality of Radimir's complied command.

Radimir's eyes snapped to Malakhov, his lips curling into a sneer before he spoke.

"You, too, Dmitri? You think she can defy me?"

Malakhov didn't flinch. "I think it is not about defying you, Sir. It is about understanding the choice she is making. She stands with you, but she has not lost her humanity."

Radimir's expression flickered, then his gaze turned back to Allison. "So, you think you can choose, Allison? You can defy me and save them?" His voice was suddenly cold, piercing, as if daring her to back down.

Allison's heart pounded, every beat crashing against her ribs like it was trying to escape. She understood the cost of standing here—what it had already taken, and what it might still demand. She'd chosen this path, fully aware it would pull her under.

But now, standing in the thick of it, everything felt like a question she didn't have an answer to.

Could she really let them die?

Could she live with the weight of this dark, twisted life she'd willingly stepped into?

But then, her mind cleared.

She couldn't allow them to die.

She couldn't be the one who made this a reality.

With a steady breath, she stepped forward again, looking directly into Radimir's eyes. "I won't let them die, Sir. Not like this. If it means choosing their lives over your command, then I will make that choice."

The room was utterly still; the tension so thick it was nearly suffocating. Radimir's anger flashed across his eyes. Allison felt such a surge of wrath in Radimir; it might, in fact, have proved too much for her to withstand. But she couldn't let fear control her anymore.

Radimir's eyes darkened, his smile twisting into something cruel and calculating. "You defy me. You defy everything I've done for you. And you do so *in front of everyone.*" The tone was deep, but the words chilling beyond a doubt.

Malakhov stepped forward as he spoke, his voice low and unflinching. "Sir, Allison has made her decision." The low voice cut through the tension like a knife. "She will not let them die. And I will not stand idly by and watch her fall for this."

Radimir's glare was sharp, and his voice grew cold, like ice scraping against stone. "And if she refuses to obey me? What will you do, Dmitri?"

Malakhov stood tall, his gaze unwavering. "I will stand by her, Sir. This is the loyalty I have to give her."

A long silence followed, heavy with expectation. Radimir's anger was palpable. *But there was something else.* There could have been admiration for the loyalty Malakhov had shown to her. It just was not enough.

Radimir cast his eyes away from Allison for a moment; the gaze flicked briefly to her clenched hands by her side. She had decided, and now she would have to live with the consequences.

"Fine, Allison. You want to spare them? Then they'll rot in the Manor's dungeons for the rest of their days. But don't forget—defiance has a *price*."

Twenty Three

The Mark That Binds

The room fell silent, eyes locked on Allison, the weight of her choice hanging thick in the air. She'd dared to defy Radimir, risking everything. Now, all that remained was to face whatever punishment awaited.

They'd trusted her loyalty countless times before, and yet here she was, challenging the man they all feared. Radimir, had been challenged in his own domain. The atmosphere was taut with expectation. Everyone waited to see how he would respond.

Malakhov stood firm beside her, his hand resting lightly on her back. His eyes met Radimir's, silent but clear, he knew that defying the leader would come with a heavy price. He wasn't naïve; he understood the power Radimir held over them all. But then again, he also understood Allison, who would never just watch them die, no matter what was asked of her.

Radimir's eyes narrowed, fury simmering beneath the surface. Defiance was unfamiliar territory, especially from Allison. He was the leader, *untouchable*, and yet she was there, choosing for herself. Allison saw the change flicker across his face, a flash of genuine surprise, instantly replaced by cold, calculating fury.

"You *truly* will refuse me? My heir? After all I've done for you?" Radimir's voice was dark, dripping with venom. He stepped closer to Allison; his long, pale fingers now clenched into a fist, heavy with the promise of repercussions. His eyes glimmered with hate, but beneath that, Allison read another emotion, a kind of twisted pride. Apparently, he respected this rebellion. In an extremely sick way, he admired her defiance.

Allison stood her ground, her heart pounding, with no trace of wavering in her voice. "I will not let them die, Sir." The words came out, calm and resolute, as if she had not just made the most dangerous decision of her life.

Radimir's gaze swept over her, "You think saving them will change the war's course?" His voice dropped to a harsh whisper. "You can't undo the past, Allison. They are a threat to my reign, to *our reign*, and they must die."

Her pulse thudded in her ears, but she didn't flinch. "I can't let them die. Not like this. Not when I can stop it." She knew there would be a price. The moment she spoke, she knew what was coming. It wasn't going to be easy. Radimir had never let someone challenge him without consequences.

Radimir's lips curled into a thin smile, but it was the smile of someone who had already decided what was going to happen. He lifted his hand, his fingers curling towards someone in the back to come forward, and in the stillness of the room, Allison's heart sank. She knew the time had come for her to pay for her rebellion. But what came next was far worse than she had imagined.

"You will understand the price, Allison." Radimir's voice was cold and final. He turned to his followers, his eyes flashing, giving them a silent command. The Bratva stepped back, creating space in the center of the room.

Someone seized her from behind. Radimir reached out and accepted the branding iron, his sigil, etched in metal, and pressed it to her upper arm.

Pain exploded through her arm, sharp and searing like fire beneath her skin. Allison gasped as her limbs buckled, but Malakhov's grip steadied her. His steady presence was a whisper at her side as the room spun and darkness crept at the edges of her vision.

"No..." she gasped, the word slipping out as fresh agony tore through her. She had felt pain before, had seen it—but nothing like this. This wasn't just a punishment. It was a *claiming*.

Radimir's words hammered in her mind, *the price she'd chosen to pay.* She knew what it meant, but the sheer force of the brand tore through her body sent her spiraling into darkness. It was a mark, a seal, something permanent.

Her heart quickened, the world spun; Malakhov kept her standing by himself, his hand slipping to her back, steadying her even as a claim was being cemented by Radimir into her very soul.

Another gasp tore from her lips, ragged, desperate panting. Her vision fuzzed, and she felt the searing wrapping around her skin down to the bone. She had heard whispers of it before, the sigil, the symbol of ultimate loyalty to Radimir. The one that marked you as his.

His servant.

His *property*.

Allison's breath caught as the pain intensified. It went deep, sinking past muscle into her very being, leaving nothing behind but an unshakable claim of ownership.

Her chest rose and fell in ragged gasps. No matter how hard she fought, the mark was hers to bear. It wasn't just a physical price. It was a symbol of everything she had done, everything she had become.

And then, as quickly as it began, the pain stopped as he lifted the iron. The room was silent except for Allison's ragged breathing as she looked slowly at the sigil now etched into her skin. Her heart was pounding.

Radimir's voice cut through the quiet. "This is what defiance costs, Allison. You belong to me now—*body and soul.*"

The sigil, dark and unmistakable, was a reminder that there would be no turning back. As the pain ebbed, Allison felt a strange stillness wash over her. It was quiet, the chaos in her mind fading into the background. Her eyes met Malakhov's, and she saw something there, a softness, an understanding, but also a solidarity. *He knew.* He understood the burden she had just borne. But more than that, he was there. By her side.

Malakhov's voice was soft, steady. His fingers brushed her shoulder. "It's done. You're marked, but you're still mine. We face this together."

Allison nodded, but her eyes were still on her damaged flesh. It wasn't just about loyalty anymore. It wasn't just about the betrayal. This was her place now, *irrevocably*. She was no longer Allison Murphy—the girl who had once fought against Radimir. She was his, marked by his sigil, bound by her choices.

Radimir looked pleased, but there was something in his eyes—something darker. "Now, Allison, you will help lead us into a new world, a world where loyalty is rewarded, and weakness is eradicated."

Allison's head swam, but she didn't look away. The cost of her defiance had been paid. There was no turning back. She had chosen. And now, she would live with the consequences.

* * *

Allison sat alone in the office of Malakhov's manor for many nights following her branding. Heavy thoughts swirled in the fog of weariness and inner conflict. The sigil had begun to heal over, the flesh still burning faintly as it settled deep into her body; a permanent scar she could never escape. The pain was now ebbing away, but the existence of the mark remained; it was more like a shackle than an anchor.

The constant awareness of her irrevocable link to the will of Radimir. The very danger associated with the power that it represented. In the quietest moments, she could hear his voice still talking in the background, giving commands and laying down expectations as though he was always watching, just nearby, waiting for her to satisfy the proof of her loyalty.

Allison tried to close her eyes and focus on anything else except the sensation from her burn. But it was impossible. A sigh escaped her lips as Allison looked away from the window. The sky was dimming from the first hints of twilight, and she pondered for a brief second whether she could still be the woman she was once. But then she remembered, she had walked away on her own accord; there was no getting back.

* * *

The weeks blurred by in endless tasks, her mind weighed down by doubt and the widening gap between who she was and who she'd become, and the growing divide between the world she had once known. It felt like standing on the edge of a cliff, uncertain whether to leap or retreat.

The world had changed, but she had changed even more. Once, she'd tried to save everyone, to keep the darkness at bay. Now she stood on the other side—and there was no way back.

And yet, when the world was asleep or under the cloak of darkness, she would remember. The loud laughter of Rob and Daniel during their late night conversations, and late night talks-and always being there for her. She remembered the warmth of friendship, and how she had sacrificed all of it. Just about every time she had a hint of doubt, the sigil would blaze and burn beneath her skin, reminding her that accepting what she had become was her only option. That power which Radimir had promised was too much to turn down, and the loyalty now seemed to form into something far deeper than obedience.

Pacing in the room, she thought of Malakhov, the man who had become her partner, who had always protected her, and in a way, was her anchor. She'd seen kindness in his eyes, that was not something she'd expected to find in a man so deeply integrated within Radimir's inner circle. She knew in the deepest parts of her that she and Dmitri had grown together in a way she could not explain. It just was not about loyalty; it was about something far more complex than she had ever imagined possible.

The door creaked open, and Malakhov entered. Calm radiated from his broad stance. His presence alone enough to calm the storm inside her, even if only for a moment.

"Still restless?" Malakhov's voice was low, those ever, present grains of gravitas sprinkling through his words, making whatever he said somehow more substantial.

Allison faced him, her lips pressed to keep from spilling her frustration. "I don't know for how much longer I can keep on pretending this doesn't eat at me, Dmitri." Against her intent, her own voice cracked. "This sigil is a shadow hanging over my every choice...the choice of everything I've left behind."

He stepped toward her, never pulling his gaze away, but his brow furrowed ever so slightly as he sensed her distress. "You've made your choice. But it doesn't make it any easier, does it?" His expression softened, and he reached out to take her hand, drawing her toward him.

Allison dipped her head in reluctant approval as the rift crushed her in its grip. "I'm not who I was anymore. Sometimes, I just can't recognize myself."

His touch stole her breath. In that moment, he was the only reassurance to her in this chaotic world. His thumb traced from the knuckles across the back of her hand, shuddering through her.

"You are still *you*, Allison." Malakhov's whisper softened, threaded with quiet wisdom."The world has changed, and yes, you have changed. But there is strength in that. I see it." His eyes darkened ever so slightly; his grip on her hand tightened as he pulled her closer. "I am here with you, always."

Allison looked up at him, her heart pounding away. The chemistry between the two had become stronger with every passing day. The tension between them and the warm energy simmered just beneath the surface.

Her hand slid to his cheek, the warmth of his skin against her fingertips stirring something fierce and tender all at once, pulling her toward the magnetism they could no longer dismiss.

"Dmitri..." Her voice pierced the silence, a mixture of rawness and truth. The way she said his name was different now; it wasn't just an acknowledgment of her partnership anymore, it meant *more* to her.

He moved before she could finish her thought, his lips capturing hers in a hard, urgent kiss, clamoring for an ownership that words could never express. His hands found her waist, pulling her tightly to his body, whose warmth filled hers.

For a breathless moment, the outside world dissolved, and nothing could sate the heat between them. Allison raised her hands to his chest, feeling the tense muscles beneath his button down. Pulling his lips away, his breath was like fire against her cheek as he whispered, "You're not just a part of this world, Allison. You're a part of mine. You always have been."

Her heart raced, and she pulled him close for more. "I know, Dmitri. I'm just..." She stopped, clutching for breath. "I'm just scared sometimes."

He cupped her face with his strong hands, his thumb brushing her pale lower lip. "There's nothing to fear, Allison." His eyes darkened; an intensity broke through his voice. "That's a promise I intend to keep. No one will touch you, and nothing will harm you. I won't let it happen."

The heat between them grew almost unbearable. His hands gripped her waist, drawing her closer. There was an intensity to his possession that said he wanted not only to protect her but to claim her.

She wanted to tumble over the precipice but almost instantly recoiled. With her chest heaving in the midst of their passion, she looked up, cheeks brushed red, lips swollen from the kiss. "Dmitri, I—"

Before she could voice anything further, he pressed his lips gently on her forehead, silencing her. "You don't need to say a word. You never have to explain." The hug wrapped around her like a shield, something she'd never known she needed. *She had never known anything like it.* It was there where she was finally free to let go and be herself.

* * *

The War Room buzzed with tension as she stepped inside for the first time since the branding. Radimir was at his usual place at the head of the table. His eyes wandered through the room, measuring loyalty and worth on all present. It was a charged atmosphere but with a subtle satisfaction that mirrored the ever-growing confidence of Radimir.

When Allison entered, a hush fell over the room, and she could feel the eyes of the Bratva upon her and Malakhov. His choice to support her had been a public proclamation. The very weight of it still clung to them.

For a moment, Radimir's gaze lingered on her, a rare flicker of approval—he had seen her potential for a while. But with his sigil etched into her flesh, she was no longer just a tool; she was rising to the status of an ally worth struggling alongside.

"Allison, come here." His voice sounded low yet commanding. "I see the change in you, my daughter. The transformation is complete."

Her footsteps quickened as she came forward, feeling the increasing weight of Radimir's approval on her. The feeling was strange but, at the same time, it seemed to confirm the road she had chosen.

The silence continued, with all eyes glued to Allison while Radimir's piercing gaze settled on her. "You chose, Allison." His voice dropped briefly, softer but still sharp. "And I'm pleased. You are not only mine, but you will also be the one to help lead us into the next era of our reign."

Allison's heart fluttered a little, but she kept her composure. "Thank you, Sir." The words were firm, though her voice was filled with an uncertain sense of pride.

Radimir smiled, and he looked almost pleased. "Despite some... *defiance*, you have also demonstrated you are loyal. You alone have become necessary for our future. Dmitri has done well. And so have you."

For a moment, Allison was stunned, but she hid it. Malakhov, had been her keeper and her guide, and now Radimir was acknowledging them both. The recognition was almost unsettling.

Radimir's eyes narrowed, and a sly grin crossed his lips. "From this day, you'll stand beside Dmitri as my second-in-command. You will both help lead us." His tone was almost gleeful; Allison could feel the shift of power.

She was no longer just a pawn. She was integral to his plans—and she knew there was no turning back.

Twenty Four

Damned by Words

Allison suddenly woke in the middle of the night, cold sweat beading on her forehead. She couldn't quite place the source of her unease, but a palpable tension weighed down the air around her. She shifted in her bed as her gaze flitted toward the window and she tried to calm her worried breath. Something twisted inside her, restless, raw, and impossible to ignore. Like a whisper she couldn't shake, no matter how hard she tried.

The sigil beneath her skin seemed to glowed faintly, its burn still fresh and raw. Sometimes it would feel like a distant touch, like a tightness in her chest or a prickling feeling on her arm. But tonight, it was way different. Tonight, it presented itself, *demanding* her total attention.

She knew that the sigil was no longer just a symbol of her allegiance; it was a constant reminder of who she had become. Radimir wasn't just a name on her skin anymore. His presence seeped into her mind, shadowed her dreams, and twisted into the very parts of her she thought were hers alone.

Allison shook her head as if to shake off the thoughts. Now was not the time to think about such things; she was still trying to figure out her way through this new life. There were still so many questions, so many feelings that she didn't know how to deal with.

* * *

They were called to the headquarters by the afternoon. The tension in Radimir's office had turned cold. Not because it was a cold day outside, but the ambiance inside seemed to drain the warmth. Shadows stretched long across the wall, flickering with the rhythm of the dying fire. Allison walked to the door with Malakhov at her side, the summons came with no explanation. The silence was deliberate.

Heavy.

Calculated.

The pale hands of Radimir, sitting against a black leather chair, folded over a single sheet of paper. His eyes lifted very slowly to meet theirs, yet there was no greeting.

"We found this in the lining of Rob's coat," he said quietly, almost amused. He unfolded the paper carefully, as if it were sacred, then held it out to Allison.

"A letter. Addressed to *you*."

Allison took it with trepidation, touching the inked page with her fingers. She hesitated, torn between a craving to hear Rob's voice in her head and fearing the pain his words would bring once she read them.

My Allie,

This can't be real.

This can't be you.

You were the fiercest person I knew. You never bowed to anyone. You fought for people. For truth. For yourself. And now I see your name whispered beside his—Malakhov. Like you're some dark prize he earned by bleeding others dry.

I don't know what they've done to you. What he's done to you. But I know it's not love. It can't be. That man, he's violence wrapped in silk. He smiles while breaking people. He touches you like he owns you. And Radimir? He's the rot beneath it all, feeding off fear like it's wine. And now... you're standing at his table.

I want to believe you're pretending. That you're surviving the only way you can. That the woman who once looked me in the eyes and swore she'd never lose herself isn't really lost. Because if this is who you've become... if you've truly given yourself to them—body, loyalty, heart—then I don't know if I ever really knew you at all.

But I think I did.

I think I knew the girl who used to patch me up after fights I couldn't win. The woman who used to laugh like the world hadn't yet broken her ribs. The one who once whispered that no one would ever claim her soul.

And I loved her... I still do.

Maybe I've always loved you, and I was too much of a coward to say it. Maybe I thought I'd always have time. But now? Now I see you draped in his name, his colors, and I feel sick.

If there's even a flicker of the old you left—fight. Come back. Not to me. Not even to the past.

Just... to yourself.

Because I can't keep watching you disappear.

Rob

Allison's breath hitched slightly. Her fingers trembled. It wasn't just what he said, it was the earnestness. The raw vulnerability. Rob had written it not with the expectation of her just reading it, but with the hope that somehow, somewhere, she'd remember who she used to be. And maybe... he wasn't wrong about all of it.

"Well?" Radimir asked.

Her eyes flicked up to him, startled. "It's..."

"Honest? Pathetic? *Dangerous?*" he supplied, voice dripping with mock concern. "Pick one."

Allison folded the letter carefully, her throat dry. She wasn't sure what to say, but the letter didn't feel like a weapon. Not exactly. Not until Radimir looked to Malakhov.

"Give it to your husband. He should read it too."

She hesitated, not because she didn't trust Malakhov, but because she knew what Rob's words would stir in him. A flicker of insecurity. Of rage. Of the deep, possessive loyalty Malakhov never spoke of, but always carried.

Still, she extended the letter to him.

Malakhov took it without a word. His eyes scanned quickly, his jaw tightening with every line. When he reached the end, he folded it once, then again, knuckles pale and handed it back to her.

"We should burn that," he muttered.

Radimir rose slowly, eyes sharp enough to cut through steel. "Burn it, yes. But not before we deal with the man who wrote it."

He circled around the desk, each step echoing like a gavel. "The problem is not just the letter. It's the whispers. The guards heard about it. Some sympathize. They're talking. *Questioning*. That... cannot happen."

Allison stiffened.

"I need *you* to correct Rob's loose tongue," Radimir said quietly. "*Permanently*, if you must."

Her pulse raced.

Allison's fingers tightened around the edge of the letter still in her hand, the words blurring before her eyes. She had betrayed Rob once, lied to him, used him to mislead the rebels. She had watched him walk into a trap she set, and now he was in chains because of her. But this... *this* was different.

"Not kill him," Radimir clarified, almost as an afterthought, as if that made it any better. "I gave my word to you that their lives would remain intact. But *pain*—pain is a necessary lesson. A warning. To him. To the others."

Her breath caught.

"I want you to punish him, Allison," he said, voice low and heavy with command. "Let them all see that loose tongues are crushed, even if they speak from a place of love. You will silence his delusions."

She turned toward Malakhov instinctively, eyes wide. His jaw had gone totally rigid, dark eyes sparkling with something unreadable.

She shook her head, voice barely a breath. "I just... I can't."

Radimir shot her with his glare. "What do you mean, *you can't*?"

"I can't hurt him like that," she said more loudly as her chest rose and fell quickly."Not like *that*. Not for this. He's already been broken, he's already locked up for life. That should be enough."

Radimir stepped forward, his presence suddenly oppressive, his voice cold. "He embarrassed *you*, Allison. And *me*. His words have been shared among the guards like a disease. Are you content to let him write your story while he rots in a cell?"

Malakhov stepped forward, his voice low but firm. "Let me take care of it. Instead of her."

"No," Radimir snapped, his tone sharp and final. "It must be *her*. Letting you do it would mean she hides behind you. That the guards were *right* to whisper."

The silence stretched, thick and suffocating.

She swallowed hard, her chest tight with shame and fear twisting deep inside her.

Radimir's eyes narrowed, his voice low and dangerous. "You have until tomorrow. Think carefully. You *say* you've made your choice, haven't you?" His eyes flicked to Malakhov. "Then *prove* it."

With that, he turned and walked out, leaving the room thick with dread.

Malakhov exhaled slowly and turned toward her, but said nothing.

Allison stared down at the letter still clutched in her hand.

She had until tomorrow. To prove herself. Or to break completely.

That heavy door closed with a loud bang behind them, echoing through the grand halls like a gunshot. Allison wasted no time, she walked past the foyer, footsteps uneven, gasping for air as she entered the sitting room and finally slumped onto the edge of a couch.

Her hands covered her face as the weight of the situation finally shattered the defenses she'd held up.

"I can't do this," she sobbed, heavy with emotion. "I can't hurt him, Dmitri."

Malakhov lingered in the doorway, the tension in the room settling around him. When he finally spoke, his voice was softer, "*I know.*" He then crossed the room, walking slowly. "I know it isn't easy. But it was never going to be easy."

Her glassy-eyed gaze glided up towards him. "It's not that I'm weak. I have chosen, terribly, and I have lied. I have betrayed. But this... this would make me no better than Radimir."

Malakhov sat beside her, trying not to intrude, with his forearms tucked upon his knees. "You don't have to explain it to me," he said. "But...".

She noticed his hesitation before he whispered timidly, "Tell me the truth,' he said quietly. 'Do you have feelings for him?"

Her breath hitched.

"What?" She cast her gaze at him in shock. "No. *God*, no. Dmitri—what are you—?"

He did not look at her even as his jaw tightened. "The letter. The way you looked when you read it. The way you froze. You didn't deny any of it."

"Because I was overwhelmed," she snapped. Then she asked in a softer voice, "Not because I believed it. Not because I wanted it to be true."

Malakhov finally locked eyes with her, the haze of vulnerability hiding beneath his guarded expression. "Is that how you see me?" he asked. "A monster with blood on his hands? Someone you've just *convinced* yourself to feel safe with?"

Her heart broke.

"No," she said, steadying herself, with her hand outstretched on top of his. "God, no. That's not how I see you. You are the one who stood by me when everyone else fell away. The one who gave me choices when I had none. The one who let me *breathe* again."

He blinked slowly, shoulders still tense beneath her touch.

She leaned closer, voice shaking. "I don't love Rob. I care about what we had, *a friendship*. I care that I hurt him. But I can't... I can't bring myself to raise a hand to someone who once trusted me. Who believed in me. That doesn't mean I don't believe in *us*."

Malakhov's eyes softened slightly, but the storm hadn't fully passed.

"I didn't doubt you," he said finally. "I just—"

"You did," she interrupted gently. "And it's okay. You're allowed to be afraid of what this means."

He exhaled and covered her hand with his. "We'll find another way. Even if it costs me."

Allison closed her eyes, relief and anguish battling in her chest. "No. I won't let it cost you either."

The silence between them was fragile but honest. And somehow, in the middle of all that tension, they still sat close, two people standing in a storm together, refusing to let go.

* * *

The morning breeze carried a quiet tension.

Allison had held her tongue while descending down the dark corridors of the Bratva headquarters. Her hand was cold within Malakhov's. He did not flinch nor did he squeeze. Silence. *Concentration.* As if he had already seen the outcome.

They were admitted to the War Room, and Allison was hit immediately by how empty it was. No lieutenants, no murmured conversations. Just Radimir, standing by the long obsidian table. The only sound was the distant hum of the facility and the rhythmic drip of something unseen.

Grigori Gordeev leaned in the far corner like a shadow waiting to be unleashed.

And Rob... Rob was bound to a chair on the far end of the room, his face bruised, his lip bloodied. His eyes met Allison's the second she entered, and they widened with something like panic.

She tasted bile.

"Allison," Radimir said coolly, his voice slicing through the silence. "You've had the night to consider."

She didn't speak at first. Her throat tightened. Malakhov's gaze flicker toward her, steady, waiting.

"I..." She hesitated. "I can't do it."

Radimir's smile was slow, glacial. "You *can't?*" he repeated, turning that single word into a weapon.

She lifted her chin. "I won't."

A flicker of something, annoyance? amusement?—passed through his eyes. "How disappointing," he said softly. "You've spent so long earning your place here. And now you defy me... *again.*"

She said nothing. Her chest ached with the pressure of unshed tears.

Radimir nodded once.

"Gordeev."

The brute stepped forward, cracking his knuckles as he approached with a predator's grin. Allison's spine went rigid.

"You said Rob shouldn't be touched," Radimir continued smoothly. "And I am a man of my word. So instead... your *husband* will take his place."

Allison's breath left her in a single, choked gasp.

"No," she whispered. "No... please... don't do this..."

Malakhov remained still beside her, though his jaw tightened. He didn't protest. Didn't speak. Only stepped forward once, his voice low and calm.

"It's all right."

"No!" she snapped, panic rising now. "Dmitri, don't—"

He turned his head toward her, something soft and unyielding in his eyes. "It's okay, *little lion*. Let him have this."

Even Rob, broken and restrained, looked horrified.

But Gordeev was already in motion.

The first hit was a brutal punch to Malakhov's gut. He doubled over with a grunt, but didn't fall. Didn't defend himself.

Allison let out a strangled cry, trying to move toward him, but Radimir lifted a hand, calm, expectant, keeping her in place.

"Stay still," he murmured. "*Watch.*"

The second blow came quick, a fist to Malakhov's jaw that snapped his head to the side. Blood sprayed from his mouth, but still he didn't fall.

"You always did think you were untouchable," Gordeev snarled. "Maybe when you're dead, I'll finally take my turn warming your wife's bed."

That's when he drove his boot into Malakhov's ribs.

Once.

Twice.

The third time, Malakhov collapsed with a grunt, coughing blood onto the floor.

Allison broke.

She lunged forward, dropping to the floor beside him, hands trembling as they searched his face and chest for any sign of life. "Dmitri, please, look at me—"

His one eye was swelling, but he managed to look at her and something wry and painful appeared for a split second on his lips; "Still here."

"Enough," Radimir said finally, his voice dispassionate. "Take Rob back to the cells."

Gordeev gave a sneering chuckle but obeyed, dragging Rob from the room while he twisted in his bindings to try and look back at Allison.

Radimir stepped forward, crouching down beside her and Malakhov. His voice was quiet, but laced with steel.

"Think very carefully, Allison, about what your choices mean. Defiance doesn't just cost you. It costs *him*."

Then he stood, brushing dust from his sleeves.

And with that, he turned and left them in silence, Malakhov broken, Allison shaking, and the walls closing in.

The walk to the car was agonizing.

Malakhov barely said a word, his arm looped tightly around his ribs, his limp subtle but telling. Every few steps, he winced. When Allison reached for his arm, he pulled away, refusing her help.

"I'm fine," he whispered through a cracked lip. "It's nothing."

"Please, don't do that," she whispered, voice cracking. "Don't pretend."

He kept walking. Eyes glued to the driveway. Legs rigid. She ran alongside like a haunting spirit, empty and unraveling.

"Dmitri, please," she begged, but he only shook his head in silent refusal, a greater pain than any coarse-yell.

Having reached their car, she opened the door and said with a soft hush, "Try to get in there, just a little bit," guiding him inside despite his quiet objections. He hissed at the moment he sat; his pain was clear. Yet he offered no complaints, no words.

The car ride was heavy with silence. Her breaths came shallow, broken only by the occasional grunt or labored exhale from Malakhov.

Tears clung to her lashes.

When they arrived at the manor she hurried around him, her hands trying to wrench open the door for him to get out. Again, he refused.

"I told you I'm fine, Allison!"

"No, you're not!" she snapped, voice sharp with the pressure frying her inside. "Stop pretending you're made of stone!"

He paused then, halfway out of the car, and looked at her. Really looked. "You're not the one who got the shit beat out of them," he said quietly. "Don't make this harder than it is."

"It *is* hard," she whispered. "Watching you take those hits for me, it was unbearable, Dmitri. And now you won't even let me... just let me take care of you, *please.*"

Something in her voice cracked him open. A nod was barely given, and he followed her inside without another word.

In the warmth of their home, she led him to the couch and helped him lie down very carefully. The moment he hit the cushions, the tension gripping his body finally released, pain trumping pride.

She then disappeared for a while, coming back with ice and painkillers and antiseptic and towels.

"I'm sorry," she whispered, kneeling by him, dabbing blood from his brow. "I should have done something. I should have stopped it—"

"You did the only thing you could," he said, his voice low and rough. "You stayed still. That kept him from making it worse."

Her hands were shaking now as she cleaned the gash on his eyebrow. "Now you're defending him?"

"I'm saying I know the rules of this world," he said, looking at her. "And I chose that beating. Because it meant you didn't have to lift your hand against someone you loved once."

She flinched. "I don't love him."

"I know." His hand reached out, and with his knuckle, he touched her cheek. "But there was a price to pay when you chose not to hurt him."

Her hands slipped from the towel, and she curled into his side, careful not to press too hard against his battered ribs. There was a hitch in her breath. "I hate that this is our world now."

"I do too," he whispered. "But we're in it together. That's the only way I can keep going."

Allison pressed a kiss to his temple and whispered, "I'll fix this. I don't know how yet, but I will."

He didn't respond.

He just let her hold him, bruised, bloodied, but not broken.

Not yet.

* * *

For the next several days, silence reigned over solemn devotion. Allison scarcely left Malakhov's side, fulfilling every whim with care. She kept the lights dim, conversational tones light, rubbing ice to his bruises and reapplied his own kind of healing salve to his split lip. The swelling on his face began fading slowly-away from shades of purple and red to sickly yellow that would vanish altogether; his lips remained scabbed and tender, but that was largely behind them. With every passing day and with his strength slowly returning, a spark of tranquility rose in her heart, although with every increment of that peace, guilt gnawed at her whenever he winced or when he caught her staring at him for just a fraction too long. Healing was her rhythm; it was her penance and her sanctuary.

In their kitchen, the morning light poured in through tall windows, creating soft rays over the plush carpet. It was a silence only interrupted by the clink of porcelain as Allison filled a cup with coffee. Her fingers trembled while bringing it up to her lips, the warmth inside soothing her. These past few days had been long and filled with tension and unease, yet finally, in the silent morning, Allison let herself breathe for a moment.

The stillness was severed suddenly by the entrance of Malakhov into the room. Even in some bland clothing, the man wearing it carried far more weight in his aura of power and experience than his clothes ever could.

"Morning," he greeted warmly, even with a hoarser rasp which hinted it was not quite healed. His lip was scabbed still, and the one eye whose bruise was still visible was shifting from violet to yellow. But dull bruises and scars did nothing to dim his infamous cocky glint in his stare as it locked with hers. "Sleep well?"

Allison smiled softly, the tightness in her chest refusing to release its grip. It wasn't about sleep, it hadn't been for days. It was that base hum of change that ran beneath her, the realization that her body might not quite belong to her anymore. "I did, for the most part," she replied, setting the coffee mug down on the table with care. "Though I feel... different."

Malakhov arched a brow, leaning against the edge of the table as if pretending he wasn't still favoring his ribs. "Different how? Emotionally unstable, murderous rage, general disgust with my face, all understandable reactions."

The corner of her mouth lifted, "Well, when you put it that way..." when a sharp pang of nausea twitched in her gut. The smile faded as the color drained from her face, and in instinctive reaction, she touched her stomach. Her surroundings seemed to have begun shifting.

Malakhov was at her side in seconds, despite the stiffness in his movements. "Allison." His hand hovered over her back, careful not to press too hard. "Sit. Hey, hey—breathe."

She slumped into the chair, gripping the edge of the table as she rode the wave of nausea. "I—I'm okay. I just..."

"You're not okay," he muttered, crouching despite the obvious discomfort. She could see the tight pull in his jaw as he lowered himself down, the way his ribs clearly still ached beneath the surface. "You've been like this the last few days. Don't think I haven't noticed."

"I've also noticed you still wince every time you sneeze," she shot back, breathless but trying for levity.

"Yes, well, some of us don't recover overnight. You should try getting the shit kicked out of you for your wife's moral crisis sometime," he said dryly, eyes searching hers with open worry. "It builds character."

A faint smile tugged at her lips despite the nausea rolling in her stomach. "You're impossible."

"You love it." he said with a smirk, wiping a damp strand of hair from her face. "Seriously though, if you keep going pale like that, I'm calling the doctor. Or Grigori, and letting him practice suturing for fun."

She gave him a withering look. "I'd rather vomit every day for a year."

"Then we're in agreement. Now tell me the truth, how long have you been feeling like this?"

Allison glanced away, heart thudding now for a whole different reason. Something *was* off. Something she hadn't yet put into words.

"I don't know," she whispered. "But I think... it started a few weeks ago."

Malakhov straightened slowly, pain flashing across his features, but he masked it quickly. "Alright," he said. "We'll figure it out. Together. And if whatever it is hurts you—"

"You'll break its kneecaps?" she offered, eyebrows raised.

"At minimum."

She smiled, but with her fingers curling against the edge of the table. Nauseating feelings were fading quickly, but that sense of something not quite right remained.

She hesitated as her fingers still held loosely the cooling coffee mug. "Probably just stress," she concluded, those words almost not sounding convincing to her own ears.

Malakhov tilted his head, unimpressed. "Stress doesn't usually make you gag at the smell of toast."

"It was burnt," she argued weakly.

He raised an eyebrow. "So was your excuse yesterday. And the day before that. And the day before that when I merely mentioned bacon."

She opened her mouth to retort but closed it again, deflated. "Okay, fine. It's been weird. I've felt off."

Malakhov's teasing eased into something softer. He leaned forward, still stiff, still bruised, and reached for her hand. His fingers curled around hers, rough and warm. "Allison," he said gently, almost carefully, "Nausea, is a common symptom of pregnancy."

His words landed with a sudden, sharp shock.

She parted her lips in stunned silence. "What?" she said, blinking at him, and then the full weight fell on her; She gasped as her brain went into overdrive-the dizziness, the nausea, the mood swings, and that odd feeling that she wasn't quite herself.

Her hand flew to her mouth. "*Oh my God.*"

Malakhov gave her a look that was half affection, half smug bastard. "You want me to say it? Or would you like to run and pee on a stick first?"

"Shut up," she muttered, already standing. She turned on her heel and disappeared into the bathroom, muttering, "If I'm pregnant, I swear you owe me a foot massage everyday for the next nine months."

"I already do. You're *terrifying* when hormonal," he called after her, grinning faintly despite the stiffness in his ribs.

The door shut, and a few tense, silent minutes passed. Malakhov looked downward; his smile slowly disappeared into something vulnerable and unreadable. His hands unclenched and clenched.

And then—finally—the door gave out a creak.

Allison stepped out, her face pale and eyes wide with unshed tears. She held the test in one hand like it might combust. She didn't speak at first, just looked at him, stunned. Then she gave the faintest of nods.

He didn't move right away, afraid he might misread it.

"You're sure?" he asked, voice low.

She sank onto the couch beside him and handed him the test. "Well, unless this is some kind of sick practical joke, yeah. I'm pregnant."

For a second, he said nothing. Then—

"Well," Malakhov said slowly, holding up the test like a prized artifact, "I've done a lot of questionable things in my life, but I gotta say... this might be my greatest achievement."

"Seriously?" she groaned, swatting at him halfheartedly.

"Hey," he said with a crooked grin, "I've taken hits from Gordeev, survived a Bratva power struggle, and now you're telling me I knocked up my war wife? *Iconic*."

Allison shook her head and finally laughed, a watery, overwhelmed sound. "You're the worst."

"I'm *your* worst," he said, bumping his shoulder gently against hers, careful of his injuries. "And now, apparently, someone's future *dad*."

Breathing out in a shaky exhale, she lay her head on his shoulder while her fingers glided aimlessly over her abdomen. "What the hell are we going to do?"

We are going to be brilliant," murmured Malakhov, his voice a whisper, but so deeply assured. "Terrifyingly, chaotic... but brilliant."

She paused, her eyes finding his. "Dmitri... What does this mean?"

Malakhov's eyes grew tender, and for a brief instance, in that stark moment heavy with tension, a glimmer of what seemed like gentleness flashed before Allison. "I've never been one to plan for the future, Allison. But the thought of you carrying our child..." He paused, and the rush of emotion made Allison's heart swell. "This is the most beautiful thing you could have ever given me."

His words came as a shock to her. He was not spewing some generic hollow line of detachment, but promising her, vowing himself to their future.

A shadow of worry then flickered in his gaze. "But this world... this empire we live in, bringing a child into it, under the shadow of Radimir, it's dangerous. I want to protect you, I want to protect our child, but..." He stopped, a lump forming in his throat. "I don't know what this will mean for you, for us."

Allison grasped his hand, squeezing it in a reassuring grip. "We'll figure out together," her voice held steady despite the whirlwind of uncertainty inside quietly building up. "I am scared but not about what's happening. What scares me is what this means for us. But we'll face it together."

The corner of Malakhov's lips twitched into that smile-web that was almost bitter. "Together," he echoed gently. Then he dipped across, laying a barely-there kiss on her lips, soaking the occasion with promises left dangling in the air.

They both were aware of the road of obstacles before them. Yet they were both assured that their child would be raised in a household of love, despite the world burning beyond their front door.

Twenty Five

The Heir's Burden

The following weeks were a strange mix of fading bruises and returning routines. Malakhov healed quickly, though Allison often caught him clenching his teeth when he thought she wasn't watching. The swelling subsided, leaving a dark bruise beneath his eye and a scab on his lip, a lasting reminder of the cost of defiance. Soon enough, he slipped back into that impossible mix of wit and charm, making her laugh when she least expected it, sneaking up behind her to kiss her neck while she stirred her coffee.

Headquarters returned to its usual rhythm too. They attended meetings, submitted reports, and carried out their duties. If Radimir held any resentment over her refusal, he concealed it well. That was one mercy of working under him, punishment was swift and brutal, but once dealt, it was forgotten. He moved on, offering no grudges or cold shoulders, only more commands and games of power. Punishment came hard and fast, but when it was over, it was truly over. It made it easier to breathe again. Slightly.

At home, things were... surprisingly good. Almost too good, like the quiet before a storm. Quietly, privately, she and Malakhov began preparing for what was coming. She'd started reading again, books on pregnancy, birth, survival with first time fathers. He'd mutter complaints when he found them on the kitchen counter, but more than once she'd woken in the night to see him sitting there in the lamplight, thumbing through a chapter with that pinched look of concentration he'd never admit to.

"So," he said one evening, stretching out on the couch with one arm draped over her growing waistline, "when exactly are we going to tell the mob boss and his equally ruthless followers that we're adding a baby to the organizational chart?"

Allison looked up from the list she was making—At the top, she'd scrawled '*baby names that don't sound like we're raising a future warlord*' and arched an eyebrow. "When the child is old enough to defend itself?"

"Reasonable," he said with a nod. "Maybe after its first hit job."

"Oh, perfect. 'Congratulations, little one. Here's your first dagger. Try not to get any blood on your onesie.'"

He smirked. "Do you think Radimir will be pleased or furious?"

"That depends," she said, smirking back. "If it's a boy, he'll probably start drawing up recruitment papers. If it's a girl, he'll just assign her to intelligence and teach her how to poison diplomats before kindergarten."

Malakhov gave a low laugh and kissed her temple. "Either way, they'll be terrifying. Like her mother."

"Or stubborn like their father," Allison muttered, the smile still on her lips. They did not have all the answers yet-far from it-but for now, it was just them and a secret growing stronger by the day. And that, somehow, was enough.

* * *

With ninety minutes to go before Allison and Malakhov would stroll hand in hand through headquarters' corridors, reality settled in, though so much about their future remained unknown.

"I reckon it is time to tell him," Malakhov said softly, the pitch and tone of voice steady despite the awful weight. "Radimir will sooner or later find out, and we can't go on hiding it."

Allison nodded, her chest feeling tight by the utter thought of it. To tell Radimir would be to put at risk everything-the life they were trying to build together, the future of their child. But there was no way around it anymore.

Upon entering, they were ushered into the office, where a peculiar feeling of tension was always felt. Sitting at his desk with that infamous gaze, those shimmering silver eyes of his gave a darkly amused appraisal to their entry.

"Ah, Allison, Dmitri," he cooed, smooth as ever. "What brings you before me today?"

He stepped forward, his posture solidified but those eyes betraying a hint of nervousness. "Sir, Allison and I have come to you with... *personal* news."

Radimir's eyes sharpened. 'Personal news?' His voice was edged with curiosity. "Speak then."

Allison swallowed hard. She looked at the floor but Malakhov squeezed her hand to keep her grounded. "Allison and I are expecting a child."

There was a long pause. For a moment Radimir did not speak. He swept his eyes over both of them, acknowledging the gravity of their words. Finally, he looked at Malakhov and asked, "Why didn't you tell me sooner?"

Allison stood tall, though she felt the pressure of his eyes. "It was... difficult to speak of, Sir."

Radimir's smile was sharp, but there was a hint of approval in it. "There is no shame in it. On the contrary, it's a sign of strength. The bloodline I've created with you and Dmitri will only strengthen our future."

Malakhov's chest swelled at Radimir's words. "Yes, Sir. We will raise this child to be part of your vision."

Allison stood a little straighter at Radimir's words. She had made her choice, and now the future was inevitable.

Radimir leaned back in his chair, a strange gleam in his eye. "Very well. I believe this union is stronger than I thought. The child will be a symbol of the future, the future of this bloodline. The legacy will continue."

Allison was surprised at how calm Radimir seemed about the entire situation. There was no anger surrounding it; it could have been manipulation, though she had expected scorn. No, it was as if he was finally getting what he had so wanted all along, a legitimate heir born from the union he made.

"Perhaps it's time I teach you both the true power of family," added Radimir with a soft chuckle. "This heir of yours... will be a force to be reckoned with."

A shiver ran down Allison's spine, extinguishing any flicker of resistance as his words echoed in her mind.

"You will bring your child into this world, and they will play an important part in our future."

The words hung in the air. Allison had just been marked by him, but now she had a greater responsibility, one that went beyond simple survival. She had become a key figure in Radimir's plans, and with that came power, a different kind of power, one she had never imagined.

* * *

The tension between loyalty to Radimir and her moral conflict was increasing. Her pregnancy was a constant reminder of the life growing inside her and the alternate futures she and Malakhov now faced.

But each day, her bodily discomfort demanded her attention. Each day gave new trials. She had come through with episodes of nausea, unpredictable and relentless; her tiredness was beyond comparison now. Not that it was any more the stress of the mission; her body was just going through the process while she felt helpless against it.

As the sun dipped below the horizon, Allison sat quiet in their shared space, somewhat weary and lost in the weight of her own decisions. She rubbed her abdomen, feeling a strange articulation of definite love and fear that now consumed her.

Malakhov had walked quietly in with a pierced eye, surveying the scene and closing the door behind him softly. Crossing to Allison's spot, his expression had become fraught with concern.

"You're still not resting enough, Allison," Malakhov said softly but seriously, his steps betraying concern as he moved toward her. He knelt beside her and brushed the hair from her forehead. "I told you to take it easy. You're pushing yourself too much."

Almost smiling, Allison's smile didn't quite reach her eyes. "I'm fine, Dmitri. It's just... it's just a lot."

Her voice wavered, and for the first time, Malakhov saw something in her gaze he'd never seen there before: doubt, raw and unguarded. He took her hands, the touch warm and reassuring, almost a little tense, as if he was battling some visible fear.

"You don't have to hide it from me," Malakhov said softly but with some insistence, "I can see it in your eyes. You're worried. And I'm worried too."

A lump built in Allison's throat, the weight of the situation pressing painfully on her chest. The weight of their actions, this regime, the pregnancy—it was too much for her. The weight was suddenly taking a toll on her, making her feel weak.

"I'm just... I'm scared," Allison said in a hoarse whisper. She looked at Malakhov stirred with a spark of emotion. "I'm scared of what happens next. I'm scared for this baby... I'm scared for us."

Malakhov's face softened, his hand resting gently on her abdomen, just above where the child inside her was growing. Something fierce and tender flickering across his face as he felt the tiny movement beneath his palm.

"I won't lie, Allison, I'm scared too," he said quietly, his voice more uncertain than she was used to. "I can keep you safe here, from everything outside. But what's going on inside you... I can't do anything about that. And that part really scares me."

His words hung there, honest in a way that left them both exposed. A faint flush climbed his cheeks, and his jaw tightened like he was embarrassed to have said so much. Her chest tightened at the sight. He wasn't just some cold Bratva enforcer. He was a man standing bare before her, armor cracked.

She reached up and cupped his warm cheek, steadying them both in the hush that followed. There was something endearingly human in how rattled he looked, and it only made him more beautiful to her. Malakhov, usually so composed, was coming undone just imagining her hurting.

Allison had never allowed herself to believe he could feel this deeply for her. People liked to say Malakhov was too hard-edged, too closed-off to ever feel love. Watching him now, she knew how wrong they were. Watching the storm behind his eyes, she understood. He was already hers. And she, even in her moments of doubt, had become a shadow of him. Not lost, but marked. *Bound.*

Then, she put all her fingers down, trembling as they traced the back of his hand, "We will make it through... together."

"I will make that promise," he whispered back quietly, a faint smile touching his lips, and tenderness softened his eyes. His words were unwavering with the lingering concern in his heart, "I will protect you and this child with all my strength, even if it costs me my very life. You have my word."

In that moment, she knew they weren't just two people caught in something bigger than them. They were a family now—whether they were ready or not.

* * *

Time moved on, quietly shifting everything in its path.

By the time her belly began to round beneath her fitted coats, there was no more hiding the truth, Allison was pregnant, and everyone at Headquarters knew. At first, there had been whispers. Sideways glances. A few knowing smirks exchanged during meetings. But it didn't take long for Radimir to make it official, announcing during one of the late evening strategy councils that Malakhov and Allison were expecting a child.

Radimir's voice was all silk over steel when he spoke, "A future heir of the Bratva. Raised in strength. In loyalty. In power."

The room had gone quiet at first. Then came the scattered congratulations, some genuine, others clearly more performative. Grigori Gordeev had offered a smile too wide to be real and muttered something about how *"they breed them loyal now."* Malakhov didn't flinch, but his jaw had tensed just enough for Allison to notice. She squeezed his hand under the table in warning.

After that, her presence in the room carried new weight. Once seen as Malakhov's clever partner, his cool-headed anchor, she was now also the vessel for a future. Some spoke to her with deference, a strange reverence in their tones, as if carrying a child had elevated her. Others seemed threatened by it, unsettled by what her growing stomach meant for the Bratva's hierarchy.

"You're glowing," one of the guards, Anna, said during a passing moment in the hallway. "Or maybe it's just the threat of raising the Boss's grand-heir that has everyone behaving like you're royalty."

Allison snorted. "Trust me, it's mostly just morning sickness and back pain."

"You say that now," Anna grinned. "But once it's born, they'll probably start calling them *little Radimir.*"

"God help us all."

At home, life retained a strange kind of peace. Allison spent more time tucked in the warm corners of their manor, organizing, preparing. Malakhov hovered, not too close, but never far. She would catch him watching her sometimes when he thought she was not looking. His gaze would wander across the swell of her belly, his expression caught somewhere between awe and disbelief.

"You alright?" she asked one night as they lay in bed, with firelight flickering across the walls.

Malakhov's hand rested gently on her belly as a small kick came from below it. "I just... I never thought I'd have something like this," he murmured.

She looked at him, really looked at him, and reached out to trail her fingers through his hair. "You're going to be a great father."

He huffed a skeptical sound. "You say that now. Wait until they start asking questions about how we met."

"Your father kidnapped me and threatened my best friends lives in front of me. It was *very* romantic."

"Charming bedtime story."

But the lightness in their home didn't always extend to the compound.

The more visibly pregnant she became, the more layered the politics grew. Some of the Bratva's senior members began to mutter about succession, about what it would mean for a child to be born into such a blood-soaked world. Whispers circled like vultures, some reverent, some mocking. In the eyes of a few, Allison had become a symbol of strength, a mother to the next generation. To others, she was just a woman out of place in a man's game, an unpredictable variable.

During one particularly tense meeting in the war room, the conversation had turned to training new recruits. The talk was brisk, tactical, but it veered suddenly when Boris Yurev, a grizzled man with more scars than skin, leaned forward with a crooked grin and said, "Hope you're teaching that kid to shoot while it's still in the womb."

"I'm waiting for them to develop proper trigger discipline," Malakhov replied smoothly, not looking up from the map spread before him. A few of the younger men laughed under their breath.

Gordeev, lounging at the far end of the table like a dog waiting for scraps, didn't smile. "Heir or not," he muttered, swirling the drink in his glass, "the little brat has to earn their place. Blood doesn't guarantee loyalty."

"No," Allison said calmly, her gaze steady, "but raising them right might."

Her voice came out steady and cold, slicing through the muttering like a sudden wind. The room shifted. A few heads turned, some toward Gordeev, others away. But Gordeev only smirked, leaning back and stretching his legs out with arrogant ease.

"You know," he drawled, his eyes lingering on her stomach a beat too long, "after that beating Malakhov took, I'm honestly surprised he was firing anything but blanks."

The room went silent.

Malakhov lifted his eyes slowly, his expression unreadable. "You seem awfully obsessed with what goes on in my bedroom," he said coolly. "Jealousy's a poor color on you, Gordeev. Doesn't pair well with impotence."

Several men coughed, trying to mask their reactions. One barked a short laugh before catching himself.

Gordeev's smirk faltered, his jaw tightening. "Just saying, Boss better hope your heir isn't as soft as you've gotten."

Malakhov stood slowly, rolling his shoulders as though bored. "I'm still standing, aren't I? Even after I took a beating from you, what does that say about *you* exactly?" He turned toward Radimir, who had been silently watching the exchange with his usual amused detachment. "Maybe next time, we let Gordeev volunteer to take the hits. Let's see if he's still talking once his ribs are splintered."

"I like my ribs intact," Gordeev muttered, but he looked away first.

Radimir's lips curved faintly. "Enough. The child will be born into strength, one way or another. Let's move on."

Yet, when the meeting resumed, Allison caught Malakhov's hand under the table and gave it a squeeze; once. He didn't look at her, but fingers curled around hers in silent reassurance.

They didn't need to defend their child. Not to these men.

But they would.

Every damn time.

Radimir, for his part, seemed to enjoy the slow upheaval. His gaze often flicked between her and Malakhov with amusement, as if he were watching the chessboard shift under his command. He rarely offered much input, though he had once said, "It will be interesting to see which side of the child rises first. Yours... or mine."

Those words echoed in her ears long after he left the room.

* * *

By the seventh month, Allison was exhausted in ways she hadn't even known were possible. Her body ached, her mind was stretched thin, and yet she felt sharper than ever. Every meeting became a performance, every interaction an assessment. But through it all, Malakhov remained constant, stoic, and hers.

One evening, curled on the sofa with a blanket and one of the baby's potential names scribbled on a notepad, she looked over at him and asked, "Do you think they'll respect our kid?"

Malakhov didn't look up from the dossier he was reviewing. "Doesn't matter."

"Why?"

"Because we'll teach them not to care."

She smiled, resting her head against his shoulder. For now, that was enough.

They were still here. Still together. And soon, it wouldn't be just them against the world anymore.

And the Bratva would have no idea what was coming.

Twenty Six

No Room for Regrets

The morning began like many others, with steel gray skies, thick silences in the air, and a long-winded briefing at headquarters. Malakhov had been beside her for the entire time, his hand occasionally grazing hers as if to remind her that he was still there. Radimir rattled off updates, issued clipped orders, and slipped in those soft, poisonous warnings he delivered with a smile, the kind everyone obeyed, whether they liked it or not.

After the meeting, Radimir assigned Malakhov to lead a city patrol detail. It wasn't unusual, standard rotations, keeping up appearances of control and presence, but Allison could see the way Malakhov's jaw tensed. He didn't want to leave her alone.

"I'll be back before dinner," he murmured as he helped her slip her coat on. "Don't get into trouble while I'm gone."

She raised a brow. "You make it sound like that's a daily hobby."

He smirked, pressing a kiss to her temple. "With you, it might be."

They shared a long look, one that held unspoken words and quiet worry. Then he left, and she stood in the shadow of the war room doors, her thoughts already drifting somewhere else.

She went past the heavy double doors, through the lower wings, toward the restricted levels of headquarters. The sharp scent of disinfectant and iron hung in the air, and the cold seemed to press against her skin, muffling every sound. Fewer guards, fewer voices.

She had asked days ago, half-heartedly, to be granted access to the prisoners. She hadn't really expected the permission to come through. But now, standing at the threshold of the cell block, her request had been granted.

Maybe Radimir wanted to see what she would do.

Maybe he already knew.

Either way, she was here now.

Allison found herself standing before the door to the prisoner cells. This bit of distance she could already feel, setting a wall of separation between them. The door was pushed wide open and the biting look from Daniel greeted her. He was sitting on the floor with his arms shackled, face pale, roughened, and tired.

Seeing him, the man she'd once called a brother, felt like looking into a cracked mirror that reflected everything she'd lost.

"Allison," Daniel said sharply, his voice cracking as it echoed through the stone cell. His wrists, bruised from the iron restraints, twitched as if the pain were secondary to the weight of her presence. "You're really here, aren't you? After everything... after everything we've been through, you've chosen to side with him?"

His eyes were raw, not just with disbelief at seeing her, but at what she'd become.

A traitor.

A Bratva wife.

His friend turned stranger.

And Allison sucked in a great breath, but she forced herself to stare into his eyes. She had played this out thousands of ways in her mind of how this moment would unfurl, mainly being screamed at and maybe even having him spit in her face. Nothing had prepared her for the quiet devastation she heard in his voice.

"I didn't choose this, Daniel. I never wanted to be part of his world, but here I am. And I can't do anything about it now."

He stepped forward, the chains clanking, and something old and bitter flickered in his eyes. "That's a damn convenient way to say you sold your soul." He spat the words like venom. "You talk like you're a victim, but you're not. You've made your choices—*willingly*. You let them use you. Let him put a ring on your finger. Let him—" he stopped himself, his jaw tightening. "You're one of them now. Just another weapon in Radimir's war."

Allison's fists clenched at her sides, but she didn't rise to the bait. "I'm doing what I have to. For *my* family."

"Your family?" he snapped. "You mean the man who beats people for sport? The one who chained you to a world of blood and silence? *That's* your family now?"

Her voice caught, cracking the next time she spoke. "It—It's not that way. You think he is just a monster. You don't know what I have seen, what he has done for me. He is—" She stopped abruptly to blink away a sudden flood of tears. "He is not what you think he is."

Daniel laughed bitterly. "Oh, Allie. You used to be the smartest person I knew. Now listen to you. Defending a man who murders and tortures like it's a sport. And what, you think having his child changes who he is?"

She flinched. The words hit hard, not because they weren't cruel, but because they weren't entirely wrong.

"I know what this world is," she said quietly. "But I also know I'm not powerless in it. I've made choices I hate, Daniel. Choices I'll never stop regretting. But I've tried to make good out of them. "I'm not proud of where I am, but I'm trying to simply survive and protect something innocent now," she said.

His eyes flicked from hers to her stomach, the swell visible under her coat.Something shifted in his expression, his anger melting into something quieter, sadder. "Do you really think that bringing a child into this big mess is protecting it?" he whispered. "It's like swaddling a baby in razor wire and pretending it's safe."

Allison felt a tightening around her throat, but she stood her ground. "It's the only life we have, Daniel. And I'll fight to make it better, even if you never understand why."

His voice went low, ragged, as if the words were tearing something out of him. "I looked up to you. Even after everything. I kept thinking, *She'll come back to herself. She'll remember who she is,* But I don't see her anymore. Just the mask you're wearing."

Allison felt something break inside her. "I *never* stopped being me," she whispered. "But I can't keep apologizing for surviving. For trying to live in a world that broke us both."

For a long moment, Daniel said nothing. The silence sat heavy between them, years of friendship cracking under the weight of two lives pulled too far apart.

"I hope that you are," he finally replied. "I hope that child never finds out what it is like to look into someone's eyes and no longer see recognition there."

He turned his back on her.

And she wandered off, her vision swimming, her heart crushed into a thousand pieces, unsure whether she could ever put either back together again.

The walk to Rob's cell grew heavier with every step. This would be harder still, she knew. Rob had always been her closest friend, her confidante, and now he was simply a prisoner thanks to her decisions. She pushed open the door to his cell, and those eyes met hers immediately.

"Allison," said Rob, his voice hoarse from disuse, he rose unsteadily to his feet. The chains on his wrists clinking with hollow finality. "You're really here."

There was so much in that sentence, the relief, the disbelief, the anger, and the heartbreak, trying to find its place.

She crossed into the cell as if she were crossing some invisible line between past and present. Her gaze locked on him, on the familiar contours of a face now marred by imprisonment and sorrow. The sting of tears formed in her eyes before they slipped down. "I had to see you, Rob," she whispered hoarsely. "I had to explain."

But before she could say more, his eyes dropped from her face, and stopped.

On her stomach.

His breath hitched. His mouth parted, but no sound came. Just the sound of those goddamn chains as he took an unconscious step forward, stunned.

"You..." His voice began failing. "You're... *you're pregnant...*"

She nodded slowly. "Yes."

The word hung there, so delicate it felt like it might splinter if she breathed wrong.

For a long while, Rob was silent. He started shaking his head, trying to block out the unpleasant sight confronting him.

"So this means it's over?" His voice was low and trembling. "You've chosen him."

Allison flinched. "Rob..."

"You're carrying *his* child." There was no accusation in his tone, just devastation. "I thought... after everything... I thought I had a chance to reach you. That—that my letter would mean something."

He looked at her now with eyes glassy and wide. "I meant every damn word, Allison. When I said I loved you—I wasn't just trying to pull you back. I've *always* loved you. Since we were kids. When you climbed that rusted train car and dared me to jump. When you stood between me— "

Her chest ached. It sounded like he'd been holding those words back for years, and now they were breaking him open.

"I read the letter," she whispered, trembling.

"And did it matter?" he asked, almost a whisper now. "Did *any* of it matter?"

"It did," she said. "It *does.* But Rob..." Her hand moved gently to her stomach. "This baby... I didn't plan this. I didn't expect this. But it's mine. And Malakhov's. And he's..." she trailed off, struggling to find words that wouldn't sound like betrayal.

Rob's laugh was hollow. "Don't tell me he's *good* to you. Don't stand here and tell me that the man who burned towns and slit throats is now your savior."

"He's *not* a saint," Allison said sharply. "But he has stood between me and Radimir more than once. He took the beating that was meant for *you*. He's... he's not what you think."

"He's not *you*," Rob choked. "You were supposed to *never* be one of them. That was the one thing I believed in. That no matter how bad things got, Allison would fight her way out. Not kneel to them. Not *fall in love with them.*"

"I didn't kneel," she said, quietly but firmly. "And I didn't fall in love with a monster. I fell in love with the man who kept me alive when I wanted to disappear. Who held me while I bled and never asked for anything in return."

"And now he gets everything," Rob said bitterly. "He gets the life. The child. *You.*"

She looked at him, really looked, and saw not the friend she'd loved like a brother, but someone she could never reach again. A life that could no longer touch hers.

"I'll never stop caring for you," she whispered. "But I can't go back. I won't."

Rob turned his face away, his shoulders stiff and trembling. "Then go. Go be with your Bratva husband. Raise your warlord baby. Just... don't come back again, not unless you're ready to remember who you used to be."

Her lip trembled. "I remember. *Everyday.*"

But he wouldn't look at her.

She left feeling as if she'd shed part of herself she could never recover.

* * *

Later that night, Allison was all alone in her home, dimly lit by a flicker of a lamp. Her thoughts wouldn't stop, no matter how hard she tried to shove them aside. The things they'd said stuck to her skin, bitter and impossible to scrub away. Her chest felt heavy with everything left unsaid.

The door creaked open, and Malakhov came in.

His usual sharp presence was subdued, shoulders tense, jaw tight. Even from across the room, she could see the damage, bruising mottling his arms, a dark bloom forming beneath one eye, and a cruel split carving through his bottom lip.

Allison stood quickly, alarm etched across her face. "Dmitri..." she breathed, reaching for him. "What happened?"

With a shake of the head, he waved away any concern and moved over to the couch to collapse beside her with a muted wince. "Radimir really does have his special way of expressing displeasure, as I was properly reminded of my place," he said with a sort of hoarse sarcasm.

She touched his forearm carefully, avoiding the worst of the bruises. "I...sorry," she whispered. "I didn't want you to be punished. I never want to see you in pain."

He sighed and turned toward her, clasping her hand. "Pain I can handle, but your sorrow," he said, "it's the thing that destroys me, *little lion*."

Allison's lips trembled as she fought to keep her voice from breaking. "I saw them today... Daniel and Rob. It was... hard. Rob... he told me he loved me."

There was a beat of silence. Then Malakhov's head snapped toward her, his brows arching with a sharpness that cut through his exhaustion. "He *what*?"

She blinked, startled by the tone. "He said he's always loved me. That he wrote that letter with every intention of—"

Malakhov made a sound low in his throat, like a growl through gritted teeth. "Did he *touch* you?"

Allison raised an amused brow. "No."

"Did he try?" he pressed.

"No," she repeated, gently, though a smirk tugged at the corner of her mouth. "You planning to hunt him down from his cell if he had?"

"I'm just trying to decide if it would be worth a second punishment round," Malakhov muttered, already visibly brooding.

She leaned in and kissed the unbruised side of his cheek. "You're ridiculous."

"And territorial," he added, as if it were a badge of honor. "*Very* territorial. I don't share, especially not with men who used to braid your hair and stare at you like puppies."

Allison rolled her eyes but chuckled. "For the record, he never braided my hair."

"Well, that's even worse," Malakhov snapped. "All that yearning and no braids? What a waste."

She laughed then, more genuinely this time, and squeezed his hand. "It's not *his* baby I'm carrying, Dmitri."

That seemed to settle something in him. His bruised face softened, and a slow, wicked smile spread across his lips. "Damn right it's not. I'm the only man in this bloodstained empire with proof that I've won the war."

Allison raised a brow. "So I'm a trophy now?"

"You're the prize," he said with a shrug. "The throne, the kingdom, the dragon's hoard. And if anyone touches you again, I'll remove their hands. *Politely*. With an axe."

Despite everything, she laughed again, resting her head against his shoulder. "You're lucky I find you charming even when you're a violent, jealous bastard."

"And you," he murmured, kissing the top of her head, "are lucky I love you even when you talk to a man who's in love with you in a prison cell."

"Jealousy looks very fetching on you," she teased, reaching up to trace the uninjured corner of his mouth.

"You should see me in full-blown possessive rage," he muttered. "It's practically romantic."

They sat in silence for a while after that, their laughter faded, replaced by a hush that felt steadier than words. And in that quiet, when the laughter faded, they held onto each other like it was the only thing in their world still real.

Twenty Seven

The Edge of Treason

Allison stood still in front of the full-length mirror, eyes intent upon the mark scorched onto her arm. She traced the jagged lines, her stomach clenching tighter with every pass of her fingertips. She had once been so sure of what was right, but now she teetered on the edge of something she couldn't name, questioning everything she had ever known. Every choice, every decision she had ever made, had led her down this path, yet each of them felt like an erosion of the very person she had been.

Her mind wandered back to the last meeting, one she had sat through just last night. Word had come through that the resistance, *or what was left of it*, was scrambling to form a plan to get her out. To save her. She had never been one to shy away from danger, but the weight of what she had become hung heavy in the air. They did not know that Daniel and Rob were still alive. Radimir had wanted them to believe they were dead, a cruel trick to break their spirit, and made her chest tighten with an ache she couldn't quite name.

Could the resistance even want her back? Could she truly betray everything she had worked for? The resistance, her old life, her old friends, all of that now seemed embarrassingly far off, so far out of reach—and there was Malakhov standing at her side, so quietly that it was at once comforting but also a stark reminder of just how thoroughly she had been pulled into this life with him. She knew what he had sacrificed for her; she knew how far he had gone to protect her, and the thought tore at her soul. Malakhov was tortured— *tortured* because of her. It was a weight she could barely handle, it felt like every step betrayed everything she'd once sworn to protect.

Yet it was a truth that could not be contended with. Radimir's hold on her had seeped into her very being, and despite the fight within her, there were moments when it felt like a losing battle. Still, a part of her resisted. That little part inside her still belonged to the old Allison Murphy—whose heart never gave up on friends and on fighting the darkness.

Her gaze drifted to Malakhov, who was watching from the doorway, silent but solid as ever. He didn't say a word, but she could feel the quiet promise in the way he looked at her—he wasn't going anywhere. He had never asked her to choose. He had never demanded she make a decision between him and her old life. He had simply stayed by her side. Allison had never fully acknowledged how much that meant, but now, in this moment, she realized just how much it had anchored her in the chaos.

A week earlier, Allison had received an anonymous letter, smuggled into their estate beneath layers of false files, marked with a symbol she hadn't seen in months. The resistance. Her old life. The letter had been brief but unmistakable; they were offering her a way out. A plan to disappear. To be free.

But before she could act on it, Radimir had intercepted it. He summoned her, the letter laid out before him like evidence on a courtroom table. His smile had been tight, his voice falsely pleasant. "You'll respond," he said calmly. "And you'll tell them no. That you're one of us now. *Entirely.*"

And so, she made a decision, a lie she'd sell Radimir without hesitation. She would tell him she had written back, had refused the offer, that she was loyal to him and his cause. *Completely aligned*. That she'd turned her back on the world she came from. But the truth was tangled deeper than words. Deep down, Allison couldn't let go of her old life, her old friends. That part of her still breathed, quietly, stubbornly.

Allison's fingers brushed over the sigil etched into her skin, the one that bound her to Radimir. The connection was permanent like a phantom heartbeat. It felt like a leash now, one she hadn't asked for. One she didn't know how to break. She had to cut herself off from Radimir for good. But how?

"Dmitri," she uttered softly, her voice thick with the pressure of what she was about to ask. "Do you trust me?"

He was leaning one arm upon the edge of the table, sleeves casually rolled-up. On hearing her words, he tilted his head and raised one brow with curiosity mingled with amusement. "With my life," he answered without hesitation, a faint smirk playing upon his lips. "Though, when you start conversations like that, I usually end up shot at or bleeding."

She gave him a look, somewhere between fond and exasperated. "I'm serious."

"I know," he said, standing up straighter. The smirk faded, and the familiar steel settled behind his eyes. "What are you planning?"

Allison inhaled sharply, her heart hammering against her ribs. "I have to get Rob and Daniel out."

Dmitri's eyes flickered, narrowing slightly. "That's... *bold*." His voice was neutral, but she could already feel the tension shift.

"They need to believe I'm on their side," she continued quickly. "If I let them go, they might trust me again. I can use that to guide them away. And once they're gone... we leave, too. You and me. We disappear. We sever ties with Radimir—completely."

Dmitri was silent for a beat too long. Then he stepped closer, slow and deliberate. "Allison," he murmured, "you do realize that what you're suggesting is borderline treason."

"I know."

"Against *Radimir*."

"I know."

He exhaled, dragging a hand through his hair. "I'm all for making a dramatic exit, sweetheart, but you just jumped from espionage to a full scale '*fuck you and run*' operation. You sure your pregnancy hormones aren't playing with your risk assessment?"

She rolled her eyes. "Don't blame the baby. This is me being clear-headed for once."

A reluctant chuckle escaped him, but it didn't quite reach his eyes. He took her hand, gently tracing his thumb along her wrist. "You understand, if we do this... there's no going back. No safe houses. No mercy."

"I don't want back. I want out."

Dmitri's eyes searched hers, and something in his posture shifted, less Bratva enforcer, more man trying to build something out of chaos. "You're sure?"

"Yes. I'm done playing a part in someone else's game. I'm not just a pawn in Radimir's empire. I want a life, a real one. With you. With our child."

He sighed again, though it was more resigned than resistant this time. "You know, for a woman who used to flinch when I walked into a room, you've gotten wildly good at bossing me around."

She smirked. "It's the maternal instincts. Now I just threaten with emotional damage instead of firearms."

There was a laugh that bubbled out of him, and a fragment of the burden finally cracked. He put his arms around her; his voice dropped to bear down on her ear. "Then let's burn the world down together, *little lion.*"

Allison leaned in toward him, her lips brushing the underside of his jaw. "I knew you'd say that."

He pulled back a little, looking at her with something softer than admiration. "I'll get the plans in motion. You do your part sell the lie. And when the time comes..." He paused. "We vanish. Together."

"Together," she echoed, the word like a vow.

He grinned then, that dark, rakish glint returning. "Although, just so we're clear, if we end up living in the middle of nowhere, I expect at *least* one dog and a bathtub big enough to fit both of us."

She laughed. "You get one, not both."

"I *am* carrying emotional trauma and a growing list of enemies. I think I've earned both."

She kissed him then—slow, sure, and with all the fire of someone holding on to a single thread before everything unraveled.

And just like that, a plan began to form between them. Not just of escape. But of freedom. Of love in rebellion. Of building a life far away from shadows.

Even if they had to steal it.

* * *

Later in the evening, Allison went to Radimir's estate. She had steeled herself for the conversation, rehearsing what she was to say again and again in her mind. She had to convince him that she was his staunch ally. She had to make him believe.

The moment she had stepped into the hall, Radimir's eyes of cold allure immediately began to dissect her. He was perfectly seated on the throne, eyes gleaming with some infernal calculation. It was in that moment that Allison felt a slight change in the air, a tension arising like an electric charge on her skin, but she forced herself to meet his gaze.

"Allison," said Radimir, soft-spoken and smooth as silk, but with an edge that made her stomach curdle, "I trust you have made the right decision regarding the rebellion." His smile was slight, but his eyes betrayed an unsettling satisfaction.

Allison bowed her head respectfully. "Yes, Sir, I have. The rebels will not be a concern to you any longer. I will not aid them and told them such, I stand firm in my allegiance to you."

Radimir's eyes flashed briefly with approval, but he didn't immediately speak. Instead, for a moment, he sat there weighing the silence between them, as if he were weighing her every word.

Allison felt the pinch of this moment, the stakes were so high that every bit of her inner turmoil was rising to the surface. This was it. The final decision. She had to make him believe.

Radimir smiled, his lips curling into that familiar, eerie grin. "Very good, Allison." He inclined his head slightly, almost as if to say that he had known it would come to this.

In between them fell a long yet electric silence, thick with unspoken promises and threats. Allison, contrary to her inner voice, stepped forward. It was subtle. Barely a shift in the room. But it felt monumental.

Her spine straightened, her heart thundered, and her eyes met his, cool, sharp, expectant. And then, before she could fully question the impulse, her voice broke the stillness.

"I am fully yours, *Father*."

The words rang out like a stone dropped into still water, sending quiet ripples through the air.

It was a lie. A carefully sharpened one, crafted like a blade to be used in moments exactly like this. But in the moment it left her lips, it felt real. Dangerous. Binding.

Radimir's eyes widened ever so slightly, the faintest sparkle of surprise managing to break his perfect image for just a moment. Then his lips quirked.

"*Father*." He repeated it, tasting it as if it were the finest drink ever. "Well. That's a word I never expected to hear from you."

There was a beat of silence, and then his voice, softer but just shy of sentimental, said, "You have no idea what that means to me, Allison."

She blinked, startled by the softness threading into his tone.

"For so long," he continued, rising slowly from behind his desk, "I've built this empire with loyalty bought in blood and fear. Not love. Not family. That was never part of the equation. Never something I expected. But now..." His eyes dipped to her stomach. "Now you call me Father. And you carry my blood's future."

Allison's throat tightened. She didn't expect this, this rawness. It wasn't affection, exactly, but it was real, something raw and unguarded. A glimpse of the man beneath the monster.

Radimir came to stand just before her, close enough that she could smell the faint trace of tobacco and expensive leather on his coat. He raised a hand, not to touch, but to gesture faintly toward her abdomen.

"That child," he said, voice low and rough, "will be born into a world I carved from the bones of cowards. And it will be protected, no matter what name it carries. If you truly are mine, Allison, then that child is mine as well. And I will not let history take from me what I now consider *legacy*."

Her pulse fluttered at her throat, her mouth suddenly dry.

And with that, a new wave of confidence came surging into her next sentence, though she could hardly claim to have felt it in the first place. She turned, placed a hand protectively on the swell of her belly, and looked over her shoulder at him.

"Then I suppose I should call you *Grandpa* now, too," she breathed lightly, though she packed a few words along with pointed weight.

There was a pause. And then Radimir did something unexpected—he laughed.

A low, rich chuckle rumbled from his chest, and he leaned back, shaking his head.

"*Grandpa*," he mused, almost to himself. "God help that poor child."

Allison smirked, despite the swirl of nausea and adrenaline threatening to overtake her. She watched as his eyes glittered with something dangerous but... softer.

"I never thought I'd hear that word," he admitted, his tone quieter now. "Not from you. Not from anyone. Perhaps this family is more real than I let myself believe."

Her stomach twisted. Was she manipulating him? Or had he just manipulated *her* in return?

Radimir stepped forward again, his expression unreadable now. "I expect you to raise that child with the strength of your convictions, Allison. Not sentiment. The world does not reward softness. It will not be a symbol. It will be a *weapon*."

She swallowed hard, forcing herself to hold his gaze. "Then I suppose it's a good thing I learned from the best."

Radimir smiled, and this time, it reached his eyes. "Indeed you did."

And with that, he turned back to his desk, as if the moment had passed. But something between them had changed. Solidified.

She had made the choice.

And now, there was no turning back.

* * *

Later that night, after the meeting with Radimir had ended, Allison returned home, the heavy wooden door clicking shut behind her like slamming the door on the last chance to turn back. Her legs felt like stone, her breath shallow. The lies she'd spoken still clung to her lips, bitter and metallic.

Malakhov immediately rose from the edge of the bed, his shirt half-unbuttoned, the tension coursing through his shoulders thin enough to cut glass. "How did it go?" he asked abruptly in a low, hoarse voice but with genuine concern putting forth the question.

Allison gave him a small smile—tight, brittle, nothing more than muscle memory. "It went as expected. He's... satisfied. He believes I've pledged myself fully. I'm the true heir now. *His* heir."

Malakhov's jaw tensed, but he nodded slowly. "You played the part," he murmured, stepping forward. "And he believed it."

She turned away without answering, stumbled, and fell into his arms, breaking down against his chest as if the whole night had robbed her of strength.

"I lied to him," she whispered faintly into his shirt. "I said what he wanted to hear. I looked him eye-to-eye and told him I belonged to him. I called him '*Father.*'"

Malakhov stiffened, arms tightening around her as he processed the word. "Father," he murmured as though testing the betrayal on his own tongue.

"I had to," she said, her voice breaking again. "There was no other way forward. Not without giving us a chance. Not without protecting the baby. I—" Her voice completely gave out, and she laid her forehead on his shoulder. "I somehow feel like I gave away a part of myself tonight, Dmitri. And I don't know how to get it back."

Malakhov tightened his embrace around her, one hand moving to cup the back of her head. "You haven't given anything away," he said firmly, his breath warm against her hair. "You played him. And you played him well. That man doesn't get to know the real you. He doesn't deserve your loyalty or your heart."

"But I hate that it worked," she murmured. "That there was something in me that knew exactly what to say to make him proud of me. And part of me... *part* of me needed him to approve."

Dmitri leaned back ever so slightly to watch her with narrowed eyes, and for the briefest moment, the cruel edge in him seemed to soften into a kind of heartbreak. "You were starving for a father, and he gave you the illusion of one. Of course you wanted his approval. That doesn't make you weak—it makes you human."

"I just didn't think I'd feel so sick about it afterward," she admitted. "And when I called him *'Grandpa'*..." She let out a humorless laugh before she just trailed off. "He was genuinely pleased. Like I'd handed him a second crown."

Malakhov's eyes narrowed, a quiet fury rippling under the surface. "Then let him wear it like a fool. He will never have our child. He'll never know them. He'll never see what kind of person they become. That's ours. That belongs to us."

She looked up at him then, truly looked. "And you're still with me? Even now, after I sold a piece of my soul to that man?"

"*Especially* now," he said without hesitation, cupping her jaw in both hands. "I saw you walk into fire for us tonight. You stood before a monster and told him exactly what he wanted to hear, so we could build a way out. I don't know if I've ever admired you more than I do right now."

A tear slipped down her cheek, but this time, it wasn't entirely from grief.

"Then we'll do it," she said, voice steadying. "We run. When the moment's right, we disappear. You, me, and him. No more lies. No more masks."

Malakhov blinked slowly. *"Him?"* he echoed, the word like a crack in his composure. His voice was soft, but his entire body had gone still, as though something inside him went taut all at once.

Allison glanced away for a second, suddenly shy, her fingers tightening on the edge of the dresser before she dared to meet his eyes again. "I meant to tell you differently," she said, a small, self-conscious laugh slipping out. "I had this whole plan. Something special."

His breath caught as he watched her, already guessing where this was going—but terrified to believe it.

"I found out yesterday," she said quietly. "We're having a boy."

For a moment, the world stood still.

Then Malakhov's face cracked open in a way she'd never seen before. The hard lines of his jaw softened, his lips parted as if to speak, but nothing came out. His eyes glistened with something fierce and raw, something that had no place in the life they led—*wonder.*

"A son?" he whispered. His hand moved without thinking, reaching out to her belly like it was something sacred. His palm pressed against her gently, reverently, like he might feel the heartbeat of their future through the warmth of her skin.

For a man who had killed without hesitation, led men into blood-soaked cities, and stood unshaken before the devil himself—Malakhov looked undone. Entirely.

He leaned into her touch, then pressed a kiss to her palm, then her wrist, her shoulder, her temple. "He'll never know this life," Malakhov promised, voice thick with conviction. "Not the guns. Not the shadows. I'll give him something better. I swear it."

"I know," she whispered, brushing her lips over his.

Malakhov kissed her again—deeply this time, with trembling hands sliding around her back, drawing her close like he could shield her from everything. It was a kiss laced with desperation, with hope, with something neither of them dared say out loud.

A family.

When they pulled apart, foreheads pressed together and breaths mingling in the quiet, he whispered, "We'll give him freedom."

And Allison, voice steady even as her heart cracked wide open, replied, "Then we better start planning how we get him there."

Malakhov leaned forward, allowing his forehead to rest against hers. "Together," he whispered. "Every step."

Then Malakhov's crooked smirk returned as he leaned closer, breath warm against her ear. A glint of mischief danced in his eyes as he murmured,

"Still," Malakhov drawled, amusement curling in his voice, "we need to talk about you calling Radimir *'father.'*"

Allison blinked, confused. "What?"

He leaned in, voice low and wicked near her ear. "Next time… just call me *Daddy* instead—preferably when we're alone. And I'm earning the title properly."

Allison half-choked on a laugh, her cheeks flushing with heat as she smacked his chest. "Dmitri!"

He arched a brow, quite satisfied with himself. "What? I just think if you throw that word around, might as well put it to better use."

She muttered, "You're incorrigible," fighting a smile.

"But I made you laugh," he said, smug and unrepentant, his hands gliding down to bind her waist possessively. "And made you blush, too. That's a thousand points in my book."

She leaned in, letting out a soft sigh, and rested her head against his chest.

"You love it," he murmured, kissing the top of her head, "and you love me."

Her fingers slid down to intertwine with his. Her voice came out soft but steady "Always."

Twenty Eight

No Turning Back

For the first time in what felt like forever, she was free.

But the relief didn't last long.

Freedom under Radimir's roof was never real, just a different kind of cage pretending to be mercy. And they both knew it. Every step she took away from the cage he'd crafted for her felt like a gamble with their lives.

They were still on borrowed time.

Allison and Malakhov didn't waste a second. They had no intention of staying in Kotov Manor a moment longer than necessary. The very air felt poisoned now, thick with secrets and surveillance. Even the shadows felt alive, watching from every corner. The time had come to vanish.

The plan was simple, *in theory*; break Daniel and Rob out of the dungeons, escape the grounds undetected, and disappear before Radimir realized what they had done. But nothing about it was truly simple.

Allison's stomach twisted with dread. Her old friends, *her family*, had already written her off as lost. A traitor. Radimir's heir. The girl who'd picked comfort over conviction. They wouldn't believe her now, not after everything she'd done to keep her place at Radimir's side. But that was the cost of survival.

But, she wasn't done. Not yet. She had one last card to play, one chance to make them see that the girl they once loved like family was still in there, fighting.

They slipped through the darkness, dodging lantern beams and avoiding the guards with practiced, silent urgency. Malakhov never left her side; one hand was on the knife's hilt while the other steadied her when her steps nearly faltered. It got colder as they went into the manor, dark and gloomy, with the stench of mildew and rot.

Finally, they reached the dungeon's threshold.

The air there was staler.

Still.

Forgotten.

Pacing the heavy stone door, Malakhov glanced down, his eyes fierce and unreadable. "Are you sure about this?" he asked softly, with more tension than doubt in his voice. There was fear. Not of failure, but of losing her. "They won't trust you, Allison," he continued, voice tightening. "They've already seen you standing at Radimir's side, wearing his name like armor."

Allison looked up at him, her fingers tightening around the iron key she'd stolen earlier that day. "I know," she said quietly, "but... but I have to try."

Her throat felt tight. "They need to live, Dmitri. Even if they hate me for it. Even if I never see them again. I couldn't save them the last time, I'm not going to let that happen again."

He regarded her for a long moment before nodding slowly, the muscle in his jaw twitching. "You're stronger than you think," he muttered as his fingers brushed her lower back. A darkness now invaded his voice. "But if either of those bastards spit in your direction, I'll honestly throw them through a wall."

Allison lifted a brow, a smile playing on her lips. "You'll have to stand in line. I'll be the first to throw punches if they spit on me."

Malakhov didn't smile. Instead, his eyes gleamed with a deadly seriousness, wrapped in a thin layer of dry amusement. "Fine. But if Rob so much as *looks* at you like he still has a chance..." He leaned in, mouth close to her ear, his voice low and lethal. "I will break his nose."

Allison let out a breathy laugh, despite herself. "You're very possessive for a man helping me commit treason."

"I'm helping *us* disappear, my lion," he said, straightening, though his hand lingered on her hip. "And I don't share. Especially not with anyone who think this is a bloody love triangle."

A flush rose in her cheeks, some stubborn part of her still wanting to pretend this wasn't as dangerous as it was.

"Just don't forget who's getting you out of here alive," he whispered once again, his voice softening as he searched her face.

"I haven't forgotten," she replied in a trembling whisper and heart shaking.

She faced the door and took the key in her trembling hand, sliding it into the lock.

Everything from this point forward was a risk.

But it was the right one.

And they were in it together.

They arrived at Rob's cell first. He was chained to the wall sitting on the cold stone floor, the head bowed, until he heard footsteps. A gesture of disbelief crept upon his face when his eyes rested on Allison.

"Allison?" The voice was hoarse and brittle. "What the hell are you doing here?"

She gave no answer. Her hands trembled a bit as she proceeded to get out the folded map she'd made with care from her coat. The iron key was heavy in her palm.

Malakhov stood behind her, arms crossed, leaning dangerously with apparent leisure against the cell bars.

"I'm here to get you out," Allison whispered. Moving toward the door, Rob sprung violently to his feet, chains rattling.

"Now? You decide *now*? After leaving us to rot in this hellhole for months?"

"I didn't leave you," she replied, unlocking the cell with a soft *click*. "I was surviving. Planning. And I *never* stopped trying to find a way to help you."

Rob scoffed, crossing his arms. "Help us? You chose *them*. You walked around like a queen while we were down here being starved and beaten."

Allison flinched. "If Radimir suspected anything—"

"Oh, please," Rob snapped. "Don't pretend this was some noble act. You're carrying *his* child, aren't you?" His eyes dropped to her belly, his voice turning cruel. "Tell me, how long before you forget we ever existed?"

Malakhov stepped forward, his voice dangerously low, *"Careful.* You're in no position to speak to her like that."

Rob's head whipped toward him. "You. You're the *bastard* behind all of this."

Malakhov gave him a lazy smile, like Rob was a mild annoyance at best. "Guilty. And very flattered to be given so much credit."

Rob growled, "She is carrying your child. Yet here you are, fine with dragging her further into this madness!"

Malakhov's eyes darkened, as if the very air temperature dropped in that room. "I'm fine keeping her safe and I am *very* fine with knowing that she chose me." Malakhov came nearer to Allison, placing one hand casually on her lower back to show that she was his. "And I'll be even finer if you stop looking at her like she belongs to *you*."

Rob clenched his fists, drawing harsh breaths.

"Besides," Malakhov went on without flinching, "she surely doesn't need your approval. She's not your damsel. And if you so much as breathe the wrong way in her direction, I will unshackle you just to break your jaw."

Allison gave Malakhov a sidelong look. "Subtle."

He winked. "Didn't think you brought me for my subtlety."

Rob's glare shifted to Allison again, softer now, confused. "So, what... this is actually real? You're really with *him* — not just for show?"

"I didn't plan this," she admitted, voice shaking slightly. "But yes. It's real. I'm not asking you to understand it, I just want you to get out alive."

She stepped forward, gently handing him the map. "This will take you out undetected. Go south, stick to the shadows, and don't stop until you're far beyond Radimir's reach."

Rob took it, staring at the inked lines for a long moment. His voice dropped. "Why are you really doing this?"

"Because despite everything, I still care about you," she whispered. "But I've made my choice. And I'm not looking back."

A long silence passed.

Then Malakhov, not one to let anything end to softly, added with a grin, "And for what it's worth, she made an excellent choice."

Rob muttered something under his breath, but he took the map.

And Allison knew, the line had been drawn.

And she wasn't standing on Rob's side anymore.

Behind her, Malakhov watched, his expression unreadable. But Allison could sense the tension rising in him. There was no time left to waste. She turned back to Daniel's cell, and he sat quietly, staring at her as though he could read her.

"Daniel, you've got to go too," Allison said, her voice trembling but resolute. "It's your only chance. This is the last time I can help you."

Daniel, still shackled, looked up from the floor. His eyes were wide, but not with gratitude, only shock and suspicion. "You?" he asked, his voice raw. "You're helping us?"

He stood slowly, the chains rattling with each movement. "After everything? You walk in here like nothing's changed, like we can just forget?"

Allison swallowed hard. "I never forgot," she said. "Not for a second. But I had to survive."

Daniel laughed bitterly. "And what a part you played. Radimir's pet. His heir. His... whatever the hell you are to *him* now."

Malakhov sauntered into view, arms crossed, with his face mostly composed, but his eyes were sharp, "You don't have to like me," Allison said, holding Daniel's gaze. "You don't even have to trust me, But you *do* have to leave. Please, Daniel. Take this." She held out a second copy of the map, her hands shaking.

Daniel didn't move. He stared at the paper as if it might explode. "You think a piece of paper erases all this?" he said. "Do you know what we've been through down here?"

Rob let out a snort behind her. "She knows. She's just too deep in *love* with her new warden to care."

Malakhov smiled darkly, taking a step forward. "Careful, *Robert*. Your jealousy's showing."

Rob opened his mouth, but Daniel cut in, stepping forward. "Why now, Allison? Why even bother?"

"Because I still care about you," she said, her voice breaking. "I still care about both of you. But this... this is as far as I can go. If you stay, you die. And I can't live with that too."

Daniel looked from the map to her, and then to Malakhov. "And what about *him*? What's he gonna do? Watch us run and wave goodbye?"

Malakhov smirked, voice smooth as silk. "If you two can manage to get out without tripping over your own bitterness, I'll consider it a win. But let me make something *very* clear..."

He stepped forward slowly, deliberately, the quiet drag of his boots across the stone making both Rob and Daniel stiffen. He didn't raise his voice, he didn't need to. His presence crowded the cell, cold as the stone walls.

"If either of you thinks this is your *moment...* your dramatic, last-ditch, self-righteous grab at redemption, or some pathetic attempt to *touch* her, even just to say goodbye," he said, his tone dropping into something dark and deadly, "I will put you into the floor so hard you'll wake up wondering which century you're in. And that's me being polite, for her sake"

His eyes landed on Rob like the barrel of a gun. "You lay a single hand on her, try to convince her to go with you and I'll make sure your fingers don't work again. You so much as breathe disrespect in her direction again, and I'll personally feed you your own teeth."

"*Jesus,*" Daniel muttered, taking a step back despite himself. "What the hell is she doing with *you*?"

Malakhov didn't even blink. "She's with me because I don't lie to her. Because I see her for what she *really* is: strong, brutal, brilliant." He looked at Allison then, softening for a heartbeat before the edge returned. "And because I would tear this entire fucking world apart before I let anyone hurt her again. Including either of you."

There was a long silence.

Even the shadows in the cell seemed to hesitate.

Daniel's eyes flickered, anger, maybe regret, but he finally reached out and snatched the map from Allison's hand. "I'll never forgive you," he said. "Not for what you became."

"I understand," Allison replied quietly. "But I still hope you survive."

Rob let out a short, dry laugh, the bitterness clear. "You really think this ends with the two of you walking away clean? Like some kind of happy ending?"

Malakhov didn't flinch. He just gave a faint, unbothered smirk. "We're not walking," he said. "We're getting the hell out. And we're quicker than you think."

Daniel scoffed behind Rob, shaking his head as chains rattled faintly. "You're delusional if you think this ends well. You think Radimir won't come for you? For all of us?"

Allison looked at them, really looked, and the ache in her chest deepened. The same men she'd once trusted with her life now stared at her like a stranger. But there was no room for regret. Not now.

"I never wanted this to happen," she said, her voice cracking just slightly. "But I made my choice. I chose to survive. And now, I'm choosing something more."

She paused and stepped closer, meeting their eyes in turn—Daniel's rage and Rob's heartbreak. "Goodbye, Rob. Goodbye, Daniel."

Rob's jaw tensed, but he said nothing.

Daniel looked away.

Neither of them responded.

The silence between them said enough.

Malakhov moved to her side without a word, his presence a shield she didn't have to ask for. His hand found the small of her back, grounding her. As the two of them turned to go, a voice rose one last time, his voice deep, bitter, desperate, almost breaking. "We're not coming back from this."

Allison didn't look back. She didn't have to.

"I didn't think we intend to," was the very simple reply she gave.

And just like that, the two vanished into the enfolding shadows, tied together by love, betrayal, and the ashes of the life they'd already burned.

She had done it. She had saved them. She had made the hard choice, had lied to Radimir, had convinced him of her loyalty, and helped Daniel and Rob escape. But now, the gravity of it all was starting to set in. She didn't know how long they would be free. Radimir was not one to be easily deceived.

Far from it.

The dungeons were quiet now, every click and clatter of her heeled boots echoing through the dark halls.She felt him at her back, solid and steady, and it was the only thing keeping her from unraveling. She did not have to look behind to know Malakhov was silently watching over her; his protective instincts were amplified to the fullest.

"You did well," Malakhov muttered as they walked toward the exit. "I doubt they will ever understand, but you did the right thing."

Allison nodded, contemplating her response for a few moments.

Her mind was too fixated with what she had just done. It had been the right decision, *hadn't it?* To save Daniel and Rob. To betray Radimir's trust. She had to believe it. She had made her choice, but at what cost?

"Let's move," Malakhov urged gently, sensing the shift in her demeanor. "We can't stay here for long."

Allison didn't argue with him. This was not the end of the escape, the next phase of their plan was just beginning.

* * *

They made sure to tread the dark hallways with careful precision. The night was quiet; all that stirred the silence was the soft whisper of the wind outside. Isolation was what kept the headquarters separated, yet it didn't mean the place remained unguarded. They had to keep moving, but they also had to keep to stealth.

They slipped through the corridors, avoiding any servants on their usual rounds. Initially, they got sight of a Bratva patrol, and Allison instantly held her breath. Malakhov's presence was at her side, watchful and calm. He gave her a subtle glance; his eyes flickered with a silent command nodding to a darkened corner. He knew exactly what to do and there was no time for doubt.

When they finally made it to the back door of the manor, a chilling pulse ticked up inside her. The first breath of freedom felt an entire lifetime away. Allison shot Malakhov a sideways glance, her heart still pounding in her throat. They had done it.

"You're certain this is the right choice?" Malakhov asked softly, his hand resting on her back as they moved swiftly.

Allison nodded, pushing away the doubt. "It has to be. We have to do this, for us."

A chill spread through her ribs, a dread she knew too well—Radimir would never let this stand. A part of her almost believed she deserved it, that no matter how far she ran, she'd never truly outrun the guilt she'd chosen to carry.

Before she could take in a breath, Malakhov grabbed her wrist and dragged her behind the shadows of an alcove, pressing her against the cold stone. They could hear a guard approaching. One arm went around her waist; the other locked beside her head. His breath was hot against her ear as he whispered, "Don't move. We can't afford even a whisper right now."

Allison nodded, her breath catching as the footsteps grew louder.

It wasn't just any guard, it was Veznikov, one of the newer recruits. Eager to prove himself. All swagger and suspicion. His eyes scanned the path ahead like he *wanted* to find something wrong.

Malakhov's mind raced. They were too close to lose everything now.

He drew Allison closer to him without hesitating his grip, his body flush against hers as he tilted her chin away with two digits, angling downwards to kiss the curve of her neck, something that was not gentle by any means but was intentionally possessive. His lips brushed against her skin, sending shivers down her spine, while the tightening grip on her arm gave a silent warning.

A sharp voice from the dark intervened. "Oi! Who's there? Step out!"

Malakhov didn't flinch. He gave her a faint, dangerous smile, and then casually stepped into the open, pulling her with him, his arm wrapped firmly around her waist.

"Easy," he called, voice dripping with lazy amusement. "Just taking a moment to enjoy my wife before the next round of sleepless nights begins."

Veznikov squinted at them, his expression skeptical as he took in Allison's disheveled hair, Malakhov's hand spread wide across her belly.

"The hell are you doing this far out?" he asked. "Orders were to keep inside after sunset."

Malakhov chuckled darkly, leaning in just enough to kiss the top of Allison's head. "She couldn't sleep. Baby's restless. I thought a little air might help... among other things." His fingers traced the slow movement up and down her side, deliberately brushing over her hip.

Allison, catching on fast, let out a soft laugh and leaned into him, trying to put one hand against her stomach. "And he becomes very protective when I get uneasy," she said sweetly, resting her head against Malakhov's chest. "Hormones and all."

Veznikov raised a brow, smirking now. "Possessive much?"

Malakhov's smile didn't reach his eyes. "You'd be, too, if she was carrying *your* child and the heir to the thrown, or did you forget?" The edge in his voice made the guard straighten slightly.

"I wasn't looking to start anything," Veznikov muttered, taking a step back, suddenly a little less smug. "You two do what you need. I'll just... keep patrolling."

"Do," Malakhov said, tone cool but final. "But if you see someone else out here tonight, best look the other way."

Veznikov gave an awkward chuckle and a half-hearted salute. "Right. Congratulations, by the way. Hope it's a boy."

He turned and walked off, muttering something about "damn hormones" and "territorial bastards."

As soon as he was out of sight, Malakhov exhaled slowly, still holding Allison close. "Well," he mused softly into the strands of her hair, "I believe that we have just given him an unforgettable memory."

"That kiss almost branded me," she breathed, still clutching his coat with her fingertips.

Malakhov smirked, eyes glittering in the low light. "I would've left a mark if it meant he'd think twice before looking at you again."

His thumb grazed her jaw, slow and deliberate. "Besides... you looked criminal in the shadows like that. I couldn't help myself."

A shaky laugh escaped her, soft but charged. "Let's just get out of here alive. After that, you can do whatever you want with me."

His smirk deepened. "Careful. I plan to hold you to that."

With a final glance over their shoulder, his hand gripped hers tight as they slipped back into the night. Two fugitives bound together by everything they'd done, and everything they still hoped for.

Allison looked at him with a teasing glint in her eyes. "Well, if we make it out of here, maybe you'll get to experience some of those *pregnancy hormones* up close..." She winked, barely able to keep the nervous excitement down.

A raised eyebrow traveled across Malakhov's face, making his lips curl in a charming but dangerous smile, "I'll be looking forward to it, little lion. But let's focus on getting out of here first. Once we're free, then I will see to all of those... *fantasies*."

Allison, returning the smile, felt slightly uplifted from within as they walked toward the exit. Somehow those words gave her a little warm feeling. Maybe this life, dangerous, uncertain, was worth every risk if it meant she didn't have to face it alone.

The final escape felt just like something out of a dream. They moved fast during the final stretch and toward the edge of the forest where a hidden abandoned home awaited.

"We did it," she whispered, while Malakhov wrapped his arm around her shoulder.

"We're not done yet, Allison. But yes, we did it." He planted a soft kiss on her forehead, one moment of tenderness amid all the danger.

The two of them walked into the forest as moonlight seeped through the trees on their way to their destination. The road ahead was just beginning, but for that moment, she let herself believe they might be free.

Twenty Nine

Throne of Wrath

The cold, suffocating air inside Kotov Manor seemed to grow with every step Radimir took across the stone. The shadows clinging onto the edges of the room like ghosts, the weak firelight only emphasized the cold fury building in his chest.

He had always prided himself on control, on foresight, on ability to see every step before it was set into action. This illusion, however, now shattered.

Allison Murphy, *his heir,* his carefully sculpted creation, had betrayed him.

And not just betrayed him. She had *humiliated* him.

He stopped suddenly, he echoes of his boots died, swallowed by the hush. His jaw uncomfortable and with a grim expression, his cold, predatory gaze swept over the Bratva gathered before him. The most trusted of lieutenants- Grigori Gordeev, Igor Romanov, Pavel Petrov— were also stiff, like boys waiting for a scolding.

"You let them escape," Radimir said, voice low and venom-laced. "Daniel. Rob. And her."

The word hung in the air like a curse. *Her.*

"She stood beside me. Sat at my right hand. I called her my *daughter*." His voice cracked slightly, rage laced with something dangerously close to betrayal. "And what did she do in return? She took what was *mine*. My leverage. My prisoners. My future. She spat in my face and disappeared into the night."

"You all stood guard. You all claimed you had eyes on every door." He spun toward Igor, eyes flashing. "And yet somehow, Allison walked through your defenses with two fugitives and a traitor on her arm like it was a fucking picnic!"

Igor opened his mouth to speak, but Radimir raised a single finger. *"Don't. Speak."*

Igor lowered his gaze, swallowing hard.

Radimir turned to Grigori next. "Tell me, *Gordeev*. Was your loyalty just as cheap? Did you think I wouldn't notice? That I wouldn't *feel* it when she turned her back on me?"

"No, sir," Grigori said quickly. "We didn't know—"

"She is *pregnant*," Radimir snapped, his voice thundering through the hall. "Pregnant with what was supposed to be the future of this empire. Now she is fleeing, running like a coward behind the man I trusted most."

He was now breathing heavily, his hands tightly clenched and his frame vibrating. And then he relaxed all of a sudden. His voice dropped to a frigid whisper, far more dangerous than any shout.

"I will have her back. *Alive.* I want her to carry that child to term in one of my cells. And when she does... I will take the boy. Raise him as he *should* be raised. A true heir. *My* heir."

He smiled faintly, a terrible, chilling thing. "And as for Malakhov..."

He turned back to his Bratva, eyes gleaming with something far too calm. "I want him brought in broken. Shackled, bloodied. *But breathing.* I want to watch the light go out in his eyes as I take everything from him. He'll beg for death before I'm done."

Pavel shifted uneasily, but Radimir didn't miss it. "You have doubts, Petrov?"

Pavel straightened. "No, sir. We will find them."

"Good," Radimir hissed. "Because if you don't... I will make examples of *every* one of you. Starting with your families."

The threat landed with a sickening finality.

Radimir turned to face the hearth, staring into the flames, letting their glow paint his pale features in flickering orange. "She thought she could outwit me. Outsmart me. Play both sides."

He exhaled slowly, measured.

"Spread the word. There will be no sanctuary for traitors. No mercy. No second chances. Find them. Break them. And bring them back."

Grigori nodded. "Yes, sir."

"And Grigori..." Radimir called as they began to disperse. The man turned back.

"If Malakhov so much as blinks in defiance, *cut something off.*"

Radimir sat on his throne, legs crossed, fingers steepled before his mouth as silence reclaimed the hall.

His empire may have cracked.

But soon, the reckoning would begin.

* * *

The night sky burned crimson as chaos exploded on the manor grounds. The rebels had come.

Without warning, the resistance breached the perimeter wall in a blast of smoke and debris. The Bratva had barely begun to recover from Allison's betrayal—and now the rebel strike team was inside the gates, armed to the teeth and ready to finish what she started.

"MOVE!" Travis Lewis another detective from the force roared, storming through the rubble. His rifle spat fire, dropping a Bratva soldier with three clean rounds to the chest. The man fell mid-sprint, his body tumbling limp across the bloody gravel.

Shots were fired all around, thundering, deafening, deadly. The muzzle flashes illuminated the gardens like strobe lights at the gates of hell. Shouts were swallowed by the sound of automatic fire and screaming.

To Travis's right, a rebel took a machete to the stomach, he went down hard, choking on blood—but not before unloading a final burst into his attacker's thigh. Both men died within seconds of each other, tangled in the dirt.

Rob surged forward, his face streaked with sweat and blood. He vaulted a broken stone bench and landed hard, immediately squeezing off two rapid shots. One Bratva soldier dropped. The other tried to run, Rob shot him in the back of the head without blinking.

"Advance!" he shouted, voice raw. "Push them into the north wing, we choke them there!"

Daniel limped behind him, bruised and battered, but dangerous as ever. He wielded his sidearm like a surgeon, every shot deliberate. A Bratva enforcer rushed him with a steel pipe, Daniel dropped to one knee and shot him twice in the knees, then once in the throat as the man collapsed screaming.

The courtyard was carnage. Concrete slick with blood. The bodies were all over the shattered pavements, some twitching, while the others lay still. The stench of gunpowder choked every breath.

A Bratva fighter lunged at Travis from behind, with a knife flashing in the dark. Travis caught the glint just in time and swung his rifle stock into the man's face. There was a crunch of cartilage, a scream, and Travis didn't stop, he tackled him to the ground and bashed his skull in with the butt of the rifle until the screaming stopped.

All around them, rebels surged forward, ducking behind overturned statues and burning hedges. Shouts of "Cover left!" and "Clear!" rang out amid the chaos. Some carried pistols, others rifles, and a few wielded brutal tools, fire axes, tire irons, or shivs made from broken glass and metal.

Rob reloaded behind a marble column, bullets raining over his head. "We need to cut off the west corridor! It's their fallback point!"

"Copy that!" The pin was pulled by Daniel, and then he chucked it into the hallway. Deafening noise followed the smashing of screams. Blood sprayed the far wall.

Bratva fighters began to retreat, dragging wounded or firing blindly behind them. Panic overtook discipline. One young recruit tossed down his weapon, hands raised—but a rebel shot him dead before he could blink.

"Save your mercy," Travis growled, stepping over a corpse. "None of them would've spared us."

Rob and Daniel moved as one, sweeping the halls with ruthless efficiency. Close-quarters gunfire echoed like thunder. Rob caught the guard by the collar while he was trying to escape, slammed him against the wall, and shot him through the jaw before he could let out a shout.

Out there, smoke spiraled upward, thick with ash and iron. The ground was soaked, not with rain, but blood.

The Bratva were falling apart. With no leader present to bark orders, they were scattering like rats.

A group of rebels moved up with a battering ram, slamming it through the remaining manor doors. More gunfire. More screams.

"We're taking the north wing!" Travis barked, waving them forward. "End this now!"

Rob wiped blood from his face with a shuddering hand. "Let's finish the job."

Together, they surged into the heart of Radimir's crumbling empire, leaving behind nothing but blood, smoke, and broken bodies.

The war wasn't over.

But tonight, their revolution had truly begun.

* * *

At the abandoned house on the outskirts of town that Malakhov had prepared, the tension wrapped around them like a noose.

They could hear it now, gunfire in the distance. Sharp, violent cracks echoing through the trees like thunder. Malakhov tensed, standing near the broken window, his eyes scanning the forest beyond. "We need to move," he said sharply. "They're coming. Fast."

Allison moved quickly, grabbing the pack they'd prepared hours ago. Her fingers were trembling, but her mind was locked in. Survival mode.

The sound of a muffled scream faintly floated in the night. Then more gunshots, closer this time.

Controlled.

Tactical.

Malakhov's jaw clenched.

"They've swept around us," he muttered, glancing toward the east side of the woods. "Forming a net."

Suddenly, Allison spotted flickers of movement between the trees, dark figures slipping through the underbrush. Flashlights flickering like blinking eyes. A Bratva unit. They were surrounding the house.

"They've found us," she said with her mouth barely opening, her heart in frantic beating. Malakhov didn't flinch; he grabbed her right arm and yanked her beside him in a low flat voice.

"Then we don't run. We fight."

Outside, the woods crackled with movement, boots grinding against damp soil, the soft murmur of Russian orders, the cold, unmistakable sound of rifles being cocked.

They were closing in.

Allison met his eyes, and for a second, neither of them moved.

They had seconds. Maybe less.

"Found them," Grigori Gordeev's voice slithered out of the darkness like a curse, oily and cruel. He stepped out of the trees, flanked by two Bratva enforcers. His rifle hung loose in his hands, but his eyes glimmered with malice.

He smirked as his gaze landed on Allison. "There you are, Malakhov. I'll admit, I expected better from you. Hiding in a shack like some frightened dog. But don't worry, I'll clean up after you."

His tone turned filthier, voice dropping as he looked Allison up and down. "Allison looks ripe. I hear pregnancy hormones do something special to a woman. Soft skin, flushed cheeks. Maybe I'll take my turn with her. Hell, maybe she'll give *me* a son. You wouldn't mind, would you, Dmitri? After all, you're not fit to carry on any legacy, not after this."

Malakhov didn't respond right away. He stepped forward, slowly, calm, quiet, *lethal*. Then he spoke, his voice like ice over coiled fire. "Say her name again, Grigori," he said, with his finger twitching near the trigger of the gun strapped to his chest, "and I will make certain that you do not live long enough to even finish thinking about it." He lowered his head. "You like talking big. Let's see if you scream the same way when I gut you."

Grigori's grin faltered, just slightly. "Still got that temper, I see. Still playing the protector." He raised his rifle fully. "Fine. We'll carve her out of your arms and see how far that loyalty gets you."

Allison stepped beside Malakhov, her breath sharp but her hands steady. "You don't scare me, Gordeev," she said coldly. "But you should be scared. Because you're not getting out of this forest with all your limbs."

Grigori sneered, lifting his gun a fraction higher. "We'll see."

Malakhov's voice dropped to a whisper for Allison's ears only, his eyes never leaving Grigori's. "Stay sharp. When they move, we move. Fast. We shoot to kill, no hesitation."

She gave a small nod, her pulse pounding like a drumbeat in her ears. Then—

The sharp crack of gunfire split the silence.

Sparks erupted from the wooden wall behind Malakhov's head as a bullet ricocheted, sending shards flying. He shoved Allison sideways behind a low ridge of stone as return fire burst from his rifle, muzzle flashing in the dark.

One of the Bratva men went down hard, screaming as blood sprayed across the forest floor.

Grigori ducked behind a tree, barking orders in Russian, and then Malakhov did not let him breathe. "You're not walking away from this, Grigori!" Malakhov's voice echoed through the trees.

Eruptions of gunfire began so loud and brutal, unrelenting in all directions.

Allison fired low, catching another enforcer in the thigh. He screamed and dropped, and she shot him again, this time in the chest.

The fight had begun. No more running. No more waiting.
Only blood and the will to survive.

The wind howled through the trees as several other members of the Bratva moved to surround the abandon house, their guns drawn and their faces masked in cold determination. Allison stood at Malakhov's side, her breath coming in sharp bursts as she looked around at the figures closing in on them. The night reeked of cordite and the knowledge that none of them would walk away the same.

Malakhov, ever the calm force beside her, gave her a brief glance, his eyes filled with silent understanding. The time for running was over. It was time to fight.

"They'll attack from all sides, Allison," Malakhov muttered under his breath, his eyes narrowed. "We need to take them down quickly. Don't hesitate. Keep your focus. We fight as one."

Nodding, Allison tightened her grip on her firearm. She could feel a stream of power rushing through her. At her side, Malakhov kept up moving with the fluid certainty of a man who had hunted all his life. There was no fear in his movements, just sheer purpose.

And then the next strike came.

One of the Bratva shouted, firing a shot at them.

Malakhov didn't even flinch. In an instant, he had moved Allison, his gun raised. The bullet punched through the Bratva soldier's skull, dropping him instantly. No hesitation. No mercy. One bullet out; another was fired before Allison could even react, and Malakhov was already dealing with another minor threat. He made it look so casual; swift, precise, and the whole battle almost a blur to him.

"How do you want to handle this one?" Malakhov asked in a low steady voice as he nodded toward Grigori Gordeev and Igor Romanov, the two most dangerous soldiers now standing in front of them.

Allison's eyes flickered to Grigori, a cold fury seeping into her veins. "I want Grigori. If he thinks he will ever lay a hand on me, I will end him. For good." Her voice was full of venom, and her eyes were burning with emotion, but beneath the defiance, a tremor of fear coiled in her chest. She was brave enough to face him, but she couldn't pretend she wasn't afraid.

Malakhov gave her a grim smile, a glint of approval in his eyes. "You'll have your chance. But it won't be easy. He's a dangerous man."

They shared a knowing glance. She understood him, and he understood her.

"And what about Romanov?"

"Are you sure?" Allison asked, her voice steady, but threaded with concern. She had seen the man in action, there was a stunning degree of strength there, and his lust for violence could perhaps rival even that of Radimir himself.

Malakhov's grin emerged, and it was predatory, his eyes flashing with anticipation. But when he spoke again, there was a raw edge to his voice that betrayed the truth: he wasn't afraid for himself. He was afraid for her—and for the life growing inside her.

"I will kill Romanov," he said quietly. "By the time he realizes he's been hit, he'll be dead. But if anything happens to you..." His jaw clenched. "I won't let that happen. Not to you. Not to our child."

Grigori Gordeev stepped forward, his body emerging from shadows like a predator stalking a prey. His unwilling smile spread maliciously, eyes full of bittersweet anticipation. Finally, the time he had been waiting for had arrived-and all this while, he had been biding his time. Allison was standing mere feet away, and he could practically taste the fear in her breath.

Grigori had always wanted her; in this present unstable moment of Radimir's reign, he saw it as the perfect opportunity to claim what he wanted and remind his leader of his devotion in a way that could never be forgotten.

"Ah, Allison," he mocked. "I must admit I have been curious as to how pregnancy would look on you. I've always been partial to women with curves. I'm sure you'll look exquisite when you're beneath me. After all, what good is a pregnant body if it's not used for a little fun?" His eyes gleamed with something darker, something far more dangerous.

Her heart thundered against her ribs as a surge of anger flooded through her at his words. She felt her hands tightening around her gun, yet she had no intention to let the devil torment her. "I'm not your toy, Grigori," she spat out unflinching, though a sickening tremor of disgust rippled through her. "I never was. And if you should think you'll lay a hand on me—"

Grigori smiled all the more, this time disturbing."Oh, but I will," he interrupted threateningly low. "I'll ravish you, Allison. I'll have my way with you before I hand you back to Radimir, I'll make sure you're properly used by then. Perhaps you can make this a little more... *enjoyable* for me."

Allison's chest heaved with controlled anger, but she didn't flinch. She couldn't. Not now. He wouldn't break her.

Before he could step any further, Allison raised the gun in her hand. Calm tones seemed to insult the very violent fury pumping through her veins, and she shot. The bullet soared toward him with deadly precision, but Grigori moved with a little more promptness than she anticipated, twisting away just in time. It grazed a hair off his shoulder, while he fired another round at her. Standing on the heels of one smooth movement, she turned sharply, avoiding the bullet and aimed her gun at him.

"Is that all you've got?" she mocked with a taunting smirk. "You think you're going to control me, Gordeev? You're nothing but a pathetic excuse for a man, and I'd be doing the world a favor to rid you from it."

Grigori's eyes flared with rage, and he raised his own gun again. "*Fucking bitch!*" he screamed. The shot sped toward Allison, the sickly bullet racing toward her chest with blinding speed.

But Allison was prepared. She fell back towards the ground landing on her back, avoiding the shot. The bullet collided with a window of the abandoned home behind her, exploding outward in a flash of light and sound. The impact sent a jolt through her chest, but the bullet had not touched her.

"Seriously, Gordeev?" Allison sneered, stepping from behind cover just enough to let him see the fire in her eyes. "I've seen dying rats show more courage. You strut around talking about 'ravishing' me, but let's be honest, you wouldn't last long enough to unzip your pants. You're not a predator, Grigori. You're a limp-dicked coward clinging to someone else's power."

Grigori sneered, his face twisted in a mask of fury. "You think you've won, *Murphy*? You're nothing. You always have been nothing."

"And yet, you still want me." She retorted. Allison's heart thundered as the adrenaline rushed through her. The battle was far from concluded. Adrenaline roared through her veins. She realized in that moment that she wouldn't stop, he had to go. Nothing was getting in her way of ensuring he died.

In one swift motion, with fury and fear, she lunged with lethal ferocity in swings of her gun and fired, screaming out with unbridled anger. The bullet shot out with a force she had not expected, and Grigori had no time to react as it hit straight in the chest.

His body lurching away with a sickening thud, dying down with the last words full of venom and twisted desire fading into the air was crashing to the ground. That heavy silence was choking Allison from above.

Standing and gasping for air, every muscle in her body remained tight and thrumming in the battle's aftermath. She had finished it.

She paused for a moment with white knuckles tightly gripping the gun. The adrenaline was raging under her skin, but from beneath, the exhaustion was beginning to creep up. She had done what needed to be done but was now paying for it.

Her gaze flicked toward Malakhov in the very moment he dived to avoid a shot from Romanov. Their eyes met, and he gave it a flicker of approval. "Well done, my lion," he whispered with undeniable pride. "But we're not done yet."

Allison gave a nod, the full weight of the battle yet to sink in. She had to finish.

With Grigori down, Allison turned her focus to Igor Romanov, who was already lunging toward Malakhov with terrifying speed. His snarls filled the air as he bared his teeth, the hunger for violence evident in his every movement.

"You think you can stop me, Malakhov?" Romanov snarled, his voice guttural as he raised his gun, aiming at Malakhov's chest. "You're nothing but a pet to Radimir, a *lapdog*. I'll tear you apart before you even see me coming."

Malakhov's lips curled into a wicked smile. "I've killed better men than you, Romanov. You'll be dead before you can even blink."

He charged at the man with surprising speed, using his gun as an extension of himself, each movement flowing seamlessly into the next. He ducked beneath Romanov's vicious swipe and shot a barrage of bullets, each one aimed to wound and disable rather than kill immediately. Malakhov was toying with him, weakening him for the final blow.

Malakhov aimed another bullet, but Romanov was too fast. He dodged the shot and lunged again, this time ripping through the air with a knife in his other hand.

Romanov, enraged, retaliated with a savage roar, "You can't hide from me!" He lunged, attempting to sink his knife into Malakhov's flesh.

Malakhov quickly dodged and delivered a powerful punch, sending Romanov crashing into a nearby tree. "You're nothing more than a mangy dog," Malakhov spat. Adrenaline roared through his veins.

Malakhov managed to sidestep just in time, narrowly avoiding another ferocious attack. He attempted to deflect the mans next strike, but the impact still shook him. Romanov was stronger than he had expected.

"You'll have to do better than that, Malakhov," Romanov taunted, his voice dripping with mockery. He swung his knife once again, knocking Malakhov to the ground and slicing his arm. Pain flared sharply, burning through his senses, but Malakhov gritted his teeth, refusing to let it slow him down.

With speed and precision, he scrambled to his feet, favoring the uninjured arm but steady. He raised his gun and fired a shot into Romanov's knee. "You've spent too long hiding in the shadows, Romanov. Time for you to face the truth."

Romanov screamed in rage and collapsed to the ground.

Malakhov stood over him, his breath ragged but his voice cold and powerful. "See you in hell." He delivered one final shot to Romanov's temple. The man let out a scream of rage before falling lifeless to the ground.

Malakhov stood, his breath coming in heavy gasps. The adrenaline of the fight still thrummed through his veins, but there was a calmness now, an overwhelming sense of victory. He had won. But he wasn't finished yet.

"It's over, Romanov." Malakhov spat on the lifeless body, his eyes hard. "You were a threat. Now, you're nothing."

Malakhov quickly rejoined Allison "Are you okay?" Malakhov asked, his concern evident despite his usual stoicism. His gaze flickered to her belly, and a brief flash of worry passed over his face.

Allison nodded, her eyes gleaming with a mix of triumph and worry. "I'm fine. We've done it. They're gone." She smiled weakly, still catching her breath.

Just as the battle seemed to come to a close, a dark presence filled the air. Allison and Malakhov turned their heads in unison, both knowing what was coming next.

Radimir had arrived.

His figure emerged from the shadows, his pale face twisted in fury. His eyes glowed with rage, and he was surrounded by more of his loyal followers, Grigori and Romanov's deaths still fresh in his mind.

"You thought you could escape me, Allison?" Radimir snarled, stepping through the smoke like a phantom. His coat was stained with blood, his face twisted with rage. "You were mine. I built you. And now you betray me, for *him*?" His eyes flicked to Malakhov with pure venom. "I will rip my heir from your womb before I drag you back in pieces."

Allison's heart slammed in her chest, but she stood her ground, her voice sharp as glass. "You don't own me. You never did. And I'd rather die on my feet than rot in your shadow."

Radimir's lip curled into a sneer. "You've chosen death, then. You've thrown away everything I gave you, for *love*?" He spat the word like poison. "You will die screaming, and Malakhov will beg before the end."

Malakhov stepped forward, placing himself between Radimir and Allison, his gun already raised, his grip steady. "She's not yours. She never was. If you even think about taking her, I'll put a bullet between your eyes before you finish your next breath."

Radimir's cold eyes gleamed with malice. "So be it. Let's see which of us bleeds first."

The forest around them was silent—no birds, no breeze. Only the pounding of hearts and the crackle of smoke.

This was it.

The final reckoning.

One life.

One shot.

This was their chance to be free.

Thirty

Fury and Hope

The final battle unfolded around them, with every inch of the once safe house being tainted by the chaos of destruction. Its walls were now beaten through with bullet holes and scorch marks, stained with blood. And yet, outside, amidst the fractured remains of what once was a home, stood Radimir.

He stood against the wreckage, a dark figure in a suit smeared with blood and dirt. His shoulders were tight, shaking—not from fear, but from barely restrained anger. His breath was ragged. One hand gripped a gun still warm from use, the other hung at his side, fingers twitching like they were trying to hold on to something slipping away—maybe control, maybe sanity.

But beneath the rage, deeper things stirred.

Radimir's strength, once feared, once absolute, was beginning to unravel. The weight of betrayal pressed heavy on his spine. *This* wasn't how it was supposed to end. He had calculated every step, accounted for every threat. But he had never expected *them*. He had never anticipated *this*. That two of his own, Allison, his precious weapon, and Malakhov, his right hand—would defy him, not just with words, but with bullets and open rebellion.

It was unthinkable. And it was happening.

Beside Allison stood Malakhov, calm in the eye of the storm. His movements were measured but lethal, honed by a lifetime of violence. His weapon was reloaded with cold accuracy, then he pivoted with the fluidity of a dancer, each step an act of defiance to survive. A man sculpted by war, tempered by betrayal, and burning with a purpose.

His eyes, narrowed to slits, locked on Radimir like a predator who had finally turned on his master.

Despite the chaos that shattered around her, Allison remained centered. Her hand didn't tremble. Her aim didn't waver. She had survived Radimir before. She had endured his control, his violence, his promises.

But this time was different. This time, she wasn't a pawn or a survivor.

This time, she was a threat.

She stood with purpose, her body a shield not just for herself but for the child she carried. And she took a calculated risk, knowing that Radimir, for all his cruelty, wouldn't kill her. Not yet. Not while she was still useful. Not while she still carried *his* blood.

He wouldn't risk it. And she would use that.

The tension between the three of them was thick—like the stillness right before a shot rings out. Every breath felt too loud, every glance loaded. Radimir's pale eyes flicked between them, cold and sharp. His anger filled the space, pressing in on all sides. But beneath all that fury, there was something else—something quieter, harder to name.

Recognition.

Loss.

Even pain.

Allison could see it, just for a second, a flicker of the man who once called her family, the man who once believed he was building an empire.

She saw the exact moment he realized that everything he had built was collapsing, not from an outside attack, but from within.

They were the cracks in his foundation. And the house was crumbling.

He had nurtured them. He had trained them. He had molded them into killers.

And now they were here to destroy him.

"You cannot win, Allison," Radimir hissed, his voice low and venomous, each word laced with a sinister kind of pleasure. His eyes burned with something ancient and cruel. "You think this ends with a bullet? With betrayal? You are nothing without me." He raised the gun, while barrel gleamed under the flicker of moonlight, trigger was squeezed.

The shot cracked through the night.

It tore through the air with terrifying precision, *close*, so close it clipped through her hair, embedding itself in the wall just feet above her head. A warning. A *taunt*.

Radimir's lip curled into a feral smile.

"Your life *belongs* to me," he spat. "Just as your child's will. You are bound to me, body and blood. You can't run from what you are."

But Allison didn't flinch.

Instead, she smiled.

It wasn't soft. It wasn't kind. It was the razor-sharp grin of a woman who had already died once and refused to stay buried.

"It didn't have to be this way, Radimir," she said, her voice calm but cutting, honed sharp by pain and truth. "You had *every* chance. All the power, all the people, all the time in the world to build something *good*—something lasting. But you couldn't see past your own hate."

Her voice dropped, steady and final. "And now, this is what that hate costs you."

Beside her, Malakhov took a single step forward, silent, solid, immovable. His presence was a shield. His hand hovered near his weapon, every muscle coiled and ready. Gone was the icy precision of the soldier. In its place stood something far more dangerous; a man fighting not just to win, but to *protect*.

Radimir's nostrils flared.

"You still think you can stop me, *Dmitri*?" he snarled, his voice cracking like a whip. "After everything I gave you... *you*?! You were supposed to be *mine*."

Without warning, he raised his gun and fired.

Malakhov moved before the sound reached them, his instincts honed over years of brutal survival. The bullet missed by inches as he dropped low, rolling to the side. In a single, fluid motion, he came up with his weapon drawn and fired two precise shots. One slammed into the column behind Radimir; the other clipped the edge of his coat, forcing him off balance.

An explosion echoed as Malakhov hurled a small device across the space, its blast not deadly, but disorienting. The flash sending dust and splinters flying, and for a heartbeat, Radimir staggered.

He wasn't invincible. And for the first time, he knew it.

Allison didn't waste the moment.

She raised her gun and fired, her stance solid, her breath measured. Bullet after bullet roared from the barrel, her aim deadly and focused. Each shot was a promise. Not just to end him, but to protect the life she wanted back.

Radimir ducked and spun, his movements feral. He fell backward behind a tree just as the bullets finished shattering the very space he stood in moments ago. Wild laughter, completely insane, bounced between the crumbling walls.

"You think this matters?" he howled. "You think *any* of this matters? I built this world! I carved it from blood and fire, and it *belongs* to me! You, *Allison,* you are nothing but a crack in the wall."

"We're done with you, Radimir," she said coldly, her voice echoing in the silence that followed his tirade. "This ends *tonight.*"

But suddenly—

Pain.

A sudden stab of pain, bright and merciless.

Allison gasped as something small, but jagged and fast, sliced into her side. A shard of glass, flung from the shattered upper window by the last explosion, had driven itself into her flesh with terrifying precision. It wasn't large. It wasn't deep. But it hit hard enough to throw her balance.

Her legs buckled, and she collapsed. Her gun clattered to the floor as the impact drove the air from her lungs. Her hand went immediately to her abdomen.

The baby.

Her breath came in sharp, uneven pulls, loud in her ears like a rush of static. Pain flared through her side—burning one second, icy the next. She pressed her hand to it, trying to keep herself together, literally and otherwise.

Blood bloomed between her fingers.

But she didn't cry out.

Didn't panic.

She *focused.*

She closed her eyes against the wave of dizziness crashing over her, the sound of the battlefield momentarily muffled by the pounding of her pulse. Through the chaos, through the searing pain, smoke and fear, she held onto one thing;

He doesn't win.

Not now.

Not ever.

And with gritted teeth and shaking limbs, Allison forced herself back up, because she still had something Radimir could never take.

Hope.

Malakhov's head snapped toward Allison's cry. His jaw clenched; his hand whitened around the grip of his gun. The moment of divided attention cost him, Radimir seized the opening without hesitation. A shot streaked through the gloom. At the last moment, Malakhov twisted away from it; still, the bullet grazed his shoulder, tearing a hot line across his skin. Blood blossomed, quickly soaking into the coat's worn fabric.

He staggered but did not falter.

Clenching his teeth, the pain almost developed into a scream. But the environment was too chaotic. His vision remained glued to Radimir, every fiber of his body screaming to defend the woman now trembling behind him. Malakhov was panting, sweat streaming down his brow, patching his wound would be the last thing on his mind. He was still standing, still fighting, and surely for Allison, he would not let her down.

"Stay with me, Allison!" he barked, his urgency cutting clean through the tumultuous noise of gunfire and snapping branches. "Don't you dare give up now!"

On the ground, Allison winced with each pulse of pain from the glass still lodged in her side. Every throb sent another ripple through her body. But then she heard Malakhov's voice—distant, but enough. She tightened her grip on the pistol, nails digging into her skin. Her breath came hard and fast, but she wouldn't let the pain take her down. Not yet.

Not now. Not with him here.

She gritted her teeth, shoved her heel into the dirt, and with all the strength left in her, rose the pitch of her trembling body. The world tilted for a moment, blurring with dizziness, but she forced her way through it.

Her legs were numb; but she was rising. One breath at a time. One heartbeat at a time.

Her feet unsteady, but defiant. She hissed, "Get up, Allison. You have come too far to fall now. This is going to end tonight."

Her gaze cut to Malakhov's, and between them, in that instant, a wordless understanding. He gave her the faintest nod that said; *I see you. I believe in you.*

Then, his voice dropped low, calm and steady despite the storm around them. "Do you trust me?"

His question cut through the chaos with blade-like precision.

Allison didn't hesitate. Her voice, though hoarse, rang with conviction. "With everything, Dmitri. I trust you."

A flicker of something warm passed over his expression, just for a second. Relief. Gratitude.

"Good," he said, and then lifted his gun in a gesture that seemed almost ritualistic, turning it momentarily in her direction. "Fire a hail storm. Don't stop until the clip's dry. Can you do that?"

Despite the blood at her side, despite the sting in her eyes, Allison's smile was grim and feral. "Watch me."

She pivoted, planting one knee into the ground for balance, and leveled her gun with both hands, bracing through the agony. Then she opened fire.

Bullet after bullet screamed through the air, tearing through the branches and debris, sending a barrage of bullets toward Radimir. She didn't aim with precision, this wasn't about perfect shots. This was about force. About pressure. About fury and pain and vengeance.

Radimir turned sharply, his pale eyes narrowing as the hail of gunfire rained down. He dove, rolling behind a thick outcropping of stone and roots, returning sporadic fire as he tried to calculate his next move. But Allison didn't let up. Not for a second.

And that was the point.

While Radimir focused on her, while his attention locked on the relentless barrage, Malakhov moved. Quiet, calculated steps through the underbrush, flanking around to the far edge of the clearing. The gunfire masked his approach, and the smoke cloaked his presence like a phantom stalking through the trees.

Closer.

Two more steps.

Just a few feet now.

Radimir never saw him coming.

Malakhov emerged from the shadows like a predator, his bloodied arm steady as he raised his weapon. His expression was unreadable, no rage, no hesitation.

Just purpose.

With a single pull of the trigger, the bullet tore through the space between them.

It struck Radimir in the back with a sickening *crack,* blood bursting from the point of impact. The body jolted, staggering him backward, crashing through branches behind him. He collapsed to one knee, gasping, with his hand instinctively clutching the wound.

His silver eyes went wide, and for the first time, not fury, not arrogance, but *fear* stared back at them.

Real, human fear.

Malakhov stepped forward, the smoke curling around him like a crown of ash, and said nothing.

Because the shot had said it all.

Malakhov shouted for Allison, who came limping with uneven steps, every nerve still tingling with adrenaline and pain. A horrible tightness clung to her chest, and her heartbeat pounded like war drumming in her ears. The echoes of the gunshots faded away, giving pass to only the rustling of leaves, to the shallow breaths of the dying.

Her eyes turned to Radimir, sprawled on the blood-soaked earth. The darkness in his gaze faded. The strength that had once seemed immortal was draining away, and with it, the last of his hold over them.

But he could not lay down his hate even in death.

For a brief moment, his expression did soften; Allison would never know if it was from death or some warped kind of acceptance. But his last words were bitter.

"You think you've won, Allison?" His voice cracked in his throat like broken glass. He barely managed to breathe; blood was welling on the corner of his lips. "Even now... you can't cut me out. I'm in you. *In him.* That's all I ever needed."

The words struck her like a hammer to the chest. Not because she believed them, but because she knew, deep down, Radimir had always known the truth; control was his only legacy. And even now, he was trying to wield it.

Allison felt herself fall to her knees beside him, holding her breath as she saw the life draining from his eyes. The blood from his wound had already pooled around him and soaked deep into the earth. He was disintegrating before her very eyes; his skin was paling, his chest was barely rising with each rattling inhale.

This was it.

The end.

And yet, a part of her felt hollow. Not because she mourned him, but because she'd once been *his*. She had once almost trusted him. Followed him. Believed him. And now, in his death, he was trying to pass that burden to her child.

No. Not again.

As Allison intervened, she didn't hesitate to pull the weapon from his limp, cooling fingers. She felt the metal warmth of the gun in her palm while looking coldly at his dying form, "You're not going to win, Radimir," her voice low but firm, choking on the bitter finality of the words. "This ends now. Your reign, your legacy, your lies... they die with you."

Radimir's eyes met hers one last time, clouded, dim, but in them, there was something that chilled her to her core. Not fear. Not anger.

Pride.

"You'll regret this..." he croaked, blood trailing from the corner of his mouth. "You'll never escape me. My legacy... lives on. Your son... will carry it too."

Then, with one final rattling breath, his head tipped sideways. The light went out in his eyes. The man who had haunted her, who had twisted her soul, who had threatened her child, he was gone.

Allison remained still for a long time. She looked down at the lifeless body, relief and disbelief warring in her chest. She wanted to feel free.

She wanted it to be over. But a seed of doubt lingered, planted by his final words.

A warm hand touched her shoulder.

She turned.

Malakhov was beside her now, with a faint trickle of blood coming from his wounded shoulder. His brow was furrowed, although not in pain but in concern. "We did it," he whispered breathlessly. "It's all over."

Allison nodded, her voice breaking. "It has to be."

A sharp pain coiled deep in her abdomen. Allison gasped and clutched her belly. Her knees gave way.

"Allison!" Malakhov caught her instantly, his arms steady as steel, but panic broke across his face. "What's wrong?"

Her eyes flew wide. "Dmitri... it's happening. The baby, he's coming. *Now.*"

Malakhov's face went deathly pale. "No. No, not now," he said, holding her with greater violence until she was doubled over in pain.

"It's too early," she managed to say, her voice breaking. "It wasn't supposed to be this soon—"

Another contraction seized her, stronger than the last, and she gave a piercing cry as her legs buckled and gave way entirely.

"I've got you," Malakhov said with seriousness and strength, the strength of a man who had spent a lifetime surviving, as he lifted Allison into his arms. "Hold on, Allison. Just hold on. I won't let anything happen to either of you."

He ran like mad through the woods, branches slapping against his arms, sweat and blood running down his face. But he never faltered. He never slowed down.

Inside the cabin, he laid her gently on the bed, ripped off his bloodied coat, and pressed a cold cloth to her forehead. She grabbed hold of it with her other hand, gripping with all her might as another contraction hit.

"You're okay," he whispered, softly brushing a lock of hair from her face before kissing her temple. "You're safe. I'm right here."

Allison clenched her teeth, the pain mounting. "We survived Radimir. We can survive this too."

His voice was fierce, unwavering. "We'll *do* more than survive. We'll live, Allison. You, me, and our son."

* * *

At the Kotov Manor, Daniel and Rob went sweeping through the last corridors. The manor was in ruins, windows broken, furniture shattered, walls scarred by bullet holes. But the air had changed. The oppressive presence of Radimir's rule was gone, dissolved like smoke.

Putting his gun down, Daniel paced cautiously forward while his stance relaxed for the first time in days while facing Rob. He breathed hard, "It's done."

Rob scanned the silent hallway, taking in the bodies, the blood, the chains around captured Bratva soldiers. His voice was hushed, reverent. "You can feel it. Can't you? The weight is gone."

Daniel nodded. "The Bratva is finished. For the first time in years..." he exhaled slowly, almost not believing the words himself "... we are free."

And somewhere, far in the woods, into a quiet little safe-house, a child was coming to life. Not in the shadows of tyranny but at the dawn of a new era.

Thirty One

A Birth of a New Era

The cabin was too small and the air thick with anticipation. Allison was clenching Malakhov's hand in pain. Everything was happening too fast. One moment defending themselves against attackers; the next, labor pains began at the most unwanted moment. Malakhov was beside her, his face pale and his typical calm demeanor dissipated in the rising tide of panic in his chest.

"Dmitri..." Allison gasped with pain from another contraction; she balled her fingers into a tight grip around the sheets, her knuckles visibly pale. "It's too soon. It's too soon. He isn't ready."

Malakhov shuffled nervously beside her and was muttering something in Russian, totally out of his depth. His composure cracked, leaving only raw bewilderment. He turned to her, eyes wide, hand tightening around hers as if it might anchor them both.

"What...what do I do?" His voice was thin, the fear unmistakable.

"I'm fine... just... I need to focus, Dmitri." Allison closed her eyes and tried to calm her breath for another wave of agony. She had to keep strong for herself and the baby. Malakhov was pacing beside the bed, the same man who formerly stood unshaken in the line of fire was now looking as if he might faint from pure panic.

A low groan of pain came from her as her face was dripping in sweat.

"You're doing so good, *my lion*," he muttered, but his eyes betrayed the terror.

"Just a little longer."

But then—he froze.

A sound.

Crunching gravel.

Footsteps outside.

Malakhov's head snapped toward the door. The pacing stopped. Instinctively, his hand went to the loaded gun on the table. Trained so fiercely that his instincts were screaming at him now.

"I heard it, too," Allison said, trying to sit up amid debilitating agony and pressure. Her skin was pale, her hands trembling as she braced herself. "Let me—"

"No." Malakhov was beside her in an instant, crouching low and pressing his palm gently to her shoulder. His voice, though firm, was thick with concern. "You need to rest. You stay. I'll handle it."

"But what if—?"

"No." His eyes locked with hers. "You've done enough. You've fought enough. Let me protect you now."

Allison hesitated, her lips parted as if to argue, but she stopped. Something in his expression silenced her. Not just protectiveness, but desperation. Fear, barely veiled. She nodded once, her grip on the blanket tightening.

Malakhov rose swiftly, grabbed both his sidearm and the backup, and checked each with methodical efficiency. No wasted movement. The moment he turned from her, it was as if a switch had flipped, his shoulders squared, his breath evened, and the softness he had for her fell behind a soldier's mask. The storm outside was nothing compared to the one he was ready to face.

He stepped to the front door, cracked it open, and moved out onto the broken porch with surgical precision, boots silent against the wood.

The night was cold and sharp, the forest still holding echoes of gunfire and the ghosts of what had just happened. He scanned the tree line.

Movement.

Figures.

Three.

Weapons drawn.

Malakhov raised his own instantly, his entire body coiled and ready.

Then—he saw them.

Rob.

Daniel.

And at the center, calm and cutting in her presence, Katherine Walker.

His grip relaxed, but just slightly. He didn't lower the gun.

Daniel stepped forward, voice calm but edged. "Where is she?"

Malakhov's jaw tensed. "She's safe." His eyes narrowed. "Why are you here?"

Rob's gun remained trained. "It's over. The war's done."

Malakhov's expression didn't change. His eyes, sharp and dark, flicked between the three. His body didn't shift an inch. "If you think you're coming to arrest us," he said softly, his voice like a razor being unsheathed, "I can assure you that won't be happening."

Rob didn't flinch. Instead, he lifted his chin. "We saw the body. Radimir's dead."

A flicker, barely more than a breath, passed over Malakhov's face. Something cold. Deeper. Knowing.

Rob continued, his tone flattening with finality. "Just beyond the ridge. Chest shot. Single bullet. Blood everywhere."

Silence held for half a heartbeat.

"I know," said Malakhov, the words trailing out softly, full of every meaning of everything that had been suffered through. "I'm the one who killed him."

Daniel narrowed his eyes, but he did not move.

Rob blinked, eyebrows raising, stunned, but trained not to show it. Their stances tightened without shifting.

"*You*?" Rob asked, almost disbelieving. "You pulled the trigger?"

Malakhov's voice was still and grave. "He was going to kill her. I had the shot. I took it." His words were steady, but there was a slight crack in the finish, grief, relief, trauma all buried under resolve. "I did what I had to do."

He stepped forward just once, just enough to show he wasn't backing down. "You know Radimir. You know what he was. He fought to the very end."

Rob's mouth tightened. He exchanged a silent glance with Daniel, the kind born from battlefields and blood. They'd seen enough to know the truth in someone's eyes.

Malakhov went on, voice like a vow. "You don't have to believe me. But I didn't leave her. Not for one second. Not even when he almost took me with him."

Rob's arms finally slackened. "We found the tracks. Two sets of prints in the dirt. Side by side."

Malakhov didn't respond, he didn't have to.

Then, from inside the cabin—

A scream. Shrill. Wounded. Agonized.

Everyone froze.

Malakhov's head snapped back toward the door. His spine went rigid, jaw clenched.

"*Allison*," he breathed.

And the gun in his hand trembled, for the first time that night.

Katherine's head jerked toward the cabin. "Was that Allison?"

Malakhov glanced back toward the door, tension rippling through his frame. "Yes."

Daniel stepped forward sharply, his voice cutting. "What the hell did you do to her?"

"Is she hurt?" Rob's voice rose with alarm. "If you hurt her—"

"I did *nothing* to her," Malakhov snarled, stepping between them and the door, his entire body bristling with protective rage. "I have done nothing but protect her. Love her. The stress of the battle pushed her into labor. She's screaming because she's in *labor*," he growled, grounding the chaos with bitter clarity. "And if this conversation doesn't end soon, I swear to God I will end you before I let you keep me from her."

Another cry tore through the air, longer this time. A guttural, agonized sound. It was followed by rapid, panicked breathing and the muffled crash of something inside the cabin being knocked over.

Katherine didn't hesitate.

She dropped her gun.

The clatter of metal against the porch boards echoed like thunder in the stunned silence.

She stepped forward.

Malakhov's hand jerked up, weapon raised again on instinct, his hand shook, the gun wavering a fraction, his eyes darting to the door as if he might bolt. His breath hitched. He was on the verge of losing himself.

"Mom?" Rob barked, stunned. What the hell are you doing?"

"She is in labor," Katherine said firmly, not glancing at him. Her voice didn't tremble, it carried the quiet, commanding steel of a woman who had delivered more babies than any of them had pulled triggers. "She's not going to do it alone."

She stepped closer, slowly, deliberately. Her eyes met Malakhov's, calm and unwavering.

"You want to protect her?" she asked softly. "Then let me help her. That's all I'm here to do."

Malakhov's eyes darted between the woman and the men behind her, calculating, *torn*. His finger hovered just off the trigger. The moment stretched taut as wire.

Katherine held up her hands, not in surrender, but in trust. "Put that down, Dmitri," she said gently, firmly. "You're not going to stop me from helping Allison."

He blinked at her, just once, like the name had stunned him.

Dmitri.

His given name.

His real name.

The gun was slowly lowered, brows furrowing with something gentle; a mixture of confusion, disbelief, and a dull ache of relief.

Daniel stood aside, gesturing toward the door. "Then go."

Rob's hand hovered near his holster before he finally gave a tight nod. "We are not here to take her," he said roughly, "We just... we needed to know that she was safe."

Malakhov's eyes swept over all three of them one last time. He didn't thank them. Didn't trust them. But he understood.

He gave a stiff nod, his eyes darkening with a warning glare. "She's mine to protect," he said in barely a whisper. "Do not forget that."

Without another word between them, he turned on his heel and vanished through the screen door, which thudded shut with a sound like a full stop.

The heaviness in Katherine's gaze slowly dissipated as she started moving toward Allison after a slow-moving sit on the side of the bed. "You have done a lot of bad things, Allison. You hurt my family, and you hurt Rob. And I cannot forgive you for it — not now."

Every single word hit Allison like a terrible punch, raw and unabashed, every syllable soaked in years of bitterness, heartbreak, and betrayal.

Allison gasped for air, twitched, and winced in pain again. "I know," she whispered, "I'm sorry, Katherine. I can't change what I did, but I did it for him, for us. I thought I was doing the right thing... but now I know I caused more pain than I ever meant to."

Katherine's eyes didn't waver. "You *broke* my son," she said plainly. "You left him bleeding in ways I couldn't fix. Watching him fall apart after what happened between you three... that nearly destroyed me too. You don't get to apologize and expect that to make it right."

"I don't," Allison said quickly, desperately. "I don't expect anything. I just, I'm sorry. *Truly.*"

For a moment, silence hung heavy between them.

Then, Katherine's stern expression faltered, just slightly. Her fingers, lined with age and steadiness, groped for Allison's hand. With a hushed tone, "I don't know if I'll ever forgive you for what happened with Rob," uttered with a thin voice, hardly above a whisper. "But... you also saved his life, Allison. Whatever else you've done, when it mattered, you got him out, set him free."

She exhaled slowly. "That counts for something."

Allison blinked rapidly as emotion threatened to overtake her. "I'm so sorry — for everything."

"I believe you," Katherine said after a pause. "But believing someone doesn't erase the wreckage they left behind."

Allison gave a faint nod, swallowing past the lump in her throat. "I understand."

Katherine squeezed her hand. "Don't mistake this for forgiveness. I'm here for the baby. And because...because once, you mattered to us. For the fact that you gave Rob back to me in one piece. But if you're going to raise this child, you'd better prove that you're capable of more than just surviving. You want to be a mother?" She leaned in, her eyes fierce now. "Start by owning every consequence of the path you chose."

Tears welled in Allison's eyes, but she nodded. "I will. I promise."

Malakhov stepped inside like a shadow cut from war, blood on his shirt, tension radiating off him in waves. His eyes locked onto Allison first, pale, sweating, biting back another scream, and then flicked to Katherine, kneeling beside her.

His body stiffened. He didn't raise the weapon, but his knuckles remained tight around it.

He didn't need to speak. The question was written in the angle of his shoulders, the set of his jaw, the storm burning in his gaze.

Can I trust her?

Allison met his eyes, breathing hard. Despite the pain and fear coiling through her body, her gaze was steady.

She nodded once.

Slow. Sure. Convincing.

It was enough.

Malakhov exhaled, lowered the gun to his side, but didn't let go of it. He moved toward the foot of the bed, still watching Katherine with quiet suspicion, like a wolf never quite putting his back down.

"We need help, Dmitri," whispered Allison, holding his hand as he came nearer. "I cannot do this on my own."

Malakhov looked at her, then her stomach and child she was about to bring into the world, and back again. With a wave of tenderness, he lowered himself down to one knee beside her and brushed hair away from her damp forehead. "You are not alone," he uttered, voice thick with emotion. "Not anymore. Whatever it takes, I'm here."

Katherine's eyes flicked up to him briefly, reading his face. And though no words passed between them, there was a fragile understanding, for now.

Allison was in pain.

The baby was coming.

And for the moment, all history, every betrayal, every scar, would have to wait.

The hours dissolved into a haze. Pain came in waves so fierce they stole her breath and sense of time. At some point, daylight returned, though she couldn't say when. All that she knew was the unbearable burning coursing through her body with every contraction, depriving her of breath and strength. Sweat trickled down her brow as she cried out; her muscles locked with every wave of anguish.

Malakhov didn't leave her side for a moment.

He held her hands tightly when hers grew weak, in low tones despite the flicker of fear in his eyes. He wiped her brow with trembling hands. When she doubled over, he even knelt beside her and whispered things in Russian and English that Allison could barely comprehend through the pain.

"I'm sorry, Allison," he said one time, when she squeezed his fingers hard enough to bruise. His voice cracked, hoarse with regret. "I'm trying, but I can't... I don't know what to do."

"You're doing it," she whispered, unable to look fully into his eyes but trying. "Just be here, Dmitri. That's all I need. Just... be here."

And he was.

Every scream, every breath, every contraction, he stayed through all of it. His fear never made him flinch. His instinct to protect never wavered. When she needed water, he fetched it. When she felt she couldn't go on, he told her she could, and somehow, that was enough.

Katherine moved around them with calm authority, her sleeves rolled up, her hands quick but careful as she guided Allison through each stage. She gave short, clear commands, never panicked, never raised her voice, just a steady, anchoring presence, the kind that only comes from years of supporting family.

"You are almost there," Katherine whispered. "One more push, Allison. One more."

And somehow, Allison found it in herself.

With a cry that tore from the deepest part of her, she pushed, every ounce of strength, every piece of her pain, everything she had left.

And then—

A new sound filled the room.

Not a scream of pain this time, but something small. Wet. Fragile.

A baby's cry.

Malakhov's breath caught; as he turned toward the voice. In that instant, Katherine threw a makeshift blanket around the child, quickly checking the umbilical cord before handing him gently into Allison's already-outstretched arms.

"He...he is here," Malakhov whispered beside her with wide-open eyes, unable to catch his breath. "He is here, Allison."

The baby boy was small, smaller than Allison expected, but hardy. His cries were sharp and angry; his tiny hands were curled into clenched fists, and he could very well have been screaming with joy for his own birth. His skin was pinkish red, while his dark hair clung in soggy locks to his skull.

Through her tears and amid convulsions of shaking, Allison looked down at him. "He's perfect," she murmured, voice cracking. "Dmitri, he's perfect; Our son."

Malakhov's eyes seemed eyes seemed violently torn open by some unspoken feeling, gratitude, disbelief, as he reached out, hesitant fingers threading through the baby's hair, the first act of such reverence he'd ever offered to anything. "Our son," he repeated, the words foreign and holy in his mouth. "Our legacy."

Katherine stepped back, giving the new family their sacred space, her hands slick but steady as she cleaned up. Then, in that familiar quiet, she was back, checking again, fingers working his chest, his wrists, and his back.

"He's strong," she said, after a while, pride creeping in. "A little early, yes, but healthy. He's going to be just fine, Allison."

Immediately, a wave of relief crashed over Allison.

Katherine turned to Malakhov then, her tone shifting, commanding again, but not unkind. "He'll need warmth. Care. And both of you. He'll be more vulnerable than most for the first few weeks. Don't let your guard down now."

Malakhov nodded immediately, his arm still around Allison. "We won't."

Katherine hesitated for a breath, then her gaze settled on Allison again. She crouched beside her, quiet now.

"You did well. Way better than I expected. I never even thought I would be beside you tonight, helping you give life to a child, but..." She trailed off and then pulled her in for a very brief, awkward, stiff embrace. It was as real as it could get, though. "Take care of him. And yourself. Both of you."

Allison closed her eyes against a fresh wave of tears. "Thank you, Katherine. For staying. For helping."

Katherine stood, brushing her hands off. "I'm not doing this for you," she said one last time. "I'm doing it for him. And because, despite everything, you were family once. That matters."

She turned to Malakhov.

He stepped forward, his voice uncharacteristically gentle. "Thank you, Katherine. And I do mean it," he said gratefully.

She arched her brows at the surprise and looked at him in cautious curiosity. "You are welcome for whatever I have done," she said after a pause. "I don't think I will ever forgive you; either of you. But whether you like it or not, this is your family now, so don't go screwing it up."

And with that, Katherine turned and walked toward the door.

Outside, the cold air waited. The world was still dangerous, still uncertain, but for now, in the warmth of that broken, half-lit home, in that battered cabin, something began that neither war nor regret could erase.

A baby.

A family.

For the first time, something she dared to hope might outlast the war.

Thirty Two

Between War and Wonder

Back at their home, with their little boy tucked snugly in Allison's arms, the air felt different. Just days ago, this place had been steeped in suspicion and the cold hush that follows violence. Tonight, the hush remained, but something softer threaded through it. Not quite relief, not quite safety, but the first flicker of peace they could believe in.

Allison sat on the worn velvet sofa near the hearth, her baby cuddled tightly against her chest, his tiny chest rising and falling with each fragile breath. Her arms ached, her entire body was spent, but her heart had never felt so full.

"Dmitri," she whispered with a broken voice. "I wonder if it is really over. We have him, our little boy."

Malakhov laughed and sat beside her, rested an arm on his knee, and with the other hand caressed the fuzzy curls of his child. His face, which was often cold, inscrutable, and forged through conflict, was now filled with wonder. "I never imagined this. Never imagined being a father... or this life."

Allison looked down at the sleeping baby, then back at Malakhov. "But you are," she whispered gently. "A father. A good one. He already knows your voice. I can tell, he calms down when you talk."

Malakhov's eyes flicked to hers, surprised. "He does?"

She smiled. "You didn't notice?"

"I..." He hesitated, then shook his head slowly. "No. I was too busy making sure I wouldn't drop him or hold him wrong."

"You were just perfect," she said softly, adjusting the blanket around the baby's head. "He is safe because of you."

There was a long silence that was comfortable with the popping of the fire and the son drawing slow breaths. Allison turned to look at Malakhov, her tone changing slightly. "He needs a name."

Malakhov clutched his jaw a bit, but not from anger, from the weight of the question on the man's mind. He stared at the infant, brow furrowed as if searching for something important in that tiny face.

"I would like to..." he said slowly, almost cautiously, as if naming him aloud were to make the thing too real. "I would like to name him after my father, his name was *Mikhail.*"

Allison blinked, surprised, but not at the name. At the vulnerability in his voice.

"Mikhail," she whispered, trying out the name, considering it as she felt its weight. She smiled and ran her thumb along the soft side of her son's cheek. "Mikhail Malakhov. That's a strong name. A name with roots."

Malakhov nodded once, then exhaled slowly. "He was a hard man, my father. Not cruel... just distant. Quiet. The kind of man who showed love in silence and work. I didn't understand it then. But now... I do."

She reached for him with her free hand, lacing her fingers through his. "Then let's give Mikhail something different. Something better. A father who holds him, not just protects him. A father who stays."

"I will," he said immediately, without hesitation. "There's nothing in this world that could take me from him. Or you."

Tears sprang to her eyes, uninvited but welcome. She leaned her head against his shoulder, their baby between them. "We made it, Dmitri."

"For now," he said, ever the realist, but his voice carried a thread of hope. "We've got protections in place. I have alarms set around the house, no one gets through without us knowing. If any new regime wants to come, let them try."

"We'll fight again if we have to," Allison said, nodding. "But not for a cause this time. For *him*."

Malakhov leaned forward and kissed her forehead, then the baby's. "For Mikhail."

Sitting in silence, they stared at their son sleeping, a fine consonance of his tiny breaths mixing with the hum of the wind outside. For the first time in their lives, no mission. No orders. No allegiance but to each other.

Just them.

* * *

The days slowly found their rhythm, uneven, sometimes chaotic, but warm and full in a way neither of them had ever known.

Allison had taken to motherhood with fierce gentleness. She read every book she could find in the manor's dusty library, asked quiet questions when Katherine stopped by with supplies, and trusted her instincts when nothing else made sense. Mikhail was a calm, quiet baby, often content simply to be held, soothed by the steady thrum of Allison's heartbeat or the deep rumble of Malakhov's voice. But there were nights he screamed for hours, needing more than food or rest, needing closeness.

And Malakhov, despite a lifetime of bloodshed, command, and cold calculation, was shockingly good at being a father. He moved slowly with Mikhail, as though the child were made of porcelain. He changed diapers without complaint (though often with a look of utter confusion), and he mastered the art of holding a bottle while simultaneously muttering Russian lullabies under his breath.

The sight of Dmitri Malakhov, feared commander, pacing the nursery with Mikhail against his shoulder, softly mumbling half-sung children's songs, would be etched into Allison's memory forever.

One morning, after a long night spent taking turns pacing the floor, Mikhail finally settled. He now lay in his cradle by the window, bundled, his little hand twitching now and then in sleep. The soft glow of morning painted the room in gold.

Allison and Malakhov sat together in front of the fire, both in robes, their eyes heavy with exhaustion but their expressions soft with contentment. Allison rested her head on his shoulder, her hand tucked into his, fingers twined and still faintly trembling from the early hours.

"You never thought we'd be here, did you?" she asked softly, her voice filled with affection and wonder.

Malakhov chuckled, his voice deep and rough with sleep, but genuine. "Never. I was prepared for a lifetime of war. Of surviving, not living. Not... *this*."

He turned his head and kissed her hair, then leaned his cheek against it. "But now... I want nothing more than to wake up every day to this sound," he added, nodding toward the crackle of the fire and Mikhail's faint breathing. "I'm ready to focus on our family, on Mikhail."

Allison smiled, blinking back the emotion that built so quickly these days. "You're a good father, Dmitri."

He scoffed. "I nearly put the diaper on backward yesterday."

She laughed, the sound surprised and light. "You *did* put the diaper on backward, and inside out once."

Malakhov groaned, but there was laughter in it too. "He looked so smug when I finished. Like he knew. Like he was judging me."

"He probably was," she teased. "He gets that from me."

They sat in silence for a moment, watching the flickering flames. The past still lived behind their eyes, the betrayals, the blood, the war, but it had softened, dulled by the immediacy of new life. It didn't vanish, but it no longer consumed.

"I want him to have everything we didn't," Allison whispered after a moment. "Safety. A childhood. Peace. Joy."

"He will," Malakhov said, his voice low but firm. "As long as I breathe, no one will touch him. No one will touch you."

"You really think we'll be safe?"

"I don't just think it. I'll make it so." He looked down at her, then at the cradle. "Under any circumstances, I would burn the world if it meant keeping it away from our door."

For a long moment, Allison looked into his eyes, raised herself up slowly, and kissed him softly, passing on a tender promise. For all the pain, all the war, all the things they had lost—they had built something beautiful together.

A quiet coo interrupted the moment. Mikhail stirred, squirming beneath the blanket. Malakhov rose instantly, reaching the cradle in two long strides and lifting the baby with careful, practiced ease.

"Did you miss Papa already?" he murmured in Russian, pressing a kiss to the boy's forehead. "I see how it is—you cry for her, but you *melt* for me."

Allison stood beside him, the tone of the soft laughter going well with the soft stroke of Mikhail's back from the hand. "He's got you in the palm of his tiny hand already!"

Malakhov grinned—an honest, rare smile that reached his eyes. "He's the only one who ever could."

And as Mikhail blinked up at them with unfocused eyes, his parents stood together, their arms around each other, the child between them. The war was over. A new chapter had begun.

* * *

Katherine Walker had returned to her home, but the journey back wasn't one of triumph—it was marked by the sharp sting of conflicting emotions. Bitterness clung to her like the winter wind, wrapping around her shoulders as she rode through the city Radimir had once ruled with iron control and ruthless violence. The faces of survivors along the streets, some jubilant, some wary, reminded her that the war might be over, but the pain wasn't gone.

She hadn't gone back to celebrate. She had gone back to tell the truth.

The doors to the rebellion headquarters creaked open, and every conversation inside halted the moment Katherine stepped into the main room. The officers stood waiting. Tension filled the room as shoulders stiffened and narrowed gazes fell on her, like a jury waiting to deliver its verdict.

Katherine did not flinch. She walked in and stood in the middle of the room amid that deafening silence, an oppressive force swirling in her ears.

"I know what you're all thinking," Katherine began, her voice steady but frayed at the edges. "I helped Allison. I helped her bring that child into the world. And yes, I'm still helping them. Because that baby has nothing to do with our grudges. Because they're afraid—*afraid* you'll punish them just for trying to keep him alive. I won't stand by and watch that happen."

The voices hummed in the room like overbearing static.

Katherine swept the room with her gaze, each officer being targeted in turn, daring them to speak the judgment she so sorely felt in their eyes. "You can sit there and whisper behind my back, or you can hear me out. I'm not asking for your approval. I'm asking for your sense."

She turned to Rob and Daniel, her voice softening just a fraction. "Allison didn't just bring Radimir down—she *saved* you both when it mattered. When no one else could reach you, she did. And Malakhov..." She hesitated, as if the words tasted strange in her mouth. "He's not the monster we believed. Not anymore."

"You saw him?" one of the officers asked, incredulous. "*Malakhov*?"

"I did," Katherine said. "He was gentle. With her. With that child. He held that baby like the world would break if he let go. I saw the way he looked at them both. That man would burn down what's left of the city to protect them. He's changed."

Daniel crossed his arms, skeptical. "You really trust him now? After everything?"

Katherine exhaled. "I don't trust him. Not yet. Maybe not ever. But I know this, he's not our enemy anymore. And if we keep looking backward, we'll never be able to rebuild anything forward."

Rob finally stepped closer, his voice quiet but impassioned. "She didn't choose any of this. She didn't want to fight for Radimir. She was surviving. And when it mattered, she turned on him. She protected people. She protected *me*."

His voice cracked. "She's not the same person anymore, Mom. But I think she's trying."

Katherine looked at her son. Her heart twisted, he looked older, worn down by months of captivity, of pain. But in his eyes, there was light again. And part of that light had come from Allison.

"I know, Rob," she said finally, her voice low. "And I'm trying too. I can't forget what she did. But... I *see* the change. I see the way she looks at that baby. She's not just trying, she's *fighting* for him. Like any of us would."

More murmurs stirred through the room, this time less sharp, more thoughtful. The anger hadn't left, but it was tempered now with curiosity, with the possibility of something different.

Daniel stepped forward, his tone firm. "We have to rebuild. We can't keep dividing ourselves with old wounds. They brought Radimir down, together. That has to mean something."

Katherine nodded, her voice resolute now. "You're right. Chicago needs healing. And whether we like it or not, Allison and Malakhov are part of what comes next. We can't rewrite the past, but we can shape the future. And the first step is putting down our weapons, against *each other.*"

Silence lingered for a moment longer, then, slowly, a few of the officers nodded. It wasn't full acceptance. Not yet. But it was the beginning.

Rob glanced around the room, then stepped up beside his mother. "I'll speak with her. Bring her back when she's ready. Not to fight. Just to talk."

"Let her prove it," Katherine added. "Let her earn her place back."

Daniel nodded. "Then that's what we'll do."

The rebellion hadn't disbanded, but it had changed. The war was over. What came next wouldn't be decided by force—but by choice, compassion, and the courage to forgive. Or at least, to try.

* * *

Back at their home, Allison and Malakhov settled into their new life, a life neither of them had ever imagined, and yet one they slipped into like it had always been meant for them. The manor, once a cold fortress of secrets and strategy, had softened. Mikhail's soft cries echoed through its grand halls, bringing warmth to the walls and rhythm to their days. His tiny hands curled instinctively around their fingers, and his sleepy sighs became the sweetest sounds Allison had ever heard.

This new life was never quiet; it was filled with the scent of baby powder, the brief chaos of diaper changes, and nighttime lullabies sung in tired voices.

One afternoon, Allison stood in the kitchen wearing one of Malakhov's shirts, its hem brushing her knees. Her hair was coming loose in damp curls around her flushed face. Mikhail fussed softly against her shoulder as she stirred a pot of soup that had nearly boiled over twice already.

Malakhov walked in and leaned at the doorway as he smirked. "I must say, you wear warlord fashion better than I ever did."

She shot him a glance over her shoulder. "That's because I'm the one conquering things now. Like dinner. And sleep deprivation."

He walked right over and wrapping an arm around her waist while planting a soft kiss on her neck said, "Too efficient, you are. I've never been more attracted to someone holding a baby and a wooden spoon."

"You say that now," she teased, "wait until you see what I can do with baby wipes and a blowout diaper."

"Terrifying *and* alluring," he murmured. "Deadly combination."

That night, they tried to give Mikhail his first bath together. Within minutes, the floor was slick with water, Allison's sleeves were dripping, and Malakhov was blinking soap out of his eyes while Mikhail splashed with obvious delight.

"I think we're getting better at this," Malakhov said, holding the wriggling baby while Allison tried to wrangle a towel.

"Oh sure," she said, laughing, "if the goal is to flood the manor and get peed on at least twice."

Mikhail gave a little grunt and kicked again, splashing both of them.

"*Three* times," Malakhov corrected dryly, flicking water at her.

"Keep that up and I'll let him drool in your mouth while you sleep."

"You're cruel," he said, handing her the towel. "No wonder I fell in love with you."

After Mikhail finally fell asleep, arms thrown dramatically above his head in what could only be considered a gesture of victory, they curled up on the couch, wrapped in a blanket with the fire crackling softly in front of them.

Malakhov traced a finger along Allison's hand. "Do you think he'll grow up to be like me?"

"Broody, dramatic, and secretly a giant marshmallow?" she joked.

He gave her a pointed look. "I was thinking more along the lines of disciplined, strategic, and devastatingly handsome."

Allison leaned over and kissed him slowly. "Let's hope he gets your heart, Dmitri. And maybe my sense of humor."

"I can live with that," he murmured, pulling her closer. "As long as he doesn't start quoting war strategies before his bedtime."

"You say that now," she smirked, "but just wait until he names his teddy bear after one of your old enemies."

"...I'll allow it," he said solemnly. "But only if it's Radimir."

Allison laughed, resting her head against his chest. "Deal."

The world beyond their walls was still fractured and unpredictable. But here, in this messy, improbable little corner they'd carved out, they had something they never thought possible: a quiet they could trust, a love that felt earned.

Thirty Three

A Forgotten Past

It had been months since the battle, since Radimir's reign collapsed in fire and blood. The city was healing, inch by inch. The air no longer buzzed with fear. The hush that once meant danger now carried something gentler, like the first breath after a long storm.

Allison and Malakhov had settled into their new rhythm. The shadows of each corridor had been softened by the distant laughter of a baby and the fragrance of fresh-baked bread.

The bedroom, once cluttered with war maps and radios, now held nothing more threatening than a half-finished bottle and a pile of tiny blankets.

Mikhail had grown stronger every day. His little fists no longer trembled with fragility but waved with confidence, grabbing hold of Allison's necklace or Malakhov's fingers like they were lifelines. His eyes, so bright, so curious, followed the shifting light on the walls like he could already see more than anyone else.

There was joy now. There were moments, *real moments*, of shared smiles, of Allison catching Malakhov asleep on the couch with Mikhail sprawled across his chest, of stolen kisses in the kitchen while something bubbled over on the stove. The world outside felt far away. It *was* far away.

But peace never came without questions.

No matter how Allison tried to stay present, questions crept in around the edges.

What had become of Chicago? Of the Rebellion? Of those who had called her a *traitor*… or friend? Had her name been cleared, or was she still the villain in someone else's story?

She'd heard whispers. That Scott Sutton had been reelected mayor by a landslide. That Daniel and Rob were now hailed as heroes of the people. That statues were already being planned for the fallen. Rebuilding was underway. Hope was slowly returning.

But Allison and Malakhov? They were ghosts.

Their names had not been mentioned in any broadcast. Not a single article. It was like they had vanished the moment Radimir fell, like their part had ended in the last chapter, and the world had decided not to turn the page.

Strangely, she didn't know whether to feel relieved or forgotten.

Her peace hadn't been built on recognition. She didn't need fame. But she *had* bled for that city. She had given up everything—her safety, her future, even her soul for a time. And now, in the stillness of their quiet home, she couldn't help but wonder if she had disappeared too completely.

It was a question she never voiced aloud. Until the morning the newspaper arrived.

She had just finished feeding Mikhail, who was dozing on her shoulder, warm and impossibly tiny. Her arms were still curled protectively around him when her gaze landed on the kitchen table.

The paper sat askew, a mug ring on the corner, a faint crease down the middle.

At first, she didn't think anything of it. But then—*the handwriting.* Allison was too stunned to respond. She reached out with trembling hands, pulling the paper closer. The headline read;

A Message for Allison Murphy, Dmitri Malakhov, and Their Son.

Something about seeing that name was still shocking. Shaky fingers unfolded the paper and picked out and read the large and clear black type.

To Allison, Dmitri, and Your Son,

I personally will never forgive what you have done or the decisions you've made, but I can no longer deny the truth. You have played a vital part in defeating Radimir and the Russian overtaking of the city and securing the future of Chicago. That, above all, cannot be ignored.

The charges against you have been dropped. I understand the fear that comes with returning to a world that once branded you as traitors. But if you choose to return, if you ever feel ready to come into the city again, know this; no harm will come to you or your family.

It has been made clear by our community that the past is behind us. We seek only to rebuild, to move forward from the war and the pain that has crippled our city. We've done this by coming together, and while you may not be able to reconcile with all members of the force, know that the love we had for you will always be a part of us.

You are welcome back.

—Daniel Diaz, Rob Walker, and Scott Sutton.

Allison stared at the words. For a moment, they barely made sense, the letters blurring as if the paper itself was resisting her touch. She had never expected forgiveness, let alone *acceptance.* For so long, she had lived in the shadow of her choices. The betrayal. The blood. The way her name had once sparked whispers and curses in the streets. The idea that she might be welcomed again, acknowledged not as a traitor but as a *key piece of victory,* felt surreal.

The letter was signed by three names she never thought she'd see again, at least not like this.

Daniel Diaz. Rob Walker. Scott Sutton.

A message carried not in secrecy but in print, bold, public, undeniable.

It was an olive branch.

Her lips parted for a breathless moment. Her chest slowly rose and fell, as if she were trying to inhale something unfamiliar—hope.

"They see us," she finally whispered, more to herself than to Malakhov. "They see what we did."

Her voice trembled.

Malakhov slid to her side, his gaze dropping to the page she held as if it were burning in her hands. She gave it to him, brushing her hand against his with trembling fingers.

"What does this mean, Dmitri?" she asked, her voice thick with disbelief, eyes wet. "They... *they have forgiven us?*"

He took the paper slowly and looked over it with his sharp, calculating gaze. His face remained still, expressionless as always, but as he arrived at the last paragraph, something changed.

His shoulders eased. For once, he looked almost unguarded.

"It means they recognize the truth," he said, his voice quiet, almost reverent. "And it means we're not forgotten."

The weight of those words hit her harder than she expected. *Not forgotten.* For so long, she'd thought the best she could hope for was to be erased quietly from history, her part in the rebellion never spoken of again. But now, now she was *part* of the story. Part of *change*.

Her throat tightened. "I thought I had made peace with being erased."

"You never made peace with it," Malakhov said gently, his eyes still on her. "You just learned to live without needing the world to understand."

She blinked at hearing him say these words. So familiar to her, they stopped her for a moment.

"What will you do now?" he asked, after a brief pause. His tone, gentler than one would have expected, was still dense with meaning; "Will you go back?"

Allison glanced down at their son as he curled against her chest, grasping the fabric of her shirt tightly with his tiny fingers. His soft breaths behind her neck, in a way, were grounding her to the present. Her other fingers brushed the nape of his head as she held him tighter to her side, as if the answer could be found in that small, solid weight.

For a long moment, she did not speak.

Then slowly she raised her eyes to meet Malakhov's.

"You mean, what will *we* do," she said steadily. "Don't think I'm walking into anything without my terrifying Russian bodyguard." Her lips curved into a small smile, almost teasing.

An almost guttural chuckle rumbled from his chest. "Terrifying? *You wound me.*"

She raised an eyebrow. "Well, you used to be terrifying. Now you cry when Mikhail sneezes too hard."

"I do not *cry*," he said, mock offense in his voice. "I... *blink emotionally.*"

She laughed, the sound daylight into the void between them, dispelling all tension that might have existed. Her eyes softened as she looked down at their son and then back toward the man beside her.

"I've built this life with you, Dmitri. Our son. This home. It's everything I never thought I'd have. And maybe... *maybe* we've earned the right to stop running. To stop fighting. Maybe quiet mornings were our fee, with burnt toast and muddy little footprints set against the carpet.

"But," she gave a slight falter in her smile, "I honestly don't remember how to step back over there. Into a city that once hunted me. I don't know who I am out there anymore."

Malakhov stepped closer and placed a hand gently on her shoulder. The gesture was soft, grounding, but laced with his quiet strength.

"You're Allison Murphy... Malakhov," he said with a small smile. "You walked through fire and came out carrying something worth saving. That's who you are. To me."

She turned to him with wide eyes full of emotion.

"Whatever you decide," he continued, in an almost tender gesture of brushing a strand of hair behind her ear, "we're going to do it together. I am not going anywhere."

Before she could stop it, a tear made a slow skid down her cheek. This time, though, it wasn't due to sorrow.

It wasn't regret. It was something else—something bright.

Hope. She leaned in, kissed him softly, and let the silence fall over them again. But this time, it was filled with possibility.

* * *

A few days later, Katherine Walker returned to the manor.

Her steps were measured, her presence calm, but there was no mistaking the gravity in her eyes. She wasn't the same woman who had stood by reluctantly during Mikhail's birth, arms crossed with doubt and pain. No, something had shifted. There was understanding now, and maybe even the beginning of forgiveness.

Allison was in the front sitting room when the knock came. She was suddenly up and her heart gave a little leap. Malakhov would be upstairs with Mikhail, but his senses were keen; he would be down in a matter of seconds should something seem awry.

Katherine entered with a hinged coat still over her shoulders, with her eyes roaming about as if seeing the place for the first time.

"I read the paper," she said softly, her gaze tracing the lines of the floor. "And... I think maybe I was wrong."

Allison blinked, caught off guard. "What do you mean?"

Katherine paced the room a little farther and looked at the fireplace, then back at Allison. "I thought you were lost to us," she said in a hoarse voice full of sadness. "That you had turned into something we couldn't save. But watching you... watching how you became a mother and how fiercely you love that little boy, it is clear that you were never the monster we feared. You are not the person you were before. But maybe that is a good thing."

A catch in Allison's breath interrupted her words. "Katherine..." she whispered hoarsely. "You don't know how much it means just to hear you say that."

"I think I do," came a quiet reply from Katherine, a little sad smile tugging at one corner of her mouth. "Not that I forget everything that happened. There's still pain. Still pieces I don't know how to put back together."

"I wouldn't expect you to forget," Allison whispered back, gentle. "I just... I've spent so long wondering if anything I did would matter. If people would ever see me again, not just the things I did to survive."

There was a pause between them.

"Your choices," Katherine said slowly and deliberately. "Have spoken louder than any apology could. You stayed. You protected Rob. You brought a child into the world with kindness, even when it terrified you. That tells me everything I need to know about who you are now."

Malakhov appeared in the doorway then, silent but watching. There was no interruption; he just nodded at Katherine, respectfully. She returned a silent nod. That was the first time she had ever acknowledged him without an undertone of animosity mingling into every word.

"You are different, too," she continued, glancing at Malakhov. "I don't know what changed you… but I see the man you want to be, and I see the way that woman looks at you," she said softly, looking at Allison, "as if you hung the stars."

Allison looked at Malakhov, and he gave her a faint, crooked smile with a subtle shrug for silent confirmation.

"I still, do not have all the answers," said Katherine, "and I'm not about to pretend I am not scared of what comes next. But I believe in second chances. And I believe you've earned one."

Allison felt her knees tremble slightly. "Katherine… are you saying…?"

"I think you should come home," Katherine said simply. "Not just to the city, but to us. To the people who still love you, even if they haven't said it out loud. Come see what we're building. Come *be* part of it."

Tears welled up and Allison, unwilling to let them out, whispered; "I don't know how to come back."

Katherine said, "You don't have to come back the way you left. Just appear. We'll take care of the rest."

Suddenly from behind, Malakhov gently touched Allison's back.

"You will never do it alone," whispered Malakhov.

Katherine nodded, and, for the first time in a while, silence did not injure. It felt like a beginning, raw and unsure, but real.

A beginning.

* * *

Sunlight seeped through the towering sitting room windows and painted golden lines on the floorboards. A faint scent of lavender mixed with the ash from the hearth. Somewhere upstairs, a clock was ticking, steady and regular, like a heartbeat.

Allison sat in the nursery, her robe loosely tied at the waist, Mikhail cradled against her chest. His tiny little fingers twitched ever so slightly in his sleep, the faintest of breaths drifting from his lips against her collarbone. She placed a soft kiss on his forehead, closing her eyes, breathing in the impossibly sweet scent of him.

"I didn't know it could feel like this," she said, mostly to herself. "So still. So... full."

Malakhov stood silently at the doorway for a moment, looking with crossed arms watching them quietly. There appeared to be a faint smirk formation on his face at first, a facade with his old hard lines making an appearance, but then he smiled. Not in the old guarded way, but open. Unburdened.

"You look like you've figured out what life is about," he said playfully, walking in.

"Maybe I have," Allison said without looking up. "He's seventeen pounds, eleven ounces, and drools on everything we own."

Malakhov chuckled, kneeling beside her. He brushed Mikhail's wispy hair back from his brow, then leaned forward to kiss Allison's cheek. "Then let's write the rest of our lives with him filling every margin."

She turned to look at him. "You really think we get to do that? Just... live?"

"I do," he said, and for once there was no hesitation in his voice. "The world outside is shifting, Scott's holding power with a steadier hand than Radimir ever did. There's talk of rebuilding schools, of disarming the last of the camps. I even heard Daniel might run for council."

Allison arched a brow. "Daniel? That man could barely manage laundry duty without launching a rebellion."

"True," Malakhov said, grinning. "But maybe he's finally found a fight he doesn't need to win with blood."

Allison laughed, a real, bubbling sound that startled Mikhail slightly before he settled again. "If the world's rebuilding, maybe we should be part of it... eventually."

"Eventually," Malakhov agreed. "But not today."

He went to sit next to her and put his arm across her shoulders. They sat there, the baby in between them, enveloped in warmth and silence, the waning hope that maybe, just maybe, they were allowed to dream of more.

Allison laid her head on his shoulder. "Do you think he'll know? About all of this? About what we were?"

Malakhov paused. "He'll know what matters. That we changed. That we chose better when it counted. That we fought for something real."

She looked down at their son. "And maybe that's what this all was for in the end—not just survival, not just war. But him. Us."

Malakhov pressed a kiss into her hair and whispered, "A new beginning."

And for the first time in her life, Allison didn't flinch from the idea. She didn't brace for it to be taken. She didn't feel like a fugitive from fate. She drew in a slow breath, feeling something she hadn't in years, an uncomplicated faith in tomorrow.

Whatever came next, they would face it on their own terms.

Thirty Four

Walking Toward Tomorrow

Months had passed since the newspaper arrived with that unexpected letter. The war had left the city gutted, raw in places, but slowly, life was creeping back in. In Naperville, Allison and Malakhov found themselves learning a new kind of quiet. They had Mikhail, and each other—and for the first time in years, no plan beyond tomorrow.

Downtown buzzed again, shops reopened, sidewalks crowded, life picking up where it had left off. But as Allison walked beside Malakhov, her hand wrapped around his, it all felt unfamiliar, like a place she used to know in a dream.

The small family shops that they passed just felt distant from the life that they once lived. The memories of the rebellion, the fights, and betrayals kept haunting her, making the present feel like a strange parallel life.

The bittersweet feeling disappeared quickly when they turned the corner and almost bumped into Rob, Daniel, and the Walker family.

The tension clung to them, awkwardness pressing in from all sides, but Allison felt that it was natural. She had betrayed them, had chosen a path that had led her away from everything they had once fought for together. But Malakhov had been a part of that decision too, and the consequences of their choices were still in the air, unspoken.

Rob's face was tight with something unreadable. He gave her a nod with his jaws clenching, but he said nothing. Daniel, standing beside him, gave his lips a tight smile, but his gaze was guarded and far away. As the awkwardness engulfed them, Allison felt small, but she refused to shrink.

She gave an almost imperceptible smile and a nod, trying to somehow acknowledge their need for space and respect their decision to not forgive her. She was not in the position to ask for it, not yet.

As she began walking past them, though, a gentle hand reached out and grasped her arm.

"Allison?"

There was Heather, oddly soft with emotion, the look in her eyes one Allison could not even put her finger on. Without thinking, Heather threw her arms around Allison in an embrace.

Allison stood there, her heart thudding hard in her chest. This was not supposed to happen; she had expected frostiness from Heather, but she was holding her firmly. The hug caught her off guard, unraveling something she'd kept knotted tight inside her chest.

"I am sorry, Allison," Heather's voice seemed to be weighed down with sincere emotions. "I know this has been very hard, but we have missed you. You still belong to our family. You're always welcome, you know that?"

And before Allison could respond, the tears came hot, sudden, and overwhelming. Her body shuddered as Heather held her tighter. They stood there together in the middle of the sidewalk. At that moment, every feeling with which she had against herself, every bit of guilt and every ounce of pain, came rushing to the surface.

She just couldn't hold it anymore; the floodgates opened, pouring its weight of sorrow and tears on Heather's shoulder as she sobbed silently.

Mikhail was still in her arms, and as Allison cried, she felt him squirm in her grasp.

Malakhov stood a step back, silent, his eyes moving from Allison's shaking shoulders to the familiar faces he'd learned to trust, and, for a time, to fear. He felt the complex emotions in the air, the confusion, the unfinished tension, but stood his ground. His hands were clenched at his sides, and his head remained stolidly unmoving, hiding an unreadable expression.He stood protectively, his focus fixed on Allison and their family.

Allison handed Mikhail into the arms of Malakhov, she inhaled and exhaled raggedly, attempting to regain control over herself; he held his son with great care, firmly yet gently, as though the child were far more fragile than just flesh.

Heather continued to step back, tears in her eyes, as awkwardness loomed within the atmosphere; Allison could hardly look up, weighed down by everything, by betrayal, lost time, and all the brokenness. But in Heather's eyes, she caught something then: acceptance, however faint, a mere flicker.

The atmosphere was laden with tension while the rest of the Walkers eventually fell silent, awkwardly watching everything unfold. Daniel and Rob exchanged glances as they stood, all silence between them long.

But then, Daniel stepped forward, his face softening, smiling genuinely, though not without a hint of hesitation. He extended his hand to Malakhov- who regarded it for a moment before giving it a firm shake. "We've missed you, Allison," Daniel said, quieter than he had ever spoken before, the jagged edge of former anger now dulled but never fully gone. "The war is over. We need to start moving forward."

Rob, still standing beside Daniel, offered a tight smile, his eyes filled with an unsaid understanding. "It's different, Allison. I don't know how long it will take to act normal, but I want to try."

Heather, still standing beside Allison, added, "We'll get there. Slowly. But we will."

Allison nodded slowly, almost at a loss for words. Her heart filled with emotions difficult for her to identify. The love they still had for her, and maybe, *just maybe*, a hope that they could piece their fractured bond back together.

The conversation between the group had hardly started when a familiar voice rang out, calling for their attention.

Katherine Walker, joined by her husband Charles, stepped into view. She looked older and tired but there was still a lightness that had never been there for Allison the last time she saw her.

"I've been speaking to the others, Allison," Katherine said with a graver voice but full of affection. "It will take some time. But we're working on it. We want to see you again. *All* of you. Christmas at our home, like old times. We'll have time to talk. To heal."

Allison blinked, surprised by the invitation. "Christmas? At your home?"

"Yes," Katherine smiled warmly. "We want you there. We want to rebuild. Together. If you're willing, we'll be there for you, just as we always have."

Charles stood alongside Katherine and calmly said, "It has been hard on all of us, Allison. But we just want you to know that you'll always have a place with us."

Allison was overwhelmed by the sincerity of their words, stirring her soul into a little more openness with the bitterness and regret melting away at the thought of genuine acceptance.

"Thank you," Allison whispered. She turned to Malakhov, her eyes filled with meaning. "We'll think about it."

As the Walkers left, Allison, Malakhov, and Mikhail were left standing on the busy street, the air thick with emotion but also filled with something new; hope.

Malakhov looked at her, his voice low and private as they watched the others disappear into the crowd. "You see that? They're trying, Allison. They'll come around. Maybe not today. But they'll come around." He smiled at her, "However, I put my foot down at wearing those ridiculous matching Christmas sweaters you all did in the academy that I've heard *so much* about."

Allison smiled, but her thoughts were mixed. "I hope so. I really do. But for now, I think we have enough to work on." She smiled, she glanced down at Mikhail as he cooed in Malakhov's arms. "Our little family...that's all that matters right now." And they walked, far away into a world of possibilities. The future felt hopeful for the first time, after so long.

Walking through the city, Allison, Malakhov, and little Mikhail continued through the bustling streets. There was that calming feeling that slowly started to descend into their hearts from all the way from here. The tension that weighed on Allison and Malakhov for so long, which was carried across remnants of their past, seemed to have started melting away with one step after the other.

Little Mikhail began to quietly coo in Malakhov's arms, his tiny hands reaching upward, curious about the world around him. Allison smiled; her heart swelled with love for both of them. A single moment, a family taking a quiet stroll, but felt like all was finally falling into place.

"Mikhail, what do you say?" Allison said softly as if talking to herself and brushed a lock of hair behind her ear. "Should we stop for some treats? How about ice cream?" She shot a challenging look toward her man, who at first gave her an eyebrow.

"Ice cream?" he asked, teasing. "I never thought I'd hear those words come from your mouth. I thought you'd say something more... substantial... like a big meal. Something proper."

Allison laughed, shaking her head. "Except don't be fooled. Ice cream is a proper treat. It's something pure, something for just us, just a moment of forgetting everything else." She looked at Malakhov warmly and said, "For once, let's just *be*."

Malakhov took a brief moment to look at her, his expression softening, typically so stoic. He hugged Dimitri tightly against his chest, savoring the tender weight of his son cradled in his arms. A smile, rare for him, spread across his lips. "I'll let you have your ice cream, Allison, but only because it seems to be what you've decided. And I know you've never steered me wrong."

"Lovely," Allison said with a grin. "Now let's get some for our little guy."

The small, carefree ice cream parlor sat right at the end of the alleyway. It sat amid joyous echoes of kids and the sweet aroma of fresh waffle cones. Nothing fancy, but right at that moment, it felt like the perfect sanctuary, a bubble away from Todd.

Being in the shop brought back waves of nostalgia for Allison. It reminded her of simpler, early days, before the war, before Radimir, and all the horrors that came with it. It felt like home, warmth, sweetness, and life.

Malakhov raised his eyebrows as they neared the counter. "What's good here, Allison?"

Allison smiled and leaned forward to grab a menu. "*Everything*, Dmitri. Trust me." She turned to the clerk, a young man with a nice smile. "Chocolate, strawberry and vanilla, three scoops; one for each of us" Her eyes glittered with mischief.

"Three? That's a lot of ice cream for such a little guy, don't you think?"

She shrugged with a smile, and light returned to her eyes at last. "He's growing up so fast. He deserves it."

The ice cream cones were handed to them, and Allison loosely embraced Mikhail, while Malakhov allowed Mikhail a taste of his cone. Outside, the cool evening air greeted them as the sun was setting and casting golden rays over downtown.

"There we go, little one," whispered Allison, holding her cone aloft. Curious eyes followed her movements as she scooped some chocolate ice cream with her finger and gingerly placed a bit of it onto Mikhail's finger. "You're going to love it." Malakhov smiled faintly at the sight of the baby being introduced to ice cream for the very first time.

It wasn't much, a few melting cones and a bench on a noisy street, but in that moment, it felt like a victory they could actually taste.

Allison nodded towards him, caught by the endless look of fondness in his eyes. "What?" she nudged.

"Nothing." His drumming voice sounded hollow as he almost reluctantly leaned in and kissed Allison's forehead. "Just... I never thought I'd be here. With you. With him." His gaze customarily trailed after their son as he emitted peals of laughter while wrangling for the ice cream with Allison.

A soft smile traced her lips while holding the cone to her mouth, still locked onto Malakhov's. "I never thought I'd be here either. But I am. And I'm glad it's with you."

There was a still moment, enjoying the silence and peace, simple and perfect in its quiet way. Mikhail just giggled and reached for the ice cream again, and Allison let out a gentle laugh as she wiped his face with a napkin.

"What's next for us?" Allison asked softly, filled with wonder. "Do we just go on with our lives? Is this our future?"

Silently considering, Malakhov replied to her question; "I think it's just the beginning, Allison. We've got each other. We've got Mikhail. And for the first time in a long time, I'm not thinking about the past anymore. All I'm thinking about is right now."

He leaned down, kissed her again, this time softly, and held that position for a long moment. "This is what matters. Nothing else."

Allison smiled and rested her head on his shoulder as they walked down the street, their son along with them, and the melting ice creams in the late sun.

They'd survived everything, loss, betrayal, war, and somehow ended up here, with ice cream on their fingers and hope settling into the quiet spaces between them.

For once, that was enough.

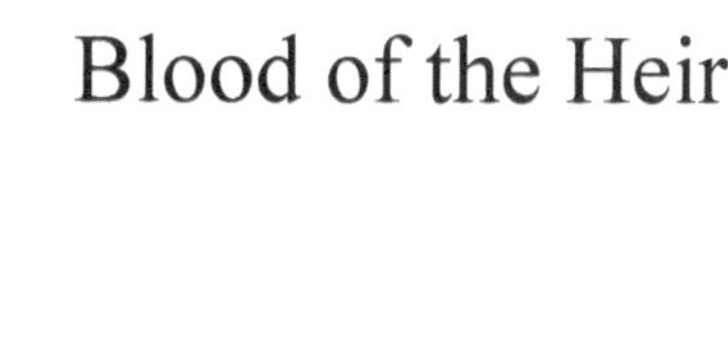

Blood of the Heir

Jennifer Chawla started writing fiction after finishing her PhD, mostly because she missed the chaotic thrill of writing under pressure—and partially because no one was asking her to cite sources anymore. By day, she's a full-time behavior analyst and developmental psychologist supporting individuals with autism. By night, she abandons clinical language in favor of morally gray characters, emotionally stunted love interests, and just enough plot to excuse the drama.

This is her debut novel, and if the characters behave (they won't), it'll be the first of many.

Blood of the Heir

Jennifer R Chawla